the deepest end of love

the deepest end of love

LISINA CONEY

PAGE
&
VINE

Page & Vine
An Imprint of Meredith Wild LLC

Paperback ISBN: 979-8-9895288-7-5

CONTENT WARNINGS

Your comfort is important to me. Before starting Lila and Reed's story, please note the following content warnings: profanity, explicit sexual scenes, and mentions of childhood domestic abuse. Additionally, Lila's mother is a survivor of sexual assault, which is also mentioned in this book. There's no abuse of any kind on page.

A NOTE FROM THE AUTHOR

The Deepest End of Love is the third and final book in The Brightest Light series. It can be read as a standalone, but please note it takes place 30 years after the main events of *The Brightest Light of Sunshine* (book 1, following Lila's parents) and 13 years after *The Darkest Corner of the Heart* (book 2, following Lila's aunt and uncle). You will see spoilers for both books.

Writing this story marked an incredibly special full circle moment for me as an author. I hope *The Deepest End of Love* feels like a warm hug goodbye to Grace, Cal, Maddie, James, Lila, and Reed.

Thank you for walking alongside me on this beautiful chapter of my life. I can't wait to show you what comes next.

To everyone who struggles with self-doubt.
You deserve all the happiness and success you dream of. Don't let
anyone convince you otherwise—not even yourself.

~~~

In loving memory of my family dog.
Wherever you are, I hope you get to play with your dog friends
at the park, have all the ham and treats, and sleep next to the
fireplace when it gets cold
(but don't fall off the couch like that one time).

We love you, B. Thank you for fifteen years of unconditional love.

chapter 1

LILA

December

Is it possible to be attracted to someone's brain?

To the way they articulate their thoughts, string them together, and create new, eye-opening concepts?

The more I think about it, the more I'm convinced that sapiosexuality is a very real, very unfair thing.

Real, because I've never—not in my twenty-three years of life—thought the shifting of organizational culture beyond psychological safety was a seductive topic of discussion. Interesting, sure. Sexy, no.

And unfair, because Reed Abner—the man capturing the entirety of my attention right now—is the last person in this university who should.

"A human-centered design perspective is needed in child-safety culture." His dress shoes make a firm, echoey thud that adds to the confident way he commands the stage. "I'm not here to point fingers and say who's to blame for the less-than-ideal mental health tool kits in foster care—although I'm dying to."

The crowd laughs despite his voice not sounding playful. And when he casually rolls up the sleeves of his light blue shirt, I'm pretty sure the girl next to me sighs.

Did I mention every single student on campus has a crush on this man?

Right on cue, the girl next to me whispers, "God, he's so hot," as she squirms in her seat.

I recognize her from my master's program, although we aren't close. I'm not the most social person as it is, but I'd like to think I'm never rude to anyone, which is why she gets a tight-lipped smile from me—getting shushed for speaking during an open lecture is never in my plans.

"I can't believe he's not married yet. Who wouldn't want to tie down a man like that?" she keeps going, oblivious to my preference for silence. To be fair, she isn't even looking at me. The man on the stage captures everyone's attention as if he had cast a spell on the whole auditorium before walking in. I'm not positive he hadn't. "I wouldn't mind if he put a baby or two in me, you know."

At that, I can't help but scrunch my nose. Sure, Dr. Abner is attractive. Like, objectively. What I think about his put-together-but-also-kind-of-rough exterior isn't relevant. Still, that doesn't make it appropriate to daydream about having his babies *out loud*.

She sinks against her seat with another longing sigh. "You're so lucky you know him. Like, so lucky."

My pulse jumps in my throat, and my palms get sweaty. An uncomfortable weight falls on my chest at her words because, no, I don't *know* him. Not really.

But the fact that people think I do could become a problem.

His voice echoes in my head once again, pulling my attention back to him.

"I'm here to discuss why it's important to ask ourselves what system improvements are needed and how we can do more for the children and their families not just in our community but on a national level," Dr. Abner concludes before moving on to the next slide with a click of the little device in his hand.

My own hand moves furiously over my notebook, scribbling every concept and idea that leaves his mouth as if my future depended on it.

Because, whether I want to admit it or not, Reed Abner is an absolute beast.

Doctor of Psychology, renowned researcher, and probably one of the most—if not the most—sought-after academics of his generation in the child welfare and foster care fields.

I've heard his current research with the state's health department holds the record for the largest grant on the East Coast, which could potentially change policies on mental health resources for kids in a very beneficial, long-awaited way.

Given his impressive background, I would be jumping at any and every given opportunity to soak up all that knowledge from the source himself...

If he weren't my mother's colleague.

And my parents' good friend.

And the man I should pretend I don't know outside of campus for the sake of my career.

My phone buzzes in my pocket, distracting me from all thoughts about Dr. Abner.

> **Oliver: Vic just booked the beach house. Wire him the money ASAP, okay, babe? I'll pay you back.**

"Workshops can play an important role in strengthening bonds within families and communities," Dr. Abner continues, but my pen won't write anymore.

There's an uncomfortable heaviness in my stomach that wasn't there five seconds ago. One that won't let me focus or think.

Another buzz of my phone skyrockets my discomfort levels, and I hate myself for it.

This is my boyfriend.

Oliver: It's cheap since we're splitting the costs between the six of us, and there are no other houses around, so we can party as loudly as we want. Win-win.

I hate the sand. I hate parties. I hate alcohol. I hate weed. I hate his friends.

But I don't hate Oliver.

"The staff should be able to deliver excellent services with respect, accountability, and transparency."

Dr. Abner changes his PowerPoint slide, but the train of thought that kept me linked to his presentation has long since derailed. I set my notes aside and type out a quick reply.

Me: We're still doing the dinner cruise, right?

A few months ago, one of my professors at my counseling master's program suggested an internship at a summer camp in Maine. I was immediately on board. She mentioned the camp coordinator had great connections to a couple of esteemed youth organizations, and if I did a good job, he'd write me a letter of recommendation, opening many doors for me.

But when I brought it up to Oliver, my boyfriend of two years, he didn't sound that enthusiastic.

"Working during summer? *Again?* Jesus, Li. You never do anything fun. You're lucky I love you, because you're not exactly the life of the party."

I gulp at the memory of his words. Oliver could've said them one day or one year ago, and he would've had a point. I'd have to attend parties to *be* the life of one, which I very rarely do. Attend them, I mean. I'm for sure never the life of one.

I'd rather stay in, while he always wants to go out. But is it such a boring thing to want to put my career first? To want to follow in my mother's footsteps and help those in need?

"Of course it's not a boring thing, babe," he'd say every time we had this conversation. "But it's our last summer before we become real adults with reals jobs and shit. Do something fun with me for once."

And every time, I didn't bother mentioning I already have a job. I've been writing articles for a renowned students' website for a couple of years now. To Oliver, though, writing about studying tips or "How to Know If a BA Program Is for You" from the comfort of my couch isn't a serious job, so he doesn't get it when I tell him that no, I can't skip work any time I feel like it.

"There's this beach house in South Carolina we've been trying to book for two years, and it's just become available for the first time," he told me a few weeks ago. "Look at the pictures. Doesn't it look sick? Please don't be boring and just say you're coming."

As soon as I spotted the outdoor jacuzzi and infinity pool, I understood why it'd always been fully booked. And sure, it was a bit pricey, but I could afford it if I wrote a few more articles this month. Agreeing was on the tip of my tongue when I saw the dates they wanted to book it for.

"The summer camp internship starts that same week," I muttered, my heart sinking with Oliver's groan.

"You'll get another internship, babe," he reasoned. "But when will we have the chance to book this insane beach house again? Think about it."

I was thinking about it, but I wasn't too convinced until he added with a knowing smirk, "Plus, there's this dinner cruise at sunset thing where we're going. It'll be romantic. When was the last time we did something romantic?"

A dinner cruise truly sounded like a dream I wouldn't want to wake up from. So, when I read his reply now, my heart sinks.

> **Oliver: My friends want to do stuff together, all of us. We'll see about the dinner cruise.**

For years, I've been working my ass off to get the best grades and opportunities that would steer me in the direction of the future I've always dreamed of—becoming a youth counselor. First with high school, then with my BA in psychology and numerous extracurricular courses, and now with my master's. A 4.0 GPA can't be maintained without hard work and discipline, but maybe I've been focusing a little too much on the textbooks.

I can't even remember the last time I went out with my best friend, Mariah. Or with Oliver, for that matter.

A couple of weeks ago, I thought a few days at a beach house with Oliver and his friends couldn't be too bad. Maybe it's not healthy to feel this way, but I'm scared Oliver and I will grow apart if I keep *not* being the life of the party.

So, I'd said yes.

I'd said goodbye to a summer internship I was dying to do and put "saving my relationship with Oliver" at the top of my list. Only for him to say the one activity I wanted us to do as a couple may not happen.

Something sharp and heavy that feels a lot like betrayal shoots through my chest as I reply to Oliver, but I ignore it.

> **Me: What are you up to?**

> **Oliver: Studying at Kev's dorm. You coming home after that lecture thing?**

> **Me: No, I'm going to the library for a couple hours to work on my thesis. Good luck on your paper :)**

I shift in my seat, trying to convince myself that not applying to the summer camp internship was the right choice. That going with Oliver and his friends to Myrtle Beach instead won't mean the end of my career. It *won't*.

I might have missed the deadline for summer internships—including the camp—but Warlington University offers plenty of internship opportunities for master's students. I'll be fine.

Something else will come up. It *has to*. I'll look into my options later when I'm at the library.

"Unfortunately, we only have time for one more question."

I snap my head up in the direction of the stage, of the man commanding it. And I know I'm not imagining the moment our eyes meet, just like they've done countless times before.

With those deep brown eyes still on me, he asks, "Does anyone have a relevant question?"

Several already-raised hands raise even higher. Some wave, trying to catch his attention.

Asking him how his model will tackle sexual education could help with my thesis.

This is a great opportunity to get a direct answer from one of the most prominent figures in psychology.

But my hand doesn't move, my mouth doesn't open, and Dr. Abner takes his eyes off me and points to a student in the front row.

I expected to feel relief about not being under his silent pressure, but the organ in my chest sinks instead.

No. I made the right choice.

People at Warlington University have heard about the children's books Dr. Abner co-writes with my mom. Some of them have gone as far as to ask me if I could give them his number—as if I had it in the first place.

Being a young woman in academia is hard enough—I don't want to deal with any whispers about me getting special treatment or opportunities because a professor works with my mom. The last thing I want is to draw attention to myself where he's concerned.

It doesn't matter that Dr. Abner is not my professor, just a professor here. To some people, that won't make a difference.

His academic articles might be fueling my literature review for my thesis, and I might have watched his talks online once or twice or seventy times, and my parents might bring him up in conversation every other day. But *I*, Lila Callaghan, have nothing to do with him.

And I hope the people around me can see that, too.

After a standing ovation once his talk is over, the auditorium clears out. As I wait for the last rows to leave, my traitorous gaze shifts to the bottom of the stage, where Dr. Abner is being accosted by a handful of professors and students.

He's so ridiculously tall, I have a clear vision of that chiseled, stubbled jaw and hard eyes that—

Crap.

Our eyes lock again, making time stop around me.

My heart does a weird cartwheel thing when he arches an inquisitive eyebrow, but it doesn't stop me from arching mine back.

A silent question.

A challenge.

What am I doing? Get away from him.

I lower my head and clutch my notebook tightly in my hand as I leave the auditorium, not looking back.

Listening to and taking notes are the only things that should tie me to Reed Abner. The only things that *will*.

Too bad my life has other plans.

chapter 2

LILA

When I was little, I would dream of finding a love like my parents'.

They met when my mom was around my age, the day she went to my dad's tattoo parlor to ink an important reminder on her skin. She didn't go through with the tattoo at that time, but it didn't matter—without knowing, they'd met their soulmate.

I've always found it interesting, the concept of soulmates. How, by chance or fate, you'll meet a seemingly insignificant person who will end up becoming your entire universe.

"I didn't know I was going to end up marrying your dad," my mom would say every time I asked her to tell me the story of how she met Dad. "All I knew was that I couldn't stop thinking about him. We seemed to always bump into each other, and he felt...familiar. Like I'd known him my whole life."

"How did you know Daddy was your soulmate?" I'd always ask, holding my breath until she gave me the answer I still find so magical to this day.

She'd smile at me, adoration written across her face. "Because my heart filled with this intense, bright light. And I knew I didn't want to live another day without him by my side."

Years later, when I met Oliver—my first and only boyfriend—I waited for my heart to fill with that bright light Mom always talked about. It was only butterflies I felt fluttering in my stomach, but I thought it was fine. I *liked* Oliver, maybe could even love him with time, and the light would eventually come.

Two years later, I finally understand why my heart is still in the dark.

Because, unlike my parents, the love I found may not be love after all.

"What the hell," I mutter under my breath as I stop the car.

When I got to the library after Dr. Abner's open lecture, I realized my laptop was dead and I'd forgotten my charger at home.

With my schedule packed, I'm in such a rush I almost miss it.

Oliver's car.

In our driveway.

I pull over to the other side of the road, just a few houses down from our shared apartment, and fish for my phone inside my bag. Scanning our text thread, I reach the conclusion that I'm not, in fact, imagining things.

Oliver: Studying at Kev's dorm. You coming home after that lecture thing?

Studying.

At Kev's dorm.

So why is his car parked in front of our apartment?

"Relax. He probably just finished early," I mutter to myself to no avail, because my fingers still shake as I type out another text to him.

Me: How's your study session going?

I take a deep breath through my nose and place a hand over

my racing heart.

Maybe that isn't his car and I'm just seeing things.

But who else has a "Make tacos not war" bumper sticker?

Plus, I know his license plate number by heart—and that is it.

I need to calm down. My plans changed, so maybe his did too. There's no reason for me to overreact like this, but at the same time I can't ignore the bad feeling swirling around in my stomach, telling me something is very wrong.

Dizziness hits me when I read his reply moments later.

> **Oliver: About to leave Kev's dorm now. Have to drive home to get my gym bag. Logan is picking me up later since I'm running low on gas, but I can tell him to drop me at the library for a quick kiss ;)**

My whole body starts trembling at the fact that Oliver is lying for no apparent reason.

He's hiding something. Why else would he lie?

As I wait for something, anything to happen, I curse at myself for having ignored my dad when he said he didn't like Oliver for me. He was fully against us moving into an apartment together a month ago, but I shrugged him off because I thought he was just being his usual overprotective, overdramatic papabear self.

I should've listened to him.

I'm still shaking when the front door of the apartment building opens minutes later.

In a way, I was expecting it. Yet I'm still shocked and heartbroken and disgusted at the sight of Oliver, my ex-boyfriend, walking a girl I don't recognize to a nearby car as she clings to his arm.

And because I must love pain, I don't look away as he backs her up against the car and presses his front to her chest, kissing her lips.

I shut my eyes when her hands tangle in his blond curls.

With every millisecond that passes, I hate myself a thousand times more.

Because I've just thrown away two years on this pathetic excuse of a man.

Because I gave up my summer internship for him since he said we weren't spending enough time together.

Maybe it's my brain trying to find a silver lining, but in a weird, messed-up way, I'm relieved to now have a valid reason to break things off.

Oliver has never had any real ambitions other than partying with his friends, which has never mixed well with my drive to climb to the top of my field. I thought he needed time to figure things out because we're still young, but months have gone by, and he's yet to show signs of real direction. It genuinely bothered me, and over the past few weeks, I've started wondering if I deserve better. If I deserve a man who takes care of himself and me. But I always concluded I was being too rigid and unfair to Oliver. That I needed to be patient.

Screw that.

I *do* deserve better. I should've been strong enough to break up sooner, to take off my rose-colored glasses and see him for who he really is.

Whatever light my mom swears by when people meet the one, now I know I will never feel it. Because I never fell in love with Oliver; I fell in love with his potential that I made up in my head. And that is all my fault.

Anger seeps into my veins—at him for being a liar and a cheater and at myself for being a stubborn idiot.

I don't move until the girl drives away and he gets back

inside the building, and only after I've taken some deep breaths and calmed myself down do I leave my car.

Despite my breathing exercises, the five-minute walk to our apartment feels nauseating. My keys jiggle between my shaky fingers as I take the elevator to the third floor, unsure of how I want to face him after I just caught him shoving his tongue down someone else's throat.

I consider calling my best friend, Mariah (she'd tell me to kick his ass), or my aunt Maddie (she'd tell me to take a deep breath and give him the cold shoulder), or even my uncle James for advice (he'd straight up kill him), but the elevator pings, and suddenly I know exactly what to do.

Because I've already wasted two years on him, and I'm not wasting another second.

"Babe?" Oliver's confused voice reaches me as I unlock the door. "I thought you were at the library."

He emerges from the bathroom, shirtless, with a gym T-shirt in his hand. When I look at him, my heart feels void.

If someone had asked me a year ago, I would've said I saw myself marrying Oliver. Maybe. With time. If he became a bit more mature and started taking adult life a bit more seriously.

How can you love someone one second and feel nothing for them the next? Just like that?

Maybe because I've never truly loved him.

My parents found love in each other many years ago, and I somehow convinced myself I'd find it too. That my first boyfriend would be the one because that's how it played out for my mom, for the person I admire the most.

I've ignored all the red flags waving right in front of my eyes because it was easier. Because it hurt less. And now I'm paying the price.

"Hey, you there?" Oliver frowns when I say nothing. "What are you doing here? I thought—"

"Did you do a lot of studying today?" I cut him off, my voice neutral despite my heart beating uncontrollably in the worst possible way.

"Um, yeah. Why?"

"Because you lied to me. Your car was here when you said you were at Kev's."

He has the sheer audacity to look me dead in the eye and say, "Fine, yeah. I didn't go to Kev's dorm. Whatever. I went to Jared's place to play some video games instead, and I just got back. I didn't tell you because you know I'm falling behind in some of my classes. I didn't want you to be upset with me. Sorry I lied, babe."

There's a part of me that doesn't believe this is real. That this whole nightmare situation is only a distasteful prank. Because there's no way Oliver thinks I was born yesterday.

"Was it Jared you cheated on me with, too, or did I imagine you kissing that girl five minutes ago?"

His silence has never been so loud.

"Lila—"

"I *saw* you kissing her, Oliver." I hate the way my voice trembles as I say it. I hate that I've put up with him belittling my priorities for so long for nothing. "Don't even try to deny it. We're done."

He curses under his breath before quickly putting on his T-shirt. "Can we talk about this later? Logan is about to come over."

"So, you're admitting it? That you cheated on me?" I ask, chin high, because he doesn't deserve to see me crumble right now.

His chest deflates with a sigh. Not a sad but an annoyed one.

"It was just a kiss, holy shit." He rakes his hands through his hair. "It didn't mean anything. If you'd just let me explain—"

"I'm not interested in knowing what reasons you think justify being unfaithful," I cut him off. The pit of anger in my stomach starts burning, consuming my patience in its wake. "How long has this been going on?"

"I don't know, Lila. A month? I don't fucking know."

I'm not dumb enough to believe whatever leaves his mouth from now on, so I quickly realize it doesn't matter if it's been a month or three or six. He *cheated* on me, period. Infidelity isn't something I'm willing to forgive and forget.

His phone pings with a notification. "Logan is downstairs. We'll keep talking about this when I get back from the gym. Okay, babe?"

"Don't call me *babe*. Are you seriously walking out of this conversation right now?"

"We'll fix this." He grabs his gym bag and leans in to give me a kiss, but I take a step back. "What's wrong?"

"Oliver, are you fucking kidding me?" I raise my voice against my better judgment. I never allow myself to lose my temper, but all my self-control goes out the window with each word that leaves his mouth. "You *kissed* someone else, probably did other things, too, since you brought her to *our* apartment. I'm breaking up with you! And while we're at it, forget about living here any longer since I'm paying for this apartment all on my own."

That makes him frown. "I live here. You can't kick me out."

"I'm paying rent for both of us," I argue. I'm glad I *did* listen to my dad when he advised me to get a month-to-month lease so I can end it whenever I want. "You don't even pay the bills. You said you would after finding a job, but I don't see you looking for one. I'm tired of your laziness and stupid excuses. What makes you think I'm going to let you stay here for free?"

Even if it means going back to my parents' house, I don't think *I'll* stay here. Too many bitter memories, too little energy to replace them with happy ones.

"Fuck this," he half shouts, yanking at the back of his hair.

"I had physical needs that you weren't meeting, that's all. It was a onetime thing."

Physical needs.

He's going there.

"So what? It's my fault that you cheated because I didn't want to sleep with you whenever you wanted?"

"I didn't say it was your fault."

"Yes, you did."

"How so?"

Is he a manipulative mastermind, or is he really that dense?

"You just said you had to get in someone else's pants because you had physical needs I wasn't meeting," I argue, losing my patience. "That implies that if I had wanted to sleep with you as many times as you wanted, you wouldn't have felt the need to see someone else behind my back. You know what that's called, Oliver? *Being a piece of shit.*"

"That's not fair," he argues back. "You're painting me as some kind of sex addict."

Pinching the bridge of my nose, I take a deep, tired breath. "It takes real talent, Oliver, to cheat on your girlfriend and make yourself look like the victim."

"I *am* a victim."

"Of what? Stupidity?"

Neither of us says anything for the next few seconds, the sound of the cars driving outside the apartment and our heavy breathing filling the uncomfortable silence. I'm about to give in and tell him I'm too tired to keep arguing when Oliver speaks again.

Sealing his death sentence.

"Yes, Lila, I had *needs.* Sorry for wanting to fuck my girlfriend, I guess. It's not my problem that you always have better things to do than pay attention to me," he snarls with a sudden bite to his voice that takes me aback. "You think you're this big shot because you're doing well in college. The perfect student, the spoiled daughter, the Goody Two-Shoes who can do no wrong. Always striving for perfection no matter what it takes. Well, guess what? You've ruined this relationship. You did. Hope your fragile little ego can take that."

Where is this coming from?

"Go with Logan, Oliver." My voice sounds less confident than before, and I hate myself for it. "Leave me alone."

"Whatever," he dismisses, typing something on his phone as he speaks. "You only care about your future. Lila, always the little savior. I've always thought you had no right to get into child counseling. You're a privileged princess—loving parents, a great childhood, access to education and whatever-the-fuck else. What do you know about struggles? Be honest with yourself and admit you just want to help kids to make yourself feel important."

The pit of anger turns into an erupting volcano. And despite his words piercing something fragile inside of me, making my self-confidence wobble, I don't let him see it.

"Nice attempt at making me feel bad for wanting a career more than I've ever wanted you." I can't hide the way my whole body starts shaking, but I don't care anymore.

"Fuck this," he spits out, rooting me into place. He's never spoken to me like this. "And you wonder why I cheated?"

I don't move or say a thing as he storms past me. And when he reaches the door, I hear him say, "I'm done with this bullshit," before he slams it with enough force to make the walls shake.

Silence wraps around me, and so do the flames of resentment fueled by his cruel words.

I've always been a peaceful person, someone who avoids conflict like the plague. But today?

Today, that Lila Callaghan is gone.

He *cheated* on me.

Blamed it on me.

Lied to my face.

Insulted me.

My feet start moving before I realize where I'm going or what I'm about to do. My judgment slips away completely, sinking into a pool of betrayal and embarrassment.

No man is ever going to disrespect me like that and get away with it.

I unplug the router from the living room wall, shoving it inside my backpack. He wants to stay here so badly? Let's see how long he lasts without Wi-Fi.

And let's see how badly he wants to stay when it smells like crap.

I don't think, just act as I yank the fridge open and grab some fish I was planning on cooking for dinner today. *Worth the sacrifice.*

My mind is fogged with rage as I bust into our former bedroom. My stomach turns with nausea at the sight of the crumpled sheets, knowing damn well I made the bed before leaving this morning.

Focus. Don't think about him and that girl.

Powering through the pain stabbing at my heart, I yank open his underwear drawer and toss the smelly fish inside.

Then I grab my suitcase and start throwing my bathroom stuff inside. Luckily, we've not been living here for long, so most of my things are still at my parents'. With so little to pack, though, the ideas keep flowing.

His toothbrush ends up in the toilet because why not.

I empty his expensive cologne and hair products down the sink because I feel like it.

And I cut the cord of his phone charger in half with a pair of scissors because *fuck him.*

Plates, glasses, and silverware disappear from the cupboards and into our moving boxes Oliver still hasn't thrown away, despite him insisting he would.

My mind is on autopilot as I pack all my clothes. The apartment came furnished, so I don't have to worry about the TV, couch, or bed.

Maybe my idea of revenge is too juvenile—I've never been a vindictive person, so I'm a little rusty—but it's still better than letting him get away without consequences. I wish I could do more damage—throwing another raw fish into the air vent couldn't sound more appealing right now—but I can't forget my name is on the lease. Getting myself into trouble with our landlord isn't worth the hassle.

I manage to put everything in my car in less than half an hour. My chest still burns with betrayal as I carry the last box with the silverware and some plates to my trunk, which explains why I do what I do next.

I may regret it in about ten seconds, but right now, revenge has never tasted sweeter.

Oliver always complains about not having enough money to pay me back for rent, but he never misses a Friday night out with his friends. He's always asking for car rides because he can't afford gas, but I've caught weed in his nightstand a few times. It's pretty clear where his priorities lie, and I've had enough.

He can't afford rent or gas? Let's add a tire to that made-up list.

The sky opens above my head, light rain clinging to my long blonde hair as I grab a kitchen knife from the last box I put in my car and stab it through his right tire. It deflates immediately.

"Fuck you," I mutter under my breath, shaking with a brutal sense of helplessness before a single tear rolls down my cheek.

Oh my God, what have I done?

A cocktail of guilt, rage, and cold seeps into my bones.

This isn't me. I don't do things like this.

I don't do revenge. I don't let other people's choices affect me to the point of losing control.

I was raised better than this, damn it.

I don't hear the car stopping in front of my apartment complex until it's too late.

And in the drizzle, I lock eyes with the last man I need or want to see right now.

Did I mention I'm still holding the kitchen knife in my hand while standing next to Oliver's ruined tire?

Reed Abner, professor at Warlington University and my parents' good friend, looks me up and down.

Goddammit.

"Get in my car, Lila."

chapter 3

REED

The first time I met Lila Callaghan, I didn't actually meet her.

Grace had mentioned her during our first work meeting, as every proud parent would, but I barely paid attention. I caught that she was a psychology student because I, too, have a BA in psychology, but that was all.

At the risk of sounding like a class-A asshole, tuning out of conversations when people start talking about their families is second nature to me. I've learned that the less interested I look and the fewer questions I ask, the less likely it is for them to ask me about my personal life in return.

Small talk isn't my thing; least of all when it involves my family.

I didn't really know anything about Lila Callaghan until she briefly caught my attention a year ago. I was mindlessly scrolling through social media one afternoon when Grace's post caught my eye—specifically, the article linked to it.

So proud of my daughter for all her grand achievements at just twenty-two years old. At the risk of sounding like an annoying mom and embarrassing her to death, I wanted to share her latest article—"Effects of Childhood Trauma in Late Education"—winner of the Warlington Research Award and published in the Warlington Science Journal.

Her dad and I couldn't be prouder!

Before I knew what I was doing, my finger clicked on the link. And then I was redirected to one of the most stunning pieces of academic writing I'd read in my goddamn life.

I scanned every line, thirsty for the next word, the next concept, the next conclusion. I didn't need to reach the last page to know that her understanding of the subject was beyond her years and education.

Lila's work would put most MA theses to shame.

Despite my momentary amazement with her brain, I closed my browser and left it at that. I never brought her up in a conversation with Grace while we discussed our next book. Nor did I go out of my way to search for Lila's information, because I had more pressing matters at hand.

When I met her in person for the first time a few months later, we exchanged a total of two words—*hello* and *goodbye*—just like the second and third times we'd been in the same room.

She's always avoided my gaze, never looking particularly interested in my presence, even though I spot her at each and every one of my open lectures. Why, though, I was never curious enough to ask.

But now *I am* intrigued.

Because why the hell is Grace and Cal's daughter holding a kitchen knife next to a car with a busted tire?

"This isn't what it looks like," she blurts out, an anxious glimmer in her eyes.

Unimpressed, I raise an eyebrow as I rest my arm on the rolled-down car window. "You're telling me I didn't just see you stab a knife through that tire."

Her throat works a swallow. "Nope. Must be an illusion."

My eyebrow arches even higher.

"Fine." Her shoulders deflate with a heavy sigh. "This is exactly what it looks like. But for the record, I already feel terrible about it. Not because he didn't deserve it, but because I don't do stuff like this."

He. Interesting.

"Good to know you don't vandalize cars on the regular."

When she throws me a glare, it takes everything in me not to smirk.

"I'm putting the knife away now," she says, slowly walking toward her trunk and placing it inside a cardboard box. She keeps her hands high where I can see them as if I were a cop.

I'm officially amused.

"Great. Now that my tires are safe from your stabbing impulses, will you get inside my car?"

Her eyes narrow suspiciously. "Why would I do that?"

"Because it's raining."

"I'm already wet," she points out. My eyes dart to her damp T-shirt for a millisecond before I remind myself *who* I'm talking to. "And I have my own car. I can just drive away. In fact, I probably should because, you know, the tire."

I scratch my jaw. "You know what's funny? I'm actually on my way to join a work call with your mom to edit her next book."

Her glare only intensifies. "I didn't take you for a snitch, Dr. Abner."

"It's Reed for you." I unlock the passenger door in an invite she doesn't take. "Get inside the car, Lila. Please."

"No, thanks."

The thing about Lila and me is that we don't *know* each other. We don't seek each other out, interact, nothing at all. In fact, it wouldn't be the first time I got the impression that she wasn't my biggest fan. Not only because she always avoids eye contact and never joins us when her parents invite me over for dinner, but also because she attends my every open lecture but still refuses to talk to me about my research or ask me any questions—just like earlier today.

It doesn't surprise me that she's hesitant to get in the car with me. What does surprise me is that I'm the one getting out of my car, the fabric of my shirt clinging to my skin as the rain falls over me.

"What are you doing?" she asks, her voice laced with skepticism as she eyes my chest so quickly, I think I've imagined the movement.

"I want to talk to you." I try not to focus on how much I tower over her or why that matters in the first place. "Specifically about why you've just slashed someone's tire."

Guilt shines in her face. "I think I lost my mind a little."

Light rain keeps falling, but neither of us seeks cover.

"You said he deserved it. Who's he?" I press.

Normal people don't go around slashing other people's tires—certainly not smart ones with a supportive family—and I won't leave without knowing why.

Lila looks around as if she expects someone to jump out of the bushes at any moment, before her hazel eyes find mine again. "Dr. Abner, I really don't think—"

"Reed," I cut her off.

She ignores me. "I don't think it would be appropriate to have this conversation right now."

That makes me frown. "Elaborate."

The impatience in her eyes tells me I should know the answer without having to ask. "Because you're a professor and I'm a student. We aren't supposed to interact outside of academic matters."

There's a nervous edge to her voice I don't quite understand. "I'm not your professor. And if you want to get technical, I only teach a couple PhD seminars. I'm mostly a researcher."

I have the feeling she already knows this, but all she does is shrug.

When she shivers, I decide I've had enough.

"You're going to get sick." I consider grabbing my jacket from my car until I realize it wouldn't make a difference. She's already soaking. "It's fine if you don't want to tell me everything. Just let me know if you're in some kind of danger or if someone did anything to you."

"I'm okay. Well, I'm not *okay,* but I'm not in danger. I..." She swallows, hugging herself. "It's my boyfriend. *Ex*-boyfriend. I just found out he cheated on me, and then he said some pretty nasty things, and I didn't take it very well. Hence the tire stabbing and...other things."

"Nasty things?" I echo, my stomach twisting with unfamiliar worry.

She waves a dismissing hand. "It's not important."

"What other things did you do?"

"I may or may not have hidden raw fish in his underwear drawer and thrown his toothbrush in the toilet. He doesn't pay me back on rent, so technically, it counts as payback. Right? It's not a crime."

"The tire thing might be, though."

She pales. "You're going to report me?"

Absolutely not. I cross my arms, widening my stance. "If you say he deserved it, I believe it. I haven't seen a thing."

Her shoulders sag with relief. "Really?"

"As long as you promise me no more tire slashing," I say, my voice serious. "I'm sure I don't need to remind you how important it is to take control of your emotions during stressful times."

Grace mentioned Lila is currently doing her master's in counseling. Of course she doesn't need the reminder, although today it may seem differently.

The rain picks up, almost drowning the gentle sound of her voice. "Wait. Does this make me a *criminal?*"

I choose to be honest with her. "What you did could be considered vandalism, but you're hardly a criminal. He could press charges if there's any kind of evidence against you. You said he wasn't paying you any rent money? Something tells me you definitely won't be getting that money back if he finds out about the tire."

"And here I thought you were going to send me straight to the police station." There's a hint of playfulness in her voice.

"I'm a busy man. But I'm sure you can get there by yourself."

"For sure. I'll be on my way."

She bites her lip, trying to force down her smile, and I find myself unable to look away.

Only when she clears her throat, her expression sobering up again, do I come back to my senses. "Can I ask you to not—"

"I won't tell anyone," I assure her, knowing exactly where she's going with this. "You're not a child, and you're also not my business. As I said, I didn't see a thing."

Her nod is short, stiff, and she somehow looks more on edge than before. I'm about to ask her if she's truly all right, if she needs anything from me at all, when she says, "I'll see you around, Dr. Abner. Thank you for...your intentional blindness."

She gets in her car so fast, I don't have time to remind her to call me Reed. Not like it would matter, anyway.

Lila Callaghan has been ignoring me since I started working with her mother two years ago, and she has no reason to stop now. Nor do I particularly want her to—she's a student, not to mention twelve years younger than me and my friends' daughter. Aside from making sure she's okay when she's clearly in distress, nothing should tie me to her.

And nothing will.

chapter 4

LILA

February

Up until this point, my life has been pretty drama-free.

A heated argument here and there used to be the most stress I put myself through socially or romantically. Then, in the blink of an eye, I turned into the worst person ever. And I don't even feel sorry for myself because it's a well-deserved title.

The past two months have taught me that it only takes one impulsive, reckless decision to bring you down completely.

Oliver found out about the slashed tire that same day, minutes before he also found his toothbrush in the toilet, saw his ruined phone charger, smelled the putrid fish, and everything else. He let me know as much in an angry text I wasn't able to read without shaking.

> Oliver: You think vandalizing private property is fucking funny, Lila? My dad's lawyer will be in touch.

But days and weeks went by, and he never sued, which my best friend, Mariah, had a very logical explanation for.

"He won't sue you when he owes you *two thousand dollars* in rent," she said when I showed her his text. She's the only person who knows about the tire incident, aside from Reed.

Dr. Abner. Aside from Dr. Abner.

"In fact, I think you should sue him. Fuck that leech."

But my guilty conscience didn't allow me to, so I discarded the idea quickly. Now that I'm back living with my parents, it's not like I need the money anyway. I'll just write some extra articles to make up for it and forget about Oliver forever.

Only, three weeks after I broke up with Oliver and Tiregate went down, guilt made me cave, and I sent him one single text. He is and will always be a liar and a cheater, but that doesn't mean I can't take responsibility for how poorly I behaved.

> **Me: You're still an asshole, but I'm sorry about everything. It was uncalled for. I should've handled it differently.**

> **Oliver: Whatever.**

And there was that.

My feelings for him vanished the second I caught him kissing that girl, and they haven't come back for a single second. I may be a terrible person for crossing the line of damaging private property, but I still respect myself enough not to go back to him.

Plus, I have better things to do—namely, find a new internship before graduation in December.

Now, ten weeks after ruining Oliver's tire—a fun fact my parents still don't know about—I summon my fakest smile and pretend I'm not dying inside.

It's a talent, if I really think about it. An art, even.

Because when all I want to do is go home, bury myself under a thick blanket, and cry for hours until my neighbors inevitably call the police because "Who the hell is being murdered next door and can they tone it down a bit," convincing the world that I'm a mentally stable girl capable of having a conversation becomes a near-impossible task.

And when my parents, the people who love me the most in the world and know me like the backs of their hands, are only a few feet away, the stakes rise even higher.

Don't ruin tonight for them.

"Your mother is a remarkable woman," Clarissa, Cassandra, or possibly Callista assures me with a smile brighter than the muted golden lights above us. They're all over the gala venue, casting a beautiful glow I'm too anxious to appreciate.

My words are sincere when I say, "Thank you," because I admire my mom more than anyone else in the world, but did I mention I'm dying inside?

It's not that I miss Oliver, not really. But my future is unclear, I still feel terrible for what I did to him because that's not me, and maybe...

He knew me well, and he still thought I had no right to get into counseling. What if he's right?

The venue where the National Book Awards ceremony is being held is packed with hundreds of guests tonight, and I try to calm my pounding heart. *Wait until you go back home to cry if you need to.*

The middle-aged woman who came up to me a minute ago— wineglass in hand, dressed in a rose gold gown, and introducing herself as one of the publicists working at my mom's publishing house—puts a hand on my bare arm and says, "She tells me you're studying for a master's in counseling and that you want to work with children. Did I get that right?"

Running a hand down the tight fabric of my black dress, I tell her, "Yes. I'm graduating at the end of this year."

Or maybe not, if I can't find an internship.

The thought of waving goodbye to my dream of becoming a youth counselor because I was an idiot makes me feel like my chest is being carved open.

"You're just as bright as your mother." Clarissa-Cassandra-Callista beams, and I can't think of anything else to do other than to thank her again.

Maybe someone else would be put off by people constantly comparing them to their mother—and I get it. But for me, there's no bigger honor than to be considered just a fraction as incredible as her. My mom, whose latest educational children's book just won Children's Book of the Year at the most prestigious awards ceremony in the book world.

Being compared to Grace Callaghan doesn't sting at all. If anything, I often find myself questioning whether I deserve to be put in the same box as her.

Mom would've never given up on her dream internship for an immature boyfriend, so no.

When did all these cotton balls get stuck in my throat?

Clarissa-Cassandra-Callista's lips keep moving, but my ears are ringing and my brain isn't processing a single word.

"Lila. There you are."

The touch of a familiar hand on my arm brings me down to Earth. Mostly.

And Clarissa-Cassandra-Callista's smile only gets wider as she takes in my mother next to me. "Grace! Oh, honey, what a wonderful accomplishment. I know I've said it enough times, but we feel so blessed to have worked on such a special project with you."

"The pleasure is mine, Clarisse." So *that's* her name. "This dinner party was incredible, too. Such a dream come true for me. Everyone is having a great time."

Guilt sinks its ugly claws into my chest and tears it up. Because no, I'm not having a great time at all, and it makes me feel even worse.

It was never in my mom's plans for her books to gain this much traction and praise, but she deserves every ounce of the love they're getting. And I'm not here—not emotionally, at least—to celebrate it with her and my dad, which makes me a terrible daughter.

Get it together.

My mom and Clarisse are still engaged in conversation, but I don't have a single clue what they're saying until my mom squeezes my arm and says, "Mind if I steal Lila away for a moment?"

"Not at all. It was lovely to see you both."

A moment later, I'm following her to the crowded bar. The dinner party has since turned into a drink-and-mingle kind of evening, which I wouldn't mind and even would enjoy if only I could get rid of the anxiety that has been clinging to my heart for two months now.

"What's with that face, Li?" The concern in my mom's eyes feels like a stab to my stomach. She pulls out two high chairs, gesturing for us to sit. "You've been acting weird all night. For weeks now, actually. I wanted to give you space, but you're clearly not doing better. So, what is it, honey?"

Oh, it's nothing, Mom. I just want to scream and cry because my cheating ex said he's always thought I'm spoiled and have no right to be a counselor. Did I also mention I'm a vandal because I slashed his tire, and he threatened to sue me?

"I'm all right," I say instead, which is much safer.

"Lila." She gives me a look. "Tell me the truth, please. Is it about Oliver?"

My parents know about the cheating, but they don't know about anything else that went down that day.

Don't tell her. Don't ruin her night.

But she's looking at me *like that,* with those eyes I swear can read minds, and I know I have to give her something.

I hate liars. I hate them with all my heart, so, in a way, I also hate myself as I say, "I'm just stressed about my thesis, is all."

She gives me a look that tells me she's seeing right through the bullshit. "You're a 4.0 student, Li. What are you worried about? You've got this."

I let out a deep sigh that isn't entirely fake. "What if it's not... you know, good enough?"

My mom frowns like I've personally offended her. "If your thesis isn't good enough, whose will be? You've got a perfect GPA, experience writing countless published articles, four extracurricular counseling courses, volunteering experience..." Her frown is going nowhere as she grabs my hands in hers. "And most of all, you're passionate about what you do. Why do you doubt yourself so much? Can't you see how *brilliant* you are?"

The backs of my eyes start stinging. I'm already way too emotional for my own good, feeling way too vulnerable, and now my mom says *this*?

"I..." But no words come out.

Because no, I don't see how brilliant I am. I don't *feel* it, no matter what my academic results say. A brilliant person doesn't lose her mind like I did.

Something to her right catches my mother's attention, and suddenly, she's waving at someone. It's probably my dad, so I don't look away from my lap, because if I focus on the black fabric of my knee-length dress, maybe I'll contain the tears.

"Reed. Do me a favor, will you?" she starts, and my heart stops. "Can you please talk some sense into my daughter? Maybe if she hears it from someone else, she'll finally believe it."

Shit, shit, shit.

"Mom, I don't—"

But she's no longer in her chair. I watch as she walks up to Dr. Abner, who's clad in an expensive-looking suit that fits him a little too well. I can't make out what they're saying over the loud throng.

The heavy weight of a tattooed hand and my dad's unmistakable voice make me school my features into something less depressed faster than lightning. "Everything okay, little sunshine?"

My dad has always been protective of me. Of all three of us, really—me, Mom, and my aunt Maddie, who grew up with us due to my grandmother's alcohol issues. He says it physically pains him to see any of us cry, so the last thing I want is to upset him right now.

I still don't know how my mom and I convinced him not to kill Oliver when I told them about the cheating.

Lying to him feels equally as terrible as lying to my mom, so I change the subject. "I haven't seen you in a bit. Where were you?"

"I was outside with Reed. There are too many people here."

He isn't a fan of crowded spaces, but he makes an effort for my mom. She isn't into the party scene, either, but her job forces her to network—and she's great at it.

It makes sense that Reed—*Dr. Abner, damn it, not Reed*—hangs out with my dad because they're both quiet, closed-off men. Their introverted natures are probably what make them such close friends, which is something I don't need to think about now.

Especially when the man in question lowers himself to the chair my mom was previously occupying.

My dad squeezes my shoulder. "Your mom and I will be around."

And they walk away.

Dr. Abner unfolds his long, muscular legs in front of himself. The dark fabric of his suit pants grazes my bare skin, giving way to a sea of goose bumps.

"If it isn't my favorite criminal."

I think of crossing my arms to shield myself from the intensity of his gaze but drop them as soon as I realize pushing my breasts up isn't the message I want to send a *professor.*

"Glad to know I'm at the top of your very long list of criminal acquaintances," I retort.

His plump lips tilt into a dangerously handsome smirk. "Wouldn't give the number one spot to anyone else."

I try to keep my gaze trained forward and not on his brown hair, short stubble, or defined jaw. Because why would I openly ogle my parents' friend, a man twelve years my senior? *Please.*

"Your mom said you were worried about your thesis, but she isn't buying it, and neither am I. So, what is it?"

I guess this is what happens when you try to hide your feelings from a renowned counselor—you get busted.

But because I didn't just inherit my dad's hazel eyes but also his incurable stubbornness, I say, "I'm just stressed about graduating and writing a good thesis."

It feels weird that he agreed to have this conversation with me. He's been working with my mom for a couple years, but we've never really talked. At least not until Tiregate.

Maybe because I keep ignoring him?

The sigh that escapes his lips next sounds tired. "You're studying to become a youth counselor. You should know bottling up your emotions isn't the answer."

Oh, I know that. I also know he's only here because my mom asked him to be, not out of the kindness of his heart. Feeling like a burden—on top of everything else going on in my head—may just be the final nail in my coffin.

With as much poise as I can muster, I get down from the stupid bar chair, doing my best not to fall face-first. Despite my heels, I'm still ant-sized.

"Thank you for your concern, but I don't want to force you to listen to my problems. I'm sure you have better places to be."

His big, warm hand catches my elbow, and my heart flutters. "Sit down, please. I'm here because I want to be. Let's just talk."

Does his gruff voice sound softer, or am I hearing things?

Thinking it's probably the latter, I press, "I'm not sure that's a good idea."

There are too many people here, some of whom have connections to Warlington University. It only takes one ill-intended person to start a rumor and ruin my career before it even begins.

When he drops his hand from my elbow, my skin suddenly turns cold.

"You can leave if you really want to. I'm not holding you hostage here, Lila. But I can tell something's eating at you, something that maybe you don't want your parents to know— which is fine. I'm here to listen if you want me to. Does it have to do with your ex?"

The soft music coming from the speakers around us engulfs me, along with the buzzing of the crowd, and my head spins.

I hate that I'm letting Oliver's words about me being too privileged to help children in need affect me this much, but I *trusted* him. Yes, he wanted me to do fun things with him, but he also used to support my career and cheer me on. Did he fake that for two years?

"Do you want to talk?" Dr. Abner asks again, but I'm not really listening.

Revenge blinded me, and I did something I deeply regret, even if Oliver deserved it a little bit.

"I want to go home and sulk" is what comes out of my mouth.

He sits up straighter, looking even bigger and taller than his six foot four. "I think talking would do you better. I can order you some water if you'd like."

My nod is smaller than I would like, and so is my voice. "Please."

He calls over a waiter, who quickly sets two small bottles of water in front of us, next to two glasses with ice cubes and a slice of lemon in each. Dr. Abner pours mine first, and I take a sip.

He doesn't drink his. Instead, he rests his arm on the bar and looks at me. "Feeling better?"

I swallow. "No."

"Okay. I'm here when you're ready to talk."

Oh, he's good. It's easy to tell why my mother would want to work with him—patient, open, reliable.

I'm no child, but his counseling magic works on me all the same. Because not even two minutes pass before I say, "It's about my ex."

"The same guy who didn't pay rent, right?"

My sigh is nothing short of exhausted. "I only have one ex, so yeah. That'd be him."

How did I not see it before, how much of a liar Oliver was?

Maybe because he never lied about anything important, anything *big.* When he'd go to a bar with his friends, he'd never mentioned any of his *girl* friends being there because, in his words, he didn't want me to get angry that he was hanging out with other women. The thing is, I'd never told him he couldn't do that. He kept things from me because he didn't want to fight, he said. He thought I would get mad over it, so he lied to avoid conflict and protect the peace.

I'm so stupid.

Flags of all shades of red were waving in front of my face, and I closed my eyes.

Because it was easier. Because it hurt less. Because I'm an idealistic coward.

"Do you need to vent?" Dr. Abner asks, reminding me I'm not alone. "How did you find out about the cheating?"

I snort. "Do you have endless patience and a taste for drama?"

"Whatever you need."

Maybe I should question why he's being so nice to me, but honestly? My heart feels numb today. I can add "venting to my mother's colleague and the man I've been trying to avoid for two years" to my list of questionable decisions.

So, I take a deep, shaky breath and let it all out.

He doesn't interrupt me once. Those intense eyes never leave my face, and I find that holding his stare makes my stomach do weird things that don't feel...terrible.

"I broke things off right away, and he said I was being unfair," I conclude when I'm done explaining what drove me to ruin his tire. My fingers find the pendant hanging around my neck—a single golden flower my parents gave me for my sixteenth birthday that I never take off. "Said we could work it out because it was a onetime mistake."

I don't know why I'm about to tell him this, probably one of the most humiliating things someone has ever said to me, but at this point, my self-love is pretty nonexistent.

So here we go.

"He blamed me for it." My voice comes out quiet, meek, and I hate that I'm letting Oliver do this to me so many months later. "He said he had needs and that I didn't...didn't always help him with those."

"Are you fucking kidding me, Lila?"

I only shrug, taking another sip of my lemony water.

We stay silent for a few moments, the noise from the party surrounding us, before he says in that deep voice, "You were brave for calling him out on his bullshit and kicking him out; I want you to know that. And I also need you to know you're not to blame for the choices he made. I don't want to hear you say that what you did or didn't do drove him to cheat on you because that's not true. It was his choice."

"I know it was his fault. But maybe if I had—"

"Absolutely not, Lila. Don't even go there."

"There's...something else." I'm already bugging him with all my drama, so what's some more? "A few months ago, I saw an opportunity for a summer internship at a children's camp for aspiring youth counselors. I would've had the chance to work under the supervision of real counselors and help kids, but you know what I did instead?"

He doesn't answer.

"I told Oliver about it, and he said I worked too hard and *he* deserved to spend a summer with me. We're only young once, he said. And I passed on the internship like an idiot. I gave up on an opportunity that would've helped my chances at getting my dream job after graduation. But the thing is, I can't graduate this upcoming December without having done an internship—I'm sure you're familiar with the university's policy—and I can't find one. That's what I get for being a tire-slashing vandal, I guess."

I hide my face in my hands, not caring if I smudge my mascara in the process. I might as well become a mess on the outside, too.

"You want to be a youth counselor because of your mom?" is what he asks next. No comment on how stupid I was.

"In part, yes." I swallow back the emotions climbing up my throat. "My mom... She's been through a lot. My aunt, too. They got the help they needed thanks to access to good mental health care, and I want to be that person for children who may need guidance. But it's more than that. I've always felt like..."

When the seconds tick by and the words won't come out, he nudges his leg against mine. An intimate gesture I'm surprised but not bothered by. "Like what?"

"I've always felt like I was born to be a youth counselor. To help children just like others helped my family." I take a deep breath through my nose. "But I lost my temper and did something so out of character for me. It may not seem like a big deal to you, but I'm a rule follower. I don't slash people's tires."

How am I supposed to teach children to be healthy when I'm

such a mess?

Dr. Abner stays silent for so long I'm starting to think he hasn't even heard me, but then he says, "If you want to work with kids and can't find an internship, I'm the board member of a youth center you could intern at if you're interested."

I blink once, twice. "You're *also* a board member at a youth center? Like a Doctor of Psychology, researcher, co-author, and what else isn't enough?"

His shoulders rise and fall. "I have many interests and great organizational skills. Why would I force myself to fit one box when I can do it all?"

Fair enough. If only I had that level of self-confidence.

"Thank you for offering, really, but I don't...you know, want things handed out to me."

Those thick eyebrows form a notch. "I'm not following."

"I don't want to take someone else's place just because you know my parents. Or because you think I'm a mess and feel sorry for me. I'm not about that."

The expression on his face is nothing short of unimpressed. "We are currently understaffed, so trust me that you wouldn't be taking anyone's place." My stomach twists at his words. "I'm a board member, but I wouldn't do the hiring. Haniyah, our director, is responsible for that. You'll also need to pass a background check and obtain a fingerprint clearance card—two things I can't just *hand out* to you."

Great, now I feel like a self-absorbed idiot.

"It's called Warlington Youth Center, on Main Street," he continues. "Your mom has visited it a few times; she can give you directions. But no pressure. I just thought I'd offer, since you want to become a youth counselor. We don't do summer internships, but we can arrange something starting in August if you're interested."

And even though I know I should avoid accepting any favors—especially from *him*—I can't deny I'm intrigued. "What kind of activities would I help with?"

He runs those big hands down the dark fabric of his suit pants, smoothing it down. Why I'm focusing on how big his hands are is something I'm not willing to dwell on, ever.

"You'll have to clear that out with your internship supervisor at the university, but mainly clinical and administrative functions, supervised counseling sessions, reporting, co-organizing workshops, that sort of thing."

It sounds...right up my alley.

It really does.

I'll find something else. I still have time to look at other options.

But do I? I was supposed to apply to summer internships in December, so those are off the table. And I've been looking at other options ever since, but youth counseling internships are scarce in Warlington, for whatever reason, and I can't afford to travel anywhere else.

I can't accept. What will happen if other students find out I'm interning with Reed Abner, who coincidentally happens to be my mom's close friend?

My inner voice is right. It'd be irresponsible to accept, not to mention it'd go against what I've been trying to avoid for years.

Am I ready to risk my reputation for an internship I could possibly do somewhere else?

I finish my glass of water under his scorching stare. He still hasn't touched his.

"Are you feeling better?" he asks.

To my surprise, I find myself giving him a genuine nod. "I'll be okay. Thank you for offering the internship."

"You know where to find me if you want to talk."

I smile at him, tight-lipped and nervous.

Why is Dr. Abner holding the flashlight at the end of the tunnel I'm in?

chapter 5

LILA

March

I tried. I really did.

Despite my attempts during the past few weeks, every time I came across an internship offer, I kept comparing it to the youth center. And just like that, they lost their appeal.

Warlington University has a very strict policy when it comes to internships; students have to find a suitable one and get satisfactory results if they want to graduate from their master's program. So, without an internship in place, anxiety ate at me until I finally gave in and emailed the youth center, asking for more information.

I can still decline, but doing some in-person research won't hurt.

Warlington Youth Center sits on a quiet street near Main Street, a historical house of red bricks, a black roof, and white windows. As I do a quick perusal of the two-story building from my car, I can't help but notice it's enormous. Is that a playground at the back?

I double-check the address my mom texted me earlier and confirm this is the place. With an accelerated pulse, I exit my car and walk across the parking lot to the main entrance. The door is locked, but I can see light coming from the inside.

No Dr. Abner, though.

Let's hope it stays that way.

I buzz the doorbell to my right, causing an older woman to snap her head up at me from behind the reception desk. A moment later, she presses some kind of button, and the door clicks open.

"Hello, dear. How can I help you?" she asks, adjusting her hijab as she stands. Her smile is warm, her eyes kind, and the soothing sound of her voice instantly puts me at ease.

I smile back. "Hi, I'm Lila Callaghan. I emailed you last week about an internship opportunity with Warlington University?"

Her eyes widen in recognition. "Why, of course! I'm Haniyah, director of Warlington Youth Center. It's great to meet you, Lila. Let me fetch someone to watch the front desk, and we'll talk in my office."

A few minutes later, I'm following Haniyah down a well-lit hallway.

"We've reached maximum capacity this year. Forty kids! Can you believe it?" She beams, her passion rubbing off on me the more she talks. "We serve children as young as five, all the way up to eighteen. We organize sports events, art classes, book club meetings, and many other activities. We help them with their homework, too, if they need any extra help. Oh, and lots of outdoor play when the weather cooperates."

"It sounds amazing," I say honestly. "I love the children's drawings on the walls. It's obvious this is a well-loved place."

Haniyah looks at me with a mixture of gratitude and kindness. "It really is, which we couldn't be more thankful for." She opens a door at the end of the hallway. "We're here. Take a seat, please."

Her office is tiny but cozy—a small fireplace to my right, a huge bookshelf to my left, and a crowded desk in front of the double windows. I don't see any aromatic candles, but it smells like fresh linen and lemons in here.

I lower myself to one of the two chairs in front of her desk as she takes her place behind it.

"Before we get to the boring part where I tell you all the internship requirements, tell me a little about yourself. What made you want to intern here?"

I've done enough internships and volunteering gigs to recognize that this is an impromptu, informal interview. And although I tend to feel nervous at those, Haniyah's presence and the good feeling I got from this place the second I walked in help rein in my nerves.

I give her an honest explanation. "I've always felt a strong calling to help others. Children, specifically. I'm graduating from my counseling MA in December, and my plan is to become a youth counselor as soon as I get all my qualifications."

"That's admirable," she says. "I looked over the CV and motivation letter you attached to your email, and I must say, I'm really impressed with your academic background. For such a young woman, you are incredibly talented. Can you tell me more about your volunteering experience at the women's shelter last summer?"

For the next twenty minutes, Haniyah and I exchange stories about our times working with different community groups. It doesn't feel like an interview—more like a casual chat with a friend over coffee, sans the coffee.

She tells me about her background as a social worker, and how becoming director of this youth center was a long-term goal she finally achieved.

And then, she sobers up.

"I'll be honest with you, Lila." She clasps her hands together over her desk, looking at me intently. "I think you'd be a fantastic fit for Warlington Youth Center. If you share the sentiment, I'd be happy to tell you more about the internship so you can think about it. No pressure, though. We want everyone here to be a hundred percent committed, so if you have any doubts, you can say no. We won't take it personally."

I shift on my chair, my heart aching to shout from the rooftops that I know this is the place for me.

I'm a walking contradiction. I've been avoiding him for two years, and suddenly I want to intern at a youth center he's a *board member* of? His role here isn't exactly a secret from the public, so what if people find out I'm an intern here and start talking?

It's what he said about Haniyah being in charge of the interns that makes me think everything will be fine. Because if he isn't my direct supervisor, other students in my master's can't say I'm abusing my privilege to be here.

Right?

"So, what is it going to be?" Haniyah asks, a whisper of a smile on her lips.

Say it. Be brave.

"I certainly share the sentiment," I tell her genuinely. "I'd love to know more about the internship. Thank you so much for this opportunity."

"That's exactly what I wanted to hear." She beams. "All right, let's get down to business. I promise I'll be quick. I don't want to take up too much of your time; I know how busy MA students are."

She does? Does she have children or nieces and nephews who are also in graduate school? I don't ask because I don't want her to think I'm prying, but I wonder.

Haniyah turns the screen of her computer so I can see the lengthy document she's just pulled up.

"This is the internship guide, which I'll email you later today so you can look it over at home," she explains. "But the essentials are—three months of consecutive internship starting in August, dedicate at least ten hours of work on-site in the first month and sixteen hours during the remaining two, and attend weekly supervisions and meetings. That's pretty much it."

"Sounds good. What would my role entail?"

"You'll start by shadowing your supervisor in group and one-on-one sessions with the kids and help them with reports and co-organizing workshops." The more she keeps talking, the more it sounds like an absolute dream. "Then, when we deem you qualified enough, you'll be on your own with the kids. These sessions will be recorded and reviewed by your supervisor, of course.

"We're a tight-knit family here. Our kids come from families dealing with all kinds of hardships—financial struggles, parents recovering from addiction, kids whose parents are or have been incarcerated..." She gives me a tender smile. "Their mental health and academic performance are our main priority, but we also do other activities, such as days out in the park or visits to local museums. We want them to know there's a life out there worth exploring and that they can explore it. They deserve to, no matter what their personal circumstances look like. If you join us, you'll also have the opportunity to get to know our kids in a more informal setting, like in the playroom or the art room—not just as a youth counselor but as a young woman who can offer them inspiration and encouragement."

Who's cutting onions right under my nose?

My eyes start to sting, and I can't find the words to ask her any questions or even thank her for her explanation.

Because something in my chest opens and tightens at the same time. And then that something sparkles, then burns, then erupts.

The light Mom always talks about.

I'm not a spiritual person, but I recognize the passion sizzling in my chest for what it is—a calling.

My calling.

The place where I'm meant to be right now, the path I'm meant to follow.

I clear my throat, willing my tears to stay locked in because crying at an internship interview must be as unprofessional as it gets.

"Your work and commitment to these children is nothing short of inspiring," I tell her. "I'd be honored to be part of it."

"You'll fit right in. You'll see," she assures me with that motherly smile. "Do you have any questions for me? If you can't think of any right now, we can schedule another visit once you've gone over the internship guide and the contract."

"I do have a couple of questions now if that's okay. Do you offer any in-house training?"

"Of course! I can't believe I forgot to tell you about that." She chuckles. "It's a pretty standard procedure. You'll have to pass a background check first. You'll also have to meet the qualifications of a mental health professional and have a driver's license. Lastly, we offer an online course and on-site training you'll have to complete before joining us in August. Does that sound good to you?"

"It sounds great." I shift on my seat. "You also mentioned I'd have to shadow my supervisor for a while and report to them?"

She nods. "A mental health professional from the youth center will be in charge of training and guiding you through this internship. You'll have your weekly meetings with them and follow them around for the first few weeks, observing. It doesn't sound like a lot of fun when I put it like that, but I promise you'll learn a lot. Think of your supervisor as a fairy godmother of sorts."

That makes me smile. "Is there any chance that supervisor will be you?"

A girl can dream. Haniyah seems like she'd be a kind, efficient supervisor I could learn a lot from.

"Oh, dear, I'd love to. Unfortunately, my responsibilities as director don't leave me much room to wiggle anything else in.

But worry not. Reed is an excellent professional, and he'd love to supervise such a bright student as you are."

The air whooshes out of my lungs.

Reed.

I clear my throat. This isn't happening right now. "Reed Abner?"

"You know him? He didn't mention you'd be applying. Well, it doesn't surprise me you're familiar with him, really. He's made quite the name for himself, that boy."

She says it with a soft smile that shows how much she cares about him, but also makes me wonder why she's calling him a boy when Reed is all man. Even if it weren't for his giantlike stature or how big he is overall, the way his mere presence commands a room denotes a kind of subtle power only experience and confidence can give.

"He's, um, he works at my university," I tell her. She doesn't need to know about my mom.

She frowns. "He's not your professor, is he? Because that may present a conflict of interest, which could change things."

"He's not my professor. He's a researcher and supervises PhD students, which I'm not."

"That's fine, then. See, we're currently a little understaffed. We're making it work while we aim to expand, but currently, Reed is the only person in charge of our Mental Health Department until we get more funding. He does an outstanding job, as you can imagine, but that means he's the only person here who's qualified enough to give you the best possible internship experience. If you say he's not your professor and you're not his student, then we're in the clear."

I gulp. "So, you're saying there's no one else here who could be my supervisor?"

"Is there a problem with Reed?" she asks, confusion lacing her words.

"No, no," I quickly say like a total liar. Because I *might* have a tiny, little problem with this whole thing, but I don't want to be an inconvenience when Haniyah is being so welcoming to me. "I was just wondering."

She eyes me like she doesn't fully believe me, but she doesn't press. "Reed is actively trying to expand our Mental Health Department through his research so we can bring more dedicated professionals into the youth center. Not only to this one, but to every other youth center, community center, and foster home in the state. We're lucky to have countless volunteers who are also social workers, therapists, and youth counselors, but he's currently the only member in his department who possesses the qualifications and the time to oversee interns. I'm sure you understand."

"I understand." My smile wavers. Not because I suddenly don't want to intern here, but because Dr. Abner being my supervisor complicates things. "I'd love to review the guide and contract with my professor, and I'll get back to you within a couple weeks. Would that work for you?"

"Absolutely. Take your time, please. It was lovely to meet you, Lila. Oh, before I forget, let me show you around. All the kids are still at school, so it's the perfect time to see everything before chaos ensues."

I follow her out of her office and down the same hallway we passed on our way here. "These doors lead to offices and supply closets. That one is Reed's office, where you'll be meeting with him if you join us."

Right. Because *meeting with Reed* sounds absolutely fantastic.

"And here's our main room," she says when we reach an enormous, open room down the hall from the reception desk.

Colorful tables and chairs, both kid and adult-sized, a few new couches and comfortable-looking beanbags, a TV, and a foosball table adorn the room. It's well-lit, and huge windows on the other side lead to a garden with a playground. It smells like a classroom, taking me right back to childhood.

"This room is incredible," I breathe out.

"We were only able to afford this renovation last year, so I'm happy you like it. See that door over there?" She points to a far corner of the room. "That hallway leads to the library and the kitchen, where we keep some snacks for the kids. Follow me upstairs."

We take the stairs, but she tells me there's also an elevator available in case anyone who's injured or uses a wheelchair ever needs it.

"All five classrooms are here, as well as the infirmary and two bathrooms. There are a couple bathrooms downstairs, too," she explains. "I don't know if you saw, but there's a playground outside and a community garden."

"I did. It's really impressive what you've done with this place."

"Thank you, honey. I'm glad you like our youth center." She looks at me with a hopeful gleam in her eyes. "Well, I believe that's all for the tour. Do you have any more questions for me?"

I shake my head. "Not really. You've explained everything perfectly."

And the more time I spend here, the more I'm convinced this is where I'm supposed to be.

Minus Dr. Abner supervising me.

I'm itching to ask Haniyah if there's absolutely any way someone else can supervise my internship, but her answer was pretty clear. Plus, being so insistent will for sure set off all her alarms, and I don't want her to think I'm a weirdo.

Once we're back on the ground level, Haniyah tells the woman at the front desk she can go back to her office, and she takes over once again.

"Let me email you all the paperwork now before I forget,"

she tells me, logging into the computer. "It'll just be a minute. Remind me, what's your email address?"

I've barely just said the words when the front door unlocks behind me.

Haniyah looks up, an easy smile on her face. "Oh, just in time."

When I glance over my shoulder and lock eyes with him, I'm confident that the universe is laughing in my face.

"Hey," that familiar deep voice says. He sounds serious, a harsh contrast to Haniyah's welcoming nature. "Lila."

I hate everything about this.

"Hi, Dr. Abner."

There, boundaries. No *Reed* nonsense will be leaving my mouth anytime soon. Or ever.

I turn to Haniyah, hoping I don't sound as panicked as I feel. "Thank you so much for taking the time to answer my questions and show me around. I have to get going, but I'll be in touch."

"Sure, honey. The pleasure was all mine." She turns to him. "Lila here is thinking of joining us in August as an intern youth counselor. I told her you'd be in charge of her supervision."

"Is that right?" he asks slowly, his intense gaze on me.

"I'm thinking about it," I quickly say. "I... I need to go now, but thank you for your time, Haniyah."

"No problem, dear. I hope to hear back from you."

I nod, itching to get out of here.

Dr. Abner's woodsy scent fills my nostrils as I pass him on my way to the door, and I swear my knees buckle a little.

Get a grip.

With my hand on the handle, I start breathing normally once again, knowing I'm seconds away from getting the hell out of his orbit.

But then that gruff voice behind me says, "Drive safe, Lila."

And I'm back to square one.

chapter 6

REED

I watch as Lila hurries down the steps to the parking lot and gets inside her car.

The sound of Haniyah typing away at the computer and mumbling to herself doesn't pull me away from the blonde until her car disappears down the road.

"Are you done ogling dear Lila?"

I snap my head toward her—the woman who gave me everything when I had nothing.

"Don't say that. It makes me sound like a creep."

I'm met with her easy laugh. "I watched you grow up into the man you are today, Reed. You're many things, and a creep isn't one of them."

"Care to share what those many things are?" I smirk, leaning over the reception desk as she continues to fiddle around with the computer. "Need any help with that?"

She throws me a glare. "I might be old, but I can handle technology just fine."

"Just teasing you, Han."

Her eye roll is affectionate. "Well, let's see. You're the sharpest and most driven person I know, for one. You're incredibly stubborn, which sometimes plays in your favor—but often doesn't. You also have the kindest, most selfless soul I've ever come across, and I know many people. What else? Oh, yeah, you're definitely not a creep, but you're hiding something from me. Something about Lila. So, what is it?"

Damn it, this woman is something else.

After nearly three decades of knowing her, I should know better than to think she can't see right through me. That's how we became family, after all.

Because, for all intents and purposes, Haniyah is like a mother to me.

"She said she knew you from the university," she presses.

"Right. She isn't my student, though." I glance at the clock mounted on the wall behind the reception desk. The kids will be here in less than an hour. "And I don't exactly know her from the university. I've worked with her mother before, the children's author—Grace."

Haniyah's eyes widen. "She's Grace's daughter? They do look alike, now that I think about it."

Grace has been to the youth center several times to talk about what it's like being an author—as some of the kids here really enjoy writing—and even co-organized a storytelling workshop with me once.

"I mostly know her through her parents, that's all," I explain.

"When I told her you'd be supervising her internship, she looked kind of freaked out." Her voice is quiet, as if someone could overhear us. "Why would that be? Have you ever taught any of her classes?"

"I haven't."

But I might have a slight idea as to why she didn't seem too excited about the idea of me supervising her.

"I looked at her résumé, and it's truly impressive. I haven't heard of a 4.0 GPA since yours, and that was years ago. She's quite the brilliant young lady, so don't scare her away. She could really help the kids here."

"I barely know her as it is," I tell her. "I'm not trying to scare her away."

"Let's keep it that way." She gives me a stern look, but I know she's messing with me. "Who do you have on for today?"

I don't need to look at my planner. "I have Cameron in for a counseling session at four. We're still working on his anger issues, but I'm not seeing much progress, so I'm thinking of changing my approach."

"Maybe Lila can help you with that when she joins us. A new perspective will be good for you," she muses.

Something tells me Lila won't be joining us at all, if her reaction to seeing me was any indicator. But I don't have it in me to tell Han not to get her hopes up.

"I'll see what I can do." I rap my knuckles on the counter. "I'll be in my office if you need me."

"Sure. Have a good day, Reed."

No matter how much time goes by, I never get used to the silence in the youth center before we open up. It feels wrong that these hallways aren't filled with laughter and the occasional excited scream. Because if I've learned anything in the past five years as a board member, it is that the word *quiet* isn't part of any child's dictionary.

And honestly? I'm more than okay with that.

I think about Cameron and the rest of the kids here who need our help, and my chest constricts. Despite the numerous improvements we've made in the past year alone—such as upgrading the main playroom and organizing more educational field trips—it doesn't feel like it's nearly enough.

More. We should be doing more. *I* should be doing more.

Hopefully, the project I'm working on with the state government will go through and give foster homes and youth centers enough funding to improve our mental health departments. It won't get approved—if it even does—until next year, but everything is going smoothly for now.

I haven't come this far—which is a miracle in itself,

considering my past—only to stop now.

"I want to run him over with a car."

I count to five in my head and take a deep, calming breath through my nose.

Here we go.

"You're twelve, Cameron. You can't drive," I say in an even voice, not looking away from the boy across from me. His eyes are glued to his jeans-clad lap where he rests his angry fists. "Which isn't the point, anyway. Running people over with cars is illegal. I bet you don't want to go to jail."

"Kids can't go to jail," he tells me, sounding so sure I wouldn't put it past him to have looked into it.

"They can." At that, his alarmed eyes snap up at me. "There are prisons built specifically for minors who commit crimes."

"You're lying." I give him a flat look that tells him no, I'm very much not bullshitting him. His throat bobs with a hard swallow before he asks, "Are you going to send me to a kids' prison?"

"Why would I do that?"

He shifts on the armchair placed in the middle of the counseling room, a layer of guilt draping over his face. "Because I just told you I want to run Sean over with a car."

"You can't go to jail for something you haven't done. What I'd like to know is why you'd want to do that to Sean in the first place."

He doesn't hesitate. "Because he made fun of my sister for having dyslexia."

Before today's session started, I already knew he'd bring this up. According to what one of the volunteers told me, a few days ago, Melody—Cameron's twin sister—was struggling with her homework when one of the other kids her age made fun of her for not getting the answers right.

Melody was diagnosed with dyslexia and ADHD three months ago, which helped us craft a more thorough study plan for her here. She's doing okay, but her brother has made it his life's mission to protect her from all harm.

And it would be noble of him if he didn't use violence to keep her safe—he didn't run Sean over with a car, but last month, he would have punched him in the face had Haniyah not intervened in time.

"How would hurting Sean help your sister?" I ask him.

Cameron looks away, arms crossed over his chest. "I don't know. He will stop bothering her, I guess."

Voices from outside of the room filter under the door, other children running up and down the hallway while getting reprimanded for running in the first place.

"All right, let's say you hurt Sean and he stops messing with Melody. What happens when another kid makes fun of your sister?" I lean back in my armchair. "Will you run them over with a car, too?"

He shrugs. "If I have to."

"Then I guess someone else will have to protect your sister when you're in jail."

That has him looking at me again, alarmed. "No. *I* will protect Melody. Nobody else."

"You can't protect anyone from jail. And depending on how badly you hurt Sean, or anyone else, you might stay in jail forever. You might never see your sister again. Is that what you want?"

"No." He sits up, agitated. "No. I don't want to go to jail."

"Let's leave jail aside for a second." I lean forward, resting my arms on my knees. "I know how you're feeling, Cameron. You love your sister and you want to keep her safe, but we all get hurt. It's part of life, and that's also how we grow. It makes us stronger. You can't control what happens to your sister."

"But it's unfair. Melody did nothing wrong. She can't control her dyslexia."

"You're right. We have very little control over what happens to us," I concede. "What Sean did was wrong. It shouldn't have happened, and it hurt your sister. But instead of threatening to run people over with your nonexistent car, I think you should focus on helping Melody instead."

He frowns. "I help her lots."

"You aren't helping her, Cameron. You get in fights with whoever so much as looks at her the wrong way, and eventually you're going to get in serious trouble."

When I catch his light intake of breath, I take it as a sign to keep going. "Both you and Sean are twelve and should know better. You're not babies anymore. Wanting to protect your sister is very honorable, but do you know what would make you an even better brother?"

"What?" he mutters, not sounding like he's that interested in my answer.

I take a quick glance at the clock on the far wall, noting we only have a few minutes left of our session.

"Teaching Melody how to defend herself," I say. "And not with her fists. You know violence isn't the answer."

"But it works."

"Not in the long run. You know why? Because you're giving other people the power to control you. Their words and actions affect you so much, you lose your temper and do bad things. Sure, punching someone may stop them from hurting your sister, but it will also get you into trouble. There are ways to stand up for yourself and for others that won't have terrible consequences for you."

"Like what?"

"Like not caring about what people say. If someone bothers your sister, what you should do is ignore that person and tell a parent or a teacher. They will deal with it and make sure it doesn't happen again."

He gives me an unsure look, like he's not fully convinced. "What's the point if Melody will be hurt anyway?"

I can't say I didn't see that rebuttal coming. "She'll get hurt even if you run someone over with your car, won't she? The damage will be done, but we can control how we react to it. You don't care about what others say about you, and that's a great thing. I think you can teach your sister to be more like you in that regard. Help her stand up for herself."

He hides his hands inside the pockets of his hoodie. "Maybe I wouldn't mind going to jail for my sister."

The alarm in my phone goes off, signaling the end of our session. But a different one rings in my head at his last statement.

"Before you go." I pass him over a small notebook. "Homework."

His groan isn't unexpected. "What is it?" he asks, scanning the blank notebook.

"Every time you feel angry or frustrated, instead of hurting someone or breaking something, I want you to write down whatever bothered you on this notebook and then rip the page you wrote on."

His eyes widen. "You're gonna let me rip the pages?"

"Yep." I give him my pen. "Go ahead. Write something that bothered you today, read it to me, and then rip it out."

Visibly enthusiastic about this idea—or at least curious enough to try—he quickly scribbles something and clears his throat, reading what he wrote. "Mom made me wear this hoodie today, and I don't like it because it has a dinosaur on it, and it makes me look like a baby."

"Very well. Now rip the page."

I don't have to tell him twice.

Cameron destroys the paper until only the smallest pieces remain. When he's done, his face has visibly relaxed.

"Feel good?" I ask, earning me a nod from the boy. "Here's

the catch, though. Once you write down what bothers you and you rip the paper, that's it—you can't think about it again or act on it. You can feel all the anger and frustration as you're breaking the paper, but once you're done, you have to move on. And clean up the mess, of course. Do we have a deal?"

He surprises me by reaching out his fist, silently asking me to bump it. "Deal."

Twenty minutes after our session is over, I'm working on his report when my phone pings with a text.

> **Cal: I have a free slot in two weeks for that tattoo. No pressure (yes pressure).**

I shake my head, smirking at his sheer determination to ink me up. To be fair, I suggested it first. It was during a moment of weakness—after a few glasses of whiskey at a social gathering neither of us wanted to be at, but Grace had been invited—and Cal, who was very sober, never let go of the idea of tattooing me.

> **Me: We don't even have a sketch, man.**

> **Cal: Throw some ideas and give me twenty minutes.**

> **Me: Maybe next time. Still unsure.**

> **Cal: You know I'm just messing with you. You shouldn't rush it. Just wanted to remind you I have a slot for you whenever you want it.**

The tender, marred skin between my shoulder blades burns, just like every time I think of covering it with ink.

Do I want to erase what happened? Choose the easy way out?

The most logical part of me knows my wounds run much, much deeper than the ones visible on my skin. Tattooing over the scar my father gave me when I wasn't strong or brave or old enough to defend myself doesn't mean my memories will go away.

But my heart refuses to accept it.

Me: Appreciate it.

I lock my phone and turn on my computer, going back to Cameron's report.

And I wonder if Cal knows why his daughter looks like she wants to run away from me every time she sees me.

chapter 7

LILA

April

I was five years old the first time someone made me question my worth.

Growing up, I'd always been a bubbly kid. I never held in my laughter, always wondered out loud when I had questions, and asked for what I needed.

I got that last trait from my aunt Maddie, no doubt.

But all that confidence didn't sit well with many, especially not when I was also on top of every class and good at sports. I wasn't rubbing my accomplishments in anyone's face, but I wasn't hiding them either. Why would I? Was I not supposed to feel proud of myself?

And I did—I felt proud and deserving of everything I worked hard for. My family cheered me on and taught me to value myself, so I didn't know how to do anything else.

Until that day.

It all started because Trish, one of my then friends, was feeling down after getting her progress report.

"I got three Unsatisfactory," she complained, and I felt for her. I truly did. I knew how much effort she put into her classes, but her results didn't always show it. "It's so bad."

"You'll get better next year," I remember saying, putting an arm around her shoulders to comfort her. It wasn't much, but I'd never been one to ignore people who needed cheering up. "Your moms will understand."

"I hope they let me go to the pool this summer." She sounded and looked defeated as the rest of our friends kept their gazes trained on the ground, uncomfortably kicking the gravel around us. "What did you get?"

"Huh?"

"On your progress report."

"Oh. All Satisfactory."

Our friends stopped kicking the ground, their gazes snapping up at me.

Trish shrugged my arm off her shoulders.

The energy shifted in an instant, and at the time, I didn't understand why.

Victor, a good friend from my very first day at preschool, spoke next. "So you think you're better than us?"

I remember the exact feeling of my stomach sinking. "What?" I repeated, dumbfounded. "I don't."

They had asked me a question, and I'd only answered. Had I said something wrong? Was I supposed to lie?

"All Satisfactory," Trish said, mimicking my voice. "You're not cooler than us."

"I'm not saying that!" I stood, agitated. "I was just telling the truth. You asked me a question!"

Trish rolled her eyes. "If you think you're so smart, you can find other friends."

I didn't have that kind of vocabulary at the time, but today I think back on that moment and the only words that come to mind are *what the fuck*.

I hadn't meant to brag. Why was everyone suddenly giving me the stink eye? Like I had just destroyed their self-confidence on purpose?

When I saw those same friends on the first day of the new

school year, everything went back to normal. They weren't angry anymore, but I was confused. Even so, I decided to ignore it because I hated conflict—still do—and maybe I had imagined it all. Or maybe they'd forgotten about it.

Whatever. Everything was fine. *I* was fine.

Until I was fifteen and I found out my group of friends had been saying not-so-kind things about me behind my back. That I was so stuck-up, *so better than everyone else*, nobody truly wanted to be my friend.

As a teenager, it was a brutal blow to my self-esteem.

And it didn't stop there—every time I achieved something, I would get a backhanded comment about how I shouldn't share how well I was doing because someone else was struggling.

Slowly, my head turned into a mess. On one side, I had my family telling me that I should be proud of myself. But on the other hand, I had "friends" telling me not to brag or to think I was better than everyone else, even though I never had. Not for one second.

Oliver told me to my face that I don't deserve to be a youth counselor because I have no idea what it's like to live a harsh childhood. That I must be in this profession just to feed my ego.

His words, piled up on top of years and years of friends and classmates telling me that it must be easy to get such good grades when all you have to worry about is your academic performance, gave way to this...this *monster* called insecurity.

But, if I really think about it, I can't complain—because they're right. I have it easy, and I shouldn't turn myself into a victim when there are people out there who have it much, much worse. People who have to take care of sick relatives or don't have the means to access higher education in the first place.

I'm just having a bad day, overreacting. All these bitter thoughts will be gone tomorrow.

"Earth to Lila."

I blink as my mother's waving hand comes into focus. "Huh?"

My dad leans over the dining room table as we're having dinner, a concerned notch between his dark brows. "Are the vegetables trying to communicate with you? Should we hold a séance?"

I try not to smile, making a point to glare at him. "Go ahead. See if we can contact your dead sense of humor."

He barks out a laugh, my mother joining him. "I probably deserved that one."

"Only probably."

My mom asks, mirth mixing with worry in her eyes, "Why do you look so out of it today, honey? Did something happen?"

If there's one downside to living with my parents, it's this. I love them, and we've always had a great relationship, but I can't hide anything from them, and sometimes it's a little inconvenient.

I tend to go to Maddie when something is bothering me—to Uncle James too—because sometimes a girl wants to talk to her cool aunt rather than to her parents. But there's no escaping this conversation tonight, if only because my dad looks a second away from panicking.

"It's not that big of a deal," I mutter.

Because it's really not.

"Then why do you look so upset?" That's my mom.

Everyone says we look alike because we have the same wavy blonde hair—although mine is considerably longer. I'm clearly her daughter, but I get my personality mostly from my dad, which is a fun fact I conveniently remind him of every time he thinks I'm being too stubborn because he's a million times worse.

My dad, with his imposing height and neck and arms fully covered in ink that make him look way younger than his sixty years, sighs. "Fine. Who do I have to kill?"

"Stop it, Cal," my mom scolds, but her eyes are smiling. "Let her talk."

He throws her a wink. "Whatever you want, sunshine."

Gag.

"I'm going to ignore that for the sake of my mental health," I say, repressing a shudder.

I love my parents and how much they love each other, but they can be disgustingly cheesy sometimes. Or all the time.

"Drama queen," my dad mutters under his breath, smirking at my killing stare.

"Anyway." I let out a deep sigh. "I'm just worried about this internship."

"Which internship?" my mom asks.

The back of my neck suddenly itches. "The one at the youth center."

My parents stay silent as they wait for me to explain something I really don't want to get into right now. But I also don't want my dad to worry, thinking something terrible is happening to me—*he's* the drama queen—so that's why I add, "I just don't know if I should take it."

The words taste sour in my mouth as soon as I say them.

It's been a little over two weeks since my interview. Haniyah has been nothing but welcoming to me, the facilities look amazing, and the internship program sounds exactly like what I've been waiting for. In fact, it sounds even better than the summer camp.

"Why are you hesitant?" my dad asks.

I shift on my seat, glancing around the open-concept kitchen and living room for a moment. This is the house where I grew up with Maddie before we both moved out at different times, my safe haven. Most of my happy childhood memories happened between these walls with my parents and my aunt, and it's sad to think I'm in this mental space right now. I don't have a right to complain about this when the people in front of me have given me so much and still do.

I look away from a framed picture of me with my little cousins, Maddie and James's children, and tell them the truth. "Because Dr. Abner would be my supervisor."

My mom blinks. "Reed? But that's good, isn't it?"

I lift my glass to my lips and take a sip of cold water, saying nothing. My throat burns.

My dad turns to my mom. "Did I miss something? Do we not like Reed now?"

"Yes, honey, we still like Reed." When she turns to me, all playfulness is gone from her voice. "He's the best counselor I've ever worked with *by far*. Went above and beyond for those books as if they were his own. Why are you having doubts?"

"I guess I just don't..." I hesitate. "I don't want to get special treatment for being your daughter. That'll get people talking, and it's not the kind of attention I need."

My mom shakes her head. "You've got it all wrong. Reed doesn't care about any of that. Take me as an example—we've been working together for years, and we're friends, but when something about my books isn't working, he never sugarcoats it."

"Mmm..." An unsure, noncommittal sound is all she's getting from me. My head is so loud that no coherent words would come out anyway.

"I'm serious, Li," she insists, probably reading my mind in that creepy way moms do. "He won't care that you're my daughter; if you don't meet his standards, he'll tell you. He won't let you do a subpar job."

"There. Problem solved," my dad declares as he finishes his food. "He doesn't care about your family tree, so no special treatment for you. You'll have to work hard for it like the rest of us peasants."

I rub my eyes with the heels of my palms and suppress a groan. "Okay, fine. He doesn't care if I'm your daughter. Great. But what if other students find out my mom's colleague is *conveniently* my internship supervisor? I don't want them to spread any rumors that I'm a snob or something. That someone else deserves all these opportunities, but I'm getting them instead because of my family's connections."

My mom blinks, looking at me like she's never seen me before. "Where is this coming from, Lila?"

My stomach sinks as I lie. "I'm just overthinking it."

"Okay, let's forget about Reed for a second," my dad says. "If he weren't in the picture, would you take this internship?"

"Yes." I don't hesitate. "The program sounds amazing, and they're doing a great job at helping the children in our community."

"There's your answer, then. Stop worrying and listen to your gut."

But I shake my head. "It's more complicated than that, Dad. I'm graduating this year. I just need to do my thing and fly under the radar. If people find out about the internship, they'll start talking."

"How would they even find out?" he asks.

"We talk about those things."

"So lie to them."

"I don't want to lie." I turn to my mom, who's been suspiciously quiet for the past few minutes. "What do you think?"

"I think..." She pauses, and I already know I'm not going to like what she's going to say next. "I think you've always worried too much about what other people think of you, Lila, and it's getting out of hand."

I freeze. "Mom, I—"

But she isn't hearing me.

She doesn't look upset or angry as she stands from the dining table, disappearing into the kitchen behind her. My mom isn't prone to dramatic outbursts, which means her silence is the scary warning sign.

I share a look with my dad, me freaked out and him amused. He mouths to me, "Good luck."

"Where are you going?" I call out to my mom. My voice is only shaking a little.

It doesn't take her more than a few moments to come back, but she isn't looking at me. She's holding her phone, her eyes glued to the screen as she types away. "Shock therapy."

That makes my heart start beating uncontrollably, and not in a good way.

"I'm inviting Reed for dinner tomorrow so you get over this weird apprehension about something terrible happening when you're around him." *No way in hell.*

"Mom, I don't think this is necessary."

"I think it's *very* necessary." She sits back down and gives me a look between concern and worry. I don't like it one bit. "I understand not wanting people to think you don't deserve what you have. But you're letting people who don't know you or care about you dictate your life choices. Your dad and I won't sit here and watch you say no to things you want to do just because someone else might think you're getting undeserved help. You know you aren't, and that should be enough."

I hate that her words make so much sense.

I hate that my brain agrees, but my heart refuses to accept it.

"We're going out for dinner tomorrow. I've just invited Reed so you can talk about your internship and hopefully see how worthwhile it'll be to say yes. Don't think I haven't noticed how you avoid him every time you're in the same room."

"It's not personal," I argue. "I truly have nothing against him. I've even read his papers and attended his talks. I admire his work a lot, but—"

"No buts," my dad interrupts. "Your mom is right, Li. This is going too far. You need to face your fears head-on. Who cares what other people think or say about you? Don't give them so much power over your life, little sunshine. You're the only one in charge of it."

I don't bother telling him that he's wrong, that I'm very much *not* in charge of anything in my life. Because if someone suddenly decides to start a rumor about how my mom got me the internship instead of my own merits, I'll be done for. Nobody likes nepotism.

How is *that* being in control?

"He's just replied," my mom says, checking her phone. "Looks like he's free tomorrow night. Wonderful."

Ground, please swallow me.

chapter 8

LILA

"Hey, Li—whoa there."

The sudden sound of Mariah's voice makes me jump and stub my foot against the door of her closet. Karla, her roommate and our friend, follows closely behind.

"*Shit,*" I hiss, crouching to check I'm not bleeding to death. But nope—I'm just dramatic. "Sorry, I didn't hear the door opening."

My best friend glances around her room, a mixture of amusement and worry dancing in her dark eyes. "What in the hurricane-tornado is going on here?"

I kneel in front of the messy pile of clothes on the ground, trying to find that one skirt the ground must have swallowed instead of swallowing *me.* "I'm pretty sure hurricane-tornados aren't a thing."

"Are you going on a date or something?" Karla asks me in a teasing voice.

That earns her a snort. "As if."

Mariah and Karla know about Oliver—the cheating, the harsh words he parted with, the lost summer camp internship, and how Dr. Abner was there when I slashed the stupid tire.

I've known Mariah since we were babies, with her dad being my dad's best friend and co-owner of the tattoo parlor, and we never hide anything from each other. Much like my aunt Maddie, Mariah is my go-to person for pretty much everything.

I first met Karla in my undergraduate psychology program, and we quickly became friends. We both prefer quiet nights in and have a passion for overworking at the library—a match made in heaven. She's also pursuing a counseling MA, which means she understands my dilemma with Dr. Abner better than anyone.

Hours ago, after I finally gave up on my own closet, I texted Mariah saying there was an emergency and that I needed to raid hers. I don't have an array of going-out clothes to choose from because...well, I rarely go out. Mariah does, and we're pretty much the same size, so it was a no-brainer.

My best friend didn't even ask what the emergency was before agreeing. I used the spare key to their apartment to get in here before she finished her shift at the tattoo parlor.

"It's just dinner with my parents," I tell them over my shoulder as I finally decide on a dark green dress. It's not the skirt I wanted to wear tonight—which is something a lot more low-key than this—but it will do.

"Why are you worked up, then?" Mariah asks. "Contrary to popular belief, your dad and I don't gossip about you during work hours. We leave the fun activities for our lunch break."

Mariah is two years younger than me, but she's already following in the footsteps of her dad, Uncle Trey—my dad's best friend—and making a name for herself in the tattooing sphere of Warlington. She began pursuing a career as a tattoo artist at seventeen and now works at Inkjection, my father's tattoo shop.

I roll my eyes, but I'm smiling. "We have a *special* guest tonight, so I don't think leggings are appropriate for the occasion."

Mariah pulls her long locs back into a ponytail. "Hey, leggings are always appropriate if you believe it hard enough."

"Why did you say *special* like that?" Karla asks, plopping down on Mariah's bed.

Rubbing my eyes with the heels of my palms, I say, "It's Reed Abner. You know, my mom's co-author. The guy who witnessed me becoming a tire-slashing criminal. The internship guy."

Karla's eyes widen. "Why is he going to your family dinner?"

"Because I may or may not have said that I was hesitant to take the internship at the youth center because of him, and my mom thought I was being unreasonable." My shoulders rise and fall with a sigh. "She invited him over for dinner so I could get over myself."

"First of all, your mom is iconic and I'm a fan," Mariah says. That earns her a glare she shrugs off. "And secondly, she's right. You *are* being unreasonable and dumb and childish about this. Get your head out of your ass and accept that internship. We all know you're dying to."

"That's not the point." I start putting her clothes back in the closet because I can't stand still right now. "The point is that people—"

"If you say you're scared of what people will say about it, I'm going to scream," Mariah continues. "You're my sister from another mister, and that's why I'm telling you this, okay? Nobody gives a shit about what you do or don't do with your life."

Ouch.

"People are obsessed with their own lives and problems, which is completely normal. They aren't as focused on yours as you think they are," she finishes.

It makes sense—it really does. So why does my heart refuse to listen?

"That's so true," Karla chimes in, twirling a blonde curl between her fingers. "It's easy to get wrapped up in your own world and think you're the most important person in everyone else's."

"Okay, yes, but..." I put Mariah's last shirt away and shut the closet. "If people in our MA find out about the internship with him, they'll start talking. And I'm not making it up or jumping to conclusions; I know it for a fact. They love gossip. Karla would know."

"Oh, yeah. They're brutal." She nods, her eyes wide as she looks at her roommate. "They found out a girl from our class does tarot, and they've been calling her Weirdo Witch behind her back ever since."

Which says a lot about people who are studying to become mental health professionals, if you ask me.

"No offense to Weirdo Witch because tarot is cool as hell, but who gives a shit?" Mariah says. "Sorry, Li, but I'm with your mom on this one. You need to start making decisions based on what you want—not what you think others will approve of. That's literally insane. You're so smart. Why are you behaving like a cute little idiot about this?"

Wouldn't I like to know that?

"We're going out with some friends tonight. Text us if you want to join when you're done with your drama dinner." She comes up to me and gives me a crushing hug. I inhale the familiar scent of lavender from her body wash. "Love you, Li. Don't make dumb decisions you'll regret later."

"Love you too." I hug her a little tighter. "And I'll try."

But I'm not so sure I'll be able to do it.

REED

I spot her the second I enter the crowded restaurant.

The satin fabric of her deep green dress catches the muted light of the chandelier, her golden hair shining with a beckoning glow. She's sitting at a round table with her parents, the only seat available being the one to her right, and I recall Grace's text.

Grace: Hi, Reed. Are you free tomorrow night? Lila has some questions about the internship, and she'd love to speak with you. How do you feel about Italian food? Our treat.

Up until that point, my only Saturday night plans consisted of maybe going out for a drink with Liam and Warren. Ditching my friends to come here wasn't a tough choice.

"Reed." Grace smiles as she spots me first, standing to give me a hug. "So glad you could make it."

"Thank you for the invitation." I hug her back before shaking Cal's hand. "Don't start," I warn him.

He barks out a laugh. "Fine, I won't try to convince you to get the tattoo you so clearly, desperately want. Scout's honor."

"You've never been a Boy Scout, honey," Grace says with a playful roll of her eyes.

"Shh. He doesn't have to know."

A chuckle coming from the other side of the table shifts my attention to Lila. She's leaning slightly on the cushioned chair, arms crossed, an unimpressed expression on her face.

"Lila." I lower myself onto the seat next to her. I don't break eye contact, although her attention is on the table despite the space being empty except for her glass of water, a fancy cloth napkin, and some cutlery. "How was your week?"

If the circumstances were different, I wouldn't have hesitated to tell her how beautiful she looks tonight. But I don't want to make things even more tense between us since I'm assuming we're here to fix exactly that.

I also don't want her dad to kill me on sight.

"Uneventful," she says, not adding anything else. She

unfolds her arms and plays with the hem of her dress, drawing my attention to her bare legs. *Get a goddamn grip.* "Yours?"

We're doing one-word conversations, apparently.

I lean back on my own chair, mimicking her position. "One of my PhD students messed up his data collection report, which set us back on our deadline. Grant holders don't like that, so I had to step in. That caused me to be late to a group meeting across campus. I pretty much sprinted to the meeting, only to get there and find out it had been canceled due to one of the faculty members going into labor. They had to drive her to the hospital."

Lila turns her head then, giving me a look between confusion and skepticism. "Did you just make that up?"

"Nope. My week has really been that eventful."

The only answer I get is a shake of her head.

Throughout dinner, Lila doesn't talk much. It's mostly her parents and me keeping the conversation alive, and although it's comfortable between us, I find myself constantly wondering what must be going through her head.

On more than one occasion, I catch her glancing around the restaurant. Looking for someone? Checking if anyone is looking at us? Could be both.

It isn't until we're done with dessert that Lila excuses herself to the bathroom and Grace follows her. After they leave, Cal leans over and says, "You'll have to forgive her. She isn't usually so quiet."

I lift my glass of wine to my mouth and take a sip. "She doesn't seem to like me very much."

"It's not that," he's quick to say. He sneaks a glance behind me to where his wife and daughter disappeared to the bathroom just moments ago.

"Look, Lila is⊠ She's fucking gifted, man, but her head isn't in the right place. She worries too much about other people's opinions, and since you're a family friend and you work with

Grace, she thinks she'll be getting some kind of special treatment from you. That's why she's hesitant to take the internship even though she wants to. She gets her stubbornness from me, so we're in for a treat," he jokes, but he can't mask his worry. "She doesn't look too keen on starting any conversations tonight. Would you mind broaching the subject? Ask her to go with you to the bar or something, have some privacy. Maybe it'll be easier if her mom and I aren't around."

"No problem. She needs a push; I can get behind that."

"You're the best, man. Thank you. She—never mind, they're coming back."

The scent of her flowery perfume alerts me to her nearness. I turn around on my seat, ready to ask her to come with me to the bar just like her father suggested, but she beats me to it.

"Reed," she starts. Her voice has a weird edge to it, as if it physically pains her to say my name. It may be the first time she hasn't called me Dr. Abner, in fact. "I'd love to talk to you about the internship. Have a drink with me?"

It surprises me that she's taking the lead after giving me the silent treatment all night. "Sure."

She doesn't wait for me before making her way to the bar. But her legs aren't exactly long, so I reach her side in a few long strides. Burying my hands in the pockets of my slacks, I resist the urge to place my hand on the small of her back to guide her through the crowd. Simultaneously, I wonder if I'm losing my mind. When was the last time I felt the slightest bit protective toward a woman?

Once at the bar, she orders a strawberry mojito, and I order a bourbon. And then I watch how she fidgets on the stool, how she actively avoids my gaze and looks two seconds away from running the hell out of here. Maybe I should find it insulting that she seems so put off by my presence, but life has taught me how to detach myself enough not to care.

"So," I drawl, "the internship you couldn't wait to talk about."

She throws me a glare. I smirk as I lift my glass to my lips and take a sip.

"I'm sure my parents have told you enough," she mutters, the voices around us almost drowning out hers.

I drag my stool a little closer, resting my foot on her footrest. "I want to hear it from you."

Instead of shutting down like I expected her to, she looks at me with a kind of fire in her eyes I've never seen before. "I don't want you to ruin my reputation."

That's not what I was expecting her to say. At all.

"Here's the thing, *Dr. Abner.*" She takes a long sip of her drink, as if needing the liquid courage. Her throat bobs as she swallows, and I follow the movement with my eyes. "People on campus know you have ties to my mother. They've asked me for your phone number on more than one occasion, just so you know."

I frown. They've done *what?*

"And when they find out you're my internship supervisor, they'll start talking about how I only got the chance to work with you because of my mom," she concludes.

"*When?* Does that mean you're taking the internship?"

"That's..." She watches my hand as I set the glass back down. "That's not the important thing to focus on right now."

"I think it's the only thing we should focus on right now," I argue. "What did you think of the facilities? Did you get to see the garden?"

"The youth center was impressive, but that's not—"

"And the library? We have some of your mother's books in there."

Did she just groan at me?

"I know you're purposely ignoring what I mean." She glares at me again. Maybe it would intimidate me if she didn't look so goddamn adorable. "Is that what you'd do as my supervisor, too? Ignore my concerns if you think they're dumb?"

"Let's get one thing straight." I lean over, her sweet scent wrapping around my lungs. "I don't think your concerns are dumb. Not one bit. What I think is that you really want to take this internship, but you won't do it because of me, and I'm not going to step back from my role just to make you comfortable. That's not what you need."

She doesn't make a move to put distance between us. "And you know what I need?"

Leaning closer, I rest my arm on the back of her stool. "You're going to deny you need someone to push you out of your comfort zone?"

I don't miss her slight intake of breath. "What if I want to get out of my comfort zone on my own? Take my time with it?"

"That won't do." My voice lowers, and it's like we're wrapped inside this invisible bubble where no one and nothing else matters. "Want to know why? Because you're taking things too far."

Her face is so close, I can see green specks in her accusatory eyes under the lamp's glow.

"Don't pretend you're oh-so-worried about me, when we both know you're only here because my parents asked you to be, *Dr. Abner.*"

"Your parents asked for my help because they love you, and I agreed because I don't want to see your potential go to waste."

"I just want to earn my place," she says. "I don't want any advantages."

"As I said, you won't get any." I tell her truthfully. "You were a straight-A student before this internship, and you will be afterward. Won't that tell people you've worked hard to earn what you have? I've never been your professor, and no other faculty members have any kind of ties to your mother, so they can't say you didn't deserve any of your previous accomplishments.

Nobody will be surprised if you ace your internship, either."

"They won't care," she argues. Her gaze drops to my mouth for a second, making my heart leap with momentary lust— an emotion I haven't felt in too long. *What the fuck?* "Once the rumors start rolling, that's it. There's no chance for redemption. And it's not like they'll care if you present them with the facts either."

I lean back, putting a safe distance between us once again, not only for my own sanity but also because there's no convincing her, and we both know it.

"Looks like you've made up your mind," I conclude, standing from my seat. "I can't say I understand it, but it's your life, and I'm nobody to interfere. I hope you find another internship you'd deem more beneficial to you."

"Wait." Her fingers wrap around my wrist, stopping me. "Where are you going?"

I don't pull away from her touch. She doesn't release me, either. "To thank your parents for dinner and call it a night."

"We were having a conversation."

"Yes, and I'm done with it."

"This whole reverse psychology thing won't work on me," she warns.

"I'm not playing any mind games with you." I tell her the truth. "We've all tried to get you to see how unreasonable this behavior is, but you're being stubborn because you're scared. You don't want to take a risk and do what you know is best for you, and that's your prerogative. This back-and-forth won't get us anywhere. It's been a hell of a week, and I'm tired, so if you'll excuse me, I'd like to go home."

My skin grows cold as soon as she releases her grip on my wrist. I refuse to ask myself why.

"Thank you for talking to me tonight," she says in a quiet voice. "And I'm sorry I wasted your time."

"Talking to you is never a waste of time, Lila."

Our eyes stay locked in for an eternal second before she breaks the contact to drink the remains of her mojito.

"You'll be okay here by yourself?" I ask. I know her parents are not far, but that doesn't stop me from worrying about someone bothering her.

She gives me a small nod. "I'll go back to our table in a moment."

I hesitate at her side, the idea of going home suddenly not feeling all that appealing anymore.

What's wrong with me?

But Lila isn't acknowledging my presence, her gaze lost somewhere behind the bar. With one last perusal to check that nobody has their sick eyes on her, I leave.

"No luck?" Grace asks me as I near our table, frowning with worry.

I glance back at Lila one last time to make sure she's okay.

"Sometimes, we need to let our loved ones choose their own path even if we don't think they're making the right choice," I tell her parents. "She's a smart girl. She'll be fine."

And I mean it. Not only because she's incredible on her own, but also because she's lucky enough to have a family who will always support her.

"Thank you for coming." Cal shakes my hand. "Don't be a stranger, Abner."

I nod. "Have a good rest of the night."

As I make the short walk to my car, I allow myself to admit one single truth—I wanted Lila to take the internship. Both because I know the experience would be beneficial for her and because I'm itching to dive deeper into that extraordinary mind of hers.

How would she approach clinical cases? What feedback would she have on my reports? How would she handle the more difficult kids?

The realization that I'll never know is unexpectedly bitter.

And it pains me, it really fucking does, that such a gifted young woman is giving up on her dreams because society has taught her that she'll be marked and defined by other people's opinions of her.

That's bullshit.

I understand where she is coming from. Once upon a time, I, too, felt that urge to fit in, to be loved, to be accepted.

Then life happened.

But Lila is protected by her parents, and she'll always be loved and accepted. I've known Grace and Cal long enough to know they'd give anything to see their daughter happy, to keep her safe, to give her the future she deserves. Yet her head isn't in the right place, and I wish she—

"Dr. Abner!"

That voice.

"Wait!"

The sound of her footsteps gets closer as I turn around.

"Don't go yet, please," Lila says, out of breath, as she finally reaches me.

"What is it?" I look behind her, alarmed. "Did something happen?"

I shouldn't have left her alone at the bar, goddammit. Her parents were there, and I know she can take care of herself, but I swear if some creep said anything—

"I'm fine," she hurries to say. "Well, I'm not *fine* because I feel terrible for behaving like a petulant child back there when you were just trying to help, and I... I want to tell you something."

My body relaxes. "All right."

She takes a deep breath, in and out. "You were right about everything. I'm making a mistake in caring so much about what other people will think of me, and I hate it. I hate it so much, but when I think of throwing all caution to the wind and just doing my thing, this...this *fear* creeps in and freezes me in place. But I'm tired.

"You're a magnificent researcher, Dr. Abner, and I've admired your work for years. I've annotated every paper, watched every talk, attended every public lecture you've given. It's no wonder my mom chose to work with you, because you're genuinely one of the greatest minds in the field, and I... I guess what I'm trying to say is that I'm still terrified, and I feel nauseous just thinking about the consequences, but I'd be honored to accept the internship and work under your supervision at the youth center. And I'm sorry, again, for being so rude to you when you've been nothing but understanding and patient with me."

For a moment, I say nothing.

Over the years, I've learned to never depend on external validation to grow my self-worth. I'm not one to look for approval in other people, least of all a woman more than a decade younger than me. But I would be lying if I said her praise didn't light something in me. Something new and not entirely uncomfortable.

The truth of her words shines in her eyes despite the darkness of the night around us.

"Being brave is all about going after what you want, even when you're scared," I say, repeating the words I would tell myself when a different kind of darkness took over me. "I'm glad to hear you'll be joining us this summer."

She smiles at me, soft and sweet and genuine, and I finally peek into the young woman within. The one who has been there all this time, buried under a thick layer of insecurities.

And I realize that I like this version of Lila.

I like it a lot.

"One last thing, little criminal," I add under her attentive gaze.

The nickname slips out, and for a moment, I'm afraid I've

fucked up.

But then she gives me a curious, amused look. "Yes?"

"Call me Reed."

chapter 9

LILA

August

Anxiety pools low in my stomach the second I open my eyes in the morning.

One quick glance at my phone tells me I've woken before my alarm again. Alas, it wouldn't be so bad if I'd managed to sleep more than five hours each night in the past month.

It's been three months since I accepted Dr. Abner's offer in the restaurant's parking lot, and this afternoon I'll finally become an intern after having passed the training courses with flying colors. At least, that's what Haniyah said about my results.

I'm also twenty-four now—my birthday was last month—which means I should have my shit together. Which, again, means no room for obsessive overthinking.

Easier said than done.

My classmates are already spamming the group chat with updates about their own internships and theses, and every day I silently hope they won't notice my radio silence. At least I'll have Karla to back me up if they say anything, but something tells me it won't be enough.

As much as it pains me to admit it, Dr. Abner was right—bravery is all about going after what I want, even if I do it in fear.

Our conversation opened my eyes and helped me see what had been so obvious to everyone around me—I *wanted* that internship, and rejecting it would've been a huge mistake.

Throughout the day, I work on my thesis until it's time to leave for the youth center. But I can't shake this weird feeling that something will go terribly wrong. That I'm making an irreversible mistake.

Everything Oliver said the day we broke up starts ringing true in my head again, and I hate myself for it because I promised I'd stop thinking about it. I *have to* if I want to move forward.

But that's the thing about overthinking—you can't help it when hurtful words or terrible scenarios keep coming back in waves. Changing unhealthy mindsets overnight would be ideal, but, unfortunately, that's not how it works.

At the same time, though, there's a bone-deep feeling in me that tells me working in this field is what I was born to do. But after losing my temper with Oliver, how could I be the right person to steer children into the right direction?

I don't recognize what's inside of me, but it feels too daunting to peek over the edge. I know I won't find the same Lila from a year ago, and the uncertainty is festering inside me.

What if I don't know who I am anymore?

Shaking my head, I focus back on the road. When I park in front of the youth center and see a hurdle of kids running inside, I take a deep breath through my nose and count to ten in my head.

I'll be able to help them. I'm qualified enough to do it. Dr. Abner will be there in case something happens.

Right. Dr. Abner.

Reed, from now on.

My supervisor.

Since Haniyah was in charge of my training, I haven't seen him in the past couple of months. We've been emailing back and forth to talk about my schedule and my professional development goals for this internship, but I haven't seen him in person since that night at the restaurant.

According to my mom, he's in the last stages of his research and has spent the summer visiting his collaborators at other university labs all over the country. The fact that I'm going to see him today shouldn't make me feel more anxious than actually starting my internship, but here we are.

I get out of the car before my thoughts become even more ridiculous.

"Lila! Welcome, dear. Are you ready for your first day?" Haniyah's smile couldn't be brighter as she ushers me inside. "You look lovely, by the way. Pink is definitely your color."

Even though I know exactly what I'm wearing, I still glance down at my pink summer dress. "Thank you," I say shyly, feeling grateful for the extra boost of confidence. "It's loud in here today."

She chuckles. "And isn't it the most beautiful sound?"

It really is.

Around us, kids and teenagers hug, chat, or play games together, the warm atmosphere only confirming that I'm in the right place.

"Do you remember where Reed's office is?" Haniyah asks me.

I nod. "Second on the left?"

"That's the one. Go look for him. A little birdie told me he has a fun activity planned for you today."

My stomach flips. "All right."

Her comforting hand lands on my arm. "Reed can be a tough cookie, but I have a feeling you'll learn a lot from each other. And if you need anything, I'll be right here."

I have no doubts Reed—it still physically hurts to call him that—will teach me endless things, but *him* learning from *me*? Haniyah is sweet but also a bit too optimistic.

Once we say our goodbyes and she wishes me good luck on my first day, I make my way to his office. I've never been inside before, and I only remember where it is from Haniyah's tour.

The sound of his deep voice is immediate when I knock on his door, my heart beating way too fast.

"Come in."

I swallow and push the door open.

His eyes meet mine briefly before they go back to his computer. "Lila, hey. Give me a second, please."

My voice is nervous as I say, "Sure."

Without glancing away from the screen, he gestures with one of those huge hands to the chairs in front of his desk. "Take a seat. We'll discuss today's schedule in a moment."

I feel like a clumsy baby elephant as I close the distance between the door and the desk. The chair makes too much noise when I draw it back so I can sit. Why are my hands so sweaty all of a sudden?

"Did you have a good summer break?" he surprises me by asking, still not looking at me.

I clear my throat. "I'm working on my thesis, so I didn't have much of a break."

He hums, like he doesn't think it's that out of the ordinary to be a loser with no fun plans. "What's your thesis about?"

"Bibliotherapy."

That makes him look at me.

"Bibliotherapy?" he repeats in that deep rumble.

I nod. "I'm exploring educational and safe ways to talk about consent and sexual education to children through bibliotherapy. Things about periods, changes in our bodies, and why they're sacred. It's a really important topic for me."

Book therapy isn't a popular field in psychology by any means. There isn't a lot of research on it—the most notable papers belonging to the man in front of me—which is partly why I want to do my bit.

But also because bibliotherapy has been part of my life since the day I was born.

After my dad became my aunt's legal guardian when my grandmother's alcohol issues landed Maddie in the ER and her father left, she started seeing a children's therapist. She wouldn't open up, couldn't even identify her own feelings—as she told me many years later—until her therapist tried a different approach.

She used fictional characters who dealt with similar problems to make Maddie realize she wasn't alone, and everything had a cure. She started healing from her emotional wounds thanks to books, which then inspired my mother to write hers.

Mom was already a published children's author by this time, but she decided to change the direction of her stories toward the psychology field. Now she writes educational books for children about sensitive topics like consent, dealing with PTSD, and even adoption—she was adopted herself by my awesome grandads.

And because she wants these books to be as accurate as possible, she partners with renowned child therapists, counselors, and social workers. That's how she met Dr. Abner.

Reed.

"Interesting. Am I right to assume you got the inspiration from your mom?" he asks, a faint smile on his lips.

Stop looking at his mouth.

"You'd be right," I say proudly.

Her journey inspires me every day, and she is a big reason why I'm pursuing a career in counseling. Because I, too, want to make a difference in whichever way I can.

"That's good." He gives me a short nod of approval as he types something into his computer. "I'm sure you know there's not much research on bibliotherapy. We could use an extra mind in the field."

I clear my throat again, suddenly realizing how small I am in his presence. Not just in a physical sense—he's a giant—but because this is *Dr. Reed Freaking Abner.* He's been to Harvard and Princeton, and apparently, he has more connections than he knows what to do with despite being a textbook hermit. My mom's words, not mine.

And he's jus...here. Talking to me. Asking about my thesis. Supervising my internship.

I realize now what should've hit me like a ton of bricks much sooner. I've been so focused on seeing him as my mom's colleague I have to avoid to protect my reputation that I couldn't see this whole situation for what it truly is—an absolute privilege.

How many students in my position would *kill* to shadow Reed Abner as he works? And I'm not appreciating the fact that I get three whole months of doing exactly that.

I'm such an ungrateful, stubborn fool.

"Sorry about the wait," he says, snapping me out of my thoughts. I blink, noticing his dark eyes on me. "Did Haniyah mention something about today's schedule?"

"She only said you had something fun planned," I answer, a new resolve settling in my chest.

Excitement.

I'm excited to be here. It's taken me too long to realize how immensely lucky I am to have this opportunity, even if it means he'll be supervising me.

I can't do anything about that, can I? I tried to ask for another supervisor, but that didn't work out. I might as well make the most out of this potential fiasco.

"I hope you're ready for a group session with the kids today."

My heart somersaults. "Today?"

He glances at the expensive-looking watch on his wrist. "In about ten minutes. I'll be running it so you can get familiar with how we do things around here."

I'm meeting the kids in ten minutes?

Shit, shit, shit.

What if they hate me on sight? What if they think I'm too young and inexperienced to help them? What if—

"Lila."

I blink.

"Don't overthink it," Reed says, his voice firm yet somehow gentle at the same time. "They're not difficult kids. We're just getting to know one another today. I'll be running the session; just sit back and observe. Nothing to worry about, yeah?"

I hesitate, nerves swirling in my stomach. "Yeah."

"Now say it like you mean it."

His command sends a thrill of *something* down my spine.

"There's nothing to worry about," I say a little louder and with a little more conviction.

He nods his approval. "Good. Ready to meet the kids?"

chapter 10

LILA

"It's a group of six kids aged twelve to fourteen," he explains while we are still in his office. "We're doing an eight-week program to improve their social skills, teamwork, and self-confidence. I've already chatted with them individually and their families to let them know you'll be joining the group as an adjunct counselor. None of them had a problem with it."

That's a good sign, right?

He stands from behind his desk, and I follow suit. "Because this is our first session, I only expect you to observe how I run the group, but feel free to interact with the kids if you feel comfortable. That would help them warm up to you faster too."

I nod, storing all the details in my head. "Is it a closed group?"

"Yes. We'll be working with the same six kids for the next couple of months," he replies. "We're going to introduce ourselves first, then do a quick check-in, and then I've planned a group activity. Lastly, we'll discuss the results with the group. It's a pretty standard outline, as you can tell."

It is, but I suspect he'll somehow make it special. Now, sitting next to him with our chairs in a circle of six fidgety but visibly excited preteens, I itch to see the great Reed Abner in action.

"Hey, everyone. Welcome to this week's group session," he starts, sounding more relaxed and open than I've ever heard him before. He makes eye contact with every kid before continuing.

"Most of you know me already, but just in case the hot summer sun has wiped out your memory—"

His words are followed by a collective chuckle.

"—I'm Reed, and this right here is my colleague, Lila. She'll be helping us in our group sessions this year."

Colleague.

He's just referred to little ole me as his *colleague.*

I wave at the kids with a smile. They all smile back politely, and one of the girls waves back enthusiastically.

Just like that, with that one simple action, I know I'm going to be fine.

"Now, a couple of things before we start."

Reed reaches into the pocket of his slacks and takes out a small yellow ball. He bounces it on the floor, catching it with his hand in one easy move.

"This is the ninth member of our group." He holds up the ball between two fingers. "Say hello to Mr. Bounce."

The kids giggle again and, to my surprise, actually say hello. I'm too mesmerized by the scene unfolding in front of me to do the same.

"What is Mr. Bounce for, you might be wondering." He bounces it again, catching it just as easily. "Mr. Bounce will be really important in our group sessions because it will determine whose turn it is to talk. One of our main rules here is that everyone gets their turn to speak, and we can't interrupt one another. Our words matter because we matter, and each one of us deserves to be heard. So, when someone is holding Mr. Bounce, we're going to focus our attention on that person and listen to them attentively and without interrupting. Does it make sense?"

They all nod.

"Very well. How about we start off today's session by getting to know one another a little better," he suggests. "I'm going to pass Mr. Bounce along to one of you now, and I want you to share with us your name, age, and what your favorite movie is and why. When you're done talking, carefully pass Mr. Bounce along to the person on your left. Ready?"

Reed throws the yellow ball to the boy sitting on his left, who catches it after it bounces on the floor once.

He runs a hand through his shaggy brown hair, flustered. "Hi. My name is Trevor. I'm thirteen, and my favorite movie is *Jurassic Park* because I like dinosaurs, I guess."

Trevor glances at Reed for confirmation. When he gives him an approving nod, he throws it to the next person.

"My name is Melody," the girl who waved at me starts, an easy smile on her face. "I'm twelve, and I really like *The Little Mermaid* because I love the sea. I played mermaids on the beach this year with my cousin, and I had so much fun. My brother, Cameron, played an evil shark."

She passes the ball along to the girl next to her, and the kids introduce themselves one by one—Trevor, Melody, Sofia, Angie, Jacob, and Santiago. It's only when Santiago is done talking and he throws the ball in my direction that I startle.

I look at Reed, hesitantly holding Mr. Bounce between my fingers, and he arches an amused eyebrow in a silent response. A *challenging* eyebrow.

Very well.

"Hi, guys." I feel surprisingly calm as I address everyone in the room. "I'm Lila. I'm twenty-four, and my favorite movie is *Pride and Prejudice*. It's quite an old movie, so you may not have heard of it. I like it because it's the prettiest movie I've ever seen, and the love story is beautiful."

Maybe they think it's lame, but everyone respects the Mr. Bounce rule and they don't make any negative comments. Then, just to be a little shit, I pass Mr. Bounce along to Reed.

"Looks like it's my turn now." He plays with the ball between his fingers. *Stop looking at his fingers.* "My name is Reed, and I'm thirty-five. I have many favorite movies, but the first one that comes to mind is called *The Book Thief*. It's about a young girl who steals books to keep them from getting burned during the war. I like it because I'm a big World War II nerd."

I tuck that piece of information away for later, for some unknown reason.

"All right, now that we already know a bit more about one another, we're going to start tackling today's topic."

He unfolds his huge body from his chair, walks to the whiteboard across the room, and writes a single word.

"Self-confidence," he reads out loud. Mr. Bounce goes up and down and up and down as he moves back to our chair circle. "I'm really interested in knowing what it means to be confident to you. I'll start. For me, having self-confidence means believing that I have the ability to go after my dreams and goals. And, hopefully, I'll achieve them."

He tosses the ball to Melody. "What does self-confidence mean to you, Melody?"

Before she can answer, he adds, "And remember, this is a safe and judgment-free zone. The key is being honest with yourselves and this group and not being afraid to tell the truth. If you aren't comfortable answering a question, just say the word, and we'll move on. I promise I won't get upset. Another important thing is that everything we talk about in our group sessions can't be discussed with other people outside of it, okay? It's confidential. Raise your hand if you agree to not share other people's stories."

All the kids raise their hands at once. Reed and I do so too.

"Awesome. So, self-confidence. Let's hear it, Melody. Share as much as you wish."

As each kid takes a turn explaining what self-confidence means to them, I can't help but feel surprised at how engaged everyone is. Last night, I went through my notes on how to deal with uncooperative preteens who don't want to talk in therapy and how I could encourage them to engage in conversation at their own pace. But I did it all in vain.

It's *him*. It's the magnetism of his words, how he moves, the calming and welcoming rumble of his voice, the confident way he speaks, how his sole presence beckons everyone's attention.

Haniyah was right—we're only fifteen minutes in, and I've learned more practical knowledge watching Reed run a group session than in last semester's classes.

Once everyone is done explaining what self-confidence means to them, Reed thanks them for sharing their answers and takes the lead again.

"Here's the thing," he starts, his voice easy and amicable. He doesn't sound or act like a therapist in an overly obvious way, which I suppose is why the kids are being so open. "People who are self-confident are okay with being themselves. That's the key. But more often than not, we struggle to define who we are, which is why we aren't as self-confident as we'd like to be. Who am I? It can be a difficult question to answer at any age, but that's why we're here—to find out together."

He stands again, moving behind a desk to retrieve three big poster boards. Each one has a question written on it.

"This week, we're going to dive a little deeper into who we are by answering three simple questions," he explains as he hangs the three posters on the wall. "Sofia, can you read the first one?"

The little girl squints her eyes. *"What are my values?"*

"Thank you." Reed smiles, and I swear I've just seen a dimple under his light stubble. A *dimple*. "What do we value the most? Each person puts value on different things. Our family? Maybe our friends? How brave we are? How creative? There are no right or wrong answers. Jacob, could you read the second one?"

The fourteen-year-old, who seems to be the shyest in the group, nods. *"What do I have to offer?"*

"We all have something to offer," Reed says confidently. "You may always help people in need, or you may take care of your little siblings when your parents are busy, or maybe you always make people laugh. Again, no right or wrong answers. Angie, can you please read the last one?"

"What do I stand for?"

"Standing up for something is important. For example, one might stand against bullying. That means we don't tolerate it, and we're willing to help anyone who's being bullied," he explains. "Now, we're all going to come up here, take one of these markers, and write our answers to each question on these poster boards. There's no need to add your name; they can be sort of anonymous. Remember to answer all three questions and take turns writing them down, okay?"

As each kid writes their answers on the poster boards, Reed walks up to me, hands in the pockets of his slacks. I tell myself I don't find his confidence attractive because I *don't.*

"So," he drawls. "What do you think so far? You have any feedback for me?"

A chuckle escapes me before I can help it. "Yeah, right."

Me? Offering *him* feedback? He must be sick.

He crosses his arms in front of his chest, the fabric on his arms stretching to the point I'm afraid it'll come undone at the seams. Does he spend ten hours a day at the gym on top of everything else?

"Yes, right. I want to know what you think because I value your opinion."

He's only saying that to make me feel good about myself. To give me a little push.

Even though I don't think he's being fully honest, I still give him a genuine answer. "I really like how you're running the group. The bouncing ball was a nice touch, too. They all seem to respect you a lot."

He hums. "No feedback, then?"

"No feedback so far." I swallow and smile up at him, hoping he doesn't notice that—ironically—my self-confidence has just plummeted once more. "You have it all figured out, and it seems to be working. I'm not sure I could give you any valuable suggestions."

He glances down at me like every single word I've just said has personally offended him.

My stomach drops as he unfolds his arms once again, puts his hands back in his pockets, and tells me, "Go up to the poster boards and write down your answers, please."

I consider arguing against it, but I suddenly get the feeling that sharing my answers will also help me get closer to the kids. Still holding his stare, I stand and move to the poster boards.

Just as I'm about to write down my values, a sweet voice calls out my name.

"You are Lila, right?" It's Melody, the girl who likes *The Little Mermaid* and waved at me.

"Hi, Melody." I smile down at her.

She beams. "I like your hair. It's really long and pretty."

My heart squeezes. "Thank you so much. I think your hair looks pretty, too."

Her fingers wrap around the braid falling over one of her shoulders. "Thank you." Her cheeks redden. "Can you help me with a word? I don't know how to spell it right."

"Sure thing. What's the word?" I smile, surprised by her boldness.

Kids are usually shy to ask for help because they're embarrassed to need it, but not Melody.

Or maybe that was just my own experience.

Melody walks me to the third and final board, fidgeting with the marker between her fingers. It's only the two of us and Sofia up here, the rest of them chatting in their seats.

"I want to say that I stand for smiling, but I can't remember if it's written with one l or two." She chews her bottom lip. "And I don't want to look dumb if I write it wrong."

"Hey, none of that," I say, but my voice isn't reprimanding. "It's okay to not know things and make mistakes. You're not dumb by any means. A dumb girl wouldn't ask for help like you just did."

"Okay." A pause. "It's just that I have this thing, dyslexia, and sometimes words get confusing."

"That's okay. I can tell you're a smart girl," I reassure her. "Smiling is with one l."

"Thanks." She quickly uncaps the marker and writes it down. When she turns to me, she's smiling proudly. "You're a cool counselor, like Reed."

That may just be the best compliment I've been given lately.

Before I can say anything else, Melody hurries back to her chair, leaving me alone at the poster boards.

I meet Reed's eyes as I move to the first one and notice he is already looking at me.

Doesn't mean anything. Move along.

"All right." Reed calls the kids' attention just as I sit back down after writing my answers. "Let's discuss the answers on the poster boards. We'll raise our hands when we have something to say, but remember to pass Mr. Bounce along. Lila, could you read the answers to the first question?"

Considerably more at ease than at the start of the group session, I start, *"What are my values? Family, friends, telling the truth, being brave, kindness, family again, and career."*

I can tell Reed knows the last one is mine just by the handwriting alone, but he doesn't comment on it.

"Thank you. Family seems to be a popular one," he comments. "All of them are great, and they define what's important to us. Does anyone want to share what they wrote and why? Remember, you don't have to answer if you aren't comfortable doing so. Yes,

Santiago?"

Reed throws the ball at the boy, who has his hand raised. "I wrote 'being brave' because my mom always tells me that people are happier when they're brave and follow their dreams."

Santiago tosses Mr. Bounce back to Reed, who catches it effortlessly.

"It's true that you have to be brave to chase your dreams. Self-confident people are usually braver, too, because they aren't afraid to fail if things don't go their way," he explains. "How many of you here have trouble making new friends because you're afraid they will think you are annoying or weird?"

All the kids raise their hands.

I want to raise mine, but I don't. Reed sneaks a quick glance at me like he knows it, too.

"That happens to all of us," he reassures. "But because making new friends makes us feel nervous and anxious, our brain thinks it's a bad thing, and it tells us to stop. What's the worst thing that could happen, though? Let's make it super ridiculous and dramatic. I'll start, and each of you will take a turn adding something new. So, if I go up to someone to try to be friends with them, they may look at me weird."

He passes Mr. Bounce to Trevor.

"They may...ignore me?" He hesitates.

Reed nods. "Good. Melody?"

She catches the bouncing ball. "They may tell me that I'm ugly."

"If they're extremely rude, maybe," Reed concedes. "Sofia?"

"They may tell me that my breath stinks," she says, earning a chuckle from the rest of the kids.

"Let's make it even more ridiculous and silly," Reed instructs. "Come on. I know you can do it."

Angie holds Mr. Bounce as she purses her lips, thinking. "Maybe they will call the police, and they will arrest me because

I'm annoying?"

"Great," Reed praises. "Keep it going."

"The president will make a public announcement and say that everyone should ignore me, including my family," Santiago says, half chuckling, before passing Mr. Bounce along to the last kid.

"The Army will kick me out of the country, but no other country will want me, either, so I'll just live out in the sea," Jacob concludes.

By this point, all the kids are openly laughing because it does sound ridiculous.

Suddenly, Mr. Bounce is on my lap, and seven pairs of eyes are waiting for me to add my piece.

I steal a quick glance at Reed, and I swear I see a twinkle in his eyes. "The Army will find out that I'm living out in the sea, and they will put me on a rocket and send me to space because I'm so annoying, they don't want me to live on the same planet as everyone else."

My words are met with another round of chuckles.

"Well done, everyone." Reed's eyes linger on me for a beat too long before looking away. "Our brains always cling to the worst-case scenario because they want to keep us safe. By not taking risks, we stay in our comfort zone, and that makes anxiety go away, which in turn makes us feel good. But that's only an illusion because staying in our comfort zone forever won't make us happy. It won't make us feel brave enough to chase our dreams.

"Here's a trick—every time your brain says you can't do something because you will fail or feel stupid or weird, think of the worst thing that could happen. And make it silly, just like we've just done. You'll see how ridiculous it is—there's no way any of those crazy scenarios will actually happen. Consider it homework for next week."

We move on to the second poster board, then the third. The

kids continue to be collaborative, some of them more openly now that almost an entire hour has passed.

After they each share one thing they've learned in today's session, we say our goodbyes and the classroom falls into a comfortable quietness.

"That was..." My lips are moving before the thoughts have fully formed in my mind. I feel tired, happy, accomplished. And I haven't even done anything, but just watching him is an otherworldly experience. "You are a natural."

He gives me a lopsided smile that looks as tired as I feel. My focus shifts to his hands as he hikes up the sleeves of his shirt, exposing those strong forearms I need to look away from this instant.

"I just love my job," he says in a quiet voice. "Do you have any feedback for me now that we're done with the session?"

"I can't think of anything right now," I tell him truthfully. "But I'd love to help you organize the next one, if...if you need the help, that is."

His eyes drift to me. "You have any ideas in mind?"

"A few," I admit. "Now that I know how you run things, I can adapt them to your session plan and sketch an outline. I can send you an email later."

"Sure," he agrees. "I'm curious to see what you come up with."

That feeling of belonging grows in my chest, becoming bigger and brighter until I feel like all this excitement is going to make me burst.

I wasn't of much help in this week's session, but I *did* help Melody with her spelling and, hopefully, with her self-confidence too.

There's a part of me that still believes I'm not good enough, that I don't belong working with children, that I will fail, that I will become a pariah when people on campus find out who my internship supervisor is.

But Reed's words ring louder—staying in my comfort zone forever won't make me happy.

Today, I'm tired of feeding my inner demons.

Today, I choose to let the light win.

chapter 11

REED

I wake up with a start.

My chest is heaving, sweat is clinging to the back of my neck, and the tender flesh between my shoulder blades is burning so hot, I can still feel the lingering pain that hasn't been there in decades.

I dreamed of him again.

My bare feet touch the cold hardwood floor a moment later, refusing to keep me in bed. I need to move.

Because being on the go, keeping busy, is the way to forget.

At my wardrobe, I reach for a clean shirt and a pair of slacks and set them over the crumpled sheets. My mind is on autopilot as I open the door to the attached bathroom, drop the boxers I sleep in, and get in the shower.

The waterfall of ice-cold water sobers me up, and I throw my head back, willing it to soothe me.

It does nothing to numb the pain—not the physical but the invisible wounds.

You're a fucking joke, boy. You're no good for nothing but a good beatin'.

My back burns despite the cold water, and I scrub my body faster just to move on to the next task. Once again, it's no use. Because the second I'm out of the shower, my eyes find my reflection in the shower glass, and it's impossible to look away from the scar marring the skin between my shoulder blades.

The vile reminder of what my father did to me. Of what my mother didn't stop.

Silence greets me when I get out of the bathroom. I bought this two-story detached home not far from campus on a whim when I moved back here to Warlington—my hometown—for good, after spending a whole decade getting my qualifications and working all over the United States.

Haniyah thought buying this place would be a good investment.

"So you can settle down," she had told me in her usual gentle voice when she'd come with me to see the listing. "There's plenty of room here if you want to start a family one day."

I said nothing to that. I didn't want to break her heart by telling her that the concept of a family was so fucked up to me, starting one of my own felt more daunting than it should.

My thoughts are interrupted by the alarm on my phone, signaling that I need to leave the house right now if I want to get to work on time.

Sighing, I decide I'll just grab breakfast somewhere on campus. There are no emails that need my immediate attention, so I take advantage of the good weather to walk instead of driving in the morning's awful traffic.

I blame the lack of good sleep for the fact that my thoughts go to Lila.

To her intoxicating scent, her sweet smile, her brilliant mind.

I know it's wrong, and I'm sick in the fucking head, but that doesn't make it stop.

It's been three days since our first weekly group session. The kids seemed to warm up to her just fine, and it's making me feel things I haven't experienced before. Things I can't name.

I can't get her out of my system.

It's possible that these thoughts are a direct result of a shitty night and the lack of breakfast. So, once I answer a couple of emails from my lab students, I head over to the only coffee shop on campus that doesn't serve watered-down coffee.

I'm mindlessly scrolling on my phone when a flash of blonde hair catches my eye.

Ignoring the way my heart leaps at the sight of her, I watch as she fishes for something inside her bag. Why is her every move so damn mesmerizing?

Standing only a few feet away from the coffee shop, she looks up as I inch closer to the front door. Our eyes lock for a fleeting second before she glances back down, her cheeks flaming.

I'm about to walk up to her to say hi when, with one of the pockets on her backpack still unzipped, she scurries away in the opposite direction like a scared little mouse.

A pinch of rejection stabs the organ in my chest at her reaction, but I brush it off. I'm just sleep-deprived and not thinking straight. So, after getting my coffee, I bury myself in work all day and don't allow myself to think of her again until she's right in front of me that afternoon.

The ticking of the clock on my office wall is all I can hear, despite us both working within these walls.

When she got to the youth center, I told her I wanted her to review one of my closed cases from last year and write down a report with things she would've done differently. She asked me a quick technical question, and we've been working in silence ever since.

I don't like it.

Because she's ignoring me.

Growing up, I never craved attention. When I was a child, getting attention meant being the target of my mother's meltdowns or the aim of my father's belt buckle, so I learned to stick to the shadows and feel comfortable there.

Years later, when I lived in foster homes, getting attention was rarely a good thing. It meant that I was being too loud, too disruptive, too much of a bother. It meant that they'd send me away, forcing me to start all over again.

Throughout the years, I've learned to ignore the attention. Sure, I'm grateful for it because I want to bring awareness to what I'm working on, but personal praise isn't my driving force.

So why am I so bent out of shape now that Lila is depriving me of hers?

I close my laptop and lean back on my chair, knowing I'm not getting shit done this afternoon. I had a terrible night's sleep, one of my PhD students messed up some equipment in the lab—by accident, but it's still a massive inconvenience—and now this.

This, meaning me losing my sanity over *Grace and Cal's daughter* ignoring me.

I'm sick beyond repair.

"So," I drawl anyway because, apparently, I have self-destructive tendencies now. "Didn't know we were back to ignoring each other."

She glances from her laptop, arching a single blonde eyebrow. "How many times are we going to have this conversation?"

"Exactly. You ran away from me this morning," I point out.

"I was in a rush."

"Don't lie to me, little criminal."

Her cheeks flush, just like they did this morning. I shouldn't like that red on her cheeks so much, yet here I fucking am.

"I'm not lying, Dr. Abner," she says, her voice small, not meeting my stare.

I scratch my jaw. "Dr. Abner? Gave up on Reed already?"

She types something on her laptop, pretending to be nonchalant. "Dr. Abner is your name."

"I told you to call me Reed. Which is also my name, by the way."

"Doesn't mean I have to use it." Her voice holds a sudden teasing edge I don't shy away from. "Or should I call you Professor

Hotshot too? Since that's what they call you on campus. But I'm sure you already knew that."

I didn't, as a matter of fact.

Against my better judgment, I tell her, "If you'd rather call me Professor Hotshot instead, by all means, go ahead."

"I think Professor Bossy suits you better," she retorts despite her cheeks turning even redder.

There's a big part of me that knows we're playing a dangerous game, but my moral compass must be broken today.

"I'm not bossy," I say, knowing damn well that's a lie.

"Professor Control Freak, then?"

This girl.

I cross my arms in front of my chest, not missing the way her gaze lingers on the movement. "Tell me how I'm bossy, then."

"That right there." She shrugs, pretending to go back to her laptop when we both know she's not looking at anything. "You could have said, 'Dearest Lila, would you please give me an example of my bossy tendencies, if that's not too much of an inconvenience for you? Thank you from the bottom of my heart.'"

"Mmm." I watch as she tucks a piece of that long, wavy hair behind her pierced ear. "Do you have any more examples for me of said bossy tendencies?"

"I might need some time to think—wait, no, I got it. That night at the awards ceremony, when I didn't want to talk, and you gave me no choice but to bare my soul to you."

"If I remember correctly—and I do—I told you multiple times that you could leave if you wanted. I wasn't holding you hostage."

"Really?" She blinks several times, innocently, knowing damn well that yes, really.

"I could tell that you needed to talk that night. Let it all out. And it worked, didn't it? You needed to vent about your ex."

I cringe on the inside, knowing deep down I'm only fishing

for crumbs about her current love life because on top of being sick in the head, I'm also curious. But only because I don't think it would be a great idea if she got back with that guy after he cheated on her. Nothing else.

Lila snorts. "I'll make a mental note to go to you the next time I think getting into another relationship would be a good idea so you can talk me out of it."

Is she saying she's single? Does she even want to talk about this with me?

I narrow my eyes at her, thirsty for more but not wanting to look or sound obvious. "If you think something is a good idea, I can't talk you out of it. You should make your own choices."

"If I ever think getting into another relationship is a good idea, it must be because I'm starting to lose it," she deadpans.

I should, but I don't stop myself from asking my next question, even though I doubt it would be appropriate. "No relationships for you ever again, then? Seems a little drastic."

Her shoulders rise and fall. "What's the point? No offense, but men aren't worth it. I'd rather focus on my career," she explains. "I gave up something I really wanted for a man once, and it won't happen again."

Her summer camp internship—I remember.

"No offense taken." Some men are pretty terrible, I'll give her that. But it surprises me that she's so quick to say that when I know she grew up with one of the best—Cal is a good man and a good father. "Focusing on your career is important."

I don't stop to think about why the thought of Lila dating someone makes my body itch.

She takes me aback with her next question. "What about you? Are you also married to your career?" A pause in which my heart skips a beat. "Or to an actual woman? Man?"

My fingers are bare of any ring, so she must know I'm not married, but she's still asking.

Interesting.

"I don't have time for relationships," I tell her the half-truth I keep telling myself. Because time isn't the issue, but I refuse to dwell on the real reason for too long. "Not into men, but I wouldn't have time for relationships with them either."

She hums. "I guess there's not much room for relationships when you're a world-renowned researcher, professor, board member, volunteer, and whatnot."

"You'd be right." I clear my throat, feeling like I'd cross an invisible line if we kept talking about relationships. "So, circling back to you ignoring me on campus but calling me names behind closed doors."

"I did not call you names."

I arch a questioning eyebrow. "Well?"

"See, you're being bossy again."

"Don't change the subject."

"Then don't be so bossy."

I'll show you bossy.

Where did that thought just come from?

I sigh. "Lila."

"Reed."

"Nice to see I'm Reed again."

An urgent knock on my office door bursts the dangerous bubble we are wrapped in.

I don't have time to instruct whoever's knocking to come in because the door flies open, and I'm met with Haniyah's worried face.

"Reed, it's Cameron," she says, breathless. "He just punched another kid in the face."

Fuck.

chapter 12

REED

I'm barely aware of Lila following me out of the room with Haniyah.

She leads us to the main hall, where a commotion of kids awaits us. One of the volunteers is talking to Cameron near the garden doors.

"What happened?" I ask calmly, not wanting to freak the boy out.

Veronica, a volunteer and retired teacher, looks at me like she already knows I'm not going to like her next words. She's right. "He got into a fight with Sean because he made fun of Melody. Not the first time it's happened, either, but this time Cameron did punch him. Kelly went to the infirmary with Sean."

"He kicked me first," Cameron spits out angrily at nobody in particular.

"Thanks, Veronica. I got it from here." Ignoring everyone and everything else around me, I turn to meet his stare. He's sitting on the ground, arms crossed, a pissed-off expression on his face. "Tell me what happened."

He doesn't look at me, doesn't talk.

His angry gaze stays locked on the ground, his breathing agitated and his shoulders rigid.

"Cameron," I insist in vain.

I know him well—if he doesn't want to talk, he won't. The more he feels pressured, the more he'll retreat, so I let it go for now.

As the volunteers clear the room, the voices and chaos fade away, but Cameron is still inside his own head. Lila takes me aback when she sits on the cold floor next to the boy.

And starts talking.

"Hi, Cameron. My name is Lila. I'm new here," she says in a friendly voice. Cameron doesn't respond, but that doesn't stop her. "I met your sister, Melody, the other day, in a group session I did with Reed. She didn't know how to spell a word, and she asked me for help."

Cameron still says nothing, but I can tell he's listening.

And I can't take my eyes off her.

"It was my first day here, and I was really nervous. So much so that I couldn't even eat breakfast that morning," she explains. "Because I was scared you guys wouldn't like me or talk to me. But then your sister came up to me and told me that she really liked my hair. It may sound like such a dumb thing, but it made me feel better. Not because of the compliment—which I'll admit was nice—but because she trusted me enough to ask me about the spelling. She said she was scared of looking silly in front of the other kids, but I thought it was brave of her to ask for help. I instantly liked her."

Cameron's shoulders aren't shaking anymore, but he still doesn't meet Lila's gaze. Once again, being ignored doesn't seem to faze her because she keeps going.

"She's your twin sister, isn't she? I'm not a twin, but I've heard twins share a very strong bond. Is that true for you and Melody?"

To my surprise, Cameron nods.

"That's amazing. I'm a little jealous," she jokes. "I guess what I'm trying to say is that Melody looks like a strong girl who isn't afraid to stand up for herself and ask for help when she needs it. Sean did a bad thing when he made fun of her, for sure, but I bet she doesn't want you to get into trouble because of her. Why don't you tell me your side of the story so we can fix this?"

I'm fully expecting Cameron to retreat into his shell even more. Lila is a stranger to him, after all.

But then he asks in a quiet voice, "You're new here?"

"Yeah. I want to be a counselor after college, so I'm learning from Reed."

"Why?"

Lila doesn't miss a beat, but my heart does when she glances at me. "Because he's a great teacher."

I hold her stare for a beat too long until Cameron's voice breaks the silence.

"Melody was doing her homework, and Sean started calling her names because she didn't know what the word *bride* meant," he explains. "He always messes with her when she's doing homework. I told him to leave her alone. He kicked me on my shin, and then I punched him. He deserved it."

It takes me a moment to realize that whatever Lila has just done worked. But I can't dwell on it for too long before I jump into action.

"Thanks for telling us. Haniyah is calling your parents, since you got into a fight, which you know is what happens to everyone who gets into trouble here," I tell him, still in a calm voice. "You and I will talk tomorrow."

I'll talk to his parents when they get here and convince them to give him space today so he doesn't come in even more agitated tomorrow. I'll have to speak with Sean's parents, too, and deal with the aftermath of a physical altercation between two members of the youth center. We'll be lucky if we don't get sued, which is the last thing we need.

"Where's my sister?" he asks, glancing around the room.

"With the other kids. I'll go find her when your parents get here," I tell him. "Do you need anything? Water? Show me where

Sean kicked you, please."

If he's bleeding and we don't get him to the infirmary, we could get into much bigger trouble.

Wordlessly, he rolls up his sweatpants, and indeed, there's a bruise forming on his shin.

"We have some ointment for that. I'll go get it," I say, not wanting him to come to the infirmary, since Sean will be there. "Lila, do you mind staying with him?"

For the next hour, my brain is on overdrive as Haniyah and I try to fix what went down this afternoon.

Sean admitted to kicking Cameron first, and his parents forced him to apologize to him and to Melody for having made fun of her.

When the twins' parents got here, I had to take them to a private room to prevent Cameron from seeing his dad's reaction.

"That boy doesn't know what's coming for him," he hissed, ignoring his wife as she pulled at his arm, begging him to calm down. "We raised him better than this, damn it."

My brain forced me to internally recoil at the hardness of his words, his gestures, his demeanor. And no matter how many times I tried to convince myself I wasn't dealing with my father because that fucker is dead, it took a while to register.

It's an unfair comparison, because Cameron's father, despite his temper, isn't a violent man toward his family—we keep a close eye on signs of abuse.

He isn't my father, goddammit.

It's been three decades. Get it together.

When I finally did, I explained to Cameron's parents that the best strategy would be to tell him that what he did was wrong and ground him if they felt like it but to stay calm. They agreed, and his father apologized for having lost his temper.

The adrenaline, paired with my lack of sleep, wears me down two hours later. All the kids are gone for the day, but I'm still restless, answering emails in my office because I don't want to go back to an empty house for some goddamn reason.

That brief interaction with the twins' father brought back memories I fight every day to keep buried. Because, unlike him, my own father didn't stop at verbal lashings.

The skin on my back burns, and I curse under my breath.

He's dead. He can't hurt me.

And whose fault is it that he's fucking dead?

A knock on my office door startles me. I'm not mentally or emotionally prepared to deal with anything or anyone else today, so I don't answer.

But then I hear her voice. "Reed? It's Lila. Are you in here?"

I curse under my breath again, hating myself for ignoring her when all I want is to get my head out of my ass and tell her how amazing she was with Cameron out there. How she shouldn't doubt, not for a second, that she's meant for this job.

I shut my eyes, begging the memories of my father to go away after three decades of raw torture. Yet her voice is the only thing that manages to break through the fog in my brain.

"I wanted to tell you that I need to leave, but I'll see you tomorrow."

A pause.

"Today was hard for you, I could tell. I'm really sorry about Cameron. I know you care for him... You may not even be in there, for all I know, so maybe I'm talking to a wall, but I still want to say that you handled it well. Altercations are something our professors always say we should prepare for, but they never actually *prepare* us. This may sound wrong, I hope you get what I mean, but I'm glad it happened when you were here. I watched how you handled the parents and the rest of the staff, and it was... It was amazing. I'm learning a lot from you."

I'm locked inside my office, with my heart beating too damn fast, wishing I was strong enough to open the door and face her.

"I just wanted to tell you that you were great, and everyone respects you a lot. Me included. Don't beat yourself up too hard over it. I know how it can affect counselors when the kids get into a fight, but you handled things well. Not that you need my reassurance, because you're you, but... Okay, now I'm rambling. Sorry. Have a good night, Reed. Or good night, wall. See you tomorrow."

It isn't until I hear distant voices down the hallway that I realize I'm smiling like a goddamn fool.

chapter 13

LILA

The human brain does this weird thing sometimes, where it knows something is wrong but forces us to make that mistake anyway.

Technically, it's not my brain forcing me to do anything—*I* control it, and therefore, *I'm* the problem. And I'm fine with that. What I'm not fine with is knowing I'm making a fool of myself, but I can't seem to stop.

The morning after Cameron and Sean's fight at the youth center, I get comfortable on my couch and dial the number of the one person I should've called days ago.

"Lila-baby." My aunt's voice filters through the speakers on my phone before her smiling face comes into focus on the video call. "How have you been?"

She's walking around the house, dressed in her ballet instructor clothes and a low bun. "Hey, Maddsy. I thought you'd be at the studio."

"I'm on my lunch break. I came by the house to check on things because Dylan isn't at school today. He said he was sick, but he's running around now, so I don't know about that."

I snort, not putting it past my little cousin to fake it so he can stay home to watch cartoons. "Is this a good time to call? If you're busy..."

"No, no, it's fine. I still have some time before I need to go back, and James is handling the two little devils just fine," she says just as Dylan's unmistakable voice screams my name.

I laugh. "Put him on the phone."

"Yeah, just a sec. Careful, Dyl. Don't drop Mommy's phone, okay?"

But the six-year-old's face is already pressed to the screen, oblivious to his mom's warnings. "Lila! I got a new dinosaur toy."

"No way." I give him my biggest smile. There's no little boy I love more in this world. "Who gave it to you?"

"Gramma," he tells me, referring to my grandmother. "Because I'm sick. She came to see me."

My grandmother has been sober for decades and, eventually, rekindled her relationship with both of her children. I'm not a fan of what she put my dad and aunt through, but if they've been able to forgive her, so can I. She's been nothing but loving and supportive to me.

"Are you going to show me?" I ask the little boy.

He doesn't need to be asked twice. I hear Maddie's warning as my cousin sprints away, the phone shaking with each of his steps until he says, "Daddy, where is Rexy?"

I can't see him, but I hear my uncle's deep voice. "Hey, buddy. Funny how you don't sound sick anymore, huh?" Dylan giggles at that. "It should be on the couch, where you probably left it while you were watching TV. Hey—what are you doing with Mommy's phone?"

"It's Lila!"

A moment later, James takes the phone from Dylan's hand and frowns at the screen.

"You look like an old man who doesn't know how smartphones work," I tease.

He's only forty-four, so he knows I'm joking. And he lets me know as much when he gives me a playful roll of his eyes, which are the same blue shade as my cousin's.

"I didn't know you guys were video chatting. Did he call you on accident? You can't trust him around phones these days."

"I called Maddsy, and he wanted to show me his new dinosaur toy."

James tells Dylan to go look for it before going back to me. "Everything okay? How's your thesis going, smarty-pants?"

The nickname makes me smile. "I'm a bit overwhelmed, but I think it's going well."

He frowns. "Overwhelmed how? They're not giving you a hard time, are they?"

James, my aunt's former physical therapist turned husband, is like a brother to me. I met him when I was eleven, and we instantly clicked. If my dad is the most protective of me, my uncle follows very closely behind.

"No, it's not like that," I assure him. "I just have a lot on my plate right now. It's why I called Maddsy."

"You need to vent. Got it." He glances to the side and smiles. "But first, there's someone here who wants to say hi."

He points the phone camera at the little girl sitting on her high chair.

She beams when she sees me. "Lili!"

"Hi, Alice." I smile at my youngest cousin. "What do you have there? Is it yummy?"

She gives me an enthusiastic nod and shoves what I'm pretty sure is a slice of avocado into the screen. James laughs. "Careful, sweetie. We're going to take a bath after you're done eating, yeah?"

"Yeah," she repeats, her dimples popping out with her smile.

Maddie reappears then. "Why is everyone talking to her but me? I need some Lila time."

James turns the camera so it's facing them again. My aunt plants a kiss on his cheek before grabbing the phone.

"Where's Dyl?" she asks her husband.

"I'm here, Mommy," a little voice says. "Lila, look at Rexy."

My aunt lowers the phone so Dylan can come into view. "I love it, Dylan. It's the coolest. Give me a big kiss."

He kisses the screen, and I do the same.

"Will you be okay if I go upstairs for a moment?" Maddie asks James.

He looks at her with adoration. "Sure. Take your time, love."

Dylan, the little minx, makes gagging sounds when they kiss, and I laugh.

Gah, I miss them so much. Since they live in Norcastle, which is hours away, we don't see each other as often as we'd like.

I say goodbye to my uncle and cousins before Maddie rushes upstairs. "Finally, you and me. What's up?"

"Are you sure you can talk right now?" I ask, feeling terrible for barging in. "I can call you tonight. Or tomorrow. Or whenever you're free."

"I'm always free for you, Li." She gives me a sisterly smile. "James has the kids under control, and I still have twenty minutes until I need to go back to the studio."

I hesitate. "If you're sure..."

"Stop stalling," she says, calling me out. "Is everything okay? Did something happen?"

"Um, not exactly." I nibble on my lower lip, sitting up straight on the couch. "It's more like...a problem in my head."

"You're overthinking," she guesses. "Spill, then. You know you can tell me anything."

I do, which is why my first instinct was to call her.

I love my parents and I love Mariah, and I know I can tell them anything, too, but the bond I share with my aunt is something else. She's always had my back and gives the best advice, since she's been through so much.

So I take a deep breath and let it all out.

How Reed offered me the internship and how hesitant I was to take it. How the thought of someone finding out I'm working with my mom's colleague still worries me, even if doesn't seem as catastrophic as before.

"I think I'm messing things up," I admit out loud for the first time.

Maddie, who hasn't interrupted me once, frowns. "How so?"

"I saw Reed on campus yesterday and freaked out because I was afraid of what others would think if they saw us together, even though I promised myself I'd get over it. He called me out on it, and I didn't apologize even though what I did was pathetic. I'm such a mess, Maddsy. I don't want him to think I'm unprofessional and childish again. I promised myself I'd get over it."

What I don't say is that I've caught myself stealing glances at him more frequently than I should. That I find his easy, confident way of working with the kids more attractive than I'd ever admit.

"First of all, breathe." Her voice is calm but commanding. "Did he tell you that you were unprofessional and childish?"

"No, but—"

"No buts," she cuts me off. "You have a tendency to assume what other people will do or say, and they're never nice things."

She is...totally right.

"I think you should start living in the present," she continues. "If this Reed guy hasn't told you he thinks you're unprofessional, stop assuming otherwise. You're incredibly talented in many ways, but I doubt you've developed mind-reading abilities just yet."

"It's just... Why would he not think I'm unprofessional?" I retort. "I ran away from him right in front of his face. That's not how mature adults behave."

She groans. "Jeez, you're as stubborn as Sammy."

She calls my dad Sammy, although everyone else calls him Cal. His full name is Samuel Callaghan, but we all tend to ignore the Samuel part, which is a shame because it's such a great name.

Also, she's right again.

"It's just... I'm annoyed and disappointed in myself. We had a group session with the kids the other day, and I finally realized how privileged I am to be working with him. I told myself I'd stop these obsessive thoughts and focus on learning and being grateful for the opportunity. But then I saw him on campus, and it all went to hell. I feel like I'm running in circles." I let my head fall back against the couch. "I think I'm doing better than I was, but I still can't get over this feeling that something terrible will happen. Maybe it's because I saw him on campus and felt judged by others. Unsafe to speak to him like I do at the youth center. I don't know."

"I understand that, Li. You're an overthinker by nature. It's good that you're aware of those self-sabotaging thoughts, but be patient with yourself. Bad habits don't stop overnight," she reasons. "But I'm going to be honest—I think you're seeing danger where there isn't any. First of all, screw what people think. I wouldn't be with James if I had worried about what your dad or my friends would think of our relationship."

That much is true. Being ten years older than her and her then physical therapist, I can see why my dad wasn't too happy about Maddie being with James. But my aunt has always done her own thing, not letting other people's views affect her choices. If only I were that brave.

"And secondly," she continues, "sometimes, the only way to get over our fears is to face them head-on."

My dad said the same thing. No wonder they're siblings. "What are you suggesting?"

"I think it'd be a good idea if you went up to him on campus." I'm about to say *no way in hell*, but she intercepts me. "Don't give me that panicked look. Start by waving at him or talking about the weather if you pass him in the hallway. You don't need to have any in-depth discussions about the universe in the middle of the cafeteria, but running away from him isn't the answer, either. Especially because you know it's wrong and want to change."

I can't fight her on that.

"I love you, Li, but you're a big drama queen. Think about

what you'd tell your future patients if they came to you with this same problem. You'd tell them to face their fear so they can see that nothing terrible will happen, right? That it won't be the end of the world because it's all in their heads."

I nod because I would. But taking one's own advice is so, so ridiculously hard.

"Then you know what to do," she concludes, as if it were really that easy. "It's going to feel uncomfortable—embrace it and get over it. Don't let others have so much power over you."

As soon as we say our *I love yous* and hang up, I open the email app and don't think twice as I type away.

I'm already doing an internship with him. The damage is done, so to speak, and I'm tired of being a victim of my own overthinking.

This is the right thing to do.

It's time to put my big girl pants on.

Dr. Abner,

I would like to speak to you regarding a new idea for my internship. Could we meet today? Please let me know your office hours if you're available.

Thank you,

Lila Callaghan

His reply hits my inbox less than five minutes later.

I'll be in my office until 2:30 p.m.

Stop calling me Dr. Abner.

Sincerely,

Not Dr. Abner

Thirty minutes later, my big girl pants hug every inch of my curves, but I'm still terrified, which isn't ideal.

Before knocking at Not Dr. Abner's office door, I dry the sweat off my hands on the fabric of my jeans. No matter how many times I repeat the words in my head that this is the right thing to do and that I'll be fine, believing them is a different story.

Reed's office sits on the third floor of the Psychology Hall, where many other professors also keep their office spaces and labs—which means the hallway is packed with students. And they're looking at me.

It's because I'm staring at them. They just think I'm nuts.

Right. It's a highly plausible explanation.

Maddie is right—my obsessive thinking won't stop overnight. But I'm tired of submitting to it when I have the power to control my brain, not the other way around.

I take a deep breath and knock on his office door.

"Come in," his deep, familiar voice says from inside.

The door squeaks as I open it, one hand hanging on to my backpack strap like an anchor.

A huge shelf full of books to my right side is the first thing that catches my eye. Tomes on child psychology and trauma therapy are piled one over the other, fighting for a spot on his overcrowded shelf.

"See any you like?"

I swivel my head in the direction of the man sitting behind the desk. Reed is leaning back into his chair, his fingers resting over his stomach—I'm absolutely not looking at how the fabric of his white shirt stretches across his chest—as he eyes me with a mix of interest and amusement.

As I turn back to the bookshelf, I strategically let my hair fall to the side of my face so as to cover the heat climbing up my cheeks.

"Yeah, um..." *Words, Lila. Use your words.* "You have so many."

I'm not winning any eloquence awards anytime soon, that's for sure.

The sound of the chair groaning as he stands does something weird to my stomach. And when I feel him getting closer, I tell myself my body is only reacting this way because I forgot to eat breakfast this morning.

"I have a few that could help you with your thesis." That huge hand reaches above my head. Moments later, he hands me a book on child psychology. "This is one of my personal favorites if you want to tackle psychotherapeutic strategies for healing trauma."

"I... Thank you."

At this point, I'm pretty sure he hasn't missed the blush on my cheeks.

"Take this one too." He hands me another book, this one strictly about bibliotherapy. "And just so you know, my office library is always open for you."

Something warm seeps under my skin. When I dare to look up at him, at this mountain of a man who towers over me by more than a whole foot, I'm grateful that my voice doesn't sound as small as I feel. "You may come to regret that offer."

I'm taken aback by the sound of his unfairly attractive laughter. Have I ever heard his laugh before?

"I'd never regret extending an invitation to my personal library to someone who values academic literature as much as I do." His eyes linger on my face before he clears his throat. "You can take these home. Any others that you like too."

I give him a sincere smile. "Thank you. I really appreciate it."

Reed perches himself on the edge of the desk as I continue my perusal of his book collection. What I love about it is that his books look used, loved, like he's read them a thousand times and they're not here merely as decoration. He dog-ears the pages, though, I notice—who's the criminal now?

"So," he starts, his voice casual. "I'm surprised to see you here."

I hold on to the books a little tighter as I turn to him. "I owe you an apology."

He watches me curiously before he says, "You don't."

"Still. I want to apologize for running away from you yesterday. It was childish of me and unfair to you. You've been a great supervisor, and I don't want you to think—"

"Lila." The way he says my name sends a thrill down my spine I suppress the second it hits me. "What I think of you isn't important. The only thing that should matter is what I think of your performance as my intern. I'm not here to judge your character."

"But you do have an opinion of me," I insist, which I'll probably regret in about two seconds. "And I want to know what that is."

He doesn't answer right away. Those dark eyes hold mine as if he were trying to read my mind, but I don't take my words back.

After an eternal beat, he says, "I think you're a great student. I think your mind is extraordinary. And I think you're wasting your time and potential worrying about what irrelevant people think of you."

You're not irrelevant.

"What else is keeping you up at night?" he presses, his voice holding a challenge.

And maybe it's the wrong choice, but I accept it anyway.

"Do you treat me differently because of my parents?" I ask, my chin high. "Be honest. Because I've heard you can be demanding and hard to please, but you've been nothing but nice and encouraging to me."

"I treat all my students equally. You just happen to be more competent than most, which is why I don't need to be as demanding with you. You please me just fine."

My heart jolts.

"Why do you insist that I don't call you Dr. Abner?" is my next question, ignoring the not-innuendo of his last sentence.

He shrugs those wide shoulders. "I don't like the formality of it. All my students call me Reed."

I know my words will cross a line, but that doesn't stop me. And I don't know what it means that I'm acting out of character, but I like this version of me. It feels thrilling, authentic. *Dangerous.*

"You looked upset yesterday," I keep going. "I went to your office to find you, but nobody answered. I just wanted to know how you're doing."

I'm not imagining that powerful body stiffening, which only fuels my curiosity. "Yesterday was a difficult day."

Something else must have happened. Someone with as much experience in the child psychology field as he has doesn't get so upset after an altercation. I'm sure he's had to handle many throughout his career, probably worse than yesterday's.

"Are Cameron and Sean okay?" I ask instead because insisting feels too invasive. Something tells me he wouldn't answer anyway.

He gives me a stiff nod. "I'm talking to Cameron today. I'll also ask his sister for her side of the story. Haniyah told me she was pretty shaken up."

My heart aches for poor Melody. She seems like such a nice girl, and it's obvious that she feels a strong bond with her twin brother. But if anyone can help her, it's Reed.

"So, that idea you mentioned in your email." He changes the subject, his body language shifting with it. His posture relaxes, and his eyes hold less tension than before.

I perk up, reaching into my backpack to put his books inside and grab a new one. "Yes. So, I was researching bibliotherapy books for my thesis—different categories and all that—and I came across this one. I think it would really help Cameron with his situation, if you approve."

He raises a curious eyebrow as I hand him *Thomas and the Little Bird* and hold my breath as he opens the first page and starts reading.

It's a short children's book I found at the local library about a young boy who finds an injured bird in his backyard and nurses it back to health. But once it's ready to fly again, Thomas refuses to let it go. This causes the bird to become really sad, and eventually, the boy realizes that sometimes love means letting the other person—or bird—go their own way.

Once he's done reading, he meets my gaze in a weird way.

Weird because I can't seem to read him right now.

"You picked this out?" he asks. His voice sounds stranger than usual too. "Why?"

"I thought of Cameron when I saw it. If I picked up on the right clues, I'd say he's overprotective of his sister," I explain, shifting on my feet. "And maybe Melody wants to fly free, just like the little bird."

When he says nothing, I quickly add, "But I could be wrong. Sorry if I'm overstepping. I thought I'd rather show it to you than keep it to myself, just in case it helps. Or maybe Cameron doesn't like reading, and this is pointless—"

"Lila."

I gulp. "Yes?"

"Stop doubting how fucking gifted you are."

Air whooshes out my lungs.

Not because he cursed and I've never heard him curse before—why does it make him look so attractive?—but because he sounds so sure, so convinced, his words get sealed into my brain.

"Okay," I whisper, not sure how to respond to that.

He remains silent, like he wants to say something else but, in the end, debates against it. I don't move, barely even breathe, until he gives me the book back.

"I'll get a copy at a local bookstore so you can return this to the library," he says. "You're right about Cameron benefiting from this book. If you have any more recommendations you think the kids will find useful, feel free to email me a list."

My stomach flips. "You really mean that?"

"You should know by now I don't say things I don't mean."

And I do.

For the first time in a very long time, I put my blind trust in someone else's words.

chapter 14

REED

A drop of sweat snakes down my neck, drifting away from the ones clinging to my forehead.

My fists find the punching bag again and again and again. A constant *thump, thump, thump* that matches the rhythm of my frantic heartbeats.

The weight of Liam's stare burns me. If he weren't teaching a class in one of the adjacent rooms, I'd feel Warren's too. It doesn't surprise me that nothing escapes my closest friends—my brothers in all the ways that count.

So, I'm fully expecting Liam's hand to set firmly on my punching bag, stopping me. "Reed."

His voice sounds underwater. My brain knows he's talking to me, but I still ignore him, hitting the bag, punch after punch, followed by another punch.

I wish the pain radiating through my fists would dissolve the one coating my soul.

"Give it a rest, man. Let's just talk," Liam says.

"I don't want to talk," I grit out. But it's like my voice doesn't belong to me. Like this moment isn't really happening. Like I'm going to wake up any second now.

You ruined our family.

If you hadn't told the neighbors, we would—

Liam pulls the punching bag away from me with a yank. When my eyes focus, my best friend's face is all lines of concern and agitation.

"You were about to lose it, man." Liam glances over my shoulder, throwing his brother a knowing look.

"I'm okay," I mutter, removing my boxing gloves as heavy footsteps approach me from behind.

Warren's voice reaches me just a moment later. "All right, brother. Enough sulking and punching bags."

Much like his actual brother, Warren—who is four years older than us—knows exactly what's going on in my head with just a quick glance. Growing up in the foster care system, always alert, always suspicious, we are all used to reading the silent cues as if they were words on paper.

"You're telling me I can't punch bags at a boxing gym," I deadpan, knowing damn well what he's about to tell me.

"I'm saying you can't zone out like that. It'll do you no good. Some mental health god you are."

Deep down, I'm aware this isn't the healthiest way to cope with today. Haniyah always encouraged me to attend therapy when life got too heavy, and I've listened to her. A handful of therapists have helped me over the years to deal with most of the burdens of my past, but those rules don't exist on this particular day of every year.

"Ignore him." Liam runs a hand through his longish blond hair. "Let's hit the bar tonight. Drinks on me."

"Count me the hell in," Warren says with a huge grin before his hand drops to my shoulder. "You're coming with us. Not open for discussion."

It's a Saturday afternoon, so they know I don't have an excuse to say no. But just because I usually don't work on weekends doesn't mean I'll say yes to their plans, which must be why Liam adds, "We know you're going to spend the night brooding in your empty house, which is frankly sad as fuck. If you don't want to go out for yourself, do it for us. We don't want to see you like this."

Goddammit.

I met Liam and Warren in my first foster home when I was seven. I'd always been the quiet kid, happy on my own, never particularly interested in making friends. But Liam had had a fight with his brother that day, and he asked me to play a video game with him instead.

By the time Warren showed up to apologize, Liam had decided I was going to be their new brother. I'm still not sure why, because I wasn't the life of the party, but something about me drew the Hart brothers in. We've been inseparable since.

Three years later, they got adopted by a couple who understood how important our friendship was. And while they didn't adopt me—nobody did—they allowed Liam and Warren to meet with me every weekend.

Our friendship grew over the years, and even the hits of adulthood weren't strong enough to separate us. Nobody and nothing will.

I love them in the same way I love Haniyah, like one loves a stranger who eventually becomes family.

And because these fuckers love me back and know what strings to pull, I find myself agreeing. "Just one drink."

I'd never spent the anniversary of the ending of my old life surrounded by alcohol before. Not once in the twenty-eight years since I sent my parents to jail.

Going for a drink seems like the obvious answer to grief, to drowning the pain, to distracting the anger. To most people, anyway.

But I've never leaned into alcohol because I crave the punishment this day brings every year.

In a fucked-up way, I'm convinced I deserve it. Therapy hasn't been able to fix this part of me, the one that feels guilty for everything that happened. My brain knows I need to move on, but my heart refuses to catch up.

Today marks the day my parents got arrested for child neglect and abuse after leaving me alone at the house for five days.

They left me—to go who the fuck knows where—with nothing but the bleeding wound on my back my dad had inflicted the night before and some stale bread. The perfect company for a seven-year-old.

Today marks the last day I saw my father, who passed from heart failure shortly after he went to jail. The coward left before I became strong enough to tell him how much I fucking hated him.

Today marks the last day I saw my mother alive. She went to jail, too, but soon was transferred to a mental health institution. Schizophrenia, they said. The next time I saw her, I was seventeen, and she was being lowered to the ground in a casket.

I gulp down the remains of my first and last whiskey of the night, fulfilling my promise to Liam and Warren, and stamp a handful of bills on the counter. It covers my drink and a couple of rounds for them—a gift of sorts to compensate for my shitty mood and even shittier company.

"See you at the gym." I stand, but Liam grabs my arm in a strong grip.

"Where do you think you're going? We've been here for ten minutes, man. Sit your ass down."

I don't.

"I said I'd have one drink, not that I'd stay for two hours," I point out, probably sounding like an asshole.

Warren takes a sip of his beer before agreeing with his younger brother. "If you wanna sulk, do it here. No need to do it at home."

The headache I've been nursing all day intensifies, not because I don't love my brothers but because I'm really not in the fucking mood.

This week has been a shit show from start to finish.

During our last counseling session, I tried to help Cameron understand the source of his anger and protectiveness, and I reassured him it was okay to walk away from a conflict to calm down. But I have a feeling that won't be enough to change his ways.

Melody didn't come to the youth center all week after the incident. Her parents assured us she'll be back, that she just wanted to take a small break, but it shouldn't be like this.

And just when I thought the week couldn't get worse, Sean's parents pulled him out of the youth center. Haniyah was told that he was transferred to another youth center in town, so at least he'll continue getting the help he needs.

The whole thing still left a bad taste in my mouth.

"Forgot to tell you earlier because we were too busy making sure you didn't annihilate that punching bag," Warren says, bringing me back to the present. "But you need to sit down first, or I won't tell you."

He gets an eye roll for that, but I do as he says. "What is it?"

Warren exchanges a quick glance with Liam. "The kids can start next month."

That sentence alone shifts my whole mood.

"You're serious?" I glance between the two of them. "You cleared it with the sponsors?"

Warren nods, smiling. "They're on board. Thought it'd be a great idea, too. They're all about helping the community and all that."

"I'll email you the information for the parents on Monday," Liam chimes in. "The kids are gonna have a blast."

As children who grew up in the foster system, all three of us know what it's like to be defenseless. Angry, confused, bitter, alone. But we had one another—and eventually, we had boxing.

Warren and Liam opened their own boxing gym five years

ago. Ever since, they've offered lessons to children who need a safe place to channel their anger and learn to control it. When I suggested donating a few lessons to the kids at the youth center, they were immediately on board. And so are the local sponsors we contacted to help us fund this project, apparently.

"Thank you," I say. "They are going to lose their minds when we tell them."

"That's the goal." Warren grins before taking another sip of his beer. His eyes travel past Liam and me as he sets down the now-empty glass. "Uh-oh. Might want to order another round before that bachelorette party takes over."

I turn just as a loud group of young women and a couple of men wearing glittery cowboy hats enters the bar. I'm about to tell Liam and Warren that there's no way in hell they're making me stay now—I have nothing against people having fun, but I'm really not in the mood tonight—when a flash of long blonde hair makes me come to a halt.

The most logical part of my brain knows there's no reason for my heart to leap. Countless people have long blonde hair—enough not to assume it's her.

Why my pulse accelerates when I think it is her is the question.

Yet all thoughts vanish from my mind as Lila lifts her head from her phone and finds my eyes across the bar.

Shit.

"Hey, dude," Warren says. "I asked if you wanted another drink."

The words *I'm calling it a night* are at the tip of my tongue. Going home like I've been wanting to for the past ten minutes crosses my mind before I catch another glimpse of Lila.

And suddenly, my plans have gone out the window.

"I'll get the next round," I tell them, convinced I'm losing my mind for good. "Two beers?"

"Yeah," Liam confirms, eyeing me with a new interest. "Glad to hear you're staying."

I don't answer. As if pulled by an invisible string, my body moves on autopilot toward the bar.

She's waiting for her drink, and it doesn't take her longer than a couple of seconds to notice me as I come to a halt by her side, pressing my warmth against her in the crowded bar. The last thing I expect her to do is look me up and down, amusement glinting on her face.

"Are you following me, Dr. Abner?" Her teasing voice makes something in the southern region of my body stir to life.

Absolutely fucking not.

I shift on my feet. "Considering I was already here with my friends when you walked in, I'd say you are the one following me, little criminal."

Her cheeks turn pink, which doesn't help my situation. A situation that shouldn't be happening in the first place.

"I see," she mutters before adjusting her cowboy hat over her head. "Thoughts on my outfit?"

I don't allow myself to look past her neck even though I know she's wearing a short skirt, heeled boots, and a pink sweater. When it comes to her, I always notice more than I should.

"Very glittery. What's the occasion?"

She throws her thumb over her shoulder to the group at her back. "Birthday party. I wanted to stay home and finish up some classwork for next week, but I can't exactly say no to Mariah."

"Mariah?"

"She's my best friend," she explains, a small smile on her glossy lips. *Stop staring at her goddamn mouth.* "Her dad works with my dad. We've known each other our whole lives."

I frown. "Wait. Trey is her dad?"

She nods.

Trey works with Cal at the tattoo parlor, and I've met him

once or twice in passing. As if summoned by our conversation, a smiley Black girl with a glittery silver cowboy hat throws her arm around Lila.

"Making new friends, Li? I feel like a proud mom."

Lila rolls her eyes at her. "Mariah, this is Reed. Reed, Mariah. The birthday girl."

I give her a smile. "Nice to meet you. Happy birth—"

"Wait," she says, cutting me off and glancing frantically between Lila and me. "This is Reed? The internship guy?"

The internship guy?

So, she told her best friend about me. Huh.

Why that makes my chest fill with an unknown emotion, I'd rather not know.

"That'd be me. Internship guy." The corner of my mouth lifts. "Happy birthday."

"Thanks. Sorry for being so forward. It's just that I've heard *so much* about you, you know? It's great to finally meet the guy Li has been running away from."

"Riah," Lila hisses.

"Sorry. I might be a tiny bit drunk. Pregaming did something to me."

By the way she's wobbling a little, I believe her.

Trey's daughter leans over in my direction, whispering in a still-too-loud voice, "Don't worry, Reed. She really likes you. She told me you were a great mentor and all that. And you're easy on the eyes, too, which helps."

"Mariah!"

She looks back at Lila, shrugging. "Hey, just telling the truth. You know I've been trying to get with Eva for months, so it's not like I'm going to steal your man over here. I promise he's not my type."

I can't help but smirk. "Is this Eva person here tonight?"

I have no idea why I'm playing along, why I have this sudden need for Lila's best friend to like me, but I lean into it.

"Oh, yeah. I told Li I'm not going home tonight, if you know what I mean."

"Forgive her," Lila chimes in, her cheeks flaming. "She's a friendly person on a normal day, but she always gets a little out of control after a few drinks." She holds Mariah around her shoulders. "No more drinks for you tonight, birthday girl."

She pouts. "How about later?"

"Once you've had a full bottle of water, maybe."

"Okay, Mom." Mariah turns to me. "I'm gonna dance now, but it was great meeting you, Reed. You're a tall guy."

I chuckle. "Have a good birthday night, Mariah. And take care. That water might be a good idea if you want to avoid a hangover tomorrow."

She rolls her eyes, but she's smiling. "Oh, Li, look at him, all worried about my hangover in the morning. Cute. You guys are a match of worriers made in heaven." She hiccups. "Okay, enough talking. Bye, Reed."

Lila hides her face in her hands as her friend goes back to their group. "I don't know what that was just now. I'm so sorry."

"The past five minutes never happened. Got it."

I smirk down at her, not really minding her friend's drunken words. Whatever allows me to see that pretty blush on her cheeks, I'll take it.

She glances around the bar before looking back at me. "Let me buy you a drink. It's the least I can do after that fiasco."

"You don't have to do that. The past five minutes never happened, remember?"

"You've been forgetting too many things about me lately, starting with the tire thing. And I owe you for being so unfair to you when I started the internship," she argues. "Which, by the way, won't happen again. Running away from you, I mean. I'm fighting my intrusive thoughts like crazy right now."

That pulls a chuckle from me. "Is that so?"

"Yep." When she pops the p, the pink gloss on her lips catches the reflection of the lights above us. "I know there are many people around, but I enjoy your company, so I'm focusing on that."

My heart does a fucking cartwheel.

"I enjoy your company too, but there's no need to buy me anything," I insist. "I was just here to order a couple beers for my friends and call it a night."

"Oh." I tell myself I'm imagining the way her face falls. "So, you're leaving?"

"Might stay around for a bit, but I'm not drinking. Just water for me."

"Then I'll get you some water," she presses, looking past my shoulders. "I'm guessing your friends are those two guys looking at us. Otherwise, I might start freaking out."

Indeed, I spot Liam and Warren focusing very intensely on us when I turn my head. I raise a questioning eyebrow their way and get two shameless smirks in return.

"Those would be my friends," I tell Lila. "Actually, I don't know if Haniyah filled you in on this, but we're offering free boxing lessons to the kids starting next month. My friends over there, Liam and Warren, own the gym where they'll be taking their lessons."

Her eyes widen in surprise. "Really? That's amazing. I bet Cameron would benefit a lot from channeling his anger through a sport. They're going to love it."

Cameron had also been on my mind when I first considered boxing lessons for them.

"Can I go say hi to them?" she asks. "I want to thank them for the boxing lessons."

Something warm settles in my chest. "Sure."

But as soon as I say the word, someone crashes into Lila.

My arms wrap around her waist before I can understand what's happening, my only concern being that she doesn't hurt herself. She clings to my upper arms, her warmth seeping into my skin and not letting me breathe.

Everything around us disappears when our eyes lock.

Enthralled, I can only focus on her uneven breaths and her lips, just inches away.

What would she taste like?

"Oh my God, I'm so sorry," a new voice squeals.

Lila blinks and pulls away, breaking the moment, and creating a safe distance between us once again.

"I'm so sorry," that voice repeats. "Are you okay?"

I shift my gaze to a girl I don't recognize. She's also wearing a glittery cowboy hat, so I'm assuming she's from Lila's friend group.

"I'm fine," Lila says, breathless.

The girl gives me a big smile and holds out her hand in my direction. "Hi, I'm Karla. Lila's friend. I don't believe we've met."

I tip my chin in acknowledgment. "Nice to meet you, Karla. I'm Reed."

"Oh, I know," she drawls as I let go of her clammy hand. "I'm a counseling MA student, just like Lila. I actually asked you a question during your last open lecture at the university. You don't remember me?"

I put my hands in the pockets of my slacks, itching to go back to when it was just Lila and me. "I don't, sorry."

Lila, who has been standing to the side since Karla pushed her into me, picks up on my stiffness. "I'll come back to our table in a minute," she tells her friend.

Karla's face drops for a moment, but her happy mask slips back on quickly. "Sure. Nice to see you again, Reed."

I give her a tight-lipped smile and say nothing.

Wrapped in Lila's magnetic bubble, I hadn't even noticed

how packed the bar has become in the past few minutes. So, when she starts in Liam and Warren's direction, placing my hand on the small of her back to guide her through the crowd comes as an instinct. She stays close, not pulling away from my touch, which once again makes the situation behind my zipper not ideal.

Why am I getting hard over my twenty-four-year-old intern? My friends' daughter, for fuck's sake.

I pull away before we reach our table. Liam and Warren each send me a questioning look before their eyes fall on the girl in front of me.

"Hi," she starts, her voice friendly. "I'm Lila. Sorry to interrupt like this. It's just that I work with Reed at the youth center, and he told me about the boxing lessons. I wanted to thank you guys for doing this for the kids. It'll really help them."

"Why, Lila, thank you. Name's Warren. So pleased to meet you." Warren's face splits into a grin. "This one over here is my brother, Liam. Anything for those kiddos. You work with Reed, you say?"

I send him a death glare that only makes his smile wider. *Asshole.*

Lila is oblivious to our silent exchange. "He's my internship supervisor."

"Please tell us he's not an asshole to you," Liam says. "Are we the only ones getting special treatment?"

The sound of her chuckle makes my chest constrict. "He's not an asshole. Only a bit grouchy sometimes."

"I thought we agreed on bossy, not grouchy." My breath grazes the shell of her ear as I lean in. "Changed your mind?"

I don't miss her uneven breath. "Both can be true at the same time."

"Mmm."

"So, what are you studying, Lila?" Warren asks, not looking particularly annoyed that I've forgotten their beers.

"I'm a grad student, on to become a youth counselor next year. Hopefully."

That makes me frown. "Hopefully?"

"Just like our baby boy over here." Liam grins, patting my arm.

I throw him a glare. "I'm older than you."

"Still our baby boy," he coos.

Lila snickers. "It was great meeting you both, but I have to go back to my friend's birthday party."

"Sure thing. Hope to see you again, Lila." Warren's smile is sincere as he adds, "Those boxing lessons aren't just for the kids, just so you know."

"Yeah. Feel free to join us anytime," Liam agrees. "Reed will be more than happy to train you, I'm sure."

She swirls her head toward me. "You practice boxing?"

"Been doing it for a few years," I answer.

"Oh. That...makes sense." Has she just looked at my arm, or am I seeing things? She's quick to add, "I mean, it makes sense that you practice boxing when your friends own the gym. That's all. Well, um, it was great meeting you guys. I'll see you on Monday, Reed."

Before it registers that what I'm about to do is definitely not appropriate, I stop her with my hand around her arm. "Wait."

When she glances down at my fingers, I drop them. "Do you have a way to get home?"

She clears her throat. "Yeah. I'll just call an Uber or my dad when I want to leave. But thanks for asking."

"I can drive you home if you want," I blurt out before I know what the fuck I'm doing.

"Thanks, but I don't want to bother you." Those doe eyes have never looked more beautiful than right now, staring up at me as the light makes those green-and-hazel specks shine even brighter. "You said you wanted to call it a night. I don't want to make you wait."

I can stay. I can stay for an hour or two or three or for as long as you need me to. Because suddenly, the thought of you not getting home safely is choking the air out of my lungs.

"All right." I put my hands inside my pockets to avoid reaching out to touch her. "If you change your mind, you know where to find me. I can come back to drive you home. It may not be safe to get in a stranger's car by the time you leave."

That makes her smirk. "If I change my mind, I'll email your faculty address. Sure."

"Smart-ass." I reach for my phone under her mirthful stare. "Here. Type in my number on your phone."

She worries her lip between her teeth. "Are you sure that's a good idea?"

But she's still reaching for her phone.

"For emergencies," I lie to myself.

Lie to her.

She nods, something electric and unfamiliar passing between us.

"For emergencies," she agrees.

Her words sound like a lie, too.

Two hours later, I'm reading in bed when my phone pings with a notification.

Unknown Number stares back at me. I don't need to read the text to check who it is because my gut simply knows.

> **Unknown Number: Just got home safe. I knew you were losing sleep over it, so this technically counts as an emergency.**

Unknown Number: This is Lila, by the way :)

Setting my book aside, I drag my hand across my jaw. I should pretend to be asleep, to have my phone on silent, *anything* but what I end up doing.

Me: Glad to hear it. Did you have a good night?

Dots appear on my screen instantly, and a few seconds later, I get her reply.

Lila: I don't go out much, so I kept wanting to go home. But I had fun.

Lila: Mariah and Eva finally hooked up (another emergency since you seemed invested)

The playfulness of her texts shouldn't light me up from the inside, and yet...

We're not being inappropriate, not exactly, but texting back and forth with my intern at night about nonacademic matters is surely frowned upon.

But my heart has had a shitty day, and this is what it wants. For once, I listen.

Me: I was indeed waiting for confirmation. Now I can sleep in peace.

Lila: Ha-ha. I need to wake up early to work on my thesis. Have a good night :)

Me: Good night, Lila. Sleep well.

It's not until the following morning that I realize I didn't fall asleep with my parents on my mind.

Blonde hair and hazel eyes took over.

chapter 15

LILA

"Lili..."

A gentle smile draws on my lips as I recognize that little voice. "Yes, Ike?"

The five-year-old boy reaches out his hand to pull at the hem of my T-shirt. "My tummy hurts." A scared look takes over his face. "Am I pregnant?"

I try my hardest not to laugh while Melody attempts to hide her smile by writing something in her English notebook. Sitting across from me in the study room, she lets out a not-so-discreet cough when she can't hold it in anymore.

"Little boys can't get pregnant, Ikey. Where exactly does it hurt?"

He rubs the middle of his stomach, pouting.

Two weeks have passed since my first day, and I already feel at home. It helps that the more time I spend with them in the common room, the more kids are starting to warm up to me.

"Did you eat too much earlier? Maybe food is upsetting your stomach," I suggest.

But he shakes his head, his eyes piercing into mine like he's never wanted someone to take his pain away so badly. "I didn't eat anything."

That makes me frown. "Didn't Mommy give you lunch?"

Ike whines. "But lunch was *ages* ago, Lili."

Realization dawns on me then. I shake my head in

amusement and relief. "You're hungry, aren't you?"

And when he nods, I finally let out the chuckle I've been holding. "You should've started with that, Ikey. I thought you were sick."

His hands go back to his stomach. "I thought I had a little baby in my belly."

I turn to the twelve-year-old across from me. "You'll be okay if I get a snack with him? Five minutes, tops."

She nods. "Sure. I'm still reading this. Will you help me with some big words later?"

I give her a soft smile. "Of course. You got this."

Melody returns my smile before going back to her book, and I can't help but feel proud of her.

After her brother's fight with Sean, she didn't come here for a few days, which set off Reed's alarms because he knows Melody loves it here and benefits greatly from group therapy. His sigh of relief was palpable when Melody finally turned up with Cameron today.

Since I'm done with the report Reed asked me to go over earlier, he suggested I come to the library in case someone needed help with their homework. Melody waved at me as soon as I walked in, and I've been helping her for the past hour.

I'm pulled away—literally—from my thoughts by Ike's little hand dragging me outside of the study room.

"What do you want to eat?" I ask him. "I can slice an apple for you if you want."

But the little boy shakes his head. "I have a sandwich in my bag, but I don't remember where it is."

I chuckle. "So where are you dragging me to?"

"I think it's in the art room," he muses out loud. "But the big kids are there, and I'm scared."

He means kids around Melody's age, who he's shy around. And I get it—when you're so small, even children only a few years older than you can be as intimidating as grown adults.

We pass by a few of Ike's friends in the hallway, who ask to go play with him in the common room. But he's a boy on a mission, and he has no problem telling them as much.

I'm smiling at his sheer determination to find his sandwich, when we round a corner and we both bump into a big, hard body.

"Careful, buddy."

That voice.

I come to my senses just in time to see a big hand holding onto Ike's arm, keeping him upright as the child giggles. It takes me a second longer to realize that his other hand, warm and firm and strong, is also holding me up.

Because it's on the small of my back.

And the muscular arm attached to it is wrapped around my body.

"Are you okay?" Reed's raspy voice asks.

I school my features and give him what I hope is an easy smile. "Yep. Sorry we bumped into you."

"You're sure you're not hurt?" he asks again.

For some dumb reason, nerves start twisting in my stomach. "Not at all. Um, are you?"

I know it's a stupid question the second it leaves my mouth. There's no way a five-foot-three woman and a child can do any real damage to this tank-shaped man. I should've guessed that he practiced boxing sooner, given the size of those arms.

Not that I'm ogling him or anything. That would be unprofessional and a really, really bad idea.

"You're not hurt," Ike tells Reed. "You're big, like a superhero!"

I tell myself my stomach doesn't jump when he drops his hand from my back and smiles fondly at him. "Where are you two going?"

"My belly hurt, and I thought I had a baby inside, but Lili told me I was hungry, and I am, so I'm gonna get my sandwich."

Reed's eyebrows shoot up at that. "You..." He steals a quick glance at me, then looks back at the boy. "You thought you were pregnant."

Ike nods, being totally serious, and my lips start twitching again. "My mommy has a baby in her belly, and she says it hurts."

He makes a thoughtful noise at the back of his throat, following along. "Ah, I get it now. Well, I'm glad to hear it's just hunger. I'll let you get your sandwich, then."

"Thanks." He beams before grabbing my hand again. "Let's go, Lili. I'm more hungry than before."

I smile. "It's *hungrier*, Ikey."

"Hungrier," he repeats. "Come on, Lili. What if someone eats my sandwich?"

Holding Ike's hand again, I can only take a single step forward.

"Lila," Reed starts.

His presence shouldn't make me this nervous. I don't feel the need to run away from him anymore, but I can't shake off the feeling that we might have crossed some invisible line that night at the bar. What was I thinking, texting him that I was home safe? Like he would even care?

I swallow past the lump in my throat and ignore Ike's annoyed groan. "Yeah?"

"Meet me in my office before you leave."

"Sure thing," I agree with an easy smile, even though my insides are crumbling by the second.

With a dip of his stubbled chin, he disappears down the hallway. Once Ike finds his sandwich in the art room, I walk him back to the common room, where his friends are coloring pictures. When he's settled, I head back to Melody.

Meet him at his office for what?

To tell me to delete his number, probably.

"Sorry about that." I let out a shaky breath as I plop down

into the chair across from her and wipe the sweat off my palms on my jeans. "Did you finish your reading okay?"

"I highlighted all the words I didn't understand," she tells me, showing me her book. Then she passes me a completed sheet. "And I answered all the questions here."

I beam. "You've done so well today. Let me grab a dictionary for you so you can look up those words."

She groans. "Do I have to?"

"Uh-huh. You need to practice how to use a dictionary."

"But I use it on my phone just fine."

"A physical dictionary. You know, one of those things called *books*," I tease her as I get back up. "Your teacher won't let you use your phone in the middle of the exam."

"Ugh. Fine. You're lucky I like you."

I shake my head in amusement and head over to one of the many bookshelves perched up on every wall of the library. As I search for the dictionary, a sense of belonging washes over me.

I can't believe how quickly the kids have accepted me. Melody was the first one to show me kindness, and other kids from our group sessions, like Santiago and Sofia, soon followed suit. Then Ike, and then one of Melody's friends, Vera.

It's no wonder Haniyah, Reed, and everyone else work so hard to help these kids—when you meet them, they truly capture your heart.

Once I get the dictionary and remind Melody how to use it, she finds all her words in twenty minutes. After we go over a couple of questions on her worksheet she didn't get right, I notice we still have a few minutes until her studying time is over.

So, even though I know Reed wanted to talk to her, I can't help but ask, "Hey, Melody. Do you feel like talking about what happened with Sean and your brother?"

She visibly stiffens. "What about it?"

I lean back on my chair, attempting to sound and look casual so as to not make her anxious. It works when Reed does it, so it may be worth a try. "I just wanted to know how you're feeling after last week."

Her shoulders lift and fall as she puts everything back in her backpack. "I don't know."

"It's okay if you don't want to talk about it," I repeat Reed's words during the group session because they're true. The last thing I want is to make her uncomfortable. "I won't be upset."

She places her bag on her lap to zip it up, giving me an unsure look. "Reed said he wanted to talk to me, and I'm a little nervous."

"He only wants to make sure you're okay," I reassure her. "What are you nervous about?"

She bites her lower lip and looks away, debating whether to keep talking about this or not. But she finally admits, "I'm a bit angry with my brother, and because Reed is his counselor, I don't want to get Cameron into trouble."

"Well, if you'd feel more comfortable talking to me instead, I'm here to listen. But don't worry about Reed. He only wants to look out for Cameron—and you. Your brother won't get into trouble."

"Okay." A brief pause. Then she says, "I know Cameron loves me a lot, and I love him, but sometimes he... Sometimes he treats me like a baby."

"Because he protects you so much?"

"Exactly! It's like he thinks I can't take care of myself," she adds. "When Sean made fun of me, I told him to get lost and leave me alone. I had it under control, but Cameron yelled at him anyway, and things got messy."

"And you don't like that," I point out.

She shrugs, a mask of sadness draping over her face. "I like that I can count on him if I need help, but he doesn't let *me* handle things. It's kinda annoying. Am I a bad sister for saying that?"

"Oh, sweetie, of course you're not," I reassure her. "You're allowed to feel like this. Have you tried talking to him about it? Help him understand your feelings?"

"Not really. I told him once, and he didn't listen, so."

"All right, here's what you can do, if you want my advice." I wait until she nods. "The next time your brother treats you like a baby, you tell him that you're strong and capable of dealing with things on your own—because you are. You can tell him you'll ask for his help if you need it, but that he should let you do things on your own. But tell him firmly, with conviction. Let's practice."

Melody sits up on her chair, an intrigued spark in her eyes. "Okay."

"Let's pretend I'm your brother and you're you." Clearing my throat, I start, "Melody, I heard someone made fun of you at school today. Is that true?"

"Yes, but I can handle it," she declares firmly.

"No, I don't think you can. I'll take care of it so it doesn't happen again."

She frowns. "You don't trust me to take care of myself or what?"

"I'm just stronger than you, is all."

"It doesn't matter. I want to do this on my own because I'm strong, too," she declares firmly. "I'll ask for your help if I need it."

My face breaks into a proud smile. "Well done. That's how you can go about it," I tell her. "Make sure to add something like 'you're a great brother, and I love you, but I want to do this on my own.' That'll reassure him you still count on him, and it may make it easier for him."

"Okay." She gives me an enthusiastic nod. "I can do that."

"Of course you can. You're a strong girl. He needs to realize it, too."

The smile she gives me is nothing short of beaming. "I'm strong. I got this."

It hits me then—how could I have ever doubted this is the

right calling for me?

REED

Cameron doesn't look impressed by the book that lands on his lap at the start of our next session. He reads the title out loud. *"Thomas and the Little Bird."* Then, he frowns. "Why are you giving me a children's book?"

I sink back into my armchair. "Because we're going to read it together."

"But we never read in our sessions," he argues, not sold on the idea. "I don't want to do homework."

"This isn't homework," I explain calmly. "Sometimes, books can help with counseling. I think you'll really like this one."

He makes a face. I know he isn't an avid reader, but if there's one kid in the youth center who can benefit from the book Lila picked out, it's him.

"Come on. Let's start reading."

"Reed," he whines.

"If you finish reading the book, I'll give you something cool at the end of the session."

"Define cool. Because you're old, like a dad, and dads usually think things are cool when they aren't."

I give him a flat look that makes him chuckle. "You'll like it."

"Fine." With a dramatic sigh, he cranks the book open and starts reading.

The book is short, meant to grab the kid's attention long enough for the message to stick without boring them to death. And it works, because Cameron doesn't get distracted or complain as he reaches the end.

"Well?" I ask him once he's done. "What did you think of the story?"

He drums his fingers on the hardcover. "It was okay."

"Do you identify with the main character? Thomas?"

He frowns. "What does that mean?"

"If you see yourself in him. If you think you two are similar."

He thinks about it. "I guess I do."

"In what way?"

His eyes stay on the cover, his finger tracing the drawing of the little bird. "Thomas takes care of his bird like I take care of my sister."

I hum. "Tell me how you take care of Melody."

"I give her hugs when she's upset," he tells me, glancing up at me. "I want to keep her safe like Thomas with the bird."

"I'm sure you remember what happened to the bird, though? When Thomas didn't let it fly away because he was afraid it'd get hurt again."

"The bird got sad, and then Thomas got sad, and it wasn't fun anymore."

Cameron is a bright kid. Despite his quick temper and tough exterior, I recognized his sensibility from the moment he walked into the youth center for the first time. He can connect the dots between the book and his own personal story just fine—to transform that consciousness into actual actions is the challenge here.

And I love a challenge.

"Remind me what happened when Thomas finally agreed to let the bird fly away," I ask him.

He sits up straighter, his voice losing those sad undertones from before. "The bird came back every day to see Thomas, and he brought some friends with him sometimes."

"It was a nice surprise, wasn't it? Because Thomas thought he'd never see the bird again once it flew away."

He fidgets. "Yeah."

"Are you afraid that Melody won't need you anymore if you stop helping her?"

Cameron snaps his head up at me in surprise—a gesture that tells me I've pretty much read his mind. "Something like that."

"It's difficult to let go of control," I concede. "It makes us anxious, and whenever we feel anxious, our brain tells us to stop because something bad will happen. But that's not true— we simply feel anxious because it's something we've never done before. Have you ever let your sister stand up for herself?"

"No," he admits in a quiet voice.

"Okay. The next time she's upset, let her handle it. Stay on the sidelines and do nothing unless she asks you to. And if she needs your help, ask her first what it is that she needs from you. Maybe she doesn't want you to pounce on anyone; maybe she just wants a hug. Does that sound like something you can do?"

When he nods, I grab a piece of paper from my folder and hand it out to him. "Here you go."

The paper crinkles in Cameron's fingers. "What is this?"

"A gym in town is offering free boxing lessons for the kids here who want to join," I tell him. "Maybe it's something you'd be interested in. That's information for your parents. If they agree to sign you up, they need to fill in that application and give it back to me."

"Is this the cool surprise you talked about?" He eyes the paper with intrigue. "Boxing? Like *Rocky*? My dad loves that movie, and we watched it together."

"Yes—to all those questions."

"But you always say punching people is bad."

"And I stand by that." I lean forward, resting my elbows on my knees. "But boxing isn't about punching people—it's about discipline and managing stress. It'll help you feel less angry too."

"Really?" he asks me like he doesn't buy any of it.

"Really. I'd know it—I practice boxing at that same gym."

"No way." His eyes almost bug out of his skull. He sits upright, intrigued. "So that's why you're so big? Now I want to do boxing, too."

"Think about it. There's no rush," I say. "If you sign up, your boxing instructors will be my closest friends, and I know them well. Which is why I also know they won't teach you how to get into fights. That's not what boxing is about. You can ask me any questions you might have and talk to your parents. But don't agree to these lessons thinking it's going to be brawl galore."

"I get it," he assures me with a quick nod. "I think I'm going to watch some videos when I get home."

"That's a good idea," I encourage. "You have a couple of weeks to sign up, so take your time."

"Thanks, Reed." He leans forward, bumping my fist with his—our signature goodbye gesture. Paper still in hand, he stands before I do. "You're coming to the park, right?"

The field trip to the park is one of our most popular activities. The kids love it there because they can play outdoors and get away from their routines. This year has been no different—they've been buzzing with excitement since the school year started.

"I'll be there," I assure him.

"Is Lila coming?" he asks next, catching me off guard. "It's just that Melody really likes her. She told me the other day."

I still haven't talked to her about it, but I don't see why she wouldn't want to come.

"I'm pretty sure she'll tag along. Be good, Cameron. I'll see you tomorrow."

Once he goes back to the common room, I busy myself drafting his report until someone knocks at my office.

Blonde hair and a nervous smile greet me from the door. "You wanted to see me?"

At my nod, Lila shuts the door behind her and walks up to my desk, but she doesn't sit down.

"I saw you with Melody earlier," I start. "I just wanted to know if she said something about last week."

"I actually, um, talked to her about it," she says, looking strangely guilty.

"What do you mean?"

She shifts on her feet. "I asked her if she wanted to talk, and she said yes. She was worried about getting Cameron into trouble if she talked to you."

"Why do you look so worried?" I ask, unable to ignore the startled look in her eyes.

"I didn't know if I was overstepping," she admits. "The last thing I want is to prevent you from doing your job."

"You're doing no such thing." I stand from behind my desk, moving toward her until only a small distance separates us. "Cameron told me his sister really likes you. I'm sure whatever advice you gave her, she'll listen to it."

"I don't know about that," she mutters, looking away. "Maybe she'll think it's silly or—"

"Lila, look at me."

Those pretty eyes lock with mine.

"How many times do I have to tell you the children like you?"

And it's true. They looked more at ease around her in our second group session last week, in which we tackled teamwork. It also helps that she's out in the common room every day, playing with them or helping them with homework.

"Haniyah is happy with your performance so far, and so am I," I tell her. "Is there anything we could do to help you feel more comfortable?"

"It's not that," she hurries to say. "Everything's perfect. I'm just in over my head."

I wonder what or who made her lose her confidence to such extremes. Is that asshole of her ex the only one to blame, or is there more to it?

Don't ask. Don't get too close. I'll ruin her.

I clear my throat. "Maybe a day off will help you put things into perspective."

"I don't want a day off." She sounds alarmed.

"Not like that. There's a field trip coming up. We're going to the park to play some group games, get some fresh air. It's technically not on your internship obligations, since it's on a Saturday, but if you want to be a chaperone, I'll save a spot for you."

"That sounds amazing," she instantly says. "Count me in."

I nod, the organ in my chest pounding at the thought of seeing her again this weekend. Why does that make me feel ten times lighter?

"So, tell me more about your conversation with Melody," I say, attempting to get back on track.

Because spending the day with her away from the safety of the youth center has the potential to turn into a very dangerous thing.

chapter 16

LILA

Someone behind me taps my shoulder. "I'm getting dizzy."

I turn in my seat to face Vera, one of Melody's close friends, and find her looking at me with a painful expression on her face.

"Are you getting nauseous? Do you want to throw up?"

Please, say no.

Before we left this morning, Haniyah told me she always packs some sickness bags with her on these bus trips, but I'd rather not have poor Vera use them.

The loud voices of the kids on the bus drown out her tired voice, but I manage to read her lips. "Don't think so."

"The park is only five minutes away," I reassure her.

She closes her eyes and pouts, leaning her head on Melody's shoulder, who's sitting next to her with her eyes shut. Taking advantage of the bus stopping at a red light, I round the empty seat next to mine until I reach the two girls.

"I'm opening the window, okay? The breeze will make you feel better. Let me know if it bothers you, and I'll close it again," I tell her.

When she nods, I get on my tiptoes and hold on to the headrest of the seat in front of me, trying not to bother a sleeping Melody as I struggle to reach the tiny window. Just when I manage to open it with the tips of my fingers, the light turns green and the vehicle moves, jerking me to the side.

Shit, shit, shit, s—

A firm grip around my waist prevents me from falling onto Vera and Melody.

"Didn't they ever tell you that standing on a moving bus is a no-no?" Reed's tone is easy, teasing.

His strong hands pull me upright until I'm standing safely in the aisle. I don't need to look at my reflection to know I'm blushing furiously. I really need to check why it is I'm always blushing around this man.

Maybe because I have a cru—

No. Nope.

"Thanks," I mutter, glancing at him over my shoulder.

Big mistake.

Since we're spending the day at the park, eating picnic lunches and playing games, the dress code is casual. I thought nothing of it until I saw Reed in dark jeans and a Henley under a leather jacket, doing absolutely nothing to conceal how much boxing is paying off.

I should stop drooling over a man twelve years older than me who happens to be my kind-of boss at the youth center and a close friend of my parents. For my career, I really should.

"Sit down, Lila," he says, sounding firmer but not angry. "I don't want you getting hurt."

But his arm is still around me, so I can't exactly move.

The bus driver hits the brake when the car in front of us abruptly stops—*damn it, man, really?*—making me lose my balance again.

One moment I'm falling, and the next I'm sitting on a very hard, very muscular seat.

"Comfortable?" Reed's breath is so close, it tickles the shell of my ear, and a shiver runs down my spine.

My brain short-circuits. It must be the only viable explanation as to why it takes me an embarrassingly long amount of time to realize I'm sitting on *Reed's lap.*

I clear my throat. "Very. Thanks for asking."

But I'm not, so I wiggle on his lap, trying to get into a real comfortable position just to be a little shit. This may be violating some sort of code of conduct, for sure, but what the administration office doesn't see won't kill them. I hope.

The huge man behind—and below—me lets out a grunt as he grabs my waist, his grip strong and warm. "Stop moving."

Just as I'm about to ask why, I feel it.

A hard bulge pressing into my leggings.

Oh my God.

My thoughts are interrupted by the bus stopping one final time. I bolt out of his lap, feeling more than a little dead inside because *did I just make him hard* and wishing the ground would just swallow me whole and end my misery.

"Sorry," I mutter as he stands next to me. At the back, Haniyah and two other volunteers are standing from their seats, too. "I didn't mean to..." *Holy shit.* "I'm so sorry."

"It's my fault." His voice sounds strained and all wrong. Not because he's lying but because he's...embarrassed? "That shouldn't have happened. It was highly inappropriate, and I'll understand if you want to report—"

I roll my eyes before he's even done talking. "I'm not going to report you, Reed. It was an accident. It was my fault for standing up on a moving bus."

The kids start grabbing their backpacks and getting louder and more excited by the second. I look at the man next to me, only to find his eyes already on mine.

"We're good," I promise. "You could never make me feel uncomfortable, Reed."

He gives me a stiff, not-so-convincing nod, and we leave it at that.

As all five of us get the kids out of the bus and into the spot we picked at the park, I keep thinking how that's true. How we've gotten to truly know each other in the last month. How I've come to the conclusion that Reed Abner is an honorable man.

Turns out my parents were right—I'm in good hands with him.

Literally.

My face flames, and I push the thought away. Because what would Mom and Dad say if they read my mind and saw all these inappropriate thoughts about *their friend*?

It helps that, for the next two hours, I don't see much of him. We set up our picnic on a patch of grass between the playground and a cafeteria, where I got Vera a sweet tea earlier because I suspected her sugar levels were too low.

A few parents decided to come, too, to help us chaperone the thirty-something kids. And as I eat lunch with Haniyah, Melody, Vera, and a few other kids, I don't feel one way or another about Jacob's tall, super attractive, super smiley mom being glued to Reed's side.

I don't care at all.

So what if they eat lunch on the same picnic blanket as she talks and talks and talks and he listens attentively? Big deal.

Reed is a single man—he can do whatever he wants. If he wants to hook up with Jacob's mom or with any other woman, so be it.

When I was little, my dad used to joke that I wasn't allowed to date until I was thirty; maybe he was onto something. After everything that happened with Oliver, I swore off men for the foreseeable future anyway. Reed can do whatever he wants, and it won't affect me at all.

Yet the invisible imprint of his hands on my waist burns as the hours go by—a lingering torture that gets worse every time our eyes lock and my heart jumps.

After I give up on my personal Stop Looking at Reed game, I notice he's not talking to Jacob's mom anymore, but only because she left for work—she told us as much when she came over to thank Haniyah for organizing this field trip.

And of course, of course, the woman smells great too. Because that's just my luck.

I bet Reed likes her smell more than he likes mine. That's why he hasn't acknowledged me in two hours.

Great, and now I'm losing my sanity.

As I do so, we capture the flag, play red light, green light, and do an obstacle course. Now some of the kids are on the swings, others are playing soccer, and I'm standing alone, making sure the little ones don't get hurt on the slides.

And then it happens.

"Lila." Melody's quivering voice makes all the alarms go off in my head. And it only gets worse when I see her teary eyes. "Lila, I think something's wrong with me."

I crouch in front of her. "Why do you say that?"

She doesn't meet my eyes. "I... I'm..." She hiccups. "I'm bleeding."

Later that day, I'd face-palm myself for not realizing it sooner. Now, I only ask, "Did you fall and hurt yourself?"

"N-No, I..." She touches her belly, right under her belly button, and it clicks in my brain just before she says, "I'm bleeding... down there."

Oh.

Oh.

Oh, shit.

"Okay," I start, ever the calm and reliable adult I'm supposed to be in these situations. "Do you know why you're bleeding?"

Periods are the most common thing in the world, and I don't want to freak her out about bodily functions. My mom always says we should talk about them with full normalcy, even when around kids, and I agree.

Melody gives me a small nod. "It's a period, right? They

taught us about them at school a little bit."

A little bit. I can work with that.

"That's correct." I search her gaze to no avail. She still won't look at me. "Have you ever gotten your period before?"

"No... This is the first time," she whispers, a mix between scared and mortified.

But I got this. And, soon enough, she will too.

My eyes meet Reed's from across the park. Something silent passes between us before I focus back on the girl in front of me.

"All right. Here's what we're going to do," I tell Melody as my hand roams around the interior of my backpack. *Bingo.* "Here, take this tissue. Let's dry those tears. There's no reason to be scared."

"Thanks." She takes it with shaky fingers. "I was playing, and then I felt something weird, and I looked down, and..."

Indeed, there's a little red spot on her green leggings. I can see how that could be mortifying for anyone, let alone a young girl, so I make sure my voice is reassuring as I talk to her.

"It's nothing we can't fix. Do you trust me?" She quickly nods. "Then let's go to the bathroom so we can get you sorted. I have some pads in my backpack you can use. Do you know what pads are?"

She sniffles. "Mrs. Crawford at school told us about them. I thought they were like diapers."

"Kinda. They come in really handy." I squeeze her arm and get back on my feet. "If you have any questions, you can ask me. I get my period too, you know? It's nothing to be worried about."

"Hey. What's wrong?"

I look up just in time to see Reed towering over us, a concerned notch between his brows. His gaze ricochets between Melody and me, stopping at the tissue in her hands.

And my heart melts a little more when he crouches in front of her and asks in that soft, calm voice he always uses with the children, "Did something happen, kiddo?"

Melody looks at me, her eyes flashing with silent concern. With how immature boys her age usually are when it comes to talking about periods, it doesn't surprise me she isn't sure whether to tell Reed. I know he'll be nothing but understanding, but she doesn't know that, and maybe—

"I just got my period," she blurts out.

Her cheeks turn pink, and she sounds a little out of breath, but she was bold and brave, and she told him. Pride swells in my chest.

"I'm afraid I have no experience with periods, but Lila will help you with everything." His smile is as gentle as his voice. "Do you need anything? I can call your mom, and she can pick you up."

Melody shakes her head, glancing between us. "I'm having fun. I want to stay." She swallows, looking down at her sneakers. "I just need to use the bathroom. I'll be okay."

"Yes, you will," Reed assures her. "You girls can handle periods and much more."

She smiles and is about to say something when her brother's worried bellow breaks through the park.

"Melody!"

I turn just in time to catch Cameron running directly to his twin sister. Ignoring Reed and me, he holds Melody by the shoulders and scans her gaze frantically.

"You're crying," he says, out of breath. "Who made you cry? Tell me, Meli. Tell me, and they'll regret it."

"Slow down, tiger." Reed settles a calming hand on the boy's shoulder. "Nobody did anything to your sister. And if they had, Lila and I are here. We'd handle it. Remember what we talked about in our last session?"

Cameron shrugs him off, his eyes never leaving his sister. "I don't care. If someone hurt you, tell me. I don't care what happens to me."

"Cameron," Reed rumbles.

But anger keeps seeping from his pores. "I will do *anything* to protect my sister. I don't care about the consequences."

"All right." Reed sounds calm but serious. The gentle authority in his voice sends a thrill of *something* down my spine that makes breathing a little more difficult. "Have you tried asking Melody what she needs instead of jumping to conclusions and upsetting her even more?"

"That's dumb. I'm not upsetting her."

"You kinda are," Melody says.

We all turn to her, who's looking at her brother with determination glinting in her eyes. "Nobody hurt me, Cam. And even if they did, I don't want you to hurt yourself to protect me. I'm not a baby anymore. I can handle it."

My lips curve into a proud smile that she doesn't see because she's focused on her brother.

"Meli, I..." Cameron starts, clearly taken aback by her unexpected words. "You know I love you, and I want to—"

Her shoulders shake with a sigh. "I love you, too, but I really need to use the bathroom right now."

I put a hand between her shoulder blades. "Come this way." I turn to her brother. "We'll talk about this later. Everything's okay."

My eyes find Reed's, and he dips his chin in acknowledgement. "I've got this."

Melody reaches for my hand on our way to the bathroom at the nearby cafeteria, and she squeezes my fingers. "That was very admirable of you," I assure her. "Telling your brother what you needed and standing up for yourself. That's what you should always do."

She worries her bottom lip between her teeth. "Do you think I upset him?"

"I'm sure you didn't. He'll understand when you talk later. And even if you upset him a little, you still have the right to ask for what you need. Let him deal with his own emotions."

The smell of food surrounds us as we enter the busy cafeteria. Nobody pays us any mind as we head for the restrooms at the back.

"At least he has Reed," she muses out loud. "He says he's a good man. Helps him a lot."

"Reed is a great counselor."

He's great at other things, too. But I don't say it out loud.

I'm taken aback by Melody's knowing smirk. "You like Reed, don't you?"

Why has my heart just jumped?

"Of course I like him." I give her an easy smile that— hopefully—doesn't give away the confusing chaos her question has just unleashed inside of me.

Melody must be on a boldness rampage today because she adds, "I mean that you like him *like that*."

A flash of his hands on me just hours earlier crosses my mind, heating me up from the inside.

"You're blushing." Melody giggles. "I knew it."

Mortified, I usher her inside the empty bathroom with one hand as I reach inside the backpack hanging over my shoulder with the other. "Let's focus on what's important right now."

She smirks, taking the sanitary pad as I hand it to her. At least she's not crying anymore. "Vera and I think he likes you like that too."

"Get inside the bathroom, you busybody." She laughs. "Do you know how to use it? The sanitary pad?"

She sobers up at that, but her teasing smile isn't fully gone. "Yeah. I think."

"I'll be waiting here. Holler if you need anything."

"Okay, Mrs. Reed's Future Wife."

She shuts the door before I can tell her that's the most insane and untrue thing anyone has ever said to me.

I'm twenty-four, damn it. I should know better than to get hung up on the words of kids who don't understand complex feelings. The girls are probably just seeing things.

Yet for as long as Melody stays in the bathroom, that's all I do—wonder if they have a point, if they're right, if Reed might just feel even an ounce of the attraction I...

Fine.

I *am* attracted to Reed.

I'm attracted to how he always has the right words, to the passion he feels for his job, to how gently he treats the kids, to how right his body feels against mine.

I'm attracted to a man twelve years my senior, a forbidden man in far too many ways.

My parents would never approve.

My reputation will be tainted, and I will forever be known as the girl who slept with a professor.

Oliver took too much from me. Men aren't worth it.

The voice in my head is right—I don't need a man. What I need is to nail my thesis, graduate, and become a youth counselor just like I've always wanted.

The last thing I want is to ruin my career before it's even begun with rumors about being involved with a professor who happens to be my internship supervisor.

"I'm done." Melody opens the door behind me, snapping me out of my thoughts. *No man for me anytime soon, let alone Reed Abner.* "The pad feels weird."

I give her an apologetic smile. "You can talk to your mom later about other options. Are you sure you don't want me to call her?"

"I want to stay here." She looks down at her green leggings, biting her lip again. "But I can't remove this stain, and I don't want people to see it. It's embarrassing."

I don't think twice before I take off my hoodie and give it to her. "You can put your jacket in your backpack and wear this instead so no one will see the stain."

She takes it, quickly replacing her jacket with it. Like I suspected, it falls just past her knees. "You look great."

Before I know what hit me, Melody throws herself at me and wraps her arms around my torso. "Thank you, Lila." My heart swells. "You're like the big sister I never had."

Don't cry, don't cry, don't cry.

I wrap my arms around her. "I'm really proud of how you've handled this whole situation with your period and your brother."

She beams at me. "I'm feeling better now. And your hoodie smells really nice."

I chuckle. "I'm glad, because it's yours for the day."

With the situation under control, we go back to our group. The second we reach the park, my eyes fall on Reed.

Vera and I think he likes you like that too.

When his dark eyes meet mine, I tell myself whatever weird infatuation I feel for Reed needs to stop. *Now.*

My future is on the line, and no man is worth sacrificing my career for.

chapter 17

REED

The first thing I notice when Lila comes back to the park is that she's not wearing her hoodie, but the visibly calmer girl next to her is.

Two emotions tug at my heart at once—complete admiration for how she handled Melody's panic over her period and raw concern when she gets close enough for me to see the goose bumps on her bare arms.

"You're cold," I point out just as she asks, "Where's Cameron?"

"With his friends," I tell her quickly, my eyes zeroing in on her skin. "Why is Melody wearing your hoodie?"

"She had a bloodstain on her leggings and didn't want anyone to see. She was only wearing a T-shirt under her jacket, so I gave her my hoodie so she wouldn't get cold. Did you tell Cameron what was going on?"

"Yeah. He made a face when I told him she'd just gotten her period, so I had to explain to him why periods aren't gross and why it's important that he makes his sister feel comfortable." The wind picks up, and I don't miss her body's reaction to it. "You're going to get sick."

She waves me off. "I'm fine. We're leaving in less than an hour, anyway."

I don't stop to ponder why the thought of Lila getting sick makes me more worried than it should; I shrug off my jacket and drape it over her shoulders. "Now you're fine."

She blinks up at me. "You didn't have to do that."

"Like hell I didn't."

"You'll be the one getting sick now, Professor Bossy." The annoyance in her voice doesn't match the blush on her cheeks.

"Don't care." I resist the urge to tighten the jacket around her. Instead, I turn toward the park. "How's Melody dealing with it?"

As if she has just read my mind, Lila tightens my jacket around her frame. The sight of her in my clothes makes my cock jump, and I internally curse myself for it.

"I was silently thanking her teacher for explaining periods to them at school," she says with a sigh. "Sexual education wasn't really a thing when I was Melody's age. I'm lucky that my mom taught me about those things and I wasn't embarrassed to ask her, but it's ridiculous out there. Periods should be discussed normally. No wonder young girls freak out about it. And let's not even tackle boys. Why do they keep making fun of us or calling us gross for something we can't control? I hate the educational system sometimes. I feel like it's failing us in that regard. That's why I want to contribute with my thesis, even if it's just a little bit."

It's the words she says and how she says them that make a light bulb go on in my head.

"What will your thesis cover, exactly?" I carefully slide my gaze toward her. She's such a beautiful sight, clad in my leather jacket.

"I want to highlight the importance of bibliotherapy in children's sexual education," she explains. "My mom used to read these books to me when I was little. Not necessarily books she wrote, just in general. But they really helped me understand things, like how my body belonged to me and no one had the right to touch it or why Mom has two dads instead of a mom and a dad. She didn't whip out a book every time I asked a difficult question, but they really complemented my learning. Stories made it fun for me and helped me see that I wasn't alone."

How do you tell someone that you're falling in love with their mind without freaking them out?

Not only with her mind.

The urge to tell her that she's the most fascinating, down-to-earth, smart, passionate, fucking beautiful woman I've ever met dies in my throat.

I don't have a right to say those words, knowing I don't deserve her.

Instead, I ask, "What kind of books did you find most useful growing up?"

I confirm I'm going insane when she shivers and all I can think about is pulling her into my arms.

She hesitates. "I'm not sure how much you know about my mom's past."

"I know what you're referring to," I tell her, my voice somber.

Grace has never hidden from me the fact that she's a sexual assault survivor. I've known for years, but the reminder of that conversation is never easy. She knows about my past, too. Things I've never repeated out loud since I talked to her.

Lila eyes me skeptically. "You do?"

My nod is stiff. "We worked on a book about abuse. She told me then."

"Right." Her gaze lowers to the grass. "Because of what happened to her, my parents always made sure I protected myself. From a very early age, they taught me that 'no' is a full sentence, that nobody has the right to touch me in certain ways—kids or adults—and things like that. Books helped too. My mom has always been very open about periods, consent, sexual health... All those things. I could always go to her with a question and never felt embarrassed. We're really close."

"And you want to help normalize that among children," I

finish her train of thought.

"Exactly. It always baffled me when I talked to my friends about sex, and they just...knew nothing," she continues. "And when I asked them why they'd never asked their moms, they looked at me like I was crazy. Said that it was embarrassing, and they'd rather die than talk to their moms about that."

"Die? And I thought you were dramatic," I mutter, smirking.

I get an eye roll for that.

She keeps going. "The thing is, I soon realized people my age didn't really talk about those things with anyone. Well, we talked about sex and periods with one another, but it isn't smart to get sex advice from your friends. Not when you're young, anyway. We ended up hurting one another more than anything else. Not physically but, like, standards-wise. Most people only had TV shows to teach them, and they don't always set the best examples."

I hum my agreement. "So, what you're saying is that there's a lack of professional sex education at schools."

"For sure. I'm glad it's changing now, at least in some schools, but it's not enough."

When I glance down at her, she's frowning, biting her lower lip with a worried expression on her face. She looks like such a fragile thing right now, but I know she's strong and sharp underneath her insecurities. I'm mesmerized by her—all of her.

"Would you like to run a sexual education workshop at the youth center?"

Her head twirls toward me. "Are you serious?"

I can't tell if she sounds more excited or freaked out. Knowing her, it's probably both.

"I'd have to review it and supervise it, and we'd have to get signed approval from the parents, but I think the kids could benefit a lot from it. Haniyah would agree."

"I..." She hesitates. "Do you really think I could run a

workshop on my own?"

I arch a skeptical eyebrow. "You've just calmly walked a crying preteen through her first period, and you don't think you can run your own workshop?"

"I mean, I'd have to come up with activities and worksheets, as well as an outline for the talk. Make it interactive and not weird." She worries her bottom lip between her teeth again. "But what if I—"

"Lila. Listen to me."

Before I know what I'm doing, and not caring that we're not standing that far away from everyone else, I grasp her chin, tilting it upward until our eyes meet.

"I've never met a more brilliant yet insecure person in my entire life," I tell her, my eyes not leaving hers. I'm gentle as I pinch her chin with my fingers, earning me a shiver. "Tell me what I have to do to bring back that self-confidence I know you have in you, and I'll do it."

"You don't have to do anything," she mutters, and her breath hitches.

It takes me a moment to realize I'm not breathing normally, either.

But it takes me even longer to remember we're not alone; we're supposed to be working.

I drop my hand. "Listen to your gut. If it's telling you to do this workshop, go ahead with it and fuck everything else— including your own self-destructive thoughts."

She pulls my jacket closer around her torso. "I hate it when you're right."

"So, all the time?"

"All right, Professor Presumptuous."

"I'm shaking in my boots, little criminal."

When she smacks my arm, I let out a loud chuckle that turns several heads in our direction. Lila retreats, a furious blush on her face.

I nudge her arm with mine. "If you keep blushing when I tease you, I'm just going to keep doing it."

Her lips part. I'm dying to hear her comeback, but I don't get the chance.

"Reed!"

Cameron.

"Reed! Lila! Come here!"

I turn to the sound of Cameron's urgent voice and find him waving at us from a nearby bush. Melody, Vera, and Santiago are crouched beside it, their backs to us.

"What's going on?" Lila frowns, but we're already moving toward them.

"No clue," I mutter, frantically trying to see if anyone's hurt.

Cameron rushes to meet us in the middle. "You have to come. Quickly," he urges, dragging me by my arm.

"Is anyone hurt?" I ask him.

The answer I get is cryptic enough to make my worry reach unhealthy levels. "No. Well, we aren't. But there's a problem."

"What kind of problem?" Lila asks.

"Cam, did you get—" Melody breaks out in a smile when she spots us. "You have to see this. Hurry!"

All three kids are crouching around the bush, making the narrow space even narrower. I place a guiding hand on Lila's arm as she walks ahead of me, watching out for loose branches she might trip over.

Her back collides with my front as she comes to a halt, a hand flying to cover her mouth. "Oh my God..."

My heart races. "What is it?"

I'm still holding on to her as I peer over her head at the children at our feet.

And I spot a tiny ball of golden fur hiding under the prickly bush.

"It's a puppy." Melody beams at us before her expression turns somber. "It isn't moving, though. We think it may be hurt."

Not moving? *Fucking hell.* The last thing we need is for the kids to have found a dead puppy.

"Let me see." Lila takes a step forward, reaching to grab my hand for support as she lowers herself to the grass. I ignore the way my heart skips a beat. She wants me to keep her safe. "Hi, sweet baby. Are you lost? Where's your mommy?"

I take it that the puppy isn't dead. Good.

"It's here all alone," Santiago explains. "No other dogs came looking for it."

"Careful," I tell Lila as she crouches lower and into the bush.

"Don't worry about me," she says.

Like that's possible.

Her hand disappears under the bush, trying to reach the dog, and I finally lose it when she hisses as she pricks her hand.

"That's enough." I kneel on the grass behind her. "You're getting hurt. Let me do it."

"Almost there," she stammers, reaching farther.

When she hisses again, I see red. "Lila."

"Got it!"

Her scratched hand comes into view, holding a tiny dog. It's not a newborn—I'd assume it's at least six or seven months old—but it's still too small and bony, like it hasn't been fed for a while.

The kids all gape at the puppy, wanting to pet it, but Lila is quick to say, "It's probably very scared right now. Let us take a look, and you'll give him or her all the cuddles later, all right?"

They nod, understanding.

I move my hands to her arms, helping her up to her feet. She keeps the dog pressed against her chest while I shield it from the cold with my body.

"Reed," she whispers, her eyes never leaving the puppy. "This dog is missing a little leg."

I frown. "What do you mean?"

Lila shifts the dog just slightly, and I see it then—its front legs kick around, but one of its back legs is completely missing.

I spot the blood on its tail at the same time Lila does. It's not much, probably not an open wound, but my stomach still sinks.

"The puppy is hurt," she whispers, not wanting the kids to hear. "What should we do?"

The puppy glances up at me as if awaiting my answer, and the words get stuck in my throat.

It's such a little thing, so fragile. Why is she asking me what to do next? Doesn't she know I'll only hurt the poor thing? That's what I do—I hurt everyone. I ruin them.

I send them to jail and kill them.

It's your fault we're not a happy family anymore, Reed.

"Reed?"

Lila's voice breaks through the fog in my brain, and so does the whimper coming from the golden ball of fur in her arms. I don't recognize the breed; it's probably a mutt. It has short, light brown fur and floppy ears that aren't too small or too big.

"Should we call a vet?" she asks next.

It's her voice, laced with pure worry, that snaps me into action.

Think of this dog as one of the kids, and you'll be fine.

"Right. Yeah." I reach for my phone in my back pocket. "Guys, let's go back to the park."

"But what about the dog?" Vera asks, peering over Lila's arm to look at it. All three other kids do the same.

"We're going to call a vet and see if it's hurt or if it belongs to someone," I tell them. "It will be fine, don't worry."

"Promise?" Melody pouts.

I glance down at the puppy in Lila's bloodied hand, protectiveness sinking its claws into me. "I promise."

chapter 18

LILA

I understand vets have the right to enjoy their weekend, but that doesn't mean I like it.

All right, maybe I'm being too harsh. They work incredibly hard and deserve time off, sure. But when I'm holding a tiny injured dog in my arms and my professor slash internship supervisor slash family friend slash not-crush spends ten minutes on the phone just trying to get ahold of someone, I kind of start losing my mind a little.

"I found an urgent care center." Reed finally lets me in on the good news. "Twenty-minute drive, but there's some traffic."

Because of course there is.

And of course neither of us drove here.

I point out the obvious. "We don't have a car."

"I'll take care of it," he reassures me before going back to his phone.

Haniyah walks up to me. "I asked around, but nobody seems to be searching for a missing dog."

Right after we found this sweet little baby under the bush, she searched around the park for the dog's possible owners.

"I come here on my walks pretty often," she adds, looking at the dog with a sad expression. "I'll keep an eye out for missing dog posters, but I don't think this cutie belongs to anyone. And if it does, they weren't good owners. It looks like it hasn't been fed in a while."

I figured as much.

Some volunteers also looked around the bush area where we found him or her, but they didn't see any other animals or paw prints. Maybe their mom got hurt, or maybe...

Maybe they *did* belong to someone who doesn't want them anymore.

The puppy in my arms is all alone, and the thought is enough to make my eyes water.

Reed chooses that moment to come back. "I called Warren, and he'll be here in about ten minutes. He'll drive us to the vet."

"You're coming?" I ask him, my voice small because I'm trying oh-so-hard not to burst into tears right now.

"Of course I am." He frowns at me, then at the puppy, before he looks away. "Haniyah, will you be okay without us on the ride back?"

She waves him off. "Don't worry about it. Just make sure this precious baby is all healthy and safe."

My eyes water even more just thinking about what could've happened if the kids hadn't been snooping around the bushes. I gently stroke the dog's fluffy head in an attempt to bring them comfort. He or she is such a cute thing; their attentive eyes are looking around, but they're not really making any noise. They're not aggressive despite being hurt, which is a small blessing.

The wind has picked up in the past few minutes, enough to make me shiver despite wearing Reed's jacket. I'm debating my options—whether I should put the dog inside the jacket or take it off and wrap it around them—when he says, "Here."

I meet Reed's eyes as he hands me one of the picnic blankets. "This should be enough to keep it warm."

"Thank you." I don't know why my voice comes out as a whisper. But I do suspect why my heart starts hammering inside my rib cage as he gently covers the dog with the blanket until only their little face is visible—but I'd rather not think about it.

"What should we name it?" Melody asks, coming up to me.

"Is it a boy or a girl?" Vera muses.

"Guys," Reed interjects when Vera tries to move the blanket to take a peek. "Let's give the dog some space, yeah? We'll tell you if it's a boy or a girl when we come back from the vet."

"Why don't you just...look?" Melody asks, a hint of a blush in her cheeks.

Reed is patient as he explains, "We don't want to shift it around too much in case it gets upset or scared. It's cold, too, so we don't want to move the blanket. We'll find out if it's a boy or a girl eventually, all right?"

"We should call it Bug," Santiago suggests. "It's funny."

But Melody shakes her head. "You can't give an animal the name of another animal."

"Says who?"

"I like Rocco for a boy," Vera suggests.

"Mom told me once that a doctor got it wrong and said she was having twin girls instead of a girl and a boy," Cameron starts, eyes never leaving the puppy in my arms. "They were going to call me Ginny. That's a cool name."

Melody laughs. "Yeah, that's true. Melody and Ginny. Nuts."

Reed sends me a playful look, and I don't fight back my smile, grateful for the distraction.

His phone pings with a text moments later; Warren is waiting for us in the parking lot. After everyone says a very enthusiastic goodbye to the puppy, we make our way to his car.

Warren glances at the bundle in my arms from the driver's seat as I climb in the back, his voice friendly. "Who do we have there?"

To my utter mortification, Reed buckles me in before getting in the back with me. "Do you want me to hold it? Are your arms tired?"

"Don't worry." Why can't I stop blushing? I turn to Warren.

"Thank you so much for driving us to the vet. They're missing one of their back legs, and the tail is bleeding."

"The leg is missing?" he asks as he drives out of the parking lot.

"I think he or she may have been born without it. There's no open wound," I muse out loud, feeling my chest constrict as I look at that little face.

Please be okay. Please be okay.

Reed shifts his focus to my hands. "You got hurt. I could've grabbed it."

"I'm fine," I reassure him. "I'll clean them up when I get home."

He grunts something under his breath that makes Warren laugh. "Don't bother trying to fight this one, Lila. He's as stubborn as a mule."

My chest feels fuzzy, appreciating the fact that he remembers my name. It's such a small detail, but a part of me can't help but feel giddy that one of Reed's best friends remembers me.

Warren makes the twenty-minute drive to the urgent care center in fifteen, despite the light traffic. "I'll wait in the car. I don't think I can park here, so I'll text you if I have to move."

Reed nods. "Thanks, man."

We rush into the vet's, the warmth of Reed's hand on my back keeping me grounded. If it weren't for him, I'd be bursting into tears right now. But he always knows what to do, always finds a solution, and I trust him blindly.

The smell of disinfectant assaults my nostrils as a smiling man opens the door for us.

"Hello there." He smiles at the puppy's head popping out of the blanket. "Someone's looking comfortable in Mommy's arms, aren't we?"

Mommy.

I'm going to cry.

"We talked on the phone thirty minutes ago," Reed cuts directly to the chase. I'm surprised to hear the edge of worry in his voice all of a sudden when he's only been calm this far. "A stray in the park. It's missing its back leg and has an injured tail."

"Yes, I remember. Please, come this way. I'll take a look."

The next few minutes pass by in a blur.

"I've checked for a microchip, but she doesn't have any," the vet—he tells us to call him Paul—confirms. "No fleas, either, which is good. She could've belonged to someone, but it doesn't look like she's well taken care of."

She.

"It's a girl," I murmur in Reed's direction, emotion clogging my throat for some reason. Because I couldn't care less if this poor puppy was a girl or a boy, but *actually* knowing makes me incredibly happy.

Reed wraps an arm around my shoulders, bringing me closer against his side. My heart stops when I feel the warmth of his lips on the top of my head, gentle and fleeting.

Paul gently strokes the puppy's head as she lies on the examining table, and Reed pulls away but doesn't go far. "I suspect she was born without her right back leg since she stands normally. It looks like she has a small cut on her tail too. I understand this is a stray dog?"

"Yes," Reed confirms. It's like he can sense I'm too flustered and anxious to speak.

"All right. Well," Paul starts. The seriousness in the tone of his voice sobers me up at once. "The wound on her tail might be infected, but I'd need to take a more thorough look. Running some blood work to check if she's healthy would be a good idea, too. I need to know if you will be covering the bills before I can continue."

"I'm covering them," Reed says without hesitation.

"Very well. Let me grab a few things, and I'll be back."

I walk up to the examining table, lowering myself to my knees until I'm eye to eye with the dog. I gently pet her head with a finger. She's so small.

"You're going to be okay," I whisper as if she can understand me. "You're a strong girl, aren't you?"

Don't cry now.

I turn to Reed to avoid the tears. "We can split the vet bills. I'm not expecting you to pay for everything."

He doesn't look at me or at the dog as he repeats, "I'll take care of it."

I don't have time to dwell on why he's so cold right now—if this is how he channels worry or if it's something else entirely—because Paul comes back holding a tablet.

"From what I can tell, she seems to be about ten months old," he informs us, and I melt. She's a literal baby. "As I said, her wound might be infected, but I'd need to check if it's severe. If this is a case of gangrenous or necrotic tissues, it may require surgery."

My stomach gives a downward jolt. "Isn't she too small for surgery?"

Paul gives me an understanding smile. "Any dog can face complications during surgery, of course, but her age isn't a risk factor."

"What are the next steps?" Reed asks, that weird edge to his voice not going anywhere.

"First, you'll need to fill in this form." He passes the tablet to Reed. "Once that's done, I'll run some quick checks so we can determine if you can take her home. If something doesn't seem right, she'll have to stay the night. As for the missing back leg, please know it's not the end of the world by any means. Animals have an incredible survival instinct. She'd be able to live a happy and comfortable life as a three-legged dog with no problem."

Logically, I know what Paul is saying makes sense. Pets with three legs can live a happy life; it's the owners who may think otherwise. But, as I look at the puppy on the examining table, the thought of her being in any kind of pain makes me want to rip this entire place apart.

"I'll clean her wound while you fill out the patient form," Paul tells us. "You can go into the waiting room if you'd prefer."

As if anything or anyone could keep me away from this puppy right now.

Reed notices. "We'll stay here," he tells me before he turns his attention back to the tablet. Then, he freezes. "It asks for her name."

I blink. "Oh."

"Any ideas?"

I think back on the kids. "What do you think of Ginny?"

His tilted smirk kills me. "I have a feeling Cameron will like it."

Once Reed fills out the form and Paul finishes up cleaning Ginny's wound—the poor thing doesn't even whimper in pain— he proceeds to do the blood work and other procedures I'm too nervous to understand. My only consolation is that Ginny seems calm enough.

Reed's hand falls to the small of my back, lighting it on fire. He leans down until his lips are grazing my ear, an intimate gesture that feels less forbidden than it is.

"I have nothing for her at home," he murmurs, his hand still on me. "I'm heading outside for a moment to call Warren, see if he can grab some things from the store. Will you be okay here by yourself?"

I give him a small nod, turning to look at him. He's so close, and I can't stop thinking about his lips on the top of my head just moments go. "I'll be fine. Thanks for taking care of everything."

Of me.

He gives me an unsure nod in return, looking at me for a

beat too long before he exits the room.

Paul hums softly as he keeps examining Ginny, the room bathed in silence until he says in a lighthearted voice, "Your boyfriend is a worrier, huh? Understandable, though. She's a small puppy."

My heart cartwheels at that one word and his assumption that we're together.

He did just press his lips to the top of my head. That tends to look a certain way to strangers.

But I don't bother correcting him because what could I possibly say? That he's a professor at my university and my internship supervisor whom I rescue injured puppies with in my free time? *Right.*

The last thing I want is to answer any of the questions I'm sure he'd have if I told him the truth, so I simply give him a tight smile and say, "She's very small indeed."

"Well, worry not, because everything looks fine so far."

A small weight falls off my shoulders, but I'm still tense when Reed comes back minutes later.

"Warren is heading to the pet shop," he tells me in a quiet voice, his unreadable eyes on Ginny. "He'll drop everything off at my house later."

"That's nice of him." I search his gaze to no avail. "How are you holding up?"

He takes a few seconds to answer. And when he does, his words don't sound convincing. "I'm fine."

When he offers nothing else, I make a mental note to talk to him later. Whatever is eating at him, I want to help him through it if I can.

"All right. I believe we're done," Paul announces some time later. "I can confirm she was born with a missing limb. She's a little scared right now, but she can move around with ease and without assistance. However, it's important to note that she'll place additional strain on her legs over time. As she gets older, this could result in injuries or wear, so it's important that you take her to her annual checkups. They'll let you know if she needs some kind of support, like a dog wheelchair. But for now, she's as healthy as can be. The wound on her tail is also taken care of. There's a small infection, but it's nothing to worry about for now."

"Is there any medication she needs to take? Does she need to come back for rechecks?" I ask him.

"Come to the front, and I'll print you some care instructions so you won't forget."

For the next few minutes, the vet explains the kind of medication Ginny will have to take at home and how often to treat the infection, her next checkup with a regular vet he recommends we take her to, and other care instructions, such as how often she needs to eat or go outside.

After the vet answers some more of my questions, Reed takes care of the bill, buys a pet carrier from the clinic to carry Ginny home, and we head outside. Since Warren isn't back, Reed calls an Uber.

He's not speaking, not looking at me, his face hermetic. The pet carrier sits in the middle seat between us, one of his hands lying protectively on top of it so it doesn't shake too much. The movements of the car make his fingers graze my arm, and I'm torn between feeling anxious about Ginny and feeling anxious about his lips on me. So, this isn't ideal.

I'm still overanalyzing a million things I have no control over when the car pulls into an unfamiliar driveway.

"Where are we?" I ask Reed.

A two-story detached home looms to my right, with a tiny but well-kept front garden.

"My place."

There's a pause in which I can hear my heart hammering inside my chest.

And I couldn't have, not in a million years, guessed the words that would leave his mouth next.

"I need you to spend the night with me."

chapter 19

REED

If there was an award for terrible ideas, I'm confident it would go to me.

Because somehow, in the past hour, I went from hermit extraordinaire to dog dad.

Ginny. Her name is Ginny. And she's *my* puppy now.

Lila's voice distracts me from the familiar anxiety pooling low in my stomach. "You want me to spend the night here?"

I carefully get Ginny's pet carrier out of the car as Lila follows me. "You can go home if you want," I tell her over my shoulder.

Suggesting she stay here slipped out during a moment of weakness. Calling a car for her to go home is probably the most sensible option, but that doesn't stop me from adding, "It's..."

Tell her, goddammit. It's Lila.

Clearing my throat, I push past the murkiness in my brain and admit, "I don't know how to do this. Take care of a puppy, I mean. I know you used to have a dog, so I thought—"

"I'll help," she cuts me off gently, a comforting hand falling on my arm. "I'm basically the dog whisperer, so you have nothing to worry about. You're not alone in this, Reed."

You ruin everything. Don't you think I deserve a son who takes care of me?

My voice comes out rough, as if I haven't used it in a long time. "Maybe you shouldn't be here. I'll figure it out."

"Nice try, but you won't get rid of me that easily. I'm actually excited to be the one teaching you for a change."

"You teach me plenty of things," I retort.

"Yeah, right. Like what? How to write shitty first drafts?"

Despite the mess in my head, I can't help a half smile. "All right. I have a spare room. If you change your mind, just let me know."

The silence of my empty house greets us when we cross the threshold. Judging by the pet shop bags by the entrance, it looks like Warren has already been here. I make a mental note to thank him later.

The sight of Lila in my house makes me wonder if this is a mistake I won't come back from. Inviting an intern to spend the night at my place surely breaks all sorts of codes of conduct—kissing the top of her head sure as fuck did—yet I can't seem to give a shit right now.

I need her.

I need her in a raw way I don't understand.

"You have a beautiful home," she says, taking everything in.

I look at the ground floor too, trying to see it through her eyes—a renovated old home that still maintains the charm of when it was first built, nearly a century ago. Minimal decorations, warm tones, comfortable furniture, no personal pictures.

And, of course, the first thing that catches her eye.

"And I thought your office was bursting with books," she teases, walking up to the living room bookshelf. "How many books do you *have*?"

Her fingertips are gentle as she grazes the spines, and I try not to lose myself in the movement. Try not to picture what her touch would feel like on my bare skin.

I clear my throat and set the pet carrier on the living room floor. "A few hundred, I think."

Her eyes widen comically when she glances at me over her shoulder. "You've read them all?"

"Most of them. The ones down here are fiction books, but I have some academic tomes in my office upstairs. You can take a look later if you want. Grab a few for your thesis."

"You know I'll never say no to books."

"Suit yourself." Who knew hearing a woman talk about her love for books would turn me on? I clear my throat again. "Do you want something more comfortable to change into?"

She looks down at my jacket, cheeks reddening as if she's just realized she's still wearing it. "Oh. No, thank you. I should probably give this back." She shrugs it off, walking up to me. "Where does this go? Oh my God, I just realized I've walked inside with my shoes on. I should've asked—"

"Sit down and relax, Lila." I take the jacket from her grip. "You don't need to take off your shoes. I don't want your feet getting cold. Wait for me on the couch while I go upstairs to change and turn on the heating system. I'll get the first aid kit and clean your scratches while we're at it."

"Thanks," she mutters, her body so close that I almost do something stupid.

I step back first. "I'll be right back. We'll take Ginny out of the pet carrier when I come back down, yeah?"

Upstairs, I take a moment to compose myself. I'm on edge because of everything that went down this afternoon, that's all. I'm not thinking clearly.

I don't regret telling Lila to spend the night, although maybe I should. But the thought of being alone with such a helpless creature after...

Don't think about Daisy.

I sit on my mattress, just for a moment, and allow myself to let that open wound bleed at my feet.

What the hell am I supposed to do with a puppy? Is this a cruel joke?

"*Fuck,*" I hiss, yanking at the hair on my nape.

If my parents taught me anything before my life went up in flames, it's that I can't take care of helpless animals. I'm not built for it.

Over the years, I've taught myself to be confident in my abilities as a children's counselor. The opposite meant not helping those kids, not giving them a shot at the good childhood I never had, and that *wasn't* an option. I grew confident because I had my many academic titles and feedback from trusted professionals to back me up.

But what do I have now?

I don't *do* feelings. I don't get attached.

Yet I know that's a lie. Because if I don't do feelings or get attached, why does the thought of Ginny in pain make me want to tear the whole world apart?

And why do I always feel such a burning ache to pull Lila into my arms and never let her go?

I groan into the silence of my bedroom.

This is so fucking wrong. All of it. I got caught up in a web of feelings I should've dusted away the second they started forming.

I'm an adult. I can control my impulses around her.

That's what I keep telling myself, over and over again, as I descend the stairs in a pair of sweatpants and a T-shirt, holding a clean hoodie in one hand and my first aid kit in the other.

And then it all goes out the window when I spot Lila bending over Ginny's pet carrier. I shut my eyes and take a get-your-shit-together kind of breath through my nose because her tight leggings hug her perfectly round ass, and that's a sight I won't be able to forget.

My cock twitches. Wearing sweatpants around her is the most idiotic idea I've ever had.

I clear my throat. "How is she?"

My voice makes her jump.

"Jesus, you scared me. I didn't hear you coming down the

stairs." She crosses her arms over her baggy T-shirt. "She's lying down, but she's not sleeping. Should we set up her playpen?"

"All right." I hand over the hoodie. "Here, put this on. The heating takes a while to kick in. This is an old house."

When she puts it on and I see it reaches her knees, I have to look away. "But first, let me check those scratches. It won't take long."

She takes a seat on the couch, her knee grazing mine when I sit next to her, and we remain silent as I carefully clean her wounds. The heat of her hand seeps into my veins, lighting me up from the inside.

"Do you really want to adopt her?" she asks out of the blue. "You didn't look too excited."

"I don't know if I'm equipped to take care of a dog." *Or anyone.* "But if the other option is to send her to a shelter, I..."

The constant fear of being moved from foster home to foster home, of not knowing if the next one would be a nightmare.

The cold nights, the fights, the screams.

"I can't."

Lila gives me an unreadable look. "My parents were very adamant about not wanting another dog after Rocket passed; it was tough for everyone. If you want, I can ask around and see if anyone would want to adopt her instead. I don't want you to feel pressured if you aren't sure. It's a big decision."

"I'm keeping her."

My words are definite as I shove my trauma back into the pits of my soul.

I'm not letting that little thing go without a home like I did.

Two hours later, the downstairs floor of my house has transformed into a puppy lair—food and water bowls, a dog bed, a playpen, training pads, and toys have fully taken over. Warren went all out at the pet shop, and I'm not even mad about it.

Ginny was shy about getting out of the carrier at first. It

took her well over fifteen minutes to step out of it, and when she did, her paws started gliding on the hardwood floor. And I swear Lila's laugh as she watched her was the most beautiful sound I've ever heard.

The puppy sniffed her hands, then mine, and slowly gained confidence in her new surroundings. Some food and bathroom mishaps later, she's snoring on her new bed as Lila and I sit on the couch, empty takeout bags on the coffee table. But neither of us is paying attention to the movie playing on my TV because surely Ginny is bound to disappear into thin air if we look away even for one millisecond.

"You okay?" I ask her, my voice hoarse from not speaking in so long.

"I've been better," she mutters.

She rests her chin on her knees, hugging her legs as she tries to hide her quivering lips.

"Lila," I start in a calm voice. "Talk to me."

But she doesn't. She barely even blinks, and her watery eyes don't move away from the puppy.

Fuck it.

"Come here."

I wrap an arm around her shoulders, pulling her to me. She comes willingly, the tears rolling down her cheeks freely as I pull her against my chest. She hugs my torso and buries her face in my hoodie, weeping quietly.

"Let it all out," I mumble against the top of her head. "I've got you, angel. I'm here."

The nickname slips out and my heart free-falls. But then she hugs me a little tighter and presses her face against me a little closer, as if silently agreeing that it feels too right to take back.

"I don't know why I'm crying. It's just..." She hiccups. "She's so *small*."

My fingers tangle in her hair, massaging her scalp. "She's

okay. She was waiting for us to find her."

"What if her wound doesn't heal or something?"

I gently peel her away from me to look her in the eye. And maybe this is a very obvious sign that I'm losing my sanity, but I cup her cheek in my hand and wipe her tears away with my thumb.

Her plump lips part. She looks so fucking beautiful right now; I wonder what would happen if the distance between us disappeared.

If I took her mouth in mine like my heart has been begging me to do for far too long.

But my head is louder. It always is.

"Focusing on the worst-case scenario is never a good idea," I tell her, blinking away the lust-filled thoughts. "We'll face the bad news if it ever comes. Right now, I want you to think happy thoughts. Ginny is right here with us, and she's okay."

She lets out a shaky breath. "You're right. It's been a long day, and I haven't had a full night's sleep in months, so." That last sentence makes my worry levels skyrocket again. "I probably just need to sleep this off, but I'm so anxious I probably won't be able to."

"Do you want me to show you the spare room upstairs?" I ask.

My heart flips when she shakes her head. "I want to be near her. And I want to stay with you."

Later, when my head is in the right place and I remember all the reasons this is a terrible idea, I'll punish myself for what I'm about to do. Now, I only grab one of the decorative pillows on the couch and place it on my lap. "Come lie down."

Lila doesn't think twice before wrapping the blanket tighter around her and resting her head on the pillow. On my lap.

I don't hesitate as my hand finds her hair, stroking her scalp gently once again.

With the constant hum of the TV in the background, the darkness in the room, and my fingers caressing her hair, her breath evens out, and she falls asleep within minutes.

And as I look down at her, I wonder what I've done to deserve her in my life.

~ ୬ ~

The movie ends a while later. Despite Lila's warmth and calming presence, I'm not tired, so I put on a historical documentary I miraculously haven't watched yet.

It doesn't do much to distract me because my head is plagued by the sight of Lila's tears and the overwhelming thoughts of the lengths I'd go to never see her cry again.

A while later, a buzzing sound makes my pulse jump. But it isn't my phone that's ringing—it's hers. She set it on top of the coffee table earlier, so I don't need to move to read the caller ID.

Mom.

I internally curse.

She hasn't had a full night's sleep in months, so the last thing I want is to wake her up. But what if Grace is calling her so late at night because there's been an emergency?

I'm not thinking straight as I reach my arm to grab her phone, still sitting on the couch but maneuvering carefully not to wake her up, and press the green button.

"Thank God, Lila." Grace sounds relieved. "Why weren't you answering our texts? Are you okay?"

I take a deep breath through my nose. *Here we go.*

"Grace."

The silence that greets me from the other side of the line is deafening.

"Reed? Is that you?"

"Yeah." I don't want to know what could be going through her head right now. "Lila is here. She's okay."

She lets out a surprised, "Oh." Then she says, "Can I ask why you're together?"

She doesn't sound angry, which is a small blessing. I'm not sure I'd be as lucky if Cal had called Lila instead.

"It's a long story." When she says nothing, I take it as my cue to keep going. "We took the kids to the park today and found an injured puppy. Lila and I took it to the vet, and thankfully she's fine. But, long story short, I now have a puppy. Lila is helping me figure out the whole dog dad thing because I'm helpless."

More silence.

Then, she responds, "That's...a lot."

I let out a deep sigh. "I know."

"I was worried about Lila, which is why I called. She told us she'd be coming home before dinner, but she wasn't answering our texts. Cal can pick her up in ten."

"She's not a bother," I tell her. Why can't I do the right thing and take the out she's giving me? Lila not sleeping here would be the right thing to do, a way to fix my mistake, but the thought of not being there for her when she's upset consumes me. "She's sleeping. It's fine."

"All right." She sounds unsure, but she doesn't press. "She's a very sensitive girl; she must be quite upset about the puppy."

"She is," I answer honestly. There's no point in lying to Grace, anyway. Her intuition is sharp as a blade. "I can wake her up if you want to talk to her."

"No, no. It's okay. Let her sleep. I have a feeling she hasn't done much of that lately." Her sigh is nothing short of worried. "Thanks for answering the phone. We were worried sick. Please let me know how the puppy progresses."

Lila shifts on my lap, but she doesn't wake up. "I'll keep you updated."

"Have a good night, Reed. Thank you for taking care of our daughter."

My stomach plummets at her words.

Our daughter.

How the fuck did I forget Lila is my *co-worker's daughter*?

That I'm friends with *both of her parents*?

They trust me to take care of her when she's vulnerable, to guide her as a mentor at the youth center. Yet here I am, thinking of taking her mouth with mine and showing her exactly what she does to me.

That thought is enough to remove myself from under her, carefully placing Lila on the couch and tightening the blanket around her. I sit on the armchair on the other end of the living room, away from her—where I should be.

It would do me well to remember Lila Callaghan is and will forever be off-limits to me.

chapter 20

LILA

Anxiety wakes me up on Sunday. I'm disoriented and alone on Reed's couch, and it takes me a few seconds to spot him reading across the room.

"What time is it?" I mumble, stealing a look at Ginny's playpen. She's still snoring in her fluffy bed, a squeaky toy lying next to her. Did Reed place it there?

He sets his book on the coffee table. "Lunchtime."

My eyes widen. "I slept that long?"

He gives me a small smile. "Sure did." His gaze shifts toward Ginny, and I don't miss the worry in his face.

It's hard for me to reconcile this insecure side of him with his usual self-confidence. He said he has no experience taking care of dogs, but for a man like Reed—a problem solver by nature, as I've come to realize—that shouldn't be an issue.

There must be something else to it, something he isn't telling me. Not that he has to, of course. We may be growing closer, but we aren't...friends. At least, I don't think we should be, given the power dynamic between us, no matter how *right* it feels to be with him.

When we got home last night, I couldn't decide which sight was more adorable—Ginny gliding across the hallway or Reed being a helicopter puppy dad. And then I went and fell asleep on his lap because I love torturing myself.

Groaning, I sit up. My pulse jumps when I glance at my

phone, suddenly remembering I never went home last night.

"*Shit*," I mutter, quickly grabbing it to text my mom. "I'm so dumb. I didn't tell my parents I was staying somewhere else. They must be worried sick."

"Your mom called last night," Reed says then, making my stomach sink for a completely different reason.

My parents know I stayed the night with Reed. Awesome.

Can this whole situation get any more mortifying?

"You're good," he reassures me, not looking one bit freaked out. Okay, then. "Are you hungry? I can order something in."

I swallow back my nerves. "I should probably go home. I need to work on my thesis."

Because that thought isn't depressing.

"All right." He looks back at Ginny, the exhaustion on his face mirroring mine. "What the hell am I supposed to do with her tomorrow?"

I frown. "What do you mean?"

"I have to stop by my lab for a couple hours," he says. "I could probably get away with working at home the rest of the day, but then I'd have to leave her to go to the youth center."

I don't even think about it before I cross yet another invisible line between us. "I could watch her tomorrow while you're at the lab," I offer. He opens his mouth, but I beat him to it. "I was going to stay home anyway or go to the library. I'll watch her while I work."

But he's already shaking his head. "You won't be able to concentrate."

"My thesis is almost done. I just have to review the whole thing. It'll do me good to get out of the house. Plus, I'll work faster knowing I have limited time before she wakes up or needs something. Let's just try it out."

"I can't let you do that, Lila."

"If you don't want me to stay at your house while you're not here, I get it."

"It's not that." He lets out a deep sigh, raking his hand through his hair. "But what happens the day after tomorrow? And every day after that? *I* adopted her. She isn't your puppy to take care of."

"Okay, how about this? I work here tomorrow while I watch her, and in the afternoon, we take her to the youth center. We can set up her playpen in your office."

When he doesn't say anything, I keep going. "And tomorrow, we'll look into doggy care."

"What's that?"

"It's basically like daycare for kids but for dogs," I explain. "She will spend a few hours with other dogs—and supervised by professional trainers, obviously—while you work. You can pick her up whenever you want. I think it's quite flexible. We can call a few dog daycare centers in the area. We'll figure it out."

When Reed doesn't say anything to that, I send my dad a text, asking if he can pick me up. He replies immediately.

"My dad is coming," I tell Reed.

"Here?"

"No, to the neighbors' house. Yes, here."

"Smart-ass."

"I thought I was a criminal?"

"You're both."

I shake my head in amusement, reaching for the shoes I took off before we collapsed on his couch last night. "Do you have any puppy questions before I go? I mean, you can text me, but it's always easier to explain things in person."

"I'll be fine." He doesn't sound that fine to me. Alas, if he doesn't want to talk, I won't force him.

We watch Ginny in silence as I think about what's happened between us in the last twenty-four hours. He kissed the top of my head, then let me sleep on his lap while he played with my hair.

And I've never been more confused.

Maybe he only feels somewhat responsible for my well-being because I'm his friends' daughter, but the hopeful side of me can't help but wonder if it's something else.

If his heart beats a little faster than usual when he looks at me, just like mine does when I look at him.

A few moments later, my phone pings. "My dad is outside."

He stands right after me. "Let me walk you to the door."

We're both careful not to wake Ginny, but the poor thing is so tired she doesn't stop snoring.

I'm about to open the front door when Reed's huge hand moves around me and shuts it again.

My breathing stops.

"Reed?"

The heat of his body behind mine seeps into my bones. With his arm above my head, cocooning me between his massive body and the door, my heart leaps with surprise and excitement.

His eyes resemble a raging storm when I glance back at him. His jaw ticks, and suddenly there's not enough air in this house for me to breathe normally.

I'm very aware that my dad is right outside. I'm also very aware that Reed is still my supervisor for another month and a half.

But mostly?

I'm aware of the way my body responds to him. Of how my lips tingle, how the butterflies in my stomach flutter, how the fog in my head clears out until all I can see is him.

"I don't know what I would've done without you," he rasps out, the intensity in his eyes almost unbearable. I don't know what it means, but I like it. "Thank you, Lila. For everything."

"It was nothing." Why am I whispering? "Do you want me to watch her tomorrow?"

His nod is small, unsure. "Please."

"Okay."

Lila, stop whispering.

He pulls away slowly, and I take it as my cue to burst this weird, alluring bubble we keep finding ourselves in.

"I'll see you tomorrow," I say, giving him a smile he doesn't return.

He dips his chin once. "Text me when you get home."

Then he opens the door for me, letting in the cold afternoon air. I try not to die inside as I make my way to my dad's car, but I do a little when he waves at Reed behind me.

They have been friends long before I exchanged a single word with Reed. It's not weird that they acknowledge each other.

Considering what happened just now, I'd argue it is.

It doesn't help that the first thing my dad tells me when I get in his car is, "You seem to be spending a lot of time with Reed lately."

I'm officially dead inside.

"What is that supposed to mean?" I can't bring myself to look at him as I buckle myself in and he drives away.

"Just an observation."

"Are you mad at me?"

He doesn't sound angry—my dad rarely gets angry in the first place—but there's a weird edge to his voice I don't like.

"I'm not mad at you, little sunshine," he reassures me. "Just worried. I don't want you to get into trouble."

His unspoken warning makes the butterflies in my stomach die at once. Because he's right.

Because if someone finds out I'm spending time with my internship supervisor outside of the youth center, at *his house,* my worst nightmare will come true.

But Ginny.

"We found an injured puppy at the park yesterday. Reed adopted her," I explain. "I was just helping him adjust because he's never had a dog before and was kind of freaking out about the whole thing."

My dad looks at me out of the corner of his eye. "You know I don't have a problem with Reed. He's a friend. It's the fact that he's your superior that worries me. You know what kind of trouble I'm talking about."

"Yeah," I mutter, wondering if I'd be okay if I jumped out of the car right now. Probably not. "I'll be careful."

The fact that my dad has voiced his concern should probably deter me from wanting to spend any more time with Reed outside of our academic obligations, but I suddenly realize I do want to.

I want to see Ginny, and I want to spend time with Reed.

I have avoided him for too long, and I've finally realized my mistake. I was missing out not only on an amazing professional who can teach me endless knowledge, but also on a good man who cares about me. Maybe not in the same way I'm starting to care about him, but he makes me feel comfortable and capable.

I *like* being around him.

For once in my life, the only voice that matters is mine—and it's telling me that getting close to Reed is worth every risk.

chapter 21

LILA

A couple days later, all my attempts at focusing on creating an outline for the sexual education workshop go out the window.

Pressure weighs on me as self-doubts creep in. *What if I'm not good enough for this?*

I can't concentrate, even though Haniyah said I'd have to send her a first draft by the end of the week; otherwise, the workshop won't fit into my internship schedule. But an hour goes by, and I have only written three bullet points that don't even make sense.

My thoughts drift to Ginny. I helped Reed look for a dog daycare place yesterday, and we found one just five minutes away from campus. He was hesitant to leave her there for so many hours in a place full of strangers, but he told me Ginny had made some doggy friends when he went to pick her up.

Unfortunately, Reed's cute puppy isn't enough to make me feel better today.

My head starts pounding when someone pulls out the chair next to mine at the library.

"Hi, cutie," Karla whispers, sending me a reassuring smile. "Rough day today?"

Since we're in a secluded corner of the library and there's no risk of getting caught talking, I let out a loud sigh. "That'd be an understatement. Tell me yours is going better?"

She sets her laptop on the spot next to mine. "Not really. I'm finishing up a research paper to submit to the Youth Counseling Expo. You've heard of it, right?"

I nod. It's one of the most prestigious conferences in the psychology world—being invited as a speaker would be a dream come true. My papers are nowhere near good enough, though, so I'd rather not disappoint myself with their rejection.

"They're accepting grad students this year, right?" I ask.

"Yeah. I'm struggling with this damn paper, though." She bites her bottom lip, thinking. "Do you think you could ask Dr. Abner to review it for me? See if it needs work?"

I hesitate. "He's busy with his research, but maybe you could send him an email."

"Oh, okay." She smiles, but it doesn't reach her eyes. "Anyway, what are you working on?"

"It's, um, a workshop type of thing for my internship."

Telling people about my internship with Reed still doesn't come naturally, even if it's Karla. In our years of friendship, she's never judged me or made me feel like I was more or less than anyone else. She doesn't treat me any differently because of my grades or academic opportunities, and she didn't bat an eyelid when I told her about the internship. So why do I feel so nervous now?

Karla leans over to read my screen. The handful of words written on it, anyway.

"Oh, wow." Her eyes widen. "They let you run workshops? Lucky. My internship supervisor has me reviewing last year's reports, as if that would help me learn something."

"Maybe you can talk to her. Ask her to give you more meaningful tasks?"

But she shakes her head. "It's whatever. I just want to graduate and move on."

Something prickles the back of my brain then. "Didn't you apply for a summer internship?"

If I remember correctly, Karla was also going to apply for the summer camp internship I ended up missing.

She lowers her gaze, studying her chipped black nails. "I didn't get it, so..."

"Oh, I didn't know." I really didn't. She never brought it up again, and I assumed it was because she had gotten in, had an amazing time, and didn't want me to feel bad. "Well, I'm sure your internship will get better soon. At the very least, you'll have some experience to add to your résumé."

"Yeah, I guess." She eyes my laptop screen again. "How's working with Dr. Abner, anyway? Is he as smart as they say?"

His hands on my hips.

My head on his lap.

His lips on my hair.

I clear my throat and hope my cheeks aren't burning red.

"He's great." I give her what I hope is an easy and totally-not-nervous smile. "His feedback is invaluable, and the kids love him. Seeing him in action is out of this world."

She returns my smile. "You're very lucky to be working with him."

I don't know what to say to that, so I turn my attention to my laptop. "Your paper isn't going well, then?"

She lets out a long sigh. "I've drafted the methodology section, like, six times. I'm about to give up and get some chai."

My phone buzzes, and I take a quick look just in case it's Reed with news about Ginny. "I can give it a quick read for you if you'd li—"

His text pops on my screen, the last person I thought would contact me or I wanted to hear from, and air whooshes out of my lungs. Not because I'm ecstatic that he reached out, but because *what the fuck?*

"You okay?"

I'm aware that I haven't finished my sentence. That Karla is waiting for me to remember how to string words back together. That she probably thinks something's wrong with me. That—

"You look pale right now. Do you need some water?"

I gulp, wondering who might be having the time of their lives with my voodoo doll right now.

"I'm..." I start, but I don't know how to finish.

My fingers tighten around my phone, as if trying to break it so he has no way of contacting me again.

The fire in my stomach roars back to life. I'm here to work my ass off, to make my dream career happen for me, not to entertain cheaters.

"Sorry," I finally let out. "I'm having a weird week."

"I get it." She waves me off. "Let me know if you need anything. I'm making a quick run to the coffee shop in a bit."

I give Karla a small nod and, without a word, go back to the outline I'm definitely not finishing today. But not before shoving my phone in the deepest pocket of my backpack, all while begging my panic levels to come down.

I must be dreaming.

Because there's no way Oliver, my ex-boyfriend whom I haven't talked to or heard from in almost a year, has just texted me.

> **Oliver: Lila, we need to talk. ASAP.
> I'm serious.**

He's going to sue me. There's no way he isn't.

Why else would he text me out of the blue so many months after our breakup?

My parents are going to kill me. And that's not even the worst part of it. Because sure, the thought of disappointing the people who love me the most in this world feels like a punch to the gut, but if Oliver sues me, I could get *expelled* from my MA.

Kicked out of Warlington University.

Three months away from graduating.

Twenty more minutes go by, and it becomes clear I'm not getting any work done today. With an uncomfortable heaviness on my chest, I say goodbye to Karla, lock myself in the nearest bathroom stall down the hall, and practice my breathing techniques for what feels like hours.

It doesn't work.

REED

Lila is anxious today. I could tell she wasn't acting like her usual self the second she stepped into my office at the youth center a couple hours ago, but I didn't press.

Now I want to.

She's chewing on her bottom lip nervously and won't stop twisting the flower pendant around her neck. I don't think she even realizes how many times she's sighed since she sat down at the desk across from mine.

"You all right?" I ask her when I can't take it any longer. "Do you need help with your outline?"

She stops chewing on her lip, glancing up at me. "What? Oh. No, I'm okay."

I level her with a no-bullshit glare. "I can tell you're worried about something."

"It's nothing."

"Lila."

She shrugs tiredly, her gaze falling to her screen again.

Very well.

"So, you'll sleep on my lap, but telling me what you're worried about is where you draw the line?"

That gets her attention.

"That's not fair," she mutters at my bold statement.

"Just tell me what's wrong, Lila. Please. I want to help if I can."

Her shoulders rise and fall with an uneven breath, and her fingers move to the flower pendant around her delicate neck again. *Stop looking at her goddamn neck.*

"Oliver texted me. My ex."

My body freezes.

Her ex.

The fucker who cheated on her.

"I don't want to get back with him, *obviously*," she rushes to add, oblivious to the tension and relief locking my body into an overwhelming prison.

Tension because I don't want that boy breathing in her direction any more than I want to be punched in the face. And relief because hearing Lila say she doesn't want to date him again brings me a confusing sense of peace I have no right to experience. I reel in it anyway because I'm a selfish bastard.

"He said he wanted to talk to me, but I don't know what he could want. It's stressing me out so much on top of everything else going on."

If the way she's pressing her lips into a thin line is any indication, she's not sharing the whole story. She has the right to keep as many details as she wants to herself, but that doesn't mean I can't press some more. Especially when seeing her like this is killing me.

"What else are you stressed out about?" I ask, my voice gentle.

"Just...everything, really." She shakes her head, a blonde wave falling over her shoulder. "I'm still not done with my thesis, and then there's the workshop. I want to do a good job for the kids, but I don't know if I have what it takes. I want to graduate this semester, and it's just... The pressure is getting to me."

"I understand that, but you're on the right track—a track

you've been on for the past six years. I've seen your academic records."

Her fingers fall from her necklace to place that same long strand of hair behind her pierced ear. "That doesn't mean I'm in the clear. I can still fail my master's."

"You won't."

"You don't know that."

"You won't fail," I repeat. "You'll nail your thesis because you've got what it takes. As for the workshop, I told you we'd work on it together. I don't care if the outline you send me is messy. Do you think my first drafts are good? Because they're everything but."

The pain in her eyes kills me. "Are you saying that because you actually believe it or because you work with my mom?"

I thought I'd seen a slight change in Lila's attitude, so her question surprises me. Although, if I think about it, backsliding into former habits when life gets stressful isn't unheard of; especially for people like her, who tend to overthink and worry about unlikely scenarios. But I don't have it in me to be frustrated with her; when it comes to Lila, I only want to be patient.

"We've talked about this, remember? Your mom has mentioned you over the years, but—no offense—I wasn't interested. Talking about my family isn't something I like to do, so whenever other people talk about theirs, I tend to zone out."

I don't know why I'm telling her this. All I know is that I need her to understand, and opening myself up to her doesn't feel as daunting as it does with everyone else.

"One day, I saw that article you published about childhood trauma. Your mom shared it, and I clicked on it." Her eyes stay locked with mine. "It was a fucking masterpiece. I couldn't fathom how such a young mind was already so bright."

Her cheeks redden. "It wasn't a big deal."

The way she says it, I know she isn't fishing for compliments or playing any fake-humble games. Which is precisely why it worries me.

But I decide to save that conversation for another day.

"We'd seen each other a couple of times before the awards show, you and I," I continue, "but we weren't friends. So yes, I talked to you that night because your mother asked me to. I wanted to do it, don't get me wrong. But offering you the internship was entirely my own doing. I wasn't going to do it until you mentioned that other internship you didn't apply to. Your parents had nothing to do with it. Why are you planting all these ideas in your own head when you know the truth?"

I'm not expecting her next words.

"Because I've convinced myself that I don't deserve this."

Silence stretches between us as I fight the urge to pull her into my chest, just like I did that night on my couch.

I lean back in my chair, which groans with my weight. "What is it that you think you don't deserve?"

"All of this. Being here. Taking someone else's spot. Having been accepted into my MA. Getting the internship when I behaved so immaturely. Being a youth counselor."

"Why do you feel this way?"

"Why shouldn't I?" She crosses her arms. A shield. "I grew up in a loving family—you know my parents. We lived comfortably and had access to healthcare, education, and everything else. Most kids who need counseling don't grow up with such luxuries. I might be good at counseling, but I feel like I don't have what it takes to *truly* help them because, no matter how much empathy I have, I don't know what it's like to be in their shoes.

"And then what happened with my ex. I should've handled things differently, like the adult I'm supposed to be. But I lost my mind instead, and I can't move on from it no matter how much time has passed. I'm consumed by guilt because I haven't told my parents; I'm too embarrassed to do it. They'd be so disappointed in me because the Lila from two years ago would've never done any of this. I don't... I don't know who I am anymore, and it scares me. Why am I getting all these great opportunities in life when I'm such a mess?"

Her breathing is uneven, agitated, and her glassy eyes are an open door to the turmoil lashing inside of her.

And I hate every fucking second of it.

Because she's wrong.

"You're missing a key aspect here, Lila—your past decisions and mistakes don't define you. Not when you learn from them."

Her throat works down a swallow as a single tear rolls down her cheek. She dries it immediately.

"Your parents will understand what you did, even if they don't agree with your choices. They love you, and that's not going to change just because you slashed a cheater's tire," I continue. "Feeling guilty for the opportunities you have isn't uncommon. Asking yourself, 'Why me and not literally anyone else?' when something good or bad happens to you is a normal reaction but also very unproductive."

What I don't tell her is that I would know.

What I don't say out loud is that, still to this day, I wonder why I had to grow up with abusive parents.

Why I never got adopted.

Why, out of thousands of foster kids who dream of going to college, I was one of the very few to beat the odds and graduate.

Why I made a name for myself when others didn't get a chance to.

"I don't know how to stop," she mutters so brokenly it takes everything in me not to hold her. "I have no right to complain because I have a good life. I'm so thankful for my family and my good health and everything else. I just feel like... I don't know. Like I haven't *done* anything to deserve this life. It was just... handed to me. I lost friends at school because they kept accusing me of thinking I was better than everyone else when I have *never* felt like that, but maybe...maybe I'm a selfish person, deep down. Maybe I can't see the real me, the real Lila others want to knock down a few pegs for a good reason."

The rawness of her pained words slices my chest open.

"You were lucky to be born into your family, sure, but nobody chooses what family they get to be born into," I say softly. "Your parents fought hard to make sure you had a happy and easy life. I'm sure you'll do your best to ensure your future kids face as little suffering as possible. That's what we should do for future generations."

I tell myself the thought of Lila having children with an imaginary man doesn't make me want to rip his imaginary head off.

I'm losing my mind.

"And like I said, one past mistake doesn't define you. You clearly feel terrible about what you did, but you've also punished yourself enough. Don't let others define you. Lila, you are one of the most selfless people I know. By far."

"I'm not—"

"You started volunteering at the soup kitchen at thirteen," I remind her, recalling her résumé for her internship application. "You've also helped at the women's shelter, at the animal shelter, and now here. That's more volunteering experience in ten years than most people get in their entire life—including me."

Her eyes meet mine again, innocent and vulnerable. "I don't need you to praise me for it. I did it because I felt called to."

"I know. I'm just reminding you that you're doing an outstanding job at helping people in need. You're not a terrible person because of what you did to your ex, no matter how out of character it was. Sometimes we can't control our emotions, but we can control how we deal with the aftermath. You don't have to suffer through life to get good things, Lila. That's not how it works. You're incredible at what you do, and the children love you. Your selflessness and kind heart are making the world a less shitty place. Don't ever let anyone tell you otherwise.

"And it's not even about your volunteer work. You're a joy to everyone around you. No matter who you're dealing with, you always offer them kindness and patience. Offer us. You weren't talking to a wall that day at my office after Cameron and Sean's fight. I was here, listening to every word. Using them to stay afloat during a difficult moment because that's what you do, Lila. You make everything better just by being you."

She chews on her lower lip, those glassy eyes never leaving mine.

"Do you really mean that?" she whispers.

"Every word."

Silence stretches between us until she breaks it in the most unexpected way.

"This may be totally inappropriate, but I really want to give you a hug."

I don't think about it before I nod.

She crosses the distance between our desks. I don't get the chance to stand from my chair before her body crashes into mine, her arms wrapping around my neck in a sealing hug that allows me to really *breathe* for the first time in my goddamn life.

My arms lock around her middle of their own accord, closing the space between us because suddenly, if a piece of paper fit between our bodies, it'd be too big of a gap.

In this moment, surrounded by her warmth and her sweet scent, everything disappears.

I don't care if someone walks in and sees us like this.

Having her in my arms is worth every risk.

When she pulls away—too soon—the softness in her beautiful face as she looks at me kills me.

"How do you always have the right words to keep me calm?"

Her fingers graze my neck. "Who keeps you calm, Reed?"

You, angel. You keep me calm.

But I say nothing. Because, for once, I don't think I'm making a huge mistake as one of my hands travels the length of her spine, earning me a delicious shiver.

For once, I don't think of the consequences of wondering what it would be like to have her on my lap, with her legs wrapped around my hips, and show her how crazy she makes me feel.

For once, crossing the forbidden line between us doesn't sound like a bad idea at all.

It sounds like fate.

And I suspect she feels it, too, when her thumb starts caressing the bare skin on my neck. When those soft lips part and her breath quickens.

I need her.

And I want her to need me, too.

"Reed..." She whispers my name, and it's never sounded so fucking sweet.

Gently, I rest my forehead against hers, our noses grazing because our lips shouldn't. She willingly presses closer to me when I give her hips a squeeze, and it takes everything in me not to lower her to my desk and devour every inch of her skin.

"Do you feel this too?" she asks, her voice charged with heat. "This pull between us?"

Fuck yes.

"We shouldn't," I rasp out. "I'm your supervisor."

But my body doesn't listen to my brain as my mouth inches closer to hers.

And then, all my inhibitions shatter when her lips brush mine. Soft, caring, painfully fleeting.

I groan at the feather-like touch when she pulls away. She's teasing me, and I'm only too happy to play the game. My hands tighten on her body, the situation behind my zipper growing with every second.

I'm about to pull her into my lap when a knock on my office door makes us pull away as if we're on fire.

Lila's eyes widen on me, her chest rising and falling with heavy breaths, her cheeks bright red.

What the fuck have we just done?

"Sit at your desk," I instruct her quickly as I try to sort out the tent in my pants before this situation gets even worse.

I almost kissed my intern. Our lips fucking brushed. I was about to pull my friends' daughter into my lap like some moron. Goddammit.

Lila sits down in record time, pretending to work on her laptop again. I clear my throat and call out, "Come in."

Haniyah enters my office with her usual kind smile, completely oblivious to the heated scene she almost walked into. "Reed, Lila. Working hard, I see."

Lila glances at me like she wants the ground to swallow her in this moment. I share the sentiment.

Han starts talking about an upcoming meeting, but I can't focus for shit. Not when Lila and I have just crossed a line we'll never come back from.

And the worst part? I can't bring myself to regret it.

chapter 22

REED

The past four weeks have been the most confusing of my entire life.

My thirty-sixth birthday was a week ago, and they surprised me with cupcakes at the youth center. Lila put a birthday hat on Ginny, which almost made me do something extremely stupid.

Like kiss her.

As if I hadn't crossed that line already, even though it was just a peck. Not even that, technically.

Still, I've made a point to redraw the line between us in the past month and keep things strictly professional. Yet I can't bring myself to erect a wall.

Being close to Lila is like seeking happiness—you revel in it, let it seep into your skin, and when you've had too much of it, you start wondering if the rope is about to snap.

The sound of a little yawn brings me back to the present moment. I snap my head up in time to see Ginny stretching in her bed inside the playpen before curling back into a sleeping position. She's gotten slightly bigger in the past month, but the vet doesn't think she'll grow much more.

My office chair groans under my weight as I stand to check on her for the millionth time this afternoon. But the puppy is fine; her tail has fully healed, and I haven't hurt her yet.

But I will.

I grab the file on my desk, sneaking one last glance at Ginny before venturing down the hall to drop it at Haniyah's office. She isn't there, so I leave the file on her desk and make my way to the common room. I'm scanning the room for Han when I feel a small tug on my slacks. "Reed."

"Hey, Ike." I give him an easy smile. "Anything you need?"

"I think Lili is sick."

Lili. That's what he calls Lila.

I frantically search the common room until I spot her. She's at one of the tables with Melody and Vera. Even from a distance, I can see the dark circles under her eyes.

"Thanks for telling me, Ike. Do you need anything?"

He shakes his head with vigor. "No, just wanted to tell you about Lili."

"I'm going to check on her, but do you want me to walk you somewhere first?"

"I was playing with Jordan over there." He points to his friend sitting on the floor a few feet away, construction blocks splayed all around him. "I'm going with him again. You promise to take care of Lili?"

"Always," I tell him firmly, hoping he can tell the honesty in my voice. "Don't worry about it."

He finally nods, convinced, before going back to his friend and their building bricks.

No other kids stop me as I make my way to Lila's table. The two girls on both of her sides are making beaded bracelets and chatting to each other, but she looks out of it. With her gaze lost somewhere on the table and her arms crossed over her chest, she doesn't notice me nearing her until Melody asks, "Hey, Reed. Do you want a bracelet with our names?"

I give Cameron's sister an easy smile. "Sure."

"What colors?"

My eyes roam the table, where a vast array of colorful beads are sorted in different plastic containers. "I like red."

"You can do that one, Vera," Melody offers before turning back to me. "Would you like a blue one too? With a smiley face charm."

"Oh, oh!" Vera chimes in, her big brown eyes pleading. "Do you like stars, Reed? Can I put stars in mine, pretty please? The golden ones."

My mouth tilts at their enthusiasm. "I love smiley faces and stars. Thanks, girls." When they go back to their bracelets, I turn to Lila. "Everything all right? Ike told me you were sick."

"I'm not sick," she tells me, craning her neck to look up at me. She looks taken aback, probably because I've made a point not to talk to her about anything other than her internship in the past month. An attempt at regaining that sense of normalcy between us. She clears her throat. "Just feeling a little tired."

"You still aren't sleeping well?"

"You could say that," she mumbles, directing her attention back to the table. "Thanks for checking on me, though."

A clear dismissal that won't do it for me, not when she looks like that. Beautiful, because Lila is beautiful, but her usual spark is gone. And I won't have it.

"I'll be right back."

I head to the vending machine at the front and grab a bag of chips. Not the most nutritious snack out there, but I've seen her have these a couple times, and right now, I only want her to eat so she feels better.

The girls are still working on their bracelets when I come back, and Lila doesn't look at me until my shadow towers over her.

"Here." I place the crinkly bag in front of her and look everywhere but at her eyes.

Yet I don't need to be looking at her to notice the breathiness in her voice. "What...? Oh." A pause. "You didn't have to, but thank you. I'm actually kind of hungry."

"Aww." Melody rests her chin on her hand as she glances between us. "That's sweet that you got her a snack. She will never admit it, but she's acting kinda grouchy today."

"I'm not *grouchy*," Lila retorts as she opens the bag and plops a chip into her mouth.

I follow the movement and zero in on her lips like a sick bastard.

Melody rolls her eyes at me. "Told you."

"I'm not grouchy," she repeats, not sounding the least bit convincing. "I'm acting normal."

"You normally smile a lot and tease me about being glued to my phone all day. You haven't mentioned it once today. So, yes, you're grouchy. But it's okay—we love you anyway."

Vera nods and hums, her eyes not leaving the red bracelet she's making for me.

Something akin to warmth spreads through my chest at the notion that Lila is so popular among the kids. Some volunteers and interns never fully fit in with them, but she seems to have them all wrapped around her finger.

"And I love you guys," she says in a soft, emotional voice. "But don't make me cry, okay? I already feel sensitive enough as it is."

A silent alarm goes off in my head. "Why? Did someone say something to you?"

I can't read the expression on her face. "It's fine."

It's fine—not *I'm* fine.

"I can tell it's not just tiredness. What's wrong?"

"Noth—"

"She's been looking at her phone all afternoon," Melody chips in. "And every time she does, she gets even grouchier."

"Melody!" Lila flushes.

Is her ex bothering her again? Maybe they got back together?

Her love life is none of my business.

"He looks worried, Li. I'm just trying to help," the girl says.

"I appreciate it, but it's fine. Really. Everything's fine," she insists before finishing up her chips. It was a small bag; I should probably get her another one. "It's just...stuff."

Stuff.

"Let's talk in my office," I suggest.

Melody groans. "But we want the gossip."

"There's no gossip," I tell the girls. "I need to talk to Lila about her internship."

"Boring."

Lila sticks her tongue out at Melody. "I'll be right back."

We're silent as we make our way to my office. Ginny wakes up with the sound of the door opening and wags her tail excitedly as Lila crouches to pick her up.

"Are you being a good puppy for Reed, little bean?" she asks her in a baby voice I shouldn't find so fucking adorable.

Ginny's only response is to lick her face, so I answer for her. "She loves it here, surrounded by the kids."

That much is true. I can't go one afternoon working in my office without at least a dozen kids knocking at my door, asking to see her.

Since she sleeps the day away, I've taken her to some of my sessions with Cameron, too, which posed an interesting situation. I had never seen him speak as gently as he does with Ginny, and he loves the fact that we gave her the name he suggested. He's careful when he pets her and always asks for permission before picking her up. The boxing lessons he's been to with Warren and Liam must be paying off, because I haven't seen him look so relaxed in a long time. Scratch that—*ever.*

Lila places Ginny back in the playpen, and she goes directly on full attack mode to her favorite toy, a plushie sheep, courtesy of Han.

I don't beat around the bush. "What is it on your phone that is making you so anxious? Is it your thesis? Are you sure you don't want me to look at it?"

She's been on edge for a couple weeks now, tying all loose ends before she has to turn in her thesis. I offered to give her one last round of feedback, but she refused right away. I'm not allowed to read it until she's defended it, apparently.

She shakes her head, avoiding my gaze, which only makes me more curious.

"Lila," I start, "I know we haven't talked much in the past few weeks, but if someone or something is bothering you—"

"I'm seeing my ex today," she blurts out.

My breathing stops, followed by my pounding heart.

I'm careful to school my features and keep my voice unbothered as I ask, "Why?"

The guilt in her eyes feels like a punch to the gut.

"He's been texting me nonstop for the past month, saying we need to talk, and I just can't ignore him anymore." With each word, she buries me deeper. "I don't want to get back with him, but I feel like... I don't know. Like I owe him some of my time for what I did."

"You don't."

If she notices my harsh tone, she doesn't comment on it.

"I know I don't, but this will be like closure to me too. I think." She lets out a shaky breath. "He didn't forgive me when I apologized for the tire, and I still feel bad about it. Maybe he will now. Maybe that's what he wants to talk about."

"It's not. He'll try to get back with you," I say, like it's any of my business.

"He won't." She sounds confident about it. "I made it clear in my texts. He has ten minutes for whatever he wants to tell me. After that, I'm out."

I cross my arms in front of my chest, the organ inside it beating in an uncomfortable, rapid rhythm. "I still think it's not a good idea."

"I don't remember asking for your opinion, Dr. Abner."

Dr. Abner.

So that's how she wants to go about this. Very well.

"Watch your tone around me, Miss Callaghan," I warn her, my voice dripping with authority but not anger. "I'm still your supervisor for another two weeks."

She arches an eyebrow like she wants to ask, *So, that's why you almost threw me on top of your desk and devoured me?*

"I might need a refresher," she muses. The fire in her voice makes my cock stir to life. "I don't remember 'giving unsolicited opinions about a student's love life' being part of your tasks as my supervisor, but maybe I'm wrong."

"Indeed, you are wrong. It was in the first section of our internship agreement."

"Right. My bad," she mutters, her lips tilting upward. "If you don't need anything else, *Dr. Abner,* I'd like to go back with the girls."

The green monster inside of me rattles its cage, demanding to be released so it can make her stay with me. But she's right— she didn't ask for my opinion, and I don't have the right to give it to her.

No matter if it kills me inside that she's going to talk to her ex and potentially get back together with him because...

Fuck.

Because I'm falling for her. For her mind, her heart, her laugh, her touch—all of her.

And it will only end in heartbreak.

chapter 23

LILA

The pungent smell of weed hits me like a slap in the face.

"Hey. Come in."

Oliver opens the door wider, giving me a clear view of his place. He used to live with two of his friends before we moved in together, and it looks like he's moved back in. But the apartment is deserted now, which is a small blessing.

It also looks exactly like I remember, even one year later—small (which is fine), clothes everywhere (possibly dirty), and a constant weird smell in the air (which is not fine).

"You can sit here," Oliver offers, making room for me on their couch.

He picks up a discarded T-shirt and throws it onto a nearby beanbag. How did I ever think moving in with such a messy person was a good idea?

I can't help but think of Reed's house—clean, tidy, with character. It feels like a home, while this apartment feels like—

Stop thinking about Reed.

Right. I should.

I should probably stop thinking about what happened in his office, too, because it won't happen again.

Things have been more tense in the past month, although not uncomfortable. He's clearly redrawing the line between us, but it doesn't keep me from thinking he sounded a tiny bit jealous when I mentioned I was coming here.

"What did you want to talk about?" I ask, not wasting time with pleasantries. I don't sit down because I don't want to give Oliver the impression that I'll be staying longer than strictly necessary.

He grabs an energy drink and takes a swig before speaking. He's not smoking now, but the redness in his eyes, paired with the smell in here, tells me he must have just stopped before I arrived.

"I don't like how we left things," he says, taking me by surprise. We broke up almost a year ago. He didn't think of reaching out before now? "But I was angry with you because of the tire thing. I think it's understandable."

"I apologized for that," I remind him.

I still feel somewhat bad about it, but Reed is right—I shouldn't be the one begging for his forgiveness or being painted like the bad guy when he was the one who hurt me first.

Oliver shrugs. "Still. I couldn't go out for a month. Kinda sucks when you unexpectedly have to buy a new tire and a phone charger."

Is he trying to make me feel bad right now? Sure, I did a terrible thing, but I'm tired of punishing myself for it. And he's not exactly a saint, either.

"You know, I always found it funny how you never had enough money to pay me back for rent, but somehow your weed stash was always full. Makes you think."

"I don't want to start a fight, Lila."

"Then stop trying me."

He sighs. "Look, I know what I did wasn't okay. I'm just saying the tire thing was a low blow, not to mention the fish in my underwear drawer."

"Did you ask me to come just so you could make me feel bad about something that happened almost a year ago? Something I apologized for?"

He runs a hand through his blond hair. It looks longer than

it did the last time I saw him around campus before the summer. "I wanted us to talk because I'm sorry for what I did."

"Okay," I say slowly, knowing he's not done.

And knowing I won't like his next words either.

"I think we should try again. Give it another chance." *Oh, no, no, no.* "Go on another first date, you know?"

"Oliver..." How can I say this without sounding like an absolute ass? "You cheated on me. I could never trust you again. You get that, right?"

"You are the one not getting it." He takes another swig of his energy drink before pinning me down with his reddened stare. "I fucked up, Li, and I'm sorry. But we were so good together, and it was just a onetime thing. I promise. It wasn't a big deal, and it won't happen again."

I count to three in my head before answering. "It's good that you're apologizing for what you did, but it was a big deal to me. You betrayed my trust. And, even after so many months, it doesn't look like you understand the gravity of what you did."

"Babe, just hear me out—"

"Don't call me that," I cut him off. "I thought I'd made it clear in my texts that I didn't want to get back together. If that's why you asked me to come, I'll be on my way now. I'm sorry, Oliver, but you're wasting my time right now. I have things to do."

"Like what? Fucking your professor?"

My entire body locks into place.

"What did you say?" I ask slowly.

Because surely he didn't just say that.

Calm down. He's just talking out of his ass because he feels rejected.

Oliver shrugs, reaching for a rolled joint on the coffee table. "You think I didn't recognize him? He works with your mom, that Reed Abner guy. Professor of psychology and whatnot. And now you're doing an internship with him? That's convenient."

Where the hell is this coming from?

But most importantly, I ask, "How do you know about my internship?"

He shrugs again. "Saw it on social media. You and Reed looked cozy at the park."

I knew Haniyah often updated the youth center's social media pages with pictures of our trips and activities, but I had no idea Oliver was so invested in my life post-breakup. For some reason, I expected him to forget about me even faster than I forgot about him.

It dawns on me, as I'm standing in the middle of my ex-boyfriend's messy living room, that this is my nightmare come true. That it finally happened—someone just insinuated that I'm sleeping with a professor and that I used him to get where I am today.

And honestly? The fear doesn't come. Neither does the anxiety.

I only find this whole thing pathetic.

"Don't throw such baseless, cliché accusations at me just because I don't want us to get back together," I tell him, my head high. He won't see me crumble because I won't. "You know firsthand how hard I worked before Reed ever came into the picture. If you're trying to make me give you a second chance—which won't happen—this isn't the way."

"Whatever," he mutters as he lights the joint and brings it to his mouth. The smell of weed intensifies as he lets out a cloud of smoke. "You're sleeping with him, which is why you don't want to sleep with me. I get it, babe. You're not a cheater. Your secret's safe with me."

Where's the hidden camera?

No, seriously. Is this a prank?

"Oliver." I pinch the bridge of my nose. "Not that it's any of your business, but I'm not sleeping with anyone. And I'm most certainly not sleeping with a professor."

Whether I want to or not is irrelevant to this conversation.

"Your secret's safe with me," he repeats, ignoring every single word I've just said. "Just be careful, yeah? Rumors spread like wildfire on campus."

"All right. I'm out." I can't take this nonsense any longer. Hiking my backpack higher on my shoulder, I look around his apartment one last time. "Take care, Oliver. And don't contact me ever again."

He doesn't look at me, his gaze lost on the coffee table as his joint burns. "Sure."

When he doesn't add anything else, I head right out of the door and don't stop until I'm in my car.

Then, my breathing gets heavier.

Not because I think Oliver will spread any rumor about Reed and me—he's too scared of my dad for that—but because I'm tired.

I'm tired of living inside the prison that is my head, built with bricks of self-made insecurities. I've had enough.

I know I didn't use my parents' connections to land my internship or any other opportunity.

I know Reed values me for my hard work and not because of my family.

I know damn well I'm not sleeping with him.

Who cares what other people think?

Sure, our relationship might not be exactly traditional, and the lines might have been blurred once or twice, but he's not using his power to get something out of me. I've been raised to catch the warning signs. After Oliver, I'm never overlooking a single red flag ever again.

And Reed? He makes me feel like I have something worth offering to the world. He helped me see the light in myself, the one I thought had been extinguished long ago.

My conscience is clear. I don't feel guilty over a single thing I've done or said to Reed. Which is why I grab my phone and don't think twice about what I'm about to do, because it feels *right*.

And I deserve to start doing what feels good to me instead of trying to accommodate everyone's feelings but mine.

> **Me: You were right. He did want to get back together (texting you because this is obviously an emergency)**

His reply comes only a minute later.

> **Reed: Telling me I'm right is always an emergency. I hope you said no.**

> **Me: What if I said yes?**

I twist my necklace, unable to rein in my nerves. He looked jealous earlier, and I want to test my theory.

> **Reed: You're too smart to have said yes.**

> **Me: Mmm**

> **Reed: You didn't say yes, did you?**

> **Me: Is that concern about my dating life I detect, Dr. Abner?**

Reed: Yes, it is. Answer my question.

Me: Bossy much? Now I don't want to answer.

Reed: Lila...

His frustration seeps through the phone, and it makes the butterflies in my stomach go a little wilder.

Me: I said no. Happy?

Reed: Very.

Me: Why?

Reed: Because you deserve the fucking best, and he isn't it.

But you are, I want to text him.
I don't.

Me: I could never get back with him. He was pretty stoned while we talked and said some dumb things.

Me: He deserved to get his tire slashed again.

Reed: Dumb how? Are you okay?

Me: All safe and sound in my car.

Reed: Good. Text me when you get home.

Me: Will do :)

I start my car, not expecting any more texts. But just as I'm about to pull away, my phone buzzes again.

Reed: Don't think I've forgotten about your tire comment, little criminal. I've got a new assignment for you.

Me: Uh-oh...

Reed: You're coming to a boxing lesson with me.

My heart stops. A boxing lesson. With Reed. At the gym. My palms start sweating.

Me: I'm not sure that's a good idea.

Reed: Why not?

Me: I don't want to humiliate you in public.

Reed: Ha. Be ready on Friday.

Reed: Sound good?

It sounds dangerous, I type in before deleting my text.

All my life, I've played it safe. Maybe it's time I hold my breath and dive in for once.

Me: Sounds good

chapter 24

LILA

"Come again?"

Mariah looks at me like I've grown a second head.

To be fair, the words that have just left my mouth aren't exactly normal.

I take another bite of my sandwich. This morning, I texted my best friend asking for an emergency lunch break. I picked her up from the tattoo parlor, wearing a calm and collected mask so my dad wouldn't suspect I was freaking out on the inside. But with just the two of us alone now at a café down the block, I allow myself to be a bit more of a mess.

"He asked me to go to a boxing lesson with him," I repeat, although I know she heard me the first time.

I don't blame her for thinking she heard wrong, though. It is kind of unexpected.

Mariah gives me her signature pointed look. "A boxing lesson. With your internship supervisor. Who you're co-parenting a puppy with. Who you *kissed*."

"I didn't technically kiss him. It was just a quick brush of the lips."

"That's what kissing means."

I ignore her. "And we're not *co-parenting*, Riah. Jeez." Although Ginny does feel like mine sometimes. "I'm just teaching him how to be a dog dad. Let's not have this conversation again."

Over the past month, I've kept her in the loop about

everything Ginny-related. She's always asking me for pictures and all kinds of updates, in which she never fails to ask me about *Puppy Daddy.*

The things a girl has to endure for her best friend.

"We're totally having this conversation again," she retorts, "because this is your supervisor we're talking about. Do you realize he's, like, the *one* man you shouldn't get involved with? What happened to your lifelong plan of ignoring him?"

"I don't know. It's just..." I take a few seconds to organize my scrambled thoughts. "Ignoring him was the plan. But then I realized he was teaching me so many things, and I was behaving like a petulant child, so I told myself I'd start getting a bit closer. Convinced myself the world wouldn't end if I acted like a normal person around him."

Riah makes a humming noise as she sips from her iced tea. "That was the right call. I'm just saying, maybe the lines are a bit blurred now. You need to be careful."

"Reed was part of my life before I became his intern, in a way. And we've been put in weird situations, like finding Ginny, that kind of brought us together."

She frowns. "But Oliver said—"

"Oliver doesn't know what he's talking about," I interrupt. "He's just saying things because he feels rejected. I'm not sleeping with Reed."

"I won't judge you if you are," my best friend says. "I believe you if you say nothing's happened between you aside from the *brush of lips*, but if it does, I want to be the first one to know."

I feel my cheeks warming up. "Nothing else will happen between us. We've been keeping our distance for the past few weeks. It's like the almost kiss never happened, and I'm fine with that."

Liar.

"Just be careful," she repeats, sounding so serious that my

sandwich starts turning in my stomach. "Okay, enough about Reed. I have something to tell you."

"Oh?"

"The day has finally come—our dads want to retire next year."

I freeze.

Retiring.

Next year.

It's not like I expected my dad to work forever. He's been a tattoo artist for the past thirty years? Forty? Many people are surprised when they find out he and Uncle Trey are still working after so long.

"Are you about to have a meltdown?" Mariah's voice breaks through the fog in my brain. "Because I get it. That was my exact reaction, too."

"It's just..." I shake my head. "*Weird.*"

"Tell me about it."

"What's going to happen with Inkjection?"

My dad opened the shop thirty-something years ago, and eventually, Uncle Trey became a co-owner. Inkjection has been the most popular tattoo parlor in town for decades, so much so that professional athletes and celebrities travel all the way here just to get their ink on their bodies. I doubt they'll want to shut it down and throw all that away, but...

My best friend shrugs. "They haven't told us anything else. The staff, I mean. They might be still deciding."

It surprises me that my dad hasn't told me about this himself, but I get it. The control freak in me hates changes, and I suppose he doesn't want to upset me before he has a clear idea of what he wants to do. But I'm *definitely* talking to him about this the next time we see each other.

Him not being a tattoo artist anymore isn't the end of the world, but it feels like the end of a chapter. And so the weight in my stomach gets a little heavier.

⁓✲⁓

"Are you sure she's okay?"

I sneak glances at Liam's tiny office in the gym, where Ginny's playpen is currently set up.

"Eyes on me, little criminal." Reed's deep voice sends chills down my spine. "You're not getting out of this gym without knowing how to throw a punch."

I roll my eyes at him. "Remind me again why I'm here in the first place?"

Not that I'm complaining. Liam and Warren have been nothing but welcoming since I stepped foot in their gym. And Reed...

Let's just say the size of his naked biceps will forever stay engraved in my brain, which is both a blessing and a curse.

"Because you need a way out for all that pent-up stress," he says, that powerful body towering over me. "Have you seen how calm Cameron is lately? Thank boxing."

That much is true. Cameron can't stop talking about how much he loves boxing and how he looks forward to his lessons.

"You don't have to come back if you don't like it," Reed adds.

"All right," I agree, if only because he always seems to know what's good for me.

It was no wonder I felt so anxious all the time when I didn't sleep enough or eat balanced meals. I'm making an effort to go to bed earlier, eat at least three full meals a day, and spend some time outside. For now, it seems to be enough.

He passes me the cotton wraps and starts folding them around his hand, instructing me how to do it. His strong hand and the reminder of how it feels against my skin are enough to distract me three times, which is how many times he has to start over because I'm not paying attention.

By the time I've somehow managed to secure the wrap correctly on my left hand, I'm already exhausted.

"Do my other hand? Please?" I'm not above begging him for it.

He sends me a look. "You're capable of doing it yourself."

I bat my eyelashes at him. "I've also had a very long day and would appreciate a little spoiling."

He barks out an unexpected laugh. "All right. Come here."

A shiver skids down my spine when his hand swallows my much smaller one. He takes his time with the wrapping, and so what if I don't want him to finish just to keep feeling his warmth?

He's silent as he does it but not stoic. He seems to be in a better mood today, which is why I ask, "So, what got you into boxing?"

I feel his touch tensing for a second before it goes back to normal.

"I had my first lesson when I was Cameron's age," he explains.

I wait for him to elaborate, but he doesn't, which makes me even more intrigued.

"That doesn't answer my question," I tease him.

I'm not dumb—there's something about Reed's past he's not telling me. Not that he has to. It's just that I've opened up so much about my own fears and insecurities to him—and he's been nothing but supportive to me—that I thought...

Reed doesn't owe me anything. And it's probably for the best if we don't get any closer, although pulling back from our maybe-friendship doesn't feel right.

"I was an angry kid growing up. Until I started boxing, that is."

Reed is one of the most laid-back men I know, so his admission surprises me.

"Is that why you wanted to help Cameron so badly?"

He finishes wrapping the bands around my hand and takes

a step back.

"I want to help all the children equally, but I do see myself in Cameron at times." He clears his throat. "Let's get started."

For the next fifty minutes, I try to convince myself Reed doesn't want to kill me—nothing could've prepared me to *feel* how unfit I am. Sweat collects in every crevice of my body, and my lungs struggle to take a simple breath.

"It's normal to be out of breath if you haven't exercised in a while," he reassures me when I almost pass out after warm-ups. *Warm-ups.*

My mom and my aunt have done ballet their whole lives, but it's never appealed to me. Despite my mom being a part-time ballet instructor when I was little, she never forced me into one of her classes because she knew it wasn't my thing. I played all sorts of sports growing up—volleyball, swimming, ice skating— but ever since I started college, I haven't had the time to work out again.

So even if by the twenty-minute mark I'm already breathless— who knew throwing punches would be so exhausting?—I'll admit I've missed getting out of the house to do something else other than studying. I'm stronger than I thought, and I'd be lying if I said I don't get giddy at Reed's approving smirks as my technique improves.

It's not surprising that Reed was right once again—by the time we're done with the lesson, my stress levels have considerably depleted. My chest feels lighter, despite having to relearn how to breathe normally.

After Warren joins us for some cooldown exercises, I hurry to unwrap the bands from my hands and go find Ginny in Liam's office.

"Hi, girlie," I coo as she starts whimpering and wagging her tail when she spots me. She wastes no time licking my face as soon as I pick her up.

Liam laughs. "Man, I miss it when my dogs were pups. Now they're too grown to lick Dad's face."

I pet Ginny's fur as I hold her against my chest like a baby. "How many dogs do you have?"

"My girl doesn't allow me to have more than four, so four it is."

"That's...intense."

He barks out a laugh. "Wouldn't change a thing, though." His lips tilt into a soft smile. "She's such a good pup. Barely noticed she was here at all."

"She's tired after playing around with other dogs in daycare, aren't you?" I kiss the top of her fluffy head.

"I'm surprised Reed agreed to take her in after—"

Liam's words come to an abrupt stop, as if he had just realized he's not allowed to finish that sentence. His smile doesn't look as genuine as he says, "He's a busy man. I didn't think he'd have the time for a puppy."

I'm surprised Reed agreed to take her in after...

After what?

Does it explain why he was so freaked out by Ginny when she first got here? Why he's still kind of fidgety around her?

Before I can dig deeper, a deep, familiar voice asks behind me, "Lila. Can I talk to you before you leave?"

My heart is still racing with uncertainty as I nod.

Liam takes the cue and grabs Ginny from my arms. "I'll take her outside to see if she needs to use the toilet."

Once he leaves, Reed leans against the doorframe, arms crossed. "How did you like the lesson?"

"I can barely stand on my own two feet, but weirdly enough, I feel great. I feel more..."

"Optimistic?" He throws me a knowing smirk. "Happy? Calm?"

"No wonder Cameron has improved so much." A light

bulb goes on in my head. "Has Melody signed up for any boxing lessons?"

"Not that I know of. Do you think she'd be a good fit?"

"Totally." I beam. "I think boxing could help her with her self-confidence. Should I talk to her about it?"

His smirk is nothing short of devastatingly handsome. "I think that's a great idea."

His praise makes my stomach sizzle with the kind of nerves I felt when I stood between his legs in his office, his body a breath away from mine.

"I wanted to talk to you about your thesis," he adds, taking me by surprise.

"What do you mean?"

For weeks, Reed has insisted—to no avail—on reading my thesis. At the risk of missing out on his feedback, I refused to send it to him until I had submitted it to my supervisor first. As much as we've grown closer, I didn't want him to have any kind of involvement with my thesis.

"I'll email you the details later, but I'll be speaking at a conference in the first week of December—the Youth Counseling Expo. There's a call for papers for graduate students. I thought maybe you'd be interested," he explains, reminding me of Karla mentioning she wanted to apply too.

My mouth feels too dry. "The YCE?"

He nods. "In Chicago. If your thesis is selected, they'll cover your travel and hotel expenses."

The YCE. In Chicago. With Reed.

Am I dreaming?

"I..." I blink. "I don't know if my thesis would be good enough for that."

"Do me a favor and apply anyway."

I bite my tongue as the word *but* is about to leave my mouth. Maybe it's the adrenaline from the boxing lesson, or maybe it's the fact that I'm finally recognizing my self-worth, but I don't want to let my insecurities get in the way of something I want to do. Not this time.

With a new resolve, I tell him, "I'll have to talk to my supervisor about it, but I'm definitely interested."

His smile tells me he also sees the internal shift in me. "Good. Keep me updated."

Later that night, after he emails me all the information for the conference, I spend an hour scrolling in bed, trying to picture myself in an auditorium full of people who are interested in what I have to say.

For once, I can see it.

chapter 25

LILA

When I started this internship three months ago, the last thing I pictured myself doing was running a sex ed workshop for the kids.

My work here has given me a much-needed confidence boost. Turns out Haniyah was right about me learning from Reed—what she doesn't know is that some of the most valuable things he's taught me don't necessarily have to do with youth counseling.

All twenty kids who signed up for the workshop fill the classroom, and it hits me that tomorrow is my last day as an intern at the youth center. I'm not ready to say goodbye.

"Hi, guys," I start, pushing the sad feelings away. "How are you today?"

"Good." Cameron is the first one to answer. And he's doing it with a smile. "I told my parents I wanted to be a boxer when I grow up, and they said yes."

I beam. "That's amazing, Cameron."

"I wanted to be a pilot, but I saw a documentary about an air crash last night, and I don't know anymore." Sofia grimaces. "Maybe I'll be a teacher."

"You still have plenty of time to figure it out. Don't worry too much about it," I reassure her. "Is everybody ready to start?"

When they all nod, their attentive eyes on me, I take a deep breath and step into the role I was always meant to fill.

After making sure the camera at the back of the classroom

is working—Reed wanted to record the session so he could watch it later, deciding not to be present to give me more of a real feel for the experience—I start with the first slide of my presentation.

"First of all, thank you so much for coming to this workshop," I tell them. "I know you're not used to these kinds of activities, but I'm glad you're open to trying them out. Now, you were given some information last week for your parents so you'd know what to expect to learn today. Does anyone remember what we're going to talk about?"

Trevor raises his hand. "Sex."

The kids giggle, and I can't help but roll my eyes playfully. Both Reed and Haniyah warned me they'd behave like this during the workshop, but I'm not bothered by it. As long as they learn something valuable today, I don't mind how much or little they giggle along the way.

"Not exactly," I clarify. "We're going to learn about something called sexual education, which has to do with sex—you're right about that, Trevor—but not exclusively. We're going to start with our bodies."

The first slide of my presentation shows the question: What is happening to my body?

I got the idea from one of the books my mom read to me when I first noticed hair growing on my legs and I didn't understand why. Up until that point, I thought only men got body hair—men as old as my dad—and I had a full-on mental breakdown until my mom stepped in.

"As we grow up, our bodies change with us," I start, looking each of them in the eye. "Just like we get taller, we also start seeing other changes, like pimples or body hair. It's important that you understand that these changes can happen to anyone. For example..."

I change the slide. This one shows the word hair in big, bold letters surrounded by a few illustrations of body hair on arms, legs, and faces.

"Do you guys think body hair is something that only happens to boys? Or do you think girls can have body hair, too? Yes, Melody?"

"It happens to girls, too, because I have little hairs on my arms," she says.

She rolls up her sleeve to show the other kids around her, who stare at her arm with interest.

A girl called Laura, who joined us for the workshop, perks up. "I've got those too!" She rolls up her sleeve as well. "A boy at school called me a gorilla because he said girls don't have body hair."

"That's precisely what I wanted you to learn today," I say. "Things like acne or body hair aren't specific to boys or girls; they happen to everyone. We can't control what our bodies do, so it's not nice to make fun of anyone."

We move on to acne, then periods. I also explain that boys need to show their support and understand periods are something natural and not gross. That it's not okay to laugh at someone with a period stain and that they should help them instead.

"The most important thing you need to know about your body is that it's yours," I continue, fighting the lump in my throat.

I know my mom is okay now and that she's healed from her sexual assault, but the reminder that she went through it still makes my chest cave in.

"What does that mean?" Angie asks.

"It means many things," I explain. "But it all comes down to consent. Consent means saying something is okay to happen. You can give consent when you want to, and you can absolutely say no if something doesn't feel right to you."

I show them a few ways in which they can ask for consent as well as deny it. Then, I give them one of the worksheets I printed earlier.

"To get a better understanding of what consent means in your daily life, we're going to do a quick activity called 'What Would You Do?' We're going to read some hypothetical scenarios and discuss if you'd give your consent in those situations or not, and why. Santiago, could you read the first one?"

"A family friend wants to give me a hug, but I don't like physical contact," he reads.

"Good. In that case, what would you say to your family friend?"

He clears his throat. "I'd say I don't like hugs, and I prefer handshakes."

"That's great, Santiago. But what if your family friend says that's nonsense and they'd like to give you a hug anyway?"

He thinks about it. "I'd say no again."

"They don't listen, and they want to hug you anyway," I press.

"I'd run for my mom."

The kids laugh, picturing the scenario.

I nod. "It's important not to give in just because someone asks many, many times. You need to listen to your belly voice—if it's telling you not to give someone a hug or to run away, you do exactly that. Cameron, can you read the next one?"

"My friend said they didn't want to sit next to me on the bus, and now I'm sad," he reads.

"This one is a little different," I explain. "In this case, you're not the one giving or denying consent—your friend is. They said they didn't want to sit with you, and it made you upset. What do you think the right thing to do would be, Cameron?"

His lips purse. "I think maybe my friend is upset about something and doesn't want to talk."

"It could be. Sometimes we want to be alone, and that's fine. Would you sit next to your friend and try to make them feel better, then?"

Cameron pauses, thinking about it. "They said they wanted to be alone, so...I don't think so."

"Good. That way, you'll be respecting their wishes. If someone wants your help, they'll ask for it. It's okay to ask them if they need any help, of course, but if they say no, that's it. There's no need to ask again. No is a full sentence—remember that."

By the time we're done with the worksheet, we only have a couple minutes left. I wish we could cover more topics, but I'm glad I even got to run this workshop in the first place.

"Unfortunately, we don't have time for anything else today. But if you liked this workshop and would like another one, I'm sure Reed will run one for you. Just let him know."

"Why not you?" Melody chimes in.

My smile wavers. "My internship ends tomorrow."

I'm not expecting all twenty kids to gasp in horror.

"You're leaving?" Melody shouts. "But you can't!"

"Don't tell Reed, but you're much cooler than him," says Cameron.

"Lila, you need to stay."

"You can't do this to us!"

"Ike will cry when we tell him."

"Will you come visit us?" Melody asks, sounding genuinely concerned.

And just like that, my heart shatters.

"Of course I will." *Don't cry now.* Changing topics to avoid the impending emotional breakdown in public, I tell them, "Thank you so much for coming today. I hope you learned something new. And remember, if you ever have any questions about this or anything else, the youth center is a safe place to ask them. You're free to go to the common room now."

But they don't leave. Instead, they ask me if I can give them a hug goodbye. We're still hugging one another and trying not to cry when Reed opens the door minutes later.

He doesn't look fazed by the hug fest in front of him. "Great work, guys. Can I talk to Lila for a second? You'll see her tomorrow."

It takes them another couple of minutes to leave the classroom. Reed doesn't move from the door, crossing his bulging arms in front of his chest.

"That was..." He shakes his head, making my still-aching heart jump. "I couldn't look away from the screen, Lila. Don't ever doubt you're a natural."

I feel my cheeks heating up. "You were watching?"

"We both were."

At first, I think he means Haniyah and him. She has been very vocal about her excitement for this workshop, so it wouldn't surprise me if she had been behind the screen.

What I'm not expecting at all is for my mom to walk in.

I blink once, twice, wondering if I've hit my head and I'm seeing things. "Mom? What are you doing here?"

She closes the space between us and wraps me in a tight hug. "I'm so proud of you, Li." The emotion in her voice makes me want to tear up again. "I was just telling Reed how confident you look. The kids were listening so attentively, too. They adore you."

"You liked the workshop?" I ask, emotion clogging my voice.

I'm not ashamed to admit my mom's opinion means everything to me. The fact that she's here today, watching me run a workshop on sexual education after what she went through, feels like a full-circle moment I will never forget.

She pulls away, the raw emotion in her gaze mirroring mine. "It was incredible, honey. You were born to do this job."

Who's sticking cotton balls down my throat?

My mom beckons Reed to us, who tells me they were watching the workshop live from his office this whole time.

"I've also recorded it for Haniyah to watch later," he explains.

"I know I say it all the time, but Dad and I are so proud of you, Lila," my mom adds, which isn't helping my tears situation.

We move our conversation to the front desk, where my mom gifts Haniyah and Reed some books for the library before giving me a hug goodbye. It's not until I'm petting Ginny back in Reed's office that I tell him what I've been pondering for weeks now.

"Reed?" I start.

He turns to look at me from his bookshelf. "Yeah?"

The late-fall moon shines through his office window, casting a glow over his chiseled body. Inside, only the soft glow of his lamp illuminates us.

"My internship ends tomorrow, but I'd like to come back as a volunteer if there's a spot for me."

He throws me a wink. "I thought you'd never ask."

chapter 26

LILA

A week before the Youth Counseling Expo I was miraculously accepted to—which I can't think about right now or I'll crumble under the pressure—my world shifts on its axis.

It starts one unassuming evening after leaving Mariah and Karla's apartment. My phone rings in the passenger seat as I stop my car at a red light on my way home. Reed's name flashes on my screen, and a weird feeling settles in the pit of my stomach.

He's never called me before.

"Reed?"

"Lila," he says, his voice sounding anxious and wrong. "I'm so fucking sorry. I don't know what I'm doing, why I'm even calling you—"

"Reed," I cut him off. "You can always call me. What's wrong? Where are you?"

There's a pause in which I only hear my own frantic heartbeat.

"I'm at home," he says, still agitated. The light turns green, and I make a turn toward his neighborhood. "It's... *Fuck*."

"Reed, tell me what's wrong," I tell him calmly. "There's nothing we can't fix together, all right?"

I can almost picture him running a nervous hand through his hair.

"It's Ginny. She swallowed something, and... *Fuck*. She started throwing it back up, but she was choking—"

"Is she okay?" I rush to ask, tightening my grip on the wheel.

"I don't know," he breathes out. "I think so. She's sleeping now."

I take another turn. "Just stay calm, okay? I'm on my way."

My voice doesn't betray my nerves despite my insides crumbling. Because Reed needs me, and I have to be the strong one right now.

REED

It finally happened—I almost killed her.

It was inevitable, given the DNA weaving through my veins.

For as long as I live, I will never get Ginny's choking sounds out of my head.

I will never forget the sight of her throwing up one of my socks, which looked bigger than her body, even though it wasn't.

I will never forget the fact that I stood there, frozen, not knowing what to do to help her. If trying to do something would make it worse.

I will never know why my first instinct was to call Lila instead of a goddamn vet.

You know why.

I told myself I could take care of Ginny, no matter how unprepared I was. I convinced myself the physical and mental trauma my family had put me through wouldn't resurface, that I would be able to think clearly and not let my emotions ruin a good thing.

A lie.

I told myself my feelings for Lila were just those of a noble man who's watching out for his friends' daughter. That I wouldn't fall for her kind heart, the light in her soul, the warmth of her touch.

Another lie.

The doorbell rings. I take in Ginny's sleeping form again before heading for the door.

When I open it and her worried eyes meet mine, the urge to pull her into my arms overcomes me like a tidal wave.

She's here. Everything will be okay.

She breezes past me and crouches next to Ginny's bed.

"How are you feeling, sweet baby?" she mumbles, delicately stroking her light fur.

The front door closes with a soft click, and I make my way back to the living room with my hands inside the pockets of my slacks because I don't trust myself not to touch her right now.

"What happened?" she asks me over her shoulder.

I move closer until I'm towering over Ginny and her, and I silently gesture for her to give me her coat.

"I was doing laundry when I got distracted by a work call," I explain as I put her coat away. "When I came back, Ginny was around, but I thought she was acting normal. Moments later though, she started choking. I should've been able to tell something was wrong."

She probably thinks I'm a monster. It should bring me comfort, thinking she'll finally pull away and we won't cross any more lines. Instead, it makes me want to tear the world apart.

I'm so deep in my thoughts that I don't hear Lila getting to her feet or coming closer until her soothing hand lands on my arm.

Our gazes crash, electricity soaring through my bones. For a second, I allow myself to imagine what would happen if we weren't ourselves.

If she weren't my former intern and I weren't her former supervisor.

If her parents weren't my good friends.

If I had been born into a family who had taught me what healthy, worthy love feels like from a young age.

"If she was acting normal, there was no reason for you to think anything was wrong. Sometimes puppies eat things they aren't supposed to. It wasn't your fault. She's okay now." Her voice is gentle as she adds, "You're taking great care of her, Reed."

I gulp. "I should've been more attentive. She shouldn't have been unsupervised for so long."

My head betrays me. As I stand with the woman who's stolen my heart, it takes me back to the people who broke it three decades ago.

The sharp pain of my father's belt hitting the flesh on my back again and again.

My mother watching her husband abuse her son and not doing shit about it.

You never take care of your mother, Reed. You deserve this.

Lila's warm hand lands on my cheek, bringing my attention back to her angelic face. An anchor.

"Where did you go?" she whispers, her thumb painting circles on my stubble.

I don't tell her where my mind just dragged me because I can't. Her pity isn't something I need or want.

"Reed."

But she insists.

And she does it in that way I find so fucking hard to say no to—by looking at me like I hold the whole world in my hands.

I shut my eyes because I don't trust myself to make smart choices while looking into hers. My hands turn into fists at my sides, preventing me from reaching out.

Her thumb keeps tracing that comforting pattern over my skin, posing a stark contrast to the wound on my back that burns every single time I think of my parents.

"It's okay if you don't want to talk," she says, and I know she means it. "I can tell you've been carrying some type of burden for a long time. You don't have to keep doing it anymore, okay? You're not alone, Reed. I'm here. I'll always be on your side."

When I open my eyes, I'm caught in her stare. And maybe it's a mistake, but I don't want to leave.

"What's the matter with you and Ginny?" she asks next, her voice soft.

Knowing exactly what she means, I consider not answering or even lying about it. But this is Lila, *my* Lila, and she makes me want to bare my soul in a way I never thought I'd be capable of.

So, I take a deep breath and crack my chest right open.

"I had a dog when I was a kid. Her name was Daisy." I haven't said her name out loud in thirty years. I wasn't sure I'd be able to. "She was my best friend. My only companion. When my parents argued so loudly I couldn't sleep, she cuddled up with me and made everything less painful."

Lila's smile is sad. "I bet she loved you very much."

"That's what I thought, too." I swallow past the lump in my throat. "Until she disappeared one day. Left without a trace."

Lila doesn't say a word. She keeps caressing my skin in those calm, soothing movements that keep me going. *She* keeps me going.

"My parents said she'd run away because I didn't take good care of her, so she stopped loving me. I never saw Daisy again. For years, I believed my parents. I didn't think I was capable enough to take care of anything or anyone. I understand now that it wasn't my fault, but I've never been able to close that wound. I don't fucking know why."

"That's why you were so nervous around Ginny," she says, reaching the right conclusion. When I nod, her face falls. "Oh, Reed. You were a baby back then. There's no way taking care of a dog was your sole responsibility."

My throat is dry, and it hurts when I speak. "The most logical part of me knows. The heart is another story."

"Your parents made you believe Daisy ran away because of

you?"

"My parents beat me up until social services put me in foster care, Lila."

Air whooshes out of her lungs. Her body locks into place so close to mine, I feel the tension seeping into each and every one of her muscles.

As soon as she blinks away the first tear, I feel like an asshole.

"I'm sorry," I rush to say, wiping her tears away with the pads of my thumbs. "I shouldn't have been so abrupt. Please don't—"

She throws her arms around my neck, hugging me close as the moisture in her eyes wets the bare skin on my neck.

"Tell me what happened," she manages to let out, a surprising streak of protectiveness lacing her voice.

I wrap my arms as tightly as I can around her frame. I've never felt the need to have her against me so strongly. To know she's here and we're okay.

"It's in the past," I reassure her. "I've gone to therapy, and I'm okay now."

"No, you're not," she retorts. "Ginny triggered something in you, Reed. Don't deny it. Not to me. It's okay if you're still not fully healed from something so brutal."

Ginny isn't the only one who has triggered something in me in the past few months. But she doesn't need to know that.

I pull away, still holding her close. "Do you want to know the whole story?"

She nods. "Please."

Wiping away her tears, I start.

"There's not much to tell other than the fact that my parents never wanted to become parents in the first place and had a few undiagnosed mental illnesses." My voice is surprisingly steady. "My dad used to beat me up, mainly with his belt. And my mom slapped me occasionally and didn't do anything when my dad punished me. A few insults here and there, too, but it never went further than that."

Lila gasps, horrified. "But you were a boy, Reed..."

"I was seven when it stopped," I confirm. "My parents left me alone in the house with a bleeding wound on my back and only some expired food to sustain me. They told me not to leave before they came back, so I didn't. But by the third day, I was so hungry I went to ask the neighbors across the street for something to eat. They saw the state I was in and called the police. It made the news—a whole media circus. I didn't see my parents again."

"What happened after that?" She's quiet, as if she were afraid to ask.

"Looking back, that's the moment my life shifted for the better," I tell her. "It didn't feel like that at the time, though. I felt alone and scared, but I was lucky the social worker assigned to my case was devoted to me. She made sure I had a second chance in life, and she's been looking out for me ever since."

Her eyes widen in realization. "Was your social worker...?"

"Haniyah." I nod with a small smile. It's hard not to smile when I think about the woman who gave me so much and asked for nothing in return. "She followed my case closely and always offered me all the help she could. I'd hop between foster homes— that's how I met Liam and Warren—but I never got adopted. When I left the system at eighteen, she took me under her wing and sent me to college because she knew that's what I wanted to do. The rest is history."

"I knew you two were close, but..." She pauses. "Wait. Is that why you're working on that project with the state government? The one about improving mental health care in the foster system?"

I nod again. "I know what it's like to have all the odds against you. I was lucky enough to succeed, but many children and teens in foster care don't because they don't have the tools to. I want to change that."

Her hand finds my cheek again, stroking it in that sweet way.

"You're something else, Reed."

"Something good, I hope?"

"The best thing," she mutters. "Thank you for telling me about your past. I'm so sorry you had to go through that as a kid, but if it's any consolation, you've become one of the best men I know."

Burying my feelings for her becomes an impossible task when she says things like that.

Her tongue wets her lower lip, a movement I follow closely until she asks, "Not that I didn't want you to, but why did you call me tonight?"

There's no point in denying it anymore. I've given her everything, showed her the ugliness of my past, and she's still here.

I can only hope she doesn't run away now.

"You once asked what keeps me calm," I rasp out, my fingers itching to move closer to her waist. "I called you because it's you, angel. You keep me calm."

Her breath hitches, but she doesn't pull away. She doesn't make a move to run away, doesn't show me any sign that she's suddenly uncomfortable around me.

Her thumb inches closer to my mouth just as I caress the small of her back.

"You keep me calm too," she whispers.

Our uneven breaths intertwine, our bodies inching closer.

"Yeah?"

I pull her to me, pressing her front against mine.

She gives me a small nod. "Although I'm not very calm right now."

I hum as I lean in, the tip of my nose brushing her cheek, earning me a shiver.

"Tell me how you feel," I rasp, making my way down her slender throat with my nose, breathing her in.

She smells like mine.

"Reed...?"

"Yes, angel?"

"Are you...?" Another shiver. "Are you sure we should be doing this?"

But she doesn't make a move to stop me, and I don't pull away.

And when my lips brush the sensitive skin on her collarbone—that one spot I've ogled a million times with a primal kind of hunger—she makes a little noise at the back of her throat I've only heard in my most forbidden fantasies.

"Do you want me to stop?" I mutter against her skin.

"No," she breathes out, pulling me closer by the back of my neck.

That's my girl.

I take my time breathing her in, savoring her intakes of breath and the delicious way she arches her back. Slowly, I drag my lips from her collarbone to her neck, to her jaw, to her cheek.

And then I stop.

A choice.

I can close the gap between our lips and taste her like I didn't get to last time, make her feel what she does to me. Or I can do the responsible thing and remind myself she might not be my intern anymore, but she's still my friends' much younger daughter, and I will only hurt her.

In the end, my heart leads the way.

A breath later, our lips collide, and I recognize her touch as if we'd kissed a thousand times before. My chest expands, her light slipping through the cracks I never thought would be mended.

It starts out slow, tentative. Nothing more than a peck we're too scared to turn into more. But unlike last time, she parts her lips, and my tongue meets hers.

The thin rope holding on to my restraint snaps with no

chance of redemption.

She pulls me closer by the collar of my shirt, sighing against my mouth like she's been waiting ages to do this. Because I have, I cradle her face with both of my hands gently, so at odds with the way we're devouring each other.

Mine, mine, mine.

When we pull away, breathless, I'm the one who hoists her up until her legs are wrapped around my middle.

I'm the one who pushes her against the nearest wall, cradling the back of her head so she doesn't get hurt.

I'm the one who bridges the distance between us once more, as if I'll never get to kiss her again. My other hand rests on her waist as she holds my face, deepening the kiss neither of us should've started.

"Reed," she whimpers, pulling away. The sight of her red, puffy lips makes me want to kiss her again, repeatedly, until I run out of air. "We should stop."

My breaths are labored. "All right."

A beat passes, and her lips are on mine again.

Passion ignites at the pit of my stomach, then climbs all the way to my chest. We kiss furiously but tenderly all at once, because we're running out of time. Because the second she leaves my house tonight, I won't get to have her like this again.

How can I miss someone I'm holding in my arms right now?

"Fuck, Lila," I grunt, pressing my hard-on against her softness. Her breath hitches, and my cock jumps. "Look what you do to me, angel. Do you feel it?"

A throaty sound escapes her before she rubs herself against me like the little minx she is. My grip on her waist tightens; I want to mark her but know she isn't mine to claim.

As much as I feel like hers, as much as she feels like mine, she can't be.

I kiss her again, slower this time, before carefully setting her back on the ground. Twenty minutes or twenty hours could've passed. Time stops when I'm around her.

The air around us shifts, stiffens, like we momentarily forgot who we are to each other, and it all comes back now.

"That was..." She runs her fingers through the new tangles in her hair, lowering her gaze to the ground. "It can't happen again."

It takes everything in me to nod. "Okay."

"I mean it this time," she says in a firmer voice, looking up at me. "It'd be too complicated."

I won't argue with her on that one. It's not only her credibility as a student that is at risk, but the continuation of my project as well. And while she's my priority, I can't deny that saving my own ass is important too. If we get caught, my position as a researcher at Warlington University would be as good as dead, along with my involvement in the project.

And that project needs to go through. I haven't devoted decades to my education to throw it all away now.

"Promise me something, though," I say.

At the end of the day, this is Lila. This is the woman who has woken something in me I thought forever gone, and I don't want to lose her over this—or anything else.

"Don't get awkward around me now, little criminal. All right?"

Her smirk gives me the tiniest bit of hope. And maybe it's a lie, all wishful thinking, but when she says, "I said you'd never get rid of me, remember?" I choose to believe her.

chapter 27

LILA

I kissed my former internship supervisor. A professor at the university I've still not graduated from. My mom's co-worker. My parents' good friend. A man twelve years my senior.

And I don't feel one bit sorry about it.

But I do feel like my dad is reading my mind right now and isn't too happy with what he sees.

"Can you grab the parmesan from the fridge?" he asks, sending me a weird look over his shoulder. Or maybe it's just a normal look, but the guilt is making me see things.

My feet move on autopilot as I grab the cheese and walk back to where my dad is getting the lasagna ready to go in the oven. "Here you go," I tell him absentmindedly.

Because there's only room in my head for the feel of Reed's lips devouring mine, his hands holding me with a mix of possession and tenderness I'd never felt before, the sounds—

"Li."

Shit.

"I'm listening," I rush out.

My dad sends me a knowing look. "Is that why you gave me a pack of shredded mozzarella instead of the parmesan I asked for? Because you were listening?"

Nerves swirl in my stomach, and I don't trust myself to answer. Instead, I grab the stupid mozzarella and put it back in the fridge, passing him the parmesan this time.

My aunt Maddie and I always joke that my mom must have some kind of psychic powers she's been keeping from us because she always knows what's up just by looking at us. Judging by the intense way my dad is glancing at me now, I'd argue her powers have finally rubbed off on him after almost three decades of marriage.

"When did Mom say she was coming home?" I ask, a poor attempt at distracting him.

He starts grating the parmesan on the lasagna. "She just texted me she's on her way."

My parents have never been big party people—my dad doesn't even drink alcohol—but my mom's editor at the publishing house called her earlier to grab a few drinks downtown with other colleagues, and she said yes.

Her Saturday night plans are far more interesting than mine, which isn't that hard in the first place. It isn't exactly a competition with a twenty-four-year-old who has sworn off men and parties in order to graduate with the best possible results, but now that she's pretty much done, she still can't find it within herself to go out.

"You seem out of it today."

He eyes me in the same way my mom does when she knows something she shouldn't. Which is why I tell him, "Just thinking about the Youth Counseling Expo."

It's not a total lie. Since my thesis got accepted, I've been drafting a shorter version for my presentation. Now that I think about it, I should probably email it to Reed for feedback. That thought isn't making my palms sweat at all.

Karla wasn't accepted, and she seemed pretty upset about it, so I avoid talking about it when I'm with her. She said she was happy for me, but I still don't want to make her feel bad. I know it was important for her.

"That's coming up soon, right?" he asks as he puts the

lasagna in the oven and sets up the timer.

When I told my parents about the conference, they were excited for me but sad because they wouldn't be able to attend. The moment I told them Reed would be there, though, they instantly relaxed.

"He'll look out for you," my dad had said.

I wonder if he would relax this much if he knew what happened between us last night.

"I'm just worried because it was such a sudden thing," he adds, wiping off the counter as I watch from the kitchen island. I'm too fidgety to help without dropping everything. "Your paper got accepted quickly, almost as if they were waiting for you to apply. Are you nervous?"

I shrug. "A little, but I'm trying to be less dramatic. This conference is important but not decisive for my future, you know?"

"It may not be decisive, but you should take it seriously. You never know who's watching." He doesn't sound angry when he says it, just his usual worried self.

"And here I was, considering wearing a swimsuit onstage and chewing gum while I did my presentation."

His tattooed knuckles rub my head, making me chuckle.

"I swear, you and Maddie will be the death of me with all that attitude," he says, referring to my aunt, whose sass I'm pretty sure I inherited somehow.

We stay silent for the next few minutes, my dad looking at something on his phone and me watching the oven because I can't concentrate on anything else other than last night.

What would've happened if I hadn't told him to stop? Would we have ended up in his bed?

"Hey, Li?"

I jump, pretty sure my cheeks are burning hot.

My dad is right there, and I'm thinking about sleeping with his friend. Classy.

"Mmm."

"Do you want the shop?"

My heart stops.

"What?"

I must be still inside this Reed-induced mental fog. Because, surely, my dad's not saying...

"Do you want Inkjection?" he repeats.

My mouth opens and closes once, twice, but no words come out. Because what the hell is he saying right now?

Is this about the retirement Mariah told me about?

Needing to make sure my brain isn't making stuff up, I ask him very carefully, enunciating every word, "Are you asking me if I want the tattoo shop?"

He nods, confirming my suspicions.

"And do *what* with it, Dad?" My voice doesn't sound accusatory, only confused. He's lost his mind—must be all those gray hairs he insists my aunt and I are responsible for.

He shrugs. "I don't know. Sell it. Find new management. Your call."

My dad has lost it. One thousand percent.

"Dad, what's going on?" I ask, fearing his answer.

Because my best friend might have warned me already, but I'm not ready to hear it from him.

"Nothing's wrong, but I'm not getting any younger. You didn't expect me to work until I dropped dead, did you?"

"Of course not, but..."

"I was thinking of retiring next year. In the summer, maybe."

I knew this, so why am I freaking out?

"Okay" is all I can give him.

My dad has been a tattoo artist since I was born. I even tattooed him once when I was five, a little heart on his wrist he swears is his favorite tattoo. He doesn't look a day older than fifty, and he's in great shape. His health is good, too, so there's no reason for me to think this is the end of the world.

And yet.

He waves a tattooed hand in front of my eyes, a hint of laughter in his voice. "You there?"

"Yeah, yeah. It's just... I wasn't expecting you to say that."

He gives me a sympathetic look. "Sorry if it caught you off guard. I just think it's time to step back and let the new generation take over. I'm proud of everything I've done with the shop. I'll still be around because tattooing will forever be part of me, but..."

I nod my understanding. "But you don't want to be there every day. I get that."

"It's not that I've fallen out of love with this work—I never could." He runs a hand over his dark hair. "I've been busting my ass since I was fifteen, learning the ropes. Then I opened Inkjection, and I haven't stopped working because I love it, but also because I had a family to support. Now that Maddie has her own ballet studio and you're on your way to becoming a badass youth counselor"—I snort at that—"I feel like it's the perfect time to take a step back. Mom and I want to travel a bit, relax more. I've been dying to go on a cruise for years now. Need to see for myself that a bowling alley really fits inside a ship, y'know?"

Nobody deserves a break more than my parents. They fought hard to make a name for themselves—my dad in tattooing and my mom in publishing. They raised my aunt when her own parents couldn't, and then they raised me with nothing but love and support.

I round the kitchen island to wrap my arms around his middle, settling my head on top of his heart. He envelops me in one of his signature bear hugs, and I chuckle when my feet leave the ground.

"I think that's a great idea, Dad." I smile up at him once he sets me back down. "You deserve a break. I was just not expecting to have this conversation right now, that's all. Although Mariah did mention something not long ago."

"I could've tried a gentler approach," he admits. "But the offer still stands. If you want the shop, it's yours. And if you don't want it, that's fine too. I just wanted to talk to you before making a decision."

"What does Uncle Trey think?"

"He wants to retire, too. We'll do it at the same time." He scratches his stubbled chin. "We've talked about the future of the shop since he's a co-owner now, but he's happy with whatever I decide. He knows it'll be for the best."

A thought creeps into my head, one that makes too much sense. "Dad, what if you—"

"I'm home!"

My dad kisses the top of my head just as footsteps start down the hallway.

"We'll finish this conversation later," he tells me. "I don't want you to worry. Tunnel vision until you nail your presentation at the conference, okay?"

I'm thinking that said tunnel vision isn't exactly working anyway because I can't get his friend out of my mind, when the devil himself walks into my kitchen right behind my mom.

"Hey, Reed," my dad greets him, giving him a friendly slap on the back and not sounding even the slightest bit surprised he's here. "How's it going?"

"Not too bad," the man in question answers, glancing at me for the briefest second before looking away. "Smells good in here."

"I'm not ashamed to admit my husband is the better cook out of the two of us," my mom chimes in before getting on her tiptoes to kiss my dad. She turns to me. "Hi, honey. Are you joining us for dinner?"

Dinner with my parents and their friend who I kissed less than twenty-four hours ago? Sure—I'm a sucker for pain and awkward situations.

"Sure," I say, hoping my tight-lipped smile doesn't look too freaked out.

Don't get awkward around me now, little criminal.

That's what Reed told me last night before I went back home, yet he's the one not acknowledging me now. He's the one who walked through the door and didn't even say hello, despite me being right here.

Standing around in the kitchen, my dad asks him about Ginny, to which Reed answers she's alone at home, but he purchased this fancy camera so he can watch her through his phone. Then they launch into an animated conversation about dog care, and I excuse myself to set the table while my mom disappears upstairs to get changed.

I have no clue as to why Reed is in my house on a Saturday night, the day after kissing me against a wall. But if he isn't interested in acknowledging me, then fine. Two can play this game.

When my mom comes down the stairs, she walks up to me and kisses my cheek. "Did you have a good day today?"

I make a noncommittal sound at the back of my throat. "How about you? How's Dianne?" I ask, referring to her editor.

"She's doing well. Prepping for a big publishing conference they have coming up." 'Tis the season for conferences, it seems. She lets out a long, tired sigh. "I don't miss going out, though. We've only been out for a couple hours, and I was ready to come home in the first ten minutes."

I chuckle. I'm my mother's daughter, no doubt. "Was it the Christmas party?"

"Kind of. It was more of an informal thing, just a few of us," she explains. "I'm surprised Reed agreed to go out with us. He's even more of a hermit than I am."

My lips tingle with the phantom touch of his kiss.

"Yeah," I mutter, betraying myself and casting a quick glance at Reed and my dad chatting in the kitchen. "Why is he here?"

"Li," my mom hisses. "Don't be rude."

"I didn't mean it like that," I say truthfully. "I'm just curious."

She looks at me for a moment too long that has me freaking out. Psychic powers.

"I invited him because he's our friend," she finally says. "But also to thank him for everything he's done for you over the past few months."

I'm about to be sick.

"He was just doing his job," I mutter.

"I know that. Still, I want to thank him for taking such good care of you."

Am I seeing things, or is my mom implying something that has nothing to do with the professional relationship between Reed and me?

There's no way she knows I kissed him.

But what if Reed told her?

No. He doesn't have a death wish.

"Why are you asking? Did something happen?" she asks in a low voice, a hint of something in her voice, which is enough to make my head spin.

She knows.

"Not particularly," I lie. "I wasn't expecting company, but I don't mind him."

"I'd assume so, seeing how much time you're spending with him now."

I'm so busted.

The urge to give up this charade, throw myself into my mom's arms, and tell her everything is almost too strong to resist. Luckily, clarity hits me first—no matter how much my parents like him, I don't know how they'll react to us being that close. I don't need to put my master's to use to guess they won't take it too well, considering the warning my dad gave me in the car not long ago.

So, I smile at my mom, channeling the purest picture of innocence, and say, "I'm going to help Dad with the salad."

I leave before she can say anything else, straight into the wolf's den.

My dad ruffles my hair as I pass him by in the kitchen, and I make a point not to make eye contact with Reed because I'm petty. Mom joins their conversation a moment later, all while I pretend to be immersed in the art of salad making. That is, until a presence looms at my back, making my senses tingle.

"Are you going to ignore me all night, little criminal?"

I bite my lower lip, taking advantage of the fact that my back is turned.

"Funny how you seem to be on the exact same mission, Dr. Abner."

Is that a grunt?

His fingers brush my hip, making me jump. I look behind me, not wanting my dad to commit a murder tonight, but my parents are engrossed in conversation at the dining room table, not paying us attention.

Reed leans in until his breath is caressing my ear. "I don't like it when you ignore me."

I glance at him over my shoulder as he steps back. "Is this the game we're playing now?"

"I have no idea what you mean."

But his eyes hold a challenge in them. One I'm eager to accept.

REED

I'm playing with fucking fire.

But the desire to get burned scorches my last traces of

common sense, so instead of retreating to the dining room with Grace and Cal, I stay with their daughter in the kitchen.

We work in a comfortable silence, the fire burning hotter in my veins every time I brush against her as we move in the kitchen, every time a whiff of her sweet scent wraps around my lungs, every time she brushes back a strand of blonde hair that falls out of her bun.

Enthralled—that's what I am by this woman. To the goddamn bone.

Minutes feel like hours when I can't touch her like my body is begging to. We both agreed last night couldn't happen again, and I had fully intended on respecting those wishes because Lila is right—this could get very complicated. I know it, too. But then I walked into her home, her light beckoning me, and all that resolve went out the window.

I feel like I'll suffocate if I don't kiss her again.

"How's the puppy?" Grace asks me as we dive into our food a while later. "Lila showed me a picture the other day, and she seems to be getting bigger."

"She's doing well. Loves daycare, surprisingly," I tell her.

"Surprising to you, maybe." Lila gives me a taunting smirk. "I knew she'd love it."

My own lips tilt. "Not all of us can be a puppy guru, I suppose."

Grace's gaze pinballs between us. "What's that about?"

"Your daughter is great with dogs, apparently."

Lila walks right into my bait. "*Apparently*? Put some respect on my name."

"Li," her mom chastises.

I pick up my glass of water. "It's fine. I can handle her."

Grace chuckles, my own smile widening until I feel it.

Lila's socked foot is rubbing my shin under the table, moving farther up until it rests on my lap.

My movements come to a halt. The rim of my glass is pressed to my lips, but I can't drink from it because she chooses that moment to inch closer to my groin.

Fucking hell.

I clear my throat. "This lasagna is delicious, Cal."

Lila presses her foot into my flesh, not directly onto my groin but close enough to make the blood start pumping in my lower area. Clearly, the fact that her parents are sitting right here doesn't faze her.

I both respect and fear her.

Cal smirks. "What can I say? Talent runs in my veins."

Lila rolls her eyes, her foot moving back and forth in a slow, taunting way. She wants to kill me. "Love your humbleness, Dad."

"Just speaking facts."

"Sure, honey." Grace shares a knowing look with Lila as she squeezes her husband's arm.

Maybe it should make me feel some type of way to be around a structured family that loves one another, but I've always felt welcomed here. And I like that Lila grew up with so much love, even if it shaped her into the little minx she is today.

A minx that is driving me insane.

I grab her foot under the table, halting her exploration of my thigh. When I dare to look at her, her teasing smirk manages to make me even harder. She doesn't make a move to free herself from my grip, and I don't release her either.

The conversation changes to Cal's day at the tattoo parlor, and the man who wanted his forehead tattooed. Lila wiggles her toes, trying to get away. I only let go when it becomes too suspicious that I'm keeping a hand under the table.

Luckily for my sanity, she doesn't attempt any more rubbings. And by the time I help Grace bring all the dishes back into the kitchen, my hard-on is under control.

"I should get going," I tell Grace as I finish loading the dishwasher. "I'm not sure how much longer Ginny will last without peeing all over my hardwood floors."

She chuckles. "Fair enough." Then she pauses, cleaning her hands with a dry towel. "Reed?"

"Yeah?"

Her gaze pinballs from me to Lila, who's still in the dining room, so quickly I might have imagined it. She shakes her head. "Forget it."

"No, you can tell me."

She shakes her head again. "It's okay."

"Grace. Come on."

"I promise it's nothing." The smile she gives me isn't as sincere as her usual ones. "Thank you for coming tonight. I'll see you next week?"

She clearly won't tell me a thing, so I drop it. Instead, I give her a parting hug and say goodbye to Cal.

"I'm going upstairs," Lila tells her parents before following me to the door.

Instead of walking up the stairs, though, she stays behind as I grab my jacket. The entrance is bathed in darkness, and we can hear her parents' voices coming from the kitchen, which gives me the dangerous impression that we're alone. When she arches a playful eyebrow at me, I know she's thinking the same.

"That's what you get for ignoring me tonight." She gives me the most fake-innocent smile known to mankind.

My cock responds to it.

"You're sure you want to poke the bear?" I ask her, my voice low.

She takes a step closer, then another, and another, until her chest is brushing mine. Her index finger travels the length from my chest to my lower stomach at a slow, torturous pace.

I hold my breath, anticipating her next move with a kind of hunger I'd never felt before her.

And then Lila leans in and whispers, "I want it more than anything."

chapter 28

LILA

Is this what it feels like to lose my mind?

Maybe rubbing his leg under the table with my foot was a step too far—no pun intended. But I feel like I'm on fire every time I'm in the same room with the one man I should never have fallen for, and I don't know how to cope.

Despite the forward way in which I came on to him during dinner at my parents' house a week ago, my confidence depletes once I calm down and realize getting involved with Reed could have very real career-ending consequences.

After all, until I graduate, I'm still a student at the university he works at. And even so, I will always be *that one student he supervised during her internship*. The rumors would follow us forever.

So, the week after the dinner with my parents, I keep my attraction for him locked away in the tiniest crevice of my heart, hoping it withers.

But then Reed picks up Ginny in his arms, and she licks his face.

And he helps the girls at the youth center with their bracelets even though his fingers are too big for the task.

And he plays racing cars with Ike in the common room.

Every time I'm confident my feelings are under control, Reed smiles at me or brushes my arm as he passes by or just stands near me. It's torture.

My feelings for Reed finally take the back burner the day before the Youth Counseling Expo as I squirm in the too-small airplane seat and try not to think too hard about the dozen ways I could die in this tin can.

Reed places his backpack between his legs, which barely fit in the middle seat. "Nervous flier?"

The plane, rolling toward the runway, makes a squeaky sound I'm pretty confident it shouldn't be making. My palms get sweatier. "Mmm."

"I didn't know you had flight anxiety."

I keep my gaze trained out of the window; these might be my last moments looking at solid ground, so I might as well soak everything in.

Dramatic much?

"More like flight panic." I shift on my seat again. "I hate airplanes."

"Well, we can't exactly road-trip to Chicago and get there on time now," he says, his voice thoughtful. "You should've told me sooner."

That makes me turn my head. The seats are so cramped up together, his face is mere inches away from mine. "What for? It's not like you would have driven me fourteen hours to Chicago."

"Of course I would have."

My heart jumps. And this time, it has nothing to do with the plane.

"Don't be ridiculous," I mutter. But the worst part is, I believe him.

The overhead announcement telling us we should prepare for takeoff interrupts whatever he's going to say next.

For the millionth time, I check that my seat belt is fastened and count to ten in my head, a failed attempt to calm my anxiety. People always say airplanes are the safest mode of transport, but realistically, how likely am I to survive a plane crash? I mean, I can't fly. However, if I were in a car crash, maybe I could limp away from the scene and get—

"Lila."

"Mmm."

"You're hyperventilating."

I'm not looking at him, but I can feel the hesitation to say more radiating off him as the plane aligns with the runway. These could be my last moments on earth, and I'm wasting them by being dramatic—how fitting.

"As a kid, I'd get anxious all the time when my parents had their screaming matches."

That grabs my attention.

Since the night we kissed, Reed hasn't brought up his past again. I didn't want to pry in case he wasn't ready to talk about it; maybe opening up to me had been a onetime thing. But he's giving me an in now. He's willingly talking about it.

All airplane noises disappear. I only hear Reed's voice, see those dark eyes, breathe in his clean scent.

"Was it really bad?" I ask, my voice quiet.

There's no one on the aisle seat, and the plane isn't too crowded in the first place, so it feels like a private conversation.

"It was a nightmare." His eyes don't leave mine. "The first few times it happened I'd sneak out to see what was going on. My mom would throw glasses at my dad, shattering them against the wall. My dad would put his hands on my mom. I'll spare you the details."

I swallow. "I'm so sorry you had to go through that. No child should."

The plane moves. The ghost of his hand brushes mine.

"It's in the past now." But I can tell it still haunts him. His eyes can't lie to me. "Do you want to know what I'd do to fall back asleep?"

My breath hitches as the plane starts accelerating down the

runway. My fingers are on a mission to crush the armrest when Reed's hand covers mine. Forgetting where I am for a blissful second, I watch him in silence as he flips my hand and laces his fingers with mine.

Thump, thump, thump.

"My dog, Daisy, would climb into bed with me, and I'd bury my face in her fur," he rumbles. "Cuddling her soothed me enough to fall back asleep."

My heart breaks just wondering what his parents might have done to his childhood dog, only to then blame it on him.

My smile is nervous but sincere. "I bet Daisy gave the best cuddles."

"She did," he confirms. "She isn't here to calm your flight anxiety, but I am."

My pulse quickens.

"Come here, angel."

My body floats as the plane takes off. I tell myself that's the only reason I don't think twice as I lift the armrest between us and bury my face in his collarbone, shutting my eyes for all sorts of different reasons.

Because the plane could drop at any second.

Because I don't ever want to let go of Reed.

Because I don't know why he calls me angel, but my heart flutters every time he does.

Because I've been dying to be this close to him again since the night we kissed.

Reed holds me tightly as the plane speeds through the clouds. Right now, I don't care who's watching. If other passengers think I'm being dramatic, I'm not worried about it.

I've never felt safer than I do in Reed's arms.

"You okay?" His breath tickles my ear. The hand that was around my shoulders moves to tangle in my hair. "I'm no Daisy, but I could hug you a little tighter if you want."

THE DEEPEST END OF LOVE

I nod against his chest, and he brings me closer.

I don't pull away until the seat belt lights go off, but then I instantly miss the warmth of his body against mine.

"Thank you," I mumble, pretty sure that my cheeks are burning hot. "Daisy must have been a genius, because that helped a lot."

His smile is devastating. "I'm glad. Let me know if my hugging services are required again during the flight."

I blame my possibly impending death by plane crash for my next move. I cover his big palm, now resting on his thigh, with my much smaller one and lace my fingers with his. When he raises an eyebrow at me, I shrug. "My flight anxiety counts as an emergency. I'd normally text you, but.."

His nod is serious, following along. "Sure. Feel free to hold my hand for the next three hours."

"Can you not remind me how long this flight is? I'm anxious enough as it is."

He flips my hand again, taking charge, and rubs a soothing pattern on my skin with his thumb. "I should keep doing this, then."

Is he flirting with me?

"Oh, definitely."

Am I flirting right back?

At thirty-five thousand feet in the air, neither of us seems to care about the boundaries we set that night. First at the dinner table and now again, I realize I can't fight the magnetic pull between us anymore. I don't *want* to.

If we're going to break the rules, we might as well do it in Chicago, thousands of miles away from home. In the shadows, where our decisions seem to have no consequences.

꩜

By the time we get to the hotel where the Youth Counseling Expo is taking place, I'm positively exhausted.

After getting our bags and checking on Ginny—Haniyah is dog sitting this weekend—Reed arranged a car to take us to the hotel. The lobby is filled with academics I recognize from watching countless talks online, and I actually have to take a moment to come to terms with the fact that I'll be sharing the spotlight with them this weekend. *Me.*

"Nervous?" Reed asks when he notices me looking around frantically.

"Not as much as I'm excited," I tell him truthfully. "Be honest with me. How likely am I to do my presentation in front of any of these people? Because I recognize most of them, and I'm kinda freaking out."

He shifts on his feet, crossing his arms. We've kept our hands to ourselves since we left the airport, and it's not too hard to understand why—to these people, we're a professor and student traveling together.

"Your presentation only overlaps with other graduate students', so it's highly possible." My stomach jumps and then drops. "There may be a whisper or two about how incredible this Lila Callaghan, future counselor is."

"Shut up," I hiss.

"Don't shoot the messenger. I'm only telling you what's being talked about in my circles."

"There's no way any of these people know who I am."

"A student who has published several articles before graduating isn't exactly common. Of course they have heard of you."

I shake my head, moving with the queue. "Nope. I don't believe it."

"I would never lie to you, Lila."

It's the way he says it, so full of conviction, that makes me want to hug him again.

The queue moves again. "Great. Now I'm more nervous than excited."

"I'm having dinner with a few colleagues tonight, but I can help you go over your notes before then," he offers. "Or tomorrow morning, before your presentation. Whatever you need, I'm here."

"Thank you, but I've got it." A forty percent, maybe. "I'll call Mariah to get my mind off things. Go for a walk around the block. There's a gym at the hotel too; I looked it up."

His hand lands on the small of my back for the briefest second as he guides me forward. "Text me if you need me, all right?" he insists. "You're not alone in this."

I look up at him and offer a small smile, unable to say anything else.

Because what are you supposed to say to the man you're falling in love with?

Once we check in and they give us a key to our respective rooms, I tell him I'll take a shower and go to bed early, which doesn't stop him from offering his help again. But I don't want to bother him if he has plans, no matter how badly the nerves start eating at me as the hours go by.

It's past dinnertime when my phone buzzes as I'm finishing up my nightly skin-care routine.

> **Reed: Everything all right? You haven't texted me all evening.**

> **Me: No emergencies so far.**

That might be a bit of a lie—my stomach has been in knots since he told me I'll have all eyes on me during my presentation tomorrow.

> **Reed: Are you sure you don't need anything? Just ask, and I'll give it to you.**

The most insane, derailed thought crosses my mind after reading his text.

He's been more affectionate with me since the night of our kiss. We said it couldn't happen again, but what if—

No. Don't be insane.

> **Me: I'm sure. Thanks for asking though :)**

> **Me: How was your dinner?**

> **Reed: Uneventful. I missed a certain someone pestering me under the table.**

My breathing comes to a halt. Is he actually bringing it up? There's a slight tremble to my hands as I type out a response.

> **Me: There won't be any tables involved, but I can pester you now if you're not too tired.**

> **Reed: Shame about the tables. I'll be there in five.**

Holy shit.
He's coming here.

I glance at my reflection in the mirror—I'm met with clean skin, my hair pulled back in a low pony, and very short sleep shorts paired with an old baggy T-shirt that has seen better days. But it's not like I expected any late-night visits during this trip— even though I secretly hoped it would happen—so I didn't pack anything sexier.

What am I even saying?

Reed wouldn't care if I wore sexy sleeping clothes or not. That's what I keep telling myself for the next five minutes. But when Reed knocks on my door and I open it to reveal him wearing a white dress shirt unbuttoned at the neck and dark slacks, my brain stops responding.

"Hey, angel."

chapter 29

REED

I sat through two hours of monotonous conversations with my phone burning in my pocket until I couldn't take it anymore and texted her.

Throughout dinner, I couldn't stop thinking about her. About how I'd much rather be spending my time with her. About how I ached to hold her again, to bring her comfort like I did on the plane.

Lila said she was going to bed early ahead of her presentation tomorrow, so I wasn't expecting a reply. What I was expecting was for common sense to knock me over because flirting with my former intern over text is probably a death sentence waiting to happen.

That didn't stop me from leaving my colleagues at the hotel's restaurant without a solid explanation and knocking at her door as soon as she texted me back. And it sure doesn't stop me from appreciating the smooth skin of her bare legs in those sinful shorts when she opens the door now.

"Hey, angel." The nickname slips out before I can stop myself.

Her smirk is nothing short of taunting. "Was the emergency that you were bored?"

The emergency was that I couldn't go another second without being near you.

"Sure was."

Lila opens the door wider. "Come on in, then. Let me entertain you with the last steps of my skin-care routine."

I shut the door behind me before following her to the bathroom. "A great Friday night plan, if you ask me."

She throws me a glare over her shoulder. "Don't sass me, or I won't let you watch."

"Wouldn't dream of it." I put my hands up in surrender as I take a seat on the edge of the tub, behind the vanity, where all sorts of different face creams and serums are sprawled out in some kind of order I don't understand. "Watching you is my favorite activity."

She smirks, looking at me through the mirror. "Watching me do what, exactly?"

"Anything."

"I need you to elaborate."

"Not happening."

She shakes her head. "Coward."

If you only knew.

Lila shifts her attention to her serums. As I watch her, I wish I'd be brave enough to tell her how mesmerizing her every move is. How being around her has become my favorite thing. How we could watch paint dry together, and I wouldn't get bored.

That thought alone scares me to death.

After what my parents put me through, I promised myself I would live my life relationship-free, without committing to or attaching myself to anyone. I've had my fair share of hookups over the years and even some attempts at a few relationships after college that didn't last long because I couldn't take the pressure of being someone else's rock. But every time I convince myself to pull away, she smiles at me, and I come undone again.

She fills the silence between us. "You're quiet."

I rest my elbows on my knees. "It's been a long day."

"You can go back to your room if you're tired," she offers,

spraying her face with some kind of mist. "You also have your presentation tomorrow."

"I'm not worried about it."

My answer gets me a playful roll of her eyes. "Must be nice, knowing people will be in awe of you no matter what you do or say."

"It's not like that." She sends me a pointed look. "All right, it may be a bit like that. I've worked my ass off for it, though."

"That's true." Her ponytail comes undone next, and she grabs a hairbrush. "Can I ask you something?"

"Go ahead."

She bites the side of her cheek, unsure, as she starts brushing her hair. "Was it hard, going to college and graduating all by yourself? You said you never got adopted, right?"

Her question takes me aback, but I find it surprisingly easy to answer.

"I was able to afford it with grants, but since I also had to cover off-campus housing—just a small studio—I had to find a job pretty early on," I tell her. Nobody knows this about me aside from Liam, Warren, and Haniyah, I realize. "I worked at a car repair shop part-time and bartended on the weekends.

"I'm sure you know how it goes, but because Haniyah had been my social worker, it was frowned upon to be so involved in a past case's life. But she helped me as much as she could behind the scenes—she found several grants for me, helped me apply, and her husband owned the car shop I worked at." I shift on the edge of the tub. "I wouldn't be where I am today if it weren't for her. She's like a mother to me."

Lila's smile is compassionate. "That was very generous of her. And I'm glad she's always been in your life despite the circumstances that got her there."

My mind takes me back to the first day I met Haniyah, less than twenty-four hours after my parents were taken away by the authorities. I remember her calming voice, her reassuring smile, that weird gut feeling telling me I could trust her.

And it's that same gut feeling that makes me stand from the edge of the tub and close the distance between Lila and me. The warmth of her body beckons mine, but I stop myself before I do something we wouldn't come back from.

Instead, I hold out my hand. "Can I?"

She frowns, confused. "You want to brush my hair?"

My fingers graze hers as I grab her brush. "I'll settle for brushing your hair."

As I'm careful to not hurt her when I find any knots, I realize I don't have a fucking clue why I'm doing this in the first place—all I know is that taking care of her like this feels right. That I'm tired of fighting my instincts.

She glances at my reflection in the mirror, her eyes glinting with interest. "Settle? What does that mean?"

My hand brushes the side of her neck.

"It means I want to do more, but I won't."

Our eyes lock in the mirror, invisible strings pulling us closer.

"Maybe I don't want you to settle for just brushing my hair."

I take a step closer. One more, and I would be pressed against her. One more, and she'd feel exactly what being near her does to me.

"We said it couldn't happen again," I remind her.

"We're acknowledging that night, I see."

I brush the last few strands of her hair and set the brush on the marble counter. Instead of stepping back, I place my hands on both sides of her, caging her in. In the mirror, her cheeks have acquired that cherry-red color I love so damn much.

"That night was a mistake," I say.

"I know."

Neither of us sounds like we believe it.

"It would be irresponsible if it happened again," I add, my voice low.

Lila presses her back to my front, my hardness digging into her lower back. "Absolutely."

"Lila," I grit out, my hand settling on her hip. "It's not a good idea."

"You're right," she whispers. "It's a terrible one."

When she presses against me a little harder, the fleeting grip I have on my sanity snaps once again.

I flip her around, grab her hips, and lift her up until she's sitting on the vanity. Pressing my forehead against hers, my voice comes out rough when I whisper, "You want to do this? Then let's fucking do this. Tell me what you need, angel, and it's yours."

Breathing heavily, she licks her lips. "Touch me, Reed."

Fucking hell.

"Where?" One of my hands lands on her bare thigh, leaving goosebumps in its wake. "Here?"

She shakes her head, looking up at me with a mixture of lust and innocence that drives me insane.

"Guide my hand where you want it."

Electricity seeps into my skin when she touches me. Slowly, she guides my hand to her warm core, right above the flimsy fabric of her sleep shorts. She lets out a small, breathy whine as she presses my hand to her center. "Right here."

I shut my eyes, not moving an inch. "Lila."

"Yeah?"

"Tell me to stop," I grit out, a desperate plea for her to do what I can't.

"No." I feel her cupping my cheek, her thumb playing with my lower lip. "I need you, Reed. I need you so badly, it hurts."

"Not fair." I bite her thumb—softly, not to hurt her. "You know I can't say no to you."

"Then don't."

But I still don't move. Her thumb on my lips, my hand between her legs, and I don't move.

Closing the slim distance between us, she pecks my lips. A brief, sweet kiss that makes my head spin.

And when she whispers, "I want to feel you stretching me out," I fucking lose it.

I take her mouth with my mine, finally breathing her in again. She wraps her arms around my neck, then her legs, urging me to get closer, to take her, to make her mine. But I won't—not like she's begging me to. Not yet.

I find the hem of her shorts and pull them down her legs, her panties coming off with them. Her T-shirt is so big it covers the lower area of her body, and I slowly inch closer until my thumb is pressed to her wet core, which elicits a whimper from the woman in my arms.

"You're soaked," I rasp out, moving my thumb in circles. She's panting, breathless, unable to answer with actual words. "How many times have you been this wet for me, sweetheart?"

When she whines again, I press my thumb a little harder until she gives me the answer I'm looking for. "Too many," she admits. "I touch myself thinking of you."

My cock hardens behind my zipper. "Fucking hell, Lila."

"What? Like you don't?"

I shut my eyes, collecting her wetness. "More times than I can fucking count."

Breathless, she says, "I feel so empty, Reed. I need your fingers inside me."

Those words alone are enough to almost make me come undone.

I'm not ready for her tightness as I try to push my middle finger inside of her and find resistance. "*Hell*," I grunt.

She shifts on the counter. "S-Sorry. It's been a while."

"Don't apologize. Never for this." I press my lips to her

forehead. "I'll go slow. I've got you."

The reminder that someone else has been inside her before me is enough to make the most possessive, primal part of me erupt. I push a little farther, careful not to hurt her.

"No one else gets to touch you like this anymore," I grunt. "No one but me. Understood?"

She nods, breathless. "Only you, Reed."

"That's my girl."

With one final push, I bury my middle finger inside her and see fucking heaven.

She throws her head back with a moan as I ease my finger in and out of her while my thumb keeps circling her sensitive core, stretching her out like she asked me to. Like I've been dying to do for longer than I'm brave enough to admit.

Lila grinds herself on my hand, testing my willpower. The urge to throw her over my shoulder, toss her onto the bed, and take her raw is so intense that I'm blinded for a moment.

She whines my name, tells me to go faster, and I obey. For her, I'd do anything—even erase the forbidden line between us for good.

"That's it, angel. Ride my hand," I praise her. "You're so tight, I don't think I could fit another finger inside you."

"T-Try."

Gently, I ease another finger into her heat. My lips find the delicate slope of her neck, kissing my way up to her earlobe. "You all right?"

A soft moan escapes her when she nods. "Never been better."

Her wetness coats my fingers, and I've never felt anything hotter. "You feel so good, Lila. Better than I'd imagined."

"You've imagined us together?"

"Every goddamn night."

She tightens around me, and I know she's close. I kiss her neck again, biting softly on her skin as I pump my fingers faster, deeper.

"Let go, beautiful," I command. "Come on my fingers."

Lila shatters around me, coming undone with a loud moan she muffles against my neck. She clings to me, and I hug her closer as she rides the last waves of her orgasm.

"Reed," she breathes out.

"I've got you." She spasms around me again as I ease my fingers out of her. "Are you okay? Did I hurt you?"

"I don't want you to regret this," she blurts out, ignoring my questions. "I don't want you to regret me."

When we pull away, I'm met with the most breathtaking view I've ever set my eyes on.

Flushed cheeks. Labored breaths. Parted lips. Shiny eyes. Ruffled hair.

"You're the most perfect woman I've ever met, inside and out." I cradle her face in my hand and press my lips to her forehead. "Nothing and no one could ever make me regret you, Lila."

Because I love you.

The sudden realization hits me out of the blue, pressing down on my chest, and it won't let me breathe.

I pull away under her vulnerable stare, ignoring the tightness in my heart. "Get some rest, yeah? Tomorrow's a big day."

"But what about—"

"Don't worry about me." I don't make a move to adjust the obvious bulge she's eyeing right now.

"It's not fair," she mumbles, sliding off the vanity.

I keep a hand on her arm just in case. The bathroom counter is too high, and she isn't exactly on the tall spectrum. Once she's safely on the ground, I take a step back. "Text me if you need anything before your presentation tomorrow. I'll be up early."

"Way to change the subject."

"I'm not—"

"You've just given me the most intense orgasm of my life, and you're telling me I can't return the favor?"

My cock twitches. She arches an eyebrow at me when she notices.

"Tonight isn't about me." I risk my sanity again by giving her another forehead kiss. "See you tomorrow."

"I'm mad at you," she says, opening the door for me.

I can't help a smirk, knowing she isn't. "All right. Sleep well."

I step toward the end of the hallway in the direction of my room when Lila grabs my hand and stops me in my tracks.

I turn just in time to sense her soft lips on my cheek. Her kiss is short, the damn sweetest thing I've ever felt. When she pulls away, the intensity in her gaze traps me. And I can tell her next words are true.

"I could never regret you either, Reed."

chapter 30

REED

The full realization of what Lila and I did last night knocks me on my ass when I check my phone the following morning.

> **Cal: Is there any way to record her talk? I swear, I'm about to catch a flight if you say no, my appointments be damned.**

I stare at his text for longer than I need to. The question he's asking is simple, yet the only thought in my head is how I made his daughter come last night and how I'd do it again.

Running a hand through my hair, I excuse myself from the group of colleagues I was having breakfast with and sit in the lobby. I still have an hour until my presentation.

> **Me: All talks are recorded and will be uploaded online sometime in the upcoming weeks. I can send you the link when Lila's is up.**

> **Cal: Great. Can always count on you.**

If only you knew.

> **Cal: I called Lila earlier, but I didn't want to overwhelm her before her presentation. Did she say something to you? Is she nervous?**

> **Me: She was okay when I saw her yesterday. She texted me today that she was going for a walk to clear her head. She'll be fine. She's resourceful.**

> **Cal: Obviously. She's my daughter.**

I catch myself smirking before I reread the *she's my daughter* part.

It's not like I have forgotten who Lila's parents are. But it isn't until now that it truly sinks in that if what happened last night somehow got out in the open, my friendship with Grace and Cal would end.

And Cal would kill me on sight.

I've worked with Grace for three years and eventually found an unexpected but genuine friendship in her and her husband. If they knew what I feel for their daughter, what we've done, our relationship would go down the drain.

Yet it's not enough to keep me away from Lila, which terrifies me. Because I'm starting to think nothing ever will.

With my mind on autopilot, I go back upstairs to get my notes before heading over to the conference hall downstairs. The auditorium is packed—as it always is for keynote speakers—and as I try to find a single empty seat in the crowd, I wonder if Lila would freak out if she saw so many people at her presentation.

Has she slept well? Eaten breakfast? Gone over her notes enough times?

She texted me this morning that she was fine, and I believe her, but I still worry.

My own presentation goes smoothly. Mental health tool kits in foster care is something I've discussed many times before in front of similar crowds, but I take it as a good sign that people are still interested in hearing what I have to say.

After I wrap up my talk and the fifteen minutes of follow-up questions, I'm tackled in the lobby by at least a dozen attendees who didn't get the chance to ask theirs. I'm about to excuse myself, reaching for my phone to text Lila, when I see her.

She's standing at the far end of the lobby, a playful smirk on her lips. When our gazes collide, she waves at me.

"Thank you for your questions," I tell the crowd around me. "I have somewhere to be, if you'll excuse me."

I don't care who's watching as I close the distance between us, stopping only when I'm next to her.

"At least five people around me sighed when you rolled up your sleeves during your talk," Lila teases.

I arch an amused eyebrow. "Jealous?"

"Maybe I am."

My cock stirs awake, pushing against my zipper.

"You have nothing to be jealous of," I tell her. "I'm yours for the rest of the day."

And all the time.

"Great, because I'm about to have a panic attack just from looking at my notes."

I glance at the watch on my wrist. "Go ahead and wait for me in your room. I'll grab us some lunch and help you go over your notes one last time. You still have two hours to go."

Her face turns from playful to concerned. "As much as I'm

craving some good sushi right now, I will literally throw up if I take a single bite of food."

"Trust me that doing a presentation on an empty stomach isn't a good idea," I say. "I'll grab you something small. Do you like apples?"

"Yes, but—"

"Just let me take care of you, all right?"

She lets out a shaky breath. I see the fight leaving her when she agrees. "All right."

Two hours later, after making sure she ate the whole apple and reminding her that she got selected to speak at this conference for a reason and she'll do a great job, I walk her through the backstage door of the auditorium.

With just a couple minutes until she's introduced, she turns to me, worry all over her face, and asks, "Any last-minute advice?"

I'm much too aware of all the people around me—lighting crew, organizers, and other speakers. But somewhere along the past few months, I've lost all self-control when it comes to her, so I pull her into my arms.

"You deserve to be here, Lila," I mutter as she hugs me back, resting her head on my chest. "You shine brighter than anyone else I've ever met. All your hard work has gotten you this opportunity—enjoy it, angel. Have fun on that stage because you've earned every second of it."

She squeezes my middle before letting go, unshed tears swimming in her eyes. "Thank you, Reed. I needed that."

I resist the urge to wipe her tears away. If we were alone, I would. "That's what I'm here for. Now go show them what you're made of."

LILA

Reed's words fill every corner of my head as I walk over to the center of the stage, my ears filled with the sound of applause. I only allow myself one second to freak out when I see a full auditorium before I open my mouth, hoping my voice doesn't give away my nerves.

It doesn't.

For the next forty minutes, I'm in a dream. As soon as I introduce myself and my research, all the pent-up anxiety and panic I've been harboring since I knew my paper had been selected go away.

It's strange, I realize as I go over my presentation on bibliotherapy and sexual education, how my own perception can change so fast. I've spent the last two decades worrying about how other people saw me, if they thought I was worthy of the opportunities I'd been given. Stupidly, I let them dictate what I thought of myself.

All it took was working with Reed to find my self-worth.

No matter how many times he told me I was doing a good job, I didn't believe him—so he showed me. He gave me the chance to prove my worth, not to him, but to myself—through the group sessions, through letting me handle the kids, through listening to my advice about Ginny, through trusting me to run my own workshop.

It's taken me twenty-four years, but I know without a single shade of a doubt that *this* is what I was born to do.

And now that I've pretty much graduated, I will show the world what it's been missing.

Despite my newfound confidence, I'm not expecting a standing ovation at the end of my talk. My mind slips for a moment, trying to convince me that these people are exaggerating, that they're only trying to make me feel good about myself, that I'm not *that* great, but I quickly recover.

Because even if they weren't praising me, I would still feel proud of myself for getting on this stage and nailing my presentation.

I, Lila Callaghan, finally believe in myself.

> **Reed: Be ready at seven. Wear casual clothes.**

His text comes through as I'm getting out of the shower later that afternoon. I may or may not have almost slipped after reading it.

What does he mean *be ready*?

Why does he want me to wear casual clothes?

What is this about?

With shaky fingers and still in my towel, I text him back.

> **Me: What happened to hello? How are you?**

> **Reed: It's called time efficiency.**

> **Me: Am I not allowed to know where we're going?**

> **Reed: Where's the fun in that?**

> **Me: See? You're bossy.**

> **Reed: See you at seven.**

A part of me wants to poke him a little harder until he answers my question, but a bigger side of me is all about the thrill of the unknown.

At seven sharp, Reed knocks at my door. Despite knowing he'd also wear casual clothes wherever we're going, I'm not ready for the sight of him in his leather jacket again.

"Cat's got your tongue?" he teases.

"Don't be mean," I mutter, closing the door behind me and starting down the hallway.

He barks out a laugh. "Cut me some slack, little criminal. Or I won't tell you what our plans are."

I arch an eyebrow as we get inside the elevator. "I don't want to know now, anyway."

He smirks. "You're a handful."

My shoulders rise and fall with a nonchalant shrug. "But you like it."

"Yeah, I like it a little too much."

The elevator stops on the ground floor just as I think of doing something very stupid—namely, pressing the button to our floor, guiding him back to my room, and returning the favor from last night.

Neither of us seems too keen on talking about what happened in my hotel bathroom just hours ago, which is fine by me—today has been eventful enough.

My body tingles as he guides me into the back seat of our ride. But then my phone buzzes with a text from my mom, and I spend most of the car ride updating my family on how today went—omitting my current plans with Reed.

The truth is, I've been dying to talk to my mom about him. Growing up, I would always go to her for love advice—not that I had much of a love life, but she was the first to know about my crushes. My friends found it weird that I was so close to her, but to me, my mom is my confidant. Instead of jumping to conclusions or getting angry, she always listens to me with an open mind. We disagree sometimes, but what I love about our relationship is that she never judges me.

When it comes to Reed, though, I'm not sure her reaction would be an understanding one.

Would she find it scandalous that he's so much older than me? My mom is eight years younger than my dad, and my aunt is ten years younger than my uncle, but maybe she'll think twelve years is too much.

I don't even want to think about my dad's reaction if he found out. I wouldn't put it past him to hunt Reed down.

Not like Reed would ever date me. Of course not. Whatever we're doing is... I don't have a name for it. Does it need one?

At this point, the attraction between us is undeniable. But beyond giving in to a tension that has been boiling for months, this is going nowhere. I tell myself my heart doesn't hurt at my own admission.

"We're here," Reed says, snapping me back into the present moment.

When I look out of the window, I can't help but smile.

"I hope you're still craving some good sushi," he adds before getting out of the car and holding the door open for me.

My stomach does a weird flip that has nothing to do with hunger. "Thank you." Why do I feel so shy all of a sudden? "This is exactly what I needed today."

My legs wobble a little as he guides me inside, his hand on my lower back, and he doesn't remove it until we're sitting by the sushi train.

"What do you want to order?" I ask him as I eye all the options, nearly salivating.

"Whatever you want. I've never had sushi before."

I audibly gasp. "You're joking."

"Never saw the appeal, but it must be good if you like it. Order two of whatever you want. My treat."

"Reed—"

"No buts." He bumps his knee against mine under the table. "I trust your good taste."

For the next hour, my belly hurts from laughing as Reed makes faces at each sushi piece he eats, only to then admit he's a fan.

"The texture is kind of weird," he argues, an adorable furrow between his brows.

I chuckle. "But it tastes good, doesn't it?"

"I would eat it again."

"That's enough for me. Welcome to the sushi lovers' club."

While we try out different types of sushi, Reed tells me all about Ginny's new advancements—she no longer uses the house as her private bathroom, and she's made a few friends at the dog park—and I tell him I'm considering signing up for more boxing lessons.

"Maybe after the holidays, once I send in some résumés," I tell him.

"Where are you applying?"

"To a few local schools and high schools." I take a sip of my soda, ignoring the flicker of anxiety that appears every time I think about my future. "I still need to get my license, so we'll see."

He smiles at me, gentle and confident. "You have nothing to worry about."

This time, I agree with him.

We don't stop chatting as we finish our dinner, in the Uber, or on the walk up to our hotel floor. Reed tells me about happier childhood memories with Liam and Warren, and I tell him what it was like to grow up with my aunt, who feels more like an older sister than anything else.

Reed walks me to my room and stops at the door when I open it. Suddenly, the ease I felt between us tonight is replaced by something heavier. Something that makes my body tingle.

"So," he starts. "I think we need to talk about what happened last night."

I search his eyes, my heart quickening. "Why?"

He pauses.

Then he shatters all my inhibitions.

"Because I want to do it again."

chapter 31

LILA

The world stops as soon as Reed utters those seven words.

Because I want to do it again.

"What do you want to do again?" I mutter in the silence of the hallway because I need to make sure he's saying what I think he's saying.

He takes a step forward, caging me in against the door.

"I want to touch you," he rasps, low so only I can hear. "I can't take it another second, Lila. I need to feel you again."

The heat between my legs pulses at his confession. Breathless, I tell him my own truth. "I need to feel you too."

At this moment, I don't want to think about the consequences of moving forward instead of going back to our old dynamic. All I see and all I want is Reed.

Things may not be the same after tonight, but I've had enough of worrying about what other people will think of my choices. I don't want to neglect my own desires anymore.

With my heart beating a million miles an hour, I move my hands up his leather jacket, hold it by the collar, and pull his mouth down on mine.

And we fall.

His lips are as soft and demanding as I remembered. I can only think about how I don't want to kiss anyone else ever again as he reaches behind me and opens the door wider, then shuts it behind us before his hands travel down my spine until he's cupping my backside.

"You drive me insane." His voice is a rough whisper against my neck. "Wrap your legs around me, angel."

There is no awkwardness, no hesitation, as he picks me up so effortlessly it makes my belly flutter. I do as he says, wrapping my legs around his middle before his mouth finds mine again.

His fingers stretch wide on my ass, squeezing it as if he knows he won't get to touch me like this again. As we kiss, my own hands tangle in his short hair, earning a deep grunt when I bite down on his lower lip.

"Reed," I whimper, grinding my core against his hard bulge. "I need you."

"I know you do, sweetheart." His mouth finds my sensitive neck. Kissing, sucking, biting. "You're gonna let me eat you like I've been dying to do for months?"

"No."

"No?"

"No," I repeat, grinding against his hardness. "It's my turn now."

"Lila..."

"Sit on the bed," I instruct, not fully convinced he'll listen to me. Reed is bossy in and out of the bedroom, and I love that about him, but I need this. I need him to feel good.

He grunts against my neck but eventually does as I say. Still holding me in his arms, he sits on the edge of the bed and places me on his lap.

His mouth finds mine again as my hands explore the broad, hard planes of his shoulders. His strength drives me crazy on a normal day, but knowing he can pick me up so effortlessly wakes up something primal in me.

The burning desire to give him pleasure blinds me. I help him take his leather jacket off, and then I start playing with the hem of his shirt.

"I want you to take it off," I breathe out, the arousal between my legs burning hot just from the thought of seeing his bare skin, of feeling his muscles under my touch.

He swallows, hesitating. "I..."

It's the sudden change in his voice from possessive to doubtful that stops me in my tracks.

"Did I do something wrong?" I ask him, alarmed. "We can stop if you want to."

"It's not that." His big hands engulf mine, placing them over his chest again. He pauses, then swallows. "I have a scar on my back. From one of my dad's beatings. It's not pretty."

His admission shatters every piece of my heart, but I do my best to focus on him. This isn't about me.

"Nothing about you is ugly to me, Reed," I tell him softly. His throat bobs at my words. "You can leave it on if it makes you more comfortable."

His eyes search mine, and I hope he sees the truth in them. His childhood made him into the man he is today—the man my heart beats for. Those horrors should've never happened, but they don't make him a monster. They never could.

Reed is perfect to me in every way.

I follow the movement with my eyes as he unbuttons his shirt, knowing how important this moment is for him, and don't look away until he says, "I feel safe with you."

Our eyes remain locked in a silent embrace as he gets undressed. As he lets the shirt fall to the ground. As I trace his torso with my careful fingers.

"Will you show me the scar?" I ask him softly, hoping he knows he can say no.

His hesitation breaks something in me. "Are you sure?"

I lean in to press a kiss on the base of his throat. "I want to see all of you if you want me to."

Gently, he picks me up and turns us around so I'm kneeling

on the bed. He towers over me; he's so imposing, so masculine, the need to make him feel good consumes me.

I pat the mattress. "Sit here."

He hesitates for a moment but finally sits on the bed, showing me the scar between his shoulder blades.

I suck in a breath—not because I'm disgusted, but because I can't even begin to understand what kind of monster would do this to their own son.

"Can I touch it?" I ask him in a whisper.

He nods.

My fingers map out his skin with care, afraid to hurt him, even though I don't think I could. My heart fills with rage for him but also with admiration—how someone could live through hell and come out of it such an honorable man with such a strong desire to give back to the world is beyond me.

Overwhelmed by what I'm too scared to admit I feel for him, I lean in and press my lips to his scar. He flinches for a second before relaxing against me. My hands find the naked skin on his back, caressing it. He deserves to be taken care of, and I want to be the one to do it.

"You're perfect," I whisper against his scar. "Every inch of you."

He lets out a shaky breath. "Come here, angel."

I give his scar one last kiss before getting off the bed. Almost instantly, his hands find my hips and pull me between his legs. I let him rest his head on my chest because I know he needs it.

"Thank you," he whispers, his voice rough.

I run my hands through his hair. "You don't have to thank me. I'm here for you."

He looks up at me then, emotion swimming in his eyes. "And I'm here for you."

His grip on my chin is gentle as he pulls me into a kiss. He sighs into my mouth, telling me everything I need to know. So,

I part his lips with my tongue, deepening the kiss, telling him without words that he's the only one for me. That his past will never scare me away because he's...

He's the man for me.

I pull away, overwhelmed by my need to make him feel as good as he makes me feel every day. "Let me take care of you."

He swallows thickly. "You don't have to."

But I'm already lowering myself to my knees between his legs, salivating at the thought of having him in my mouth. We don't break eye contact as I undo his slacks, as he helps me lower them to his ankles, and as I start palming his massive bulge through his boxers.

Hissing, he shuts his eyes as I grab his cock through the fabric and squeeze him. "Fuck."

The sound of his pleasure makes my own arousal grow. I press my legs together as I keep stroking him.

"Do you like me on my knees before you?" I drawl.

"I fucking do." He opens his eyes again and strokes my hair. "You look so beautiful right now."

I press my lips to his covered bulge in a soft kiss, then another, and another. His grip on my hair tightens as he curses under his breath.

"You're killing me," he rasps.

I smirk, enjoying this power I wield over him a little too much. When I grab the hem of his boxers and start pulling them down, down, down, he throws his head back with a groan.

I salivate at the size of him. Just the thought of struggling to take him in my mouth makes me blind with need.

His eyes are already on me when I look up at him. I don't break eye contact as I take the tip into my mouth deliberately slowly, then take some more until he's hitting the back of my throat.

"Shit. That's it, angel. You suck me so well," he praises,

pulling my hair back and watching me with blazing heat in his eyes.

When I hum against him, his hips jolt forward, making me choke. He's quick to put a hand on my cheek, caressing me. "Are you okay?"

My only response is to take him deeper.

"Lila," he chokes out. "Stop, baby, or I'm going to come."

I hum again, enjoying that idea too much, but he gently pulls away.

"I need to be inside you," he says. "Stand up and undress for me."

His command sends a thrill down my spine. It's the thought that I have such an effect on him, that he wants me, that boosts my self-confidence as I strip to my underwear. He watches me in silence, one big hand wrapped around himself, stroking those generous inches in a lazy rhythm.

It's the most erotic thing I've ever seen.

"Don't take them off." He stops me as I'm about to roll my panties down my legs. "Those are mine."

Holy shit.

"Lie on the bed for me."

I do as he says and watch him undress completely before he climbs onto the mattress, hovering over me.

He presses a soft kiss on my stomach and mutters, "You were made for me, angel."

I whimper as his lips make their way up my torso, sucking on the sensitive skin above my breasts.

"I want to hear you scream while my tongue is inside you," he rasps.

My back arches involuntarily, just from the possessive edge of his voice. "Take it off. *Please.*"

His fingers tease the clasp of my bra. "This?"

I nod, out of breath.

My nipples harden at the contact with the cold air of the room, then some more when he sucks one into his mouth. I moan his name, clinging to his neck like I'd fall to my death if I didn't.

All sorts of grunting noises leave the back of his throat as he sucks one nipple, then moves to the other, kissing and sucking and biting. My hips move up of their own accord, colliding with his hardness. Only the thin fabric of my panties separates me from pure bliss.

"I need you inside me," I breathe out.

He comes to a sudden stop, cursing his breath. "I don't have any condoms."

My stomach sinks. "Me neither."

He holds himself up with one arm, staring down at me. "Are you on birth control?"

I bite down on my lower lip, shaking my head. "No."

My doctor said I'd have a higher risk of blood clots if I took birth control pills, but I guess talking about my medical history right now wouldn't be too sexy.

"It's okay." He places a loose strand of hair behind my ear with so much care, my heart leaps. "You're gonna come in my mouth."

My breath hitches. "Am I?"

He winks before scooting back on the mattress so he's kneeling on the ground, just like I was mere minutes ago. His strong grip holds me by the hips and pulls me to the edge of the bed.

Reed starts kissing the inside of my thigh, then the other, as wetness pools between my legs.

"I wanted to taste you so fucking bad last night," he admits. "I'm going to eat you until your body starts shaking."

I don't have time to react before his mouth descends between my legs, kissing me through my panties. My back arches, my breath hitches, and I become blind with need. Those thick fingers move the fabric of my panties aside, his eyes on me. Starving.

I thought I'd feel self-conscious, baring myself like this to such an imposing and older man, but now I realize how stupid I've been. This is Reed—there's nobody I trust more.

"You're perfect." When he presses his thumb to my clit and I moan, he smirks. "So responsive, my girl."

My girl.

It hits me that, yes. Yes, I am. I want to be.

I'm his girl—nobody else's.

And he's mine.

His mouth descends on my core, undoing me with the first faintest touch of his lips. He kisses me slowly, groaning under his breath, his eyes shut as if he were rejoicing over every second of it.

When his tongue pierces my entrance, a high-pitched whimper gets stuck at the back of my throat. He starts slow, taking his time, before he picks up the pace when my hips start bucking. I can't think straight as he devours me like I'm his last meal, like I'm the best thing he's ever tasted.

With my hands in his hair, I pull him closer, begging him to go faster, harder, deeper. He obliges.

When I can't take it anymore and start clenching around him, he pulls away long enough to say, "Come on my tongue, angel. Soak my face."

My release hits me in powerful, overwhelming waves. He puts his mouth back on me, hitting all the right spots, helping me come down from my high with gentle kisses.

I'm breathless, shaking, sated, when he stands up minutes later. "Are you okay?"

Still regaining my breath, I give him a tired smile. "Do you really have to ask?"

He lets out a low chuckle, but my attention shifts to his cock. It rests against his stomach and is so hard I hurt just looking at it.

"Where do you want to come?" I ask him, taking him off

guard by the way his eyebrows shoot up. "On my stomach? My tits? Somewhere else?"

"Baby..." He shuts his eyes, grabbing a fistful of his length and pumping it up and down. "If you don't want—"

"Choose, Reed."

He groans. "You're a fucking dream come true."

I smirk. "Come here."

He hovers over me again, supporting his body weight with one hand. His eyes don't leave mine as he says, "I want to mark your stomach."

The word *mark* sends a thrill directly to my already too-sensitive nub. I've never liked possessive guys—at least, I thought I didn't—but Reed's bossy nature in and out of the bedroom brings out something primal in me. It's raw and it's new, and it feels liberating.

I start touching myself at the same time he does, not breaking eye contact, breathing like one.

"I'm going to come," he grunts after no more than a few minutes. "Are you gonna come for me again, angel?"

I whimper, nodding, too aroused to remember how to use my English.

He kisses me again, hard and fast, before he explodes on my stomach. Hot waves hit my skin as I come for a second time with his name on my lips and a silent scream in my throat.

Breathing heavily, Reed pulls away and asks me if I'm okay again, telling me he's going to clean me up. That I don't have to move. That I did so good for him.

And my chest opens wide as my heart admits what I've been too scared to.

I've fallen in love with the one man I can't have.

chapter 32

LILA

It's been three days since we came back from Chicago.

Three days since we crossed a line we will never come back from.

Three days since I unapologetically chose myself for the first time in twenty-four years.

Three days since I realized I'm in love with a man who has the power to ruin everything I've so carefully built.

"Lili, do you know if Santa is allergic to peanut butter?"

Ike's voice is almost drowned by the dozen kids running around the common room at the youth center. When I look down at him, he's wearing one of the Santa hats we surprised them with for today's party. But his face is a true expression of concern.

I crouch so we're at eye level. "I'm pretty sure Santa isn't allergic to anything. Why are you asking?"

"Mommy and I are making cookies for Santa, and I love peanut butter ones, but I don't know if he'll like them too," he explains, making me melt.

My heart cartwheels when a tall shadow is cast over me. I don't need to look behind me to know who it is.

"Don't worry about it. Santa will love whichever cookies you leave out for him," I reassure him.

He nods, convinced. "Yeah, I think so. But maybe I'll do the chocolate chips just to be sure."

"Those are my favorites," Reed rumbles from behind me.

Ike looks up at him before gasping, a finger pointed at him. "You're not wearing your Santa hat!"

A blush crawls up my neck when Reed rests his hand on my back, helping me stand back to my full height.

"I forgot it in my office," he says, still touching me. *What is happening?* "Actually, I came to ask Lila if she can help me find it."

I send him a look that tells him he's not being slick. He smirks in return, wordlessly saying he doesn't really care.

"Ike, do you need anything else?" I ask him, purposely ignoring the menace next to me.

He shakes his head. "No. I'm going to fish for some candy canes now."

The little boy sprints to the opposite side of the room, where Haniyah is supervising a group of kids attempting to fish some candy canes out of a plastic cup. I had no idea the youth center organized a Christmas party every year, but I can tell all the kids love it. And as a new volunteer, I was eager to help out with all the preparations. I also still help Reed with his workshops—we're planning a new one on sex education for next month—and I couldn't be more excited to be back with our group. I've found a family here I never want to say goodbye to.

Reed's warm breath caresses my ear. "Come with me?"

Nobody looks at us as we leave the common room. I have no clue if Reed has told Haniyah about Chicago—it wouldn't surprise me, and I wouldn't mind it—but if anyone notices Reed has been affectionate toward me recently, they don't comment on it.

When we reach his office—now empty since Ginny is staying at dog daycare—he gently cradles my face in his hand, presses me against the wooden door, and captures my lips with his.

There's a familiarity to kissing him now that no longer feels forbidden. Maybe it's because he's not my supervisor anymore or because I no longer care for other people's perceptions of me, but

I swear his lips taste sweeter.

When he pulls away, he caresses my bottom lip with his thumb. "Sorry if I came on too strong, but I couldn't go another second without kissing you."

I suck his thumb into my mouth, remembering that night in my hotel room. When his eyes darken with lust, I know he remembers, too.

"What about the Santa hat?" I tease him.

"Fuck the hat."

"You're going straight onto the Naughty List this year, Dr. Abner."

A grunt escapes his throat as he presses his erection against my stomach. "Call me that one more time and see what happens."

My hands find the collar of his shirt, pulling his mouth closer to mine. "What would you do about it, *Dr. Abner*?"

I squeal as he picks me up in his arms and slides my back against the door. It's second nature, the way my legs wrap around his waist now, as if our bodies have known each other's for eons.

He rests his forehead against mine. I'm not expecting the change in his voice from rough to soft as he says, "This terrifies me, angel."

I find the short hairs at the nape of his neck. "Tell me what you're worried about."

"Everything."

"Don't give me that nonanswer."

It takes him a moment, but he finally says, "I don't want to hurt you."

"Why would you hurt me?"

"Because I don't know how to take care of the people who are important to me."

My chest caves in. "Reed..."

"It's okay." He places a strand of hair behind my ear so carefully, his words make even less sense. "It has nothing to do

313

with you. It's my own head that's fucked up."

"I get it," I reassure him. "You didn't have an easy childhood. But, Reed, you started taking care of me long before you realized you were."

He searches my gaze with a kind of intensity I'd never seen before. "You're too good for me," he whispers. "I don't deserve you."

"Stop saying things like that," I retort. "Let's just live in the moment, all right? I can't believe *I'm* telling *you* this, but you need to stop worrying about the future."

"Your dad will kill me."

I roll my eyes. "My dad will have to accept that his daughter is an adult woman who can do whatever she wants."

"Your mom will hate me."

"Same answer."

Carefully, he sets me back down on the ground and presses his lips to my forehead. "You're right. My head's a mess these days."

He walks up to his desk, but I don't move. I wonder, and not for the first time, what exactly we're doing here. And most importantly, what do I *want*?

To date him? I swore men off a year ago, when the whole Oliver fiasco went down. Now that I've almost graduated—it's a matter of days before I get confirmation and defend my thesis—my plan is to get my license and start job hunting. That hasn't changed, and men are still not on my radar.

But Reed...

He's something else.

He's *Reed*. Plain and simple.

He means so much to me, it's scary to put into words. He certainly means more to me than a one-night stand or whatever we're doing right now.

I grab my phone when it pings inside my pocket, but I'm

distracted. Maybe we should talk about all of this instead of swimming in uncertain waters, always against the current. Does he even see a future with me? Because I'm starting to see one with him.

Reed finishes typing something into his computer. "Your thesis defense date?" he asks.

I give him a nervous smile as I fiddle with my phone. "Maybe."

He knows I've been stressed about it because Warlington University doesn't allow students to defend their theses unless they've passed all their courses. In true Reed fashion, though, he insists I have nothing to worry about. A part of me believes him, but another...

I stop.

It's an email, but it's not about my thesis defense.

I scan it once, twice, five times, because my brain refuses to take in the words.

"Lila?"

My hands start shaking.

My phone makes a loud noise as it falls to the ground.

Rushing steps.

Firm arms holding me.

"Lila, what's wrong?"

I can't speak.

I can't.

Reed picks up my phone.

Scans the email on the screen.

And mutters, "Fuck."

Fuck, indeed.

Because in just a second, all my future has gone down the drain.

Dear Lila Callaghan,

Good afternoon. This is Kelly Russo, Dean of Psychology at Warlington University.

At your earliest convenience, please stop by my office so we can discuss the results of your internship with Dr. Reed Abner. At this time, the grade of your internship is [UNSATISFACTORY]. Therefore, you do not meet all requirements necessary for graduation.

I would like to discuss with you the alarming reason why your internship was deemed unsuccessful.

Best,

Kelly Russo

Dean of Psychology

I read the dean's email over and over again, but the contents don't change.

I don't wake up, either, despite this feeling like a cruel nightmare.

"Wha-What does she mean by alarming reason?" I stammer, my body shaking from head to toe as if I were standing in the middle of a blizzard. "I didn't do anything wrong."

"You didn't," Reed says firmly. "Your internship results were immaculate."

Tears start rolling down my cheeks before I even realize I'm crying. "I-I can't graduate. She said it."

"Like hell you won't graduate, Lila." His firmness has been replaced by anger. "This doesn't make any sense. Come on. I'll drive you to her office now. I was your internship supervisor; I'll gladly list all the reasons why she shouldn't fail you."

I don't try to convince him to stay here with the kids or tell him that I can handle this on my own and drive to campus myself.

Because I can't.

Because the future I was so sure was mine a minute ago is now gone.

And something tells me I won't get it back.

Campus is hauntingly deserted as I follow Reed into the Psychology Hall, the oxygen in my lungs getting scarcer with each step I take.

What will my parents say when they find out I'm not graduating this month?

What could that *alarming reason* Dean Russo mentioned be?

Nausea hits me when we get to her office. Reed knocks once, not bothering to wait for an invitation before he walks in. I feel like a mere spectator in my own life right now. A very unfortunate one.

"Dean Russo," he greets her. His voice has an angry edge to it I've never heard before.

The dean looks up from a stack of papers, her eyes widening through her glasses. "Dr. Abner. I wasn't expecting you."

"I came to review my student's internship grade," he adds, that anger visibly seeping out of his every pore.

I step slowly into her office, terrified of the person I'll be once I leave, and shut the door behind me. "Hi."

"Miss Callaghan, hi." Dean Russo's bright red hair glints under the fluorescent lights of her office. "Take a seat. You, too, Dr. Abner. I was about to email you also."

I don't utter a word as I sit in one of the chairs in front of her desk. Reed sits on the other one, his knee brushing mine in what I'm assuming is a comforting gesture. Too bad I'm about to throw up all over his shoes.

"I'm concerned about Lila's internship grade," Reed starts.

"I'll be frank with you—she's the best intern we've ever had at Warlington Youth Center. I struggle to believe her results didn't meet the university's criteria because I supervised her myself."

"That's precisely what brings us here," she says.

If I thought I was going to get sick before, it's nothing compared to the punch to the gut that hits me when Dean Russo turns her computer monitor in our direction.

And shows us a picture of Reed and me at a bar, the night of Mariah's birthday. He has his arms around me, hugging me so I wouldn't fall when Karla accidentally pushed me into him.

No, no, no.

I know what this must look like to Dean Russo because it *looks* like it—me pressed against my supervisor's chest, his arms around me, gazing into each other's eyes in the middle of a crowded bar.

My head starts spinning.

"This picture isn't what you think it is," Reed argues, his voice even and sure while I fall apart. "We saw each other by chance. I was there with my friends, and she was with hers. We didn't meet up. Someone tripped and pushed Lila; I was only holding her upright so she wouldn't fall."

Despite it being the truth, the concern in Dean Russo's face tells me she believes none of it.

"It's not just this picture that has landed in my inbox, Dr. Abner," she says solemnly.

A few clicks later, she shows us three more.

Reed and I getting in his car after leaving the youth center together.

Reed with his arm around me as I held Ginny the day we found her.

Reed walking me out of his house the morning after I spent the night with him and Ginny.

Nausea swirls in my stomach, and I bite the inside of my

cheek so I don't burst into tears.

"I'm sure you understand why this is concerning," Dean Russo starts. "These pictures don't showcase a traditional relationship between a student and her academic supervisor. It gives me the impression that your relationship may go beyond strict professionalism. For that reason, the department has decided that Miss Callaghan will have to retake her internship module next semester, just to make sure her results are true and fair, thus postponing her graduation until further notice."

"No." Reed's firm voice echoes in the room. "Absolutely not. These are baseless accusations. You're relying on pictures with no context behind them—any academic board would agree with me. This isn't reasonable, Kelly."

She adjusts her glasses over the bridge of her nose. "I'll admit it's our fault for not considering your relationship with Miss Callaghan's mother before accepting her internship request, but there's nothing we can do about it now."

With my mother.

"My working relationship with her mother has nothing to do with Lila's internship grade," Reed argues. "You're familiar with her academic accomplishments long before I started collaborating with this university. You can't possibly disregard that."

"I'm not," she argues back. "All I'm saying is, these pictures suggest Miss Callaghan may have had some...advantages in her internship. Possibly. We're asking her to retake her module with someone else just to make sure. You know how important it is for this university to offer every student the same advantages. We're doing you both a favor by sweeping these pictures under the rug as long as you agree to our demands. I'm sure I don't need to remind you that involvement with a professor is enough for a student to be expelled."

It's that last sentence, the accusation in it, that finally makes me snap.

"Dr. Abner keeps all the reports I've worked on during my internship, as well as recordings of all sessions I've participated in," I start, my voice firm, despite my hands shaking. "Anyone can go over them and decide whether I deserve to fail my internship. As for those pictures, they don't prove an explicit affair between us. Any lawyer would agree with me."

I really hate pulling the lawyer card, but what else can I do?

Dean Russo wasn't expecting that turn of events, if the surprise in her eyes is any indication. It's as if she expected me to submit and not defend myself at all.

I don't turn my head to look at Reed, but I can feel his eyes on me.

After a brief pause, she lets out a tired sigh. "Despite what you may be thinking, I don't want to be the bad guy here. Dr. Abner, you know your work with us over the past three years has been invaluable, and your reputation precedes you. Miss Callaghan, your reputation as a student is also remarkable. You're a top performer at this university, and I know how important it is for you to graduate as soon as possible."

I can feel a *but* coming.

"But I can't ignore these pictures. Students and professors shouldn't spend time together outside campus, let alone at a professor's home. I understand this was an internship, so you had to spend some time together, but this behavior is... It doesn't look appropriate. I have to ask you, and I expect full honesty so we can take care of the situation in a way that benefits us all. Are these pictures true? Have you ever been romantically involved?"

A charged silence falls over the room, and my ears start ringing.

Reed's knee brushes against mine, telling me all there is to know.

This was my greatest mistake.

"Yes," he admits.

A single word.

A lifelong sentence.

"Just to clarify, Dr. Abner. Have you and Miss Callaghan ever been involved romantically? Or are you currently?"

"Yes," he repeats. "Not when those pictures were taken, but lines have been crossed recently."

The older woman stiffens, directing her gaze at me. "Was this consensual, Miss Callaghan?"

"One hundred percent."

The last thing I want is for those kinds of rumors to follow Reed around when he's everything but.

Dean Russo sighs. "This isn't an ideal situation, as you can imagine. The pictures I've been sent may not depict a romantic relationship at the time, but the point is that you were involved at some point; perhaps you still are, and that is an issue."

"I'll send my resignation letter by the end of the week."

I turn to Reed, my heart beating with alarm, but he isn't looking at me.

"Now, Dr. Abner—"

"I would never want to taint this university's reputation," Reed continues. "I was aware of the risks when I decided to get involved with a student. I'll be happy to resign as long as you consider having an external committee review her internship grade."

"Reed—" I start.

His hand lands on my knee for a brief second, and he gives it a squeeze before he draws back.

Dean Russo pauses, her eyes following Reed's movements.

"Thank you both for your honesty," she dismisses us. "I will bring this information forward to the board and let you know when we reach a satisfactory decision."

In other words—goodbye to my dream of becoming a youth counselor.

Because who in their right mind would want to hire someone who got involved with a professor?

Just like those pictures magically appeared in Dean Russo's inbox, word will get out about this on campus. I'll forever be the girl who slept with her mother's professor friend.

Breathing becomes an arduous, unbearable task. Before I know it, I'm up from my seat.

"Thank you," I think I mutter to Dean Russo.

My body doesn't feel like mine as I leave her office without permission or as I rush down the hallway or as I hear Reed call my name or as a familiar hand grabs my arm.

"Let me go," I growl, yanking myself out of his grip.

My voice doesn't sound like mine either.

Regret shines on his face. "I'm so fucking sorry, Lila. I handled it as best as I could. I had no idea this would happen."

I shake my head. I know it's bad when the tears don't even come—my burning anger has evaporated them all.

"This was a mistake. All of it." Rage blinds me, not caring who gets burned in its wake. "I promised myself I wouldn't let a man ruin my life again. But I was careless, thinking nothing would happen because I felt safe with you. I made an exception for you because I..."

Because I fell in love with you.

"Lila."

He makes a move to close the distance between us, but I step back.

"I'm not even mad at you," I say truthfully, my breath uneven. "I'm angry at myself for having such low self-worth. I should've known better than to get involved with a professor and jeopardize my future like this."

I can't believe I've let a man ruin me again. The stupid realization that I can't go back in time to fix this makes me want to scream, to yank out my hair.

I wish I'd never met him.

"Don't resign," I grit out. "Don't do it for me. You resigning won't make me graduate on time; you don't need to be the hero."

"I'm resigning because it's the right thing to do," he argues back. "You failing your internship because of me *isn't* right. That's what I'm fighting for."

"I don't want you to fight for me." My voice sounds louder now, but I don't care that we're in the hallway where anyone can hear. Not anymore. "Don't you get it, Reed? Nothing good will ever come out of us being together. *Nothing.* We are a mistake. I... I can't do this anymore."

My hands start shaking again. I hate that my stomach falls as Reed's face does.

"All right," he says, his voice quieter than I've ever heard it.

Whatever guilt I feel for being so harsh with him, I choke it to death. It doesn't matter that he showed me what it's like to feel worthy, to be healthy, to be happy in my own skin. It. Doesn't. Matter.

Why didn't I stop this when I had the chance?

Who even am I?

I thought I didn't recognize the Lila who lost her temper and slashed Oliver's tire, but *this* Lila, the one who threw all caution to the wind for a professor... She's a total stranger.

We don't say goodbye.

We don't exchange another word as I look at him for the last time and leave the Psychology Hall with a shattered heart.

It isn't until I'm inside an Uber that the first tears start falling quietly.

And it hits me who sent Dean Russo those pictures.

chapter 33

LILA

I knock on Oliver's door so hard, I'm surprised I don't bust it down.

It's so pathetically obvious he's behind all this. I still remember his words from the day he asked me for a second chance—how he thought I was sleeping with Reed and how he warned me that rumors spread like wildfire on campus.

My ex is as good as dead right now.

"I'm coming, I'm coming. Holy shit."

When he yanks open the door, his eyes widen comically.

"Lila? What are you doing here?" he asks with such confusion that I almost think it's genuine.

"I came to ask you what the fuck you think you're doing," I blurt out, anger rising in my throat. "Taking pictures of us, Oliver? Really? And emailing them to the dean with false accusations? Are you kidding me right now?"

He blinks once, twice. "Are you...okay?"

My hands start trembling. "Answer me."

Oliver glances over his shoulder to check on his roommates and shuts the door. Once we're alone in the hallway, he tells me, "I honestly don't know what you're talking about. Why did you just bang on my door like that?"

Am I going crazy? Is that what's happening right now?

I wrap my arms around myself, fighting the urge to scream and cry. "The pictures. You know exactly what I'm talking about."

"I really don't."

I take a deep breath. "Oliver. Be honest with me, just once. The last time I was here, you accused me of sleeping with my professor, Reed Abner. Remember?"

He rolls his eyes. "Yeah."

"You *warned* me that rumors spread quickly on campus," I add. "And now you're telling me you have nothing to do with the fact that Dean Russo has just failed my internship because *someone* sent her pictures of us together?"

"Wait." His confused frown looks too convincing. "What do you mean, you failed your internship? You really fucked that guy?"

I groan into my hands. "Did you do it or not, Oliver?"

"What? Of course not. I have nothing to do with this."

"You lied to me for months when you cheated on me," I point out. "Why should I believe you now?"

"Good point." My ex reaches into the pocket of his gym shorts to grab his phone. As he starts scrolling, he tells me, "You said someone emailed the pictures to Russo, correct? Here are all my email accounts. Feel free to check my messages—even the deleted ones."

I shamelessly search every corner of his three inboxes but come out empty-handed. Still, I'm not convinced he's innocent.

"You could've deleted the emails from the bin," I suggest, thinking out loud.

He shrugs. "Search my camera roll, too. I have nothing to hide."

If he thinks I won't agree, he's very mistaken. For the next ten minutes, I conduct another FBI type of search on his camera roll and, once again, get nothing.

Something feels very wrong right now. A part of me wants to find Oliver guilty and move on from this mess. He's the obvious answer, the *expected* culprit.

But what if he's telling the truth?

Oliver takes his phone back once I'm done. "Look, I know I said some pretty harsh things the last time we saw each other, but I was high and angry and sad, and I didn't mean any of it. I'm in therapy now, and I'm doing better. Despite what happened last year, I wouldn't do this to you. I don't have that much free time now with my job, and I also don't care what you do in your personal life anymore. No offense."

Maybe this makes me the stupidest girl on the planet, but I believe him. There's something in the way he says it that tells me he isn't lying. After all, I've known him for years. He might have fooled me before, but I've learned to look for the signs.

Most importantly, though, I've learned to trust my gut—and it's telling me Oliver didn't send those pictures.

But if he didn't do it, who the hell did?

"All right, Li. Relax. That vein in your forehead is about to pop."

I keep pacing my best friend's apartment back and forth, just like I've been doing for the past twenty minutes. Karla is meeting a friend for coffee, which only leaves Mariah as a witness to my meltdown.

"Riah, don't you get it? My career is *over*."

The worst part is, I deserve it. I was careless, put my feelings before my goals like I promised I wouldn't do, and now my worst nightmare has come to life.

"Those are some intense words," Mariah says. "I won't deny that the situation you're in sucks, and I understand why you're freaking out, but your career is far from over. It hasn't even started."

"And now it won't." I don't wipe the tears rolling down my cheek. I can't be bothered to anymore. "I'll forever be the student who fucked her professor for a good grade."

"Lila," my best friend starts, far calmer than I am right now. "You may have fooled around with him a little bit—a brush of the lips hardly counts—but you certainly didn't do it for a grade."

I didn't.

I did it because I was falling in love with him.

Because I still am.

I shake my head, willing the thoughts to go away. They hurt too much.

"That doesn't matter," I argue, my anger slowly leaving my body to make room for self-deprecation. "When they find out about this on campus, I'll be done for. I can't even graduate."

"Yes, you can." She shakes my shoulders, no doubt trying to get me out of my head. It doesn't work. "You may not graduate this month, but you *will* next year. How's that the end of the world?"

"My parents will be so disappointed," I mutter, feeling my lower lip tremble.

She pulls me into a hug. "Your parents will always support you. They won't care if you graduate this month or next year. I promise."

They may not, but I do. The last thing I want is to disappoint them. Not like this, of all ways.

I'm supposed to be the easy child, the one they don't need to worry about. Maddie went through so much, even in her adult years, and she didn't deserve any of it. I love her to death, and I don't blame her for any part of my life at all, but I can't deny the truth—after all the drama that went down with her when I was a child, I made myself into the quiet, easy daughter so my parents could take a break after all the ups and downs they'd been through.

Getting good grades, being at the top of my class, not partying or getting drunk, never breaking the rules—that's my thing.

But the role of the perfect child has consumed me. I've been living the life of someone else, someone I'm *supposed* to be, but I'm not. Not fully.

Because sometimes I wanted to be able to underperform at school without feeling like a failure to my parents. Sometimes I wanted to stay out late with my friends instead of studying for an exam that, in the grand scheme of things, was never going to make or break my future. Sometimes I wanted to be a little rebellious and go boy crazy like my friends did instead of burying my face in my textbooks.

There's no point in regretting my choices now, but at the same time, I can't help but feel that I've never allowed myself to be authentic. I've never allowed myself to be anything other than the perfect child, friend, student. And for what? For my future to go down the drain anyway—and now I'm left without an identity.

I let my grades and accomplishments define my self-worth, and now I don't know who I am outside of my education.

"Mariah..." I let out a shaky breath as the realization dawns on me, bulldozing everything in its wake. "I...I don't know who I am."

"What do you mean?" She frowns.

"I don't know who I am outside of this...this person I've created to please everyone else." She takes my now-shaky hands in hers, walking me to the couch so we can sit down. "All my life, I've only paid attention to what others wanted and expected of me. I've neglected myself. I've put all my value into my studies, my career...but now I have none of that. And I don't know who I'm supposed to be."

She dries my tears with her sleeve. "We're young. We still have time to learn who we are."

I shake my head. "I don't have a *life*. Not even a hobby. What do I enjoy doing outside of studying and working? My dad likes working out, my mom's escape has always been ballet, and my aunt loves drawing. But me? I don't enjoy any of those things. I don't even know what I *like*."

"Don't beat yourself up over it. You've been working your ass off all this time, and that isn't a bad thing. You'll have plenty of time to try out new hobbies when you graduate," she says, attempting to calm me down. "Let's just do something fun today, get your mind off things. You can sleep here if you don't want to see your parents."

God, my parents. I'm not ready to become their biggest disappointment.

And Reed? I'm getting sick just thinking what my dad will do to him when he finds out.

Stop thinking about him.

"I don't want to do anything," I breathe out.

"I won't let you sit here and feel bad about yourself," she argues, patting her pockets. "Shit, where's my phone?"

"Well, I happen to want to do just that."

Ignoring me, she grabs Karla's laptop from the coffee table and leans back on the couch. "I'm grabbing us some tickets for the bowling alley tonight, okay? Fair warning though—I'm kicking your ass."

But I shake my head again. "I'm not in the mood."

My best friend rolls her eyes. "That's what you say now, but wait until we—"

When she doesn't finish her sentence, I nudge her with my foot. "What?"

"I...I think you have to see this," she says, not looking away from the screen.

There's a weird edge to her voice that makes my stomach drop. Slowly, I peel Karla's laptop from her grip. "You look like you've just seen a ghost."

She doesn't add anything else—she doesn't have to. Because only a second later, I understand exactly what's going on.

I've taken so many blows today that I convinced myself nothing could possibly make me feel worse.

I was wrong.

As I look at Karla's screen—my longtime friend, a trusted confidant—and I see an email with the pictures sent to Dean Russo from her account, it's like the ground beneath my feet shakes and then opens wide.

"She sent the pictures," I breathe out, scanning the screen again to make sure this isn't a joke. The more I scroll, the sicker I feel. "She wrote she was concerned about an abuse of power between Reed and me. *What the actual fuck?*"

"I'm texting her right now," Mariah says as she rushes to her room. She reappears a moment later with her phone. "I'll tell her there's a leak or something in her room so she doesn't run away, that coward."

I'm unable to look away from the email. "Why would she do this? What have I ever done to her?"

Mariah shakes her head. "Between you and me, she always seemed a bit...off when it came to you. To me, too, honestly."

"What do you mean?" I frown. "I thought we were friends."

She hesitates like she doesn't want to say the words.

"Mariah," I warn her. "If something is going on, I want to know."

A beat passes before she lets out a long sigh and admits, "She makes some weird comments sometimes, like how I have it easy at my job because my dad is my boss, so I don't have to work hard for a paycheck."

"Wait, *what*?" I sit up straight. "Riah, why have you never told me this?"

"Because I don't give a shit what anyone says about me. I do my own thing. And she's also your friend, so I didn't want to make things weird between us," she says. "We live together, but we're not super close. Not like the two of us are."

"What else has she said to you?" I press.

"Lila..."

"Tell me."

Defeated, she gives me a sorry look and says, "She looks down on me sometimes because I didn't go to college. Like, when we get the water bill and such, she says she'll look at it because I can't understand it or whatever since I didn't go to college. I thought I was overreacting, that she didn't mean it like that, and it was all in my head, but now with the pictures..."

"Don't listen to her, Riah. You're a powerhouse, and she's clearly not okay," I reassure her. The last thing I want is for my best friend to feel inferior in any way. For all intents and purposes, she's like a little sister to me.

It hits me then. "She told me she'd applied to the Youth Counseling Expo in Chicago. I got accepted, but she didn't. Do you think that's why she did all this?"

"I wouldn't put it past her," she muses.

I'm about to suggest something else when the door opens and a worried-looking Karla walks in.

"I was just on my way back. Are my clothes ruined?" she asks, alarmed.

I'm fully expecting Mariah to start a fight, so instead, I take the lead.

"Can you explain this?" I ask my so-called friend, showing her the laptop screen with the email on display.

She freezes, all color draining from her face. "What are you doing on my laptop?"

"It was on the coffee table, and I wanted to look something up because my phone was charging in my room," Mariah chimes in, not a single trace of friendliness in her voice. I don't have it in me to feel bad for Karla. "It's not the first time we've borrowed each other's laptops."

"You had no right to go on my email." Her voice raises,

getting defensive. "That's *illegal*."

"We didn't do shit." My best friend—my *only* friend in this apartment—rolls her eyes. "Your inbox was the first thing I saw when I opened your laptop. You can check your history if you don't believe me, but do it after you give Lila an explanation for why you did such a shitty thing."

Karla huffs. "I don't have to explain myself to you. I did what I had to do."

"You didn't have to accuse me of having an affair with a professor," I throw back. "What have I ever done to you, Karla? You owe me an explanation. You can't just do something like this and expect me to be okay with it."

"I don't care if you're okay with it or not," she snarls. There's a mean edge to her voice I've never heard before, and it slices me up like a knife. "You've always thought you were better than everyone, but I knew there was foul play. Your mommy's friend giving you an internship only proved my point."

"How did you even take that picture at the bar?" Mariah asks her, stealing the words right from my mouth. "You were with us the whole time."

"I paid some random frat boy ten bucks to do it," she says, like it means nothing to her. Like ruining my career is an insignificant achievement. "I knew the dean wouldn't believe me if I didn't have proof, so I *accidentally* bumped into you, and you fell into his arms. I had instructed the guy to snap the picture when that happened."

"And the other pictures?" I ask.

"You'd told us about the field trip, so I just showed up. You guys made it easy for me, being glued to each other every goddamn second. So, thank you for that, I guess."

"And the one leaving Reed's house?" I press.

She shrugs. "A guy I was hooking up with lives on that same street. I happened to be doing the walk of shame at the same time you did. A fun coincidence, if you will."

I ignore her walk of shame comment because my blood starts boiling in a rapid, surely unhealthy way. "Karla, *why*? Do you know what this could do to my reputation? To Reed's? All because you're a bitter, jealous loser?"

"I don't care what happens to either of you," she snaps. "Stop looking at me like that—we all know you have feelings for him, so it's not like my setup was much of a setup in the first place."

"So, you're admitting it," Mariah chimes in. "That it was a setup. That you weren't concerned with any abuse of power; you were just jealous. You made everything up."

"I just wanted to get back at you for taking my spot at the Youth Counseling Expo. At the youth center, too," she admits, venom in her voice and eyes as she pins me down.

"Wait, what?" I frown. "What do you mean, the youth center?"

"I wanted to work with Reed, but *somehow* you got the internship instead." She rolls her eyes. "I wonder why."

"You don't know what you're talking about."

"I know exactly what I'm talking about, Lila. Do I think you have a pathetic crush on your mommy's little friend? Yes. Do I know for a fact you're together? No. I don't care either."

I can't believe she'd stab me in the back after so many years of friendship. Was it all a farce for her?

"You know what the sad thing is, Karla?" I start, my heart beating a thousand miles an hour. "Ruining my reputation won't get you any internship opportunities because you don't have what it takes. You could be the only student applying, and they still wouldn't accept you. They were recruiting several interns at the youth center, you know? There wasn't just one spot. They were looking for several students, yet they still rejected you—that has nothing to do with me and everything to do with your poor academic performance. Same goes for the Youth Counseling

Expo."

Karla's ears have turned red, a telltale sign that I hit a sore spot. "It's not like your academic performance got you that internship either. Who knows, maybe your mommy's friend has a sick crush on you, too, and that's why he hired you."

Despite the pang of hurt in my heart, I roll my eyes. Karla knows better than anyone how hard I've worked to get here, even before Reed came into the picture, which makes her betrayal even crueler. "Whatever helps you sleep better at night, Karla. I'm not wasting any more of my time with you."

"I *am*," Mariah interjects. "Because I still have questions—namely, how you were planning to explain yourself if we ever found out. Did you really think we wouldn't?"

"You weren't supposed to," she argues.

I can't help it as I say, "So you were just going to pretend to be my concerned, supportive friend while my life fell apart because of *you*?"

"You need serious help." Mariah shakes her head when Karla only shrugs. "This isn't normal behavior, Karla. You're sick in the head."

"And what are you going to do about it?"

"Kick you out, for one," Mariah says easily. "This is my uncle's apartment, so you can pack your things and leave before the day ends, or I'll throw your stuff in the street myself."

"You wouldn't dare," she seethes.

"Don't test me, you psycho."

"Whatever. I don't need either of you." She storms inside her bedroom, slamming the door closed before she starts speaking on the phone to someone—or maybe she's pretending to do it; I wouldn't put it past her—saying how crazy her roommate is and that she needs to move out immediately and file a restraining order.

Mariah rolls her eyes. "Her rich parents spoil her; she'll be fine. It's not like I'm kicking her out onto the streets."

I rub my tired eyes with the heels of my palms and try to take a deep breath, but it becomes a near-impossible task.

It happened again. Just like at school, another friend betrayed me for something I *didn't* do. What am I doing wrong? Who am I supposed to become so this doesn't happen again?

"Her confession changes nothing," I mutter, not wanting Karla to hear. "The dean already knows Reed and I got involved at some point. We admitted to it. My career is still ruined."

Mariah gives my arm a comforting rub. "She said she had to speak to the board, right? And Reed is like a celebrity on campus, from what you've told me. His research brings a shit ton of money. If nothing else, they'll listen to him for that reason—he'll protect you."

Her words don't make me feel better. I'm still stuck in my self-destructive loop. "This shouldn't have happened. I should be graduating this month."

"Yes, but..." Mariah hesitates. "Okay, maybe it's not the right time to bring this up, but allow me to play devil's advocate for a second. You clearly have feelings for Reed, and I'm pretty darn confident he feels the same for you. Everything's already ruined, as you say, and you're going to have to pay the price for being together. So why don't you just...be together? If nothing else, at least love will win."

But I'm shaking my head before she's done. "Love can't win, Mariah. Not this time. Getting into a relationship would destroy my reputation even further, and his. People talk, especially when it's something illicit."

Illicit. The word tastes bitter in my mouth, wrong, because I have never felt more like myself than when I was with Reed.

But none of that matters now.

Karla's high-pitched voice filters through her bedroom door as she keeps screaming to the poor soul on the other side of the line.

"All right. I get where you're coming from. I'll just grab the tickets for the bowling alley, yeah? Let's get your mind off things," Mariah offers gently.

"I love you, Riah. I'm so grateful for you right now, but I want to be alone." Wrapping my arms around her, I give my best friend a hug goodbye. "I'll text you later. Tell me if you need help with this whole mess."

"Where are you going?"

The word gets stuck in my throat. "Home."

Even though seeing my parents is the last thing I want right now, I need their safety and comfort. And if they want to kick me out after what I've done...well, Mariah has an empty bedroom now.

The drive to my house goes by too fast. It's almost dinnertime, so I know both of my parents will be waiting for me inside.

This afternoon alone has felt like a thousand lifetimes. Its weight presses down on my shoulders as I grab my keys and wipe off the remainder of my tears, mentally preparing myself to become my parents' biggest disappointment.

My phone buzzes then, and I make the mistake of checking who it is.

> **Reed: I'm so sorry, Lila. I'll fix this.**
> **You're graduating this month.**
> **Whatever it takes, I'll do it. I**
> **promise.**

I don't answer.

Instead, I use up the little courage I have left and walk inside.

My parents are making dinner in the kitchen, laughing with each other, and I hate that I'm about to crush their happiness.

I've ruined everything.

My grip on my bag slips, and it drops on the floor, the tears running freely now. The sound echoes through the house and turns their alarmed heads in my direction.

"Lila," my mom gasps. "Sweetie, what's wrong? Why are you crying?"

Say goodbye to your old life, Lila.

"I...I have to tell you something."

chapter 34

LILA

"I'm going to fucking *kill him*."

I can't meet my dad's gaze because the disappointment in it will completely destroy me; the one in his voice is already starting to.

I can't look at my mom either, but I know she's standing next to him. She's barely said a word since I confessed everything, which to me is way worse than my dad's outburst.

My hands haven't stopped trembling since I sat down on the couch what feels like hours ago, but it's probably been no more than twenty minutes. The tears have stopped, but I'm not confident they'll stay at bay.

"I'll drive to his fucking house right now and gut him alive."

"Cal..." my mom warns him, the first word she's spoken in long, agonizing minutes.

"I love you, sunshine, you know I do, but I don't want to hear it right now. Nobody hurts my little girl and lives. Over my dead fucking body."

"Dad..." My throat hurts when I speak, my voice no higher than a whisper. I don't see them because I can't bring myself to look at them, but I feel my parents turning in my direction. "My career is ruined. Beating him up won't fix that."

"But it will make me feel a whole lot better about it," he argues before he pauses, and then lets out a tired sigh. Carefully, he sits on the couch next to me. "All right. I'll let it go for now.

How are you feeling?"

I shrug. My emotions are so confusing and contradicting right now, I can't put them into words.

My head is still spinning from confessing everything to my parents. The hurt in their faces as I told them about Reed and my failed internship, then the anger, will chase me forever.

"I can't graduate," I whisper thickly, feeling my eyes watering again. "I threw everything down the drain. I'm sorry I've disappointed you so much."

"Hey." My dad wraps an arm around my shoulders, pulling me closer. "You will graduate. The worst thing that can happen is that you'll have to retake your internship, but you'll get your Master's."

The couch dips under my mom's weight as she sits on my other side and holds my hand. "I'll admit everything you told us was quite shocking, but Dad and I aren't disappointed in you, honey."

"How are you not?" I shake my head. "I don't believe you."

"Well, you should," she says. "You've always been a good daughter, Li. You still are. This is...not ideal, but it's also not the end of the world."

"How can you say that?" I ask, agitated, as I stand from the couch. I can't sit still. Breathing heavily, I glance at my parents as if they were pulling some kind of elaborate prank on me. "How can you say I'm a good daughter when I got involved with a professor—*your friend*—and failed my internship for it? I *knew* the consequences, and I still did it. I sacrificed my career and my reputation for nothing. After all you went through with Maddie and her dad and everything else, how can you say I'm *good* when I make such stupid choices?"

Air barely fills my lungs. I dry my tears with the back of my sleeve and wait for them to inevitably change their minds and tell me that I'm right, that I'm not a good daughter after all.

Only, that's not what happens.

"Lila..." my mom starts, tentatively, as if she were talking to a wild animal on the loose. "What's all this about Maddie?"

I let out a shaky breath, not wanting to beat around the bush. I might as well give them another reason to see how terrible I am. "You had to raise her, and then her dad came back and you had to deal with that. I love Maddie, I really do, but I..."

"You what, little sunshine?" my dad encourages me when I stop to take a deep breath because suddenly there's not enough oxygen in this room for all three of us.

My eyes fill with tears again, and the dam keeping the words inside me finally breaks.

"I feel horrible for saying this because I love you all so much, and I love Maddie like a sister, and I don't want to sound selfish, but it affected me too. What happened with her," I start, my hands trembling again. "You'd been through enough, and I wanted to make things easier for you. Be the easy child. I tried so hard to always behave, to get good grades, to never disappoint you like teenagers do to their parents, so you could get a break because you deserve it so much after everything. But I just did it now, as an adult woman who should've known better, and I don't... I don't even know who I am anymore. I feel so confused and lost."

"Oh, sweetie." My mom gets to her feet and pulls me into a tight hug.

Burying my head in her shoulder, I let the tears fall. And when my dad stands too and hugs us both against his chest, I cry harder.

"I'm so sorry we made you feel that way," my mom says as she caresses the top of my hair. "I'm so sorry we didn't see it before, Lila."

"It's not your fault," I say, my voice muffled, but loud enough for them to hear. "I never said anything."

"We should've noticed it," my dad says, emotion clogging his voice. "It wasn't fair to you."

I pull away from our hug so I can look at them and make sure they know I mean every word. "Please, don't beat yourselves up over it. I love you so much, and I love Maddie. I could never feel resentful for anything when you've given me such a happy childhood. You're great parents, and I'm so proud of being your daughter."

My dad's eyes aren't completely dry as he kisses my forehead. "And we love you, Lila. We've done everything in our power to raise you the best we could, and we couldn't be prouder of who you're becoming."

"But I—"

"You didn't disappoint us," my mom interjects, her eyes glassy too. But she's smiling softly now. "Sure, you broke some rules. But it's fixable, isn't it?"

I sniffle. "I don't know."

I pause, our conversation sinking in as the minutes pass. And then I remember something else I haven't told them yet. So, for the sake of honesty, I blurt out, "I stabbed a knife through Oliver's car tire for cheating on me."

They blink, probably wondering if they've heard right. And then my dad throws his head back in laughter and my mom starts chuckling.

Now *I'm* the one who's blinking in confusion. "You're not mad at me for that either? I'm basically a criminal."

Reed's nickname for me pops into my head, and my heart takes a deep dive into a pit of agony again.

"Does he know it was you?" Dad asks.

"Yeah, but he doesn't have proof, so he couldn't do anything about it."

"Then fuck him. He deserved it."

My mom smiles. "I'm with your dad on that one."

I shake my head, somewhat amused for the first time since

I walked in here tonight. That momentary bliss might be the reason I don't think my words through and I add, "Reed saw me do it."

My dad's face sobers up. "He did?"

I swallow. "He kept the secret."

"How chivalrous of him." His words are laced with irony.

My mom glances between us before she asks what I've been dreading since I confessed everything, "What's going on between you and Reed, honey?"

Unsure, I slide my gaze to my dad, who shakes his head. "I won't say a word. Promise."

I let out a deep sigh that does nothing to erase my anxiety.

"Nothing." That word hits me like a bullet aiming for my heart. "Whatever it was, it's over now."

"But there *was* something," my mom says. It's not a question.

I find myself nodding as my stomach sinks. *We were never meant to have a happy ending. I have to forget about him and move on.*

"We... We had feelings for each other. Not since the start, but somewhere along the way we just... The lines blurred, slowly. I don't know how it happened."

My dad's sigh brings my attention back to him. "Say the word and I'll end him, Lila. I mean it."

I resist the urge to roll my eyes because I adore him, even when he's being dramatic. I couldn't be luckier to have a father who will protect me no matter what.

"Don't do anything to him, Dad. Please," I say. "I'm not even mad at him. Not exactly. It was always consensual between us. We tried to fight it, but..."

I can't bring myself to keep going, to relive a story that will never continue.

"I should've stopped it," I conclude. "I'm not a child. I knew what was at risk, but I did it anyway. It's my fault."

"He should've stopped it, too," my dad says, anger rising in his voice.

"All right. Tonight has been intense for all of us," my mom interrupts with a calming hand on my arm. "Don't worry about your internship because I'm sure you won't have to wait long to graduate. There's no point in worrying about what you can't control anyway, so go upstairs and try to distract your mind. How about a calming bath before bed? We'll keep talking in the morning, okay?"

When I nod, she pulls me into her arms again and kisses my cheek. "Dad and I just want to see you happy, honey. We've always trusted you to make the right choices, and that hasn't changed."

My dad hugs us tight again. "We'll always love you, whether you graduate later than you wanted or you slash someone's tires. Everyone goes through tough times, but what counts is how we deal with them. And we couldn't be prouder of the incredible woman you're becoming, Lila."

Their words stay with me all night as I toss and turn in bed hours later. I'm relieved that I still have their support after everything else has gone up in flames, but my heart still doesn't beat like it used to.

I don't think it will ever again.

chapter 35

REED

Lila doesn't return my texts. After what went down in the dean's office, I knew she wouldn't.

The part of me she nurtured and shined her light onto hoped we could talk about this, but now I've realized how much of a fool I'd been to think we had a future. To think I could take care of her. To think I wouldn't hurt her in the end.

My parents were right all along—I'm destructive. My only regret is that I ruined her on the way.

Lila doesn't come back to the youth center after Christmas break. Haniyah told me she'd gotten on a video call with the kids, but I wasn't there to hear it. I didn't allow myself to be.

Not long after that, Han finally got the truth out of me. How I fell in love with the only woman I shouldn't have, and how I ruined both of us.

"You can't control what the heart wants," she offered. "If it's meant to be, you'll come back to each other."

For the first time in three decades, I didn't believe her.

The only sliver of hope comes in the form of an email on my first day back at the research lab in January.

Dr. Abner,

I hope your Christmas break was restful.

As Lila Callaghan's internship supervisor, I'm pleased to inform you that an external committee has reviewed all the provided materials from her internship and has found her results satisfactory. The board has decided to make an exception due to these unprecedented circumstances and allow Miss Callaghan to graduate this month, per your suggestion.

As for your involvement with Miss Callaghan, upon further review, I have deemed the rumors false, since there is no solid proof of a romantic relationship in the pictures I was sent.

Warlington University hopes you will keep collaborating with us in the future.

Best,

Kelly Russo

Dean of Psychology

I'm knocking on her office door three minutes later.

"Dr. Abner," she greets me, surprised. "Did you get my email?"

"I did."

"Good. Did you have any questions?"

"I'm here to resign."

Her office becomes so silent, you could hear a pin drop. "Pardon me?"

The thought has been on my mind since that day, and it feels like the only right thing to do. Like the only thing I can do to protect Lila. If I haven't done it sooner, it's because I needed to tie all loose ends before I step back from my role, no matter how badly it fucking hurts just to think about what I'm about to leave behind.

"I'm here to resign," I repeat. "I'm in talks with one of my colleagues from Stanford who would be happy to take over my lab here until the research concludes in May."

I know what this means. *She* knows what it means.

My reputation, my name, won't be attached anymore to the project I've dedicated every piece of my soul to for the past three years.

I let my heart, *love,* lead the way, and it's time to face the consequences.

"Reed," she starts. The use of my first name is a dead giveaway of her nerves. "Please think this through. We would love for you to stay until the project has concluded this spring."

"A professor and a student getting involved goes against the policy of this university," I remind her because, for some reason, she seems to have forgotten it. "My decision to resign from my position is final."

Kelly takes a long, unreadable look at me. "I understand, but please take some time to consider your resignation. We have no plans to fire you over this...incident."

It's funny, I think to myself, how at first, I didn't understand why Lila was so scared to accept the internship because she didn't want to get any special treatment from me. I see her reasoning clearly now, as I stand in front of someone who's supposed to abide by the rules but is overlooking my mistakes instead. And I know why—because of the generous funding I bring to this institution through my research.

Much like Lila, though, that's not what I'm about.

"I appreciate all you've done for me in the past three years," I conclude. "But I will be turning in my two-week notice tomorrow."

Two days later, the rumors start. I hear them because it's impossible not to, when it's the only thing students talk about on campus.

"I heard they hooked up in a classroom once."

"He's, like, twenty years older than her. That's disgusting."

"Apparently he got Lila pregnant, and that's why she had to graduate early."

"Sleeping with a professor? Really? No wonder she got such good grades."

After the media circus that went down when my parents got arrested, this is nothing. Knowing my days as a researcher here are numbered, too, I ignore the whispers around me and thank the universe Lila isn't here to hear them. That's my only consolation.

It's late February, two months since I last saw her, when Haniyah knocks at my office door in the youth center one snowy afternoon. "Reed, dear," she starts softly.

If it weren't for her, Liam, and Warren, I would've lost my mind these past few months. And Ginny—that dog has stolen my heart and refuses to give it back.

"Yes, Han."

She hesitates. "There's someone here who wants to see you."

"Reed."

That voice.

My heart falls to the pit of my stomach when Grace appears behind Haniyah. I haven't seen her since that dinner at her house, and I almost convinced myself I would never see my friend again.

Although I'm not sure she considers me a friend anymore.

I swallow, my mouth dry. "Grace."

"I was hoping we could talk," she starts, her voice even. It doesn't give away her real emotions, and it makes me even more anxious.

Haniyah sends me a worried look before giving us some

privacy.

"Of course. Sit down, please," I offer.

Lila's mom lowers herself into the chair in front of mine. "I think you know why I'm here."

I give her a stiff nod. "I'm sorry, Grace."

"For which part?"

Fuck.

"I'm sorry for hurting her." I can't bring myself to apologize for my feelings. It doesn't feel right. "I'm sorry for not stopping it before it went too far."

In all the years I've known her, Grace's face has never been this unreadable before. She pauses, lacing her fingers together on her lap, as if she doesn't know how to say her next words. Considering she's an author, it concerns me. This won't end well for me, and I'll deserve every piece of me she destroys.

"Lila told us everything," she says. My heart skips a beat just hearing her name. "Apparently, it was one of her friends who sent the photos. She's now spreading rumors on campus, as I've heard."

"I'll speak to the dean," I offer immediately. "Just give me a name."

But Grace ignores me. "She told us about what she did to her ex-boyfriend's tire, how she felt pressured to prove her worth to us." The sadness in her voice cracks my chest open. "She told us there was something between you two."

"Grace—"

"I just have one question."

I hold my breath.

"Out of all the women in the world, Reed, why my daughter?"

"Because she's the only woman in the world for me."

The silence that follows my confession is deafening.

"Reed..." Her expression morphs into one of concern. "We've talked about your past before. What it did to you."

I don't say anything. I can't.

Sharing my past with her wasn't in my plans, but when she told me about her sexual assault, something in me shifted. For the first time, I felt safe enough to talk about it. Like she would understand what I'd gone through. Our friendship began after that, and I never looked back with regret.

"I know you've avoided relationships because you don't feel worthy of love," she says matter-of-factly—it's true. Every word. "But you've always looked different around Lila. Softer. Lighter. Like the weight of everything you've ever endured wasn't heavy at all. I'd be encouraging you if this were anyone else, but this... This won't end well."

"I don't care if it doesn't end well for me. How's she?"

She searches my gaze for something I'm not sure she'll find. "She's hanging in there."

Her response is vague, probably because she doesn't want me to know more than necessary. I'd normally pick up on such cues and respect them, but just the thought of not knowing how Lila is really doing kills me.

So that's why I ask her mom, "Did she graduate?"

"She did," she confirms. "I heard you resigned."

"It was the right thing to do," I say. "I know Lila is a responsible adult, but I'm older and I was in a position of power— I'm supposed to know better. I didn't stop when I had the chance. Dealing with the consequences is the least I can do."

She hesitates, looking away. "I'll be honest with you, Reed. I'm not...mad at you. I want to be. I *should* be, but I know you. You're not a bad man."

She's lying. I knew how it was going to end, and I still did it out of selfishness.

"And, frankly, I saw this coming."

That makes my self-deprecating thoughts come to a halt. "What do you mean?"

"That night, when you came for dinner at our house, I could see something between you two," she admits. "Cal told me I was just seeing things, but a mother's instincts never lie."

I run a hand across my jaw. "I'm sorry."

"It's not my place to accept your apology."

It's Lila's. But how is she going to when I doubt I'll ever see her again?

No matter how many times I apologize or how deeply I mean it, though, she can choose not to forgive me. She has every right to after everything I've put and still am putting her through. I've done nothing to deserve her forgiveness.

"All this would've happened no matter what you did," Grace says, sadness coating her gaze. "Sure, maybe you and Lila should've never happened in the first place. But the fact that you were a professor and she a student in the same university at the same time would've followed you forever, no matter if you'd gotten together one month or one year after graduation. People love gossiping about that stuff because it sounds scandalous."

I know she's right, but still, I say, "It should've never happened."

"There's nothing you can do about it now." The emotion in her voice sounds a lot like pity.

I pause before asking the dreaded question. "What does Cal think?"

I'm surprised he hasn't hunted me down yet.

"He's..." She hesitates again. "He needs time. Space, too."

Not the answer I wanted, but surely the one I deserve.

"Are we okay, Grace?" I ask, unsure if I'm ready to hear the answer.

"Like I said, I don't think you're a bad man," she starts, "but I also need some time. I hope you understand."

I give her a stiff nod.

She gets to her feet, her expression unreadable once again.

"Take care of yourself, Reed. I mean it."

She's about to exit my office when I stop her.

"Is Lila coming back?"

Slowly, she turns. "To the youth center?"

I nod. "The kids miss her."

I miss her.

Those words don't leave my mouth, but I can tell she has picked up on them all the same.

"She isn't here, Reed."

My stomach drops. "What do you mean?"

"She isn't in Warlington. She left."

"Where?" I ask, like I have a right to know.

For a moment, I think she's not going to answer. But finally, she says, "To Norcastle. I don't know if she wants to come back."

Norcastle. That's a big city, far more crowded and dangerous than our small college town. Hours away.

She left because of me. She left, and she may never come back.

"All right," I concede, schooling my features so she doesn't see the devastation in my face. "Thank you for stopping by. It means a lot."

She nods. "Take care."

Silence washes over the room when she shuts the door behind her. Despite the brightness in my office, my heart has never felt so dark.

I've lost her.

I've lost Lila, the only woman I've ever loved, all because I thought I was deserving of her light. But I've only extinguished it.

What if she never shines again?

The thought of flying to Norcastle crosses my mind before I tell myself I've already ruined her life enough.

Lila will never be mine, even if my heart will only ever beat for her.

chapter 36

LILA

The strong smell of coffee clings to my clothes as I peel them off in the bathroom, the steam of the shower adding to the layers of sweat from my shift. Goosebumps pepper my naked skin as I walk under the waterfall, letting the warm water drown my loud thoughts.

It's been five long months since I saw him, but the imprint of his hands on my skin, of his words in my heart, of the pain in my soul still linger.

Forget about him. It's done.

I reach for the shampoo, humming the tune of a pop song in an attempt to distract myself, just like every time I find myself thinking of the one man I never should've fallen in love with. The man I've sacrificed my career for.

Think happy thoughts.

Right. Happy thoughts. A cute kid came by the café today and asked for an extra cup of whipped cream, which I gladly gave her. She was wearing the cutest frog rain boots, reminding me of the kids at the youth center.

My heart constricts as I think of Melody, Cameron, Ike, Vera, and everyone else. What are they up to today? How are the boxing lessons going?

So much for happy thoughts.

Deciding to leave them behind to come to Norcastle was one of the hardest decisions I've ever had to make, and I try not to think too often of the day I said goodbye unless I feel like bawling my eyes out.

I keep telling myself leaving my old life behind was the right thing to do, but it doesn't lift the weight off my heart.

"You can't catch me!" a familiar little voice shouts right outside the door, loud enough for me to hear, followed by an evil laugh.

"Dylan, I won't repeat myself. Put your shirt on or you'll catch a cold," my aunt yells behind him.

The sound of their footsteps echoes in the hallway outside the spare bathroom, now full of my beauty products. I turn off the water and wrap a fluffy towel around my body, drying myself quickly. After putting on my pajamas, I open the bathroom door to find my cousin pushing toy cars down the stairs. His shirt is on, so at least there's that.

"Uh-oh. Someone's getting into trouble when Mommy and Daddy find out."

He shushes me with a finger on his lips. "Don't tell."

Turns out I don't have to—Maddie exits his bedroom at the end of the hallway just in time to see the fire truck flying down the stairs. She groans. "Are you kidding me?"

I chuckle. "I've got this."

It's the least I can do after they let me stay in their spare bedroom rent-free.

Easily, I pick up Dylan from under his armpits, making him laugh as I carry him downstairs. "Not funny, little guy. You have to take care of your toys, or Santa won't bring you any more."

He frowns at me over his shoulder. "He won't?"

"He just saw you pushing them down the stairs, buddy. One more, and you would've been on his Naughty List. You don't want that, do you?"

"No!"

I lower him to the ground. "I'm pretty sure he'll overlook this if you pick up all your toys and bring them back to your room."

He nods quickly. "I'll do it. I don't want to be on the Naughty List."

"Agreed—that's not a fun place to be."

My cousin is quick to pick up the three toy cars he pushed down the stairs and take them to his room. I follow him, making sure he doesn't trip on the stairs. Just as we reach the second floor, my uncle emerges from baby Alice's bedroom.

"One asleep, another one to go." He sighs, picking up a giggly Dylan with one arm and draping him over his shoulder like a sack of potatoes. "What did I hear about some toy cars being pushed down the stairs?"

My cousin shakes his head rapidly. "Nothing, Daddy. Li is helping me tidy up, right?"

"Right." I exchange an amused look with my uncle. "Good night, Dyl. Don't let the bedbugs bite."

"Never. I'm stronger than them," he puffs out.

I head downstairs as Maddie and James put him to bed. I'm still scanning the fridge for something to eat when they enter the kitchen.

"Go sit on the couch with Maddie," my uncle tells me. "I'm in charge of dinner tonight."

"He's feeling generous," she chimes in, smirking.

"I'm all about that." I yawn, dragging my feet across the kitchen and into the living room.

I plop down on the couch, my aunt joining me a moment later, and we put on some reality TV show as James makes dinner. An hour later, our burritos and green salad are long gone, though the reality show still playing on TV. They sit on the couch, Maddie's feet on James's lap, as I nurse a hot cup of chamomile tea on the armchair in a pink mug I made last month.

"How was work today?" she asks me.

"It was all right." I take a small sip; it's still too hot.

"Uneventful."

Working in a café isn't the most exciting job in the world, but it's peaceful—and that's exactly what I came here searching for.

"They're still sending you work from that agency?" James asks.

He means the website I've been writing articles for. "Yeah, but I'm thinking of quitting that after the summer. I don't know yet."

They exchange a quick look before Maddie voices what we've been avoiding since I got here three months ago.

"Li, I think we should talk about what happened in December."

Suddenly, I can't stomach any tea. "I'm okay."

"No, I don't think you are."

I shift on the armchair, thinking of a hundred ways I could run away from this conversation.

"Stop running away, smarty-pants," James warns. Unfortunately for me, my uncle is also a mind reader now. How fun. "Mentally *and* physically. You know we love having you here, but we have the feeling you're staying not because you love Norcastle but because you're avoiding Warlington."

Wrapping my arms around myself—when did it get so cold in here?—I try my best to sound nonchalant. "I like it here. I like living far away from Mom and Dad."

"And that's good," Maddie reassures me. "You've grown more independent here. You've even made some friends at work and at that pottery class, haven't you?"

I nod. Ann, my co-worker, and Kim and Selena from my pottery class have become my unexpected allies here.

When I moved here after my graduation, the first thing I did was go job hunting. Writing articles would keep me at home all day—which I *didn't* want—so I applied for all sorts of jobs, including a clothing shop and restaurant at the mall. They called me from the café the next day; I went in for the interview and got hired on the spot.

That's how I met Ann, who took me under her wing and introduced me to her friend group, a bunch of lovely girls I've gone out with a few times now. Mariah says she's proud.

I met Kim and Selena not long after that when I walked by a pottery workshop on my way to work one morning and saw spots open for a class. I had never given pottery a single thought, but after my first lesson, I became a devoted fan—it keeps my mind quiet, and there's no feeling like making something beautiful with your own hands.

Norcastle has given me so much in the past three months, so why do I still feel like something's missing?

"I think being here has helped you in many ways," Maddie adds. "But I also think you're avoiding the big-ass elephant in the room."

My silence is loud enough.

"You know what I was just thinking about today," my uncle starts, his eyes on me. "The first time we met. Remember?"

That day was one of the hardest of Maddie's life, being her dad's funeral, and James traveled all the way to our hometown to be with her. That's when I met him.

"You asked me if I had games on my phone," he recalls, "and you only accepted me into the family when I said yes."

I shake my head in amusement, recalling my embarrassing obsession with phone games. "I had my priorities straight."

"So why don't you anymore?"

That question wipes away my short-lived mirth.

Maddie sits cross-legged on the couch, looking at me with intent. "Fine, I'll say it, since nobody else wants to—what's up with you and that Reed guy? Have you spoken to him since December?"

My heart skips a beat at the sound of his name. I haven't allowed myself to say it out loud in months even though he crosses my mind at least a thousand times every day.

Why the hell can't I get him out of my system?

"No." My mouth feels too dry. "I haven't."

"You don't know what he's up to? Anything?"

I do. I do know some things, but not because I asked. My mom brings him up sometimes when we talk on the phone, even if it's far less frequently than before. She probably thinks I want to know about him, but I'm too afraid to ask.

She wouldn't be wrong.

"I know he isn't working at the university anymore," I tell them, repeating Mom's words. "That's about it."

"He was fired?" James asks.

"Mom said he quit."

"And the rumors?" My stomach sinks at my aunt's question. "How does that make you feel?"

Sick. They've been making me sick for the past four months.

Eva, Mariah's now girlfriend, told me someone—namely, Karla—had gone around campus spreading all sorts of nonsense about Reed and me. How we had sex in a classroom, how I had to graduate early because I was pregnant... My head pounds with dizziness just thinking about it.

Eva assured me that not everyone believes it, but the fact that some do haunts me.

"Not great," I admit.

"Is that why you don't want to go back home?" James asks.

I lock eyes with my uncle, someone who loves me as if I were his own daughter, and find myself unable to lie to him. I can't lie to Maddie, who I love more than life itself, either.

And I can't lie to myself.

"I... I don't feel strong enough to go back."

Maddie's expression softens. "Oh, Li."

"Why not?" asks my uncle.

I pull my knees against my chest. "I don't want the whispers to follow me around or feel like everyone is pointing at me, judging me, every time I try to network. My professors surely know about the rumors, and they have so many contacts in the field. Maybe I'm blowing things out of proportion, but I'm so scared."

My aunt leaves her spot on the couch and sits on the floor right by my feet. She grabs my hand in a comforting gesture. "I understand how unfair all this is, Li. I really do. But you can't let these people control your life. If you don't want to go back to Warlington, that's fine. But make that choice because you want to, not because you're scared of what people will say."

I worry my bottom lip between my teeth. "You don't get it, Maddsy. I tried. I went with my heart, blocking all intrusive thoughts about what others would think, and that's how I ruined everything. If I had been worried about others' opinions, I wouldn't have crossed any lines with Reed."

"But you still would've fallen in love with him."

The words *I'm not in love with him anymore* sit at the tip of my tongue.

But I can't say them.

"You can't help who you fall in love with," says James.

"Do you think I would've chosen to fall in love with my much-older, asshole physical therapist if I'd had a choice?" Maddie asks in a playful voice. "Duh. Of course I would have."

"But you guys are different. You *wanted* to fall in love. You were open to it."

James snorts. "I didn't want to fall in love with her."

"Hey!"

"You know what I mean, love," he tells my aunt. "When I met Maddie, I had also sworn off women. I wanted nothing to do with relationships."

I didn't know this. "Why?"

"Because when I was in college, I found my brother in my then-girlfriend's bed," he confesses, shocking me to my core. *What the hell?* "That tends to traumatize you a little."

I knew James had an older brother, and I also knew they weren't on speaking terms—I could've never imagined *this* was the reason.

"That's...horrible." I blink away my surprise. "How did you even deal with that?"

"I didn't. I avoided the problem, just like you're doing now. You get cheated on? The answer is to close off and never give love a chance again, obviously."

"Sammy got cheated on, too, when he was younger," Maddie adds.

"*What?*" I gasp. "My dad got cheated on? When? How did I not know this?"

"It happened before I was born, I think, or shortly after." Maddie purses her lips, thinking. "It was ages ago, before he met your mom. But that didn't stop him from finding love again; you're proof of that."

I let my tense shoulders sag and release Maddie's hand to rub my eyes. "What's wrong with people?"

"Plenty of things, which is why you shouldn't let them dictate your life. Tell me this, Li—if the rumors stopped, would you go back to Warlington right now?" my aunt asks.

"Maybe," I admit quietly.

"And would you go find Reed?"

My heart jumps. "What for?"

"To start living the life you want once and for all."

"He's my former internship supervisor," I argue, running out of excuses. "And twelve years older than me. That's not exactly ideal."

"Your mom once told me relationships with significant age differences *can* be healthy if both of you fight for it," Maddie offers. I didn't know my mom had such opinions; we'd never talked about age gaps because my only boyfriend was my age. "Your parents have an age gap, and so do we. It may not be ideal, but it's far from the end of the world. As for Reed being your former supervisor... Li, it won't be easy, but you can make it worth it." She looks back at James with a soft smile. "We have."

I allow myself, only for a moment, to picture what it would be like to be so brave. To take the reins of my own life. What would I even do?

Go back to the youth center.

End this pointless gap year and get my license to become a youth counselor like I've always dreamed of.

Find Reed and tell him he was never a mistake. That he's the one for me. That there's never been anyone else, and there never will be.

The fog in my brain clears when Alice's baby monitor goes off, her cries signaling she's awake.

"I'll go get her," James offers, standing from the couch. Before he leaves, he squeezes my shoulder affectionately. "Living an inauthentic life isn't worth it. Remember that."

And I do.

For the next few weeks, I think about my conversation with my aunt and uncle on repeat—at the café, at the pottery studio, while I work from home, as I play with my cousins, when my parents check on me, during my weekly video calls with Mariah.

And by the time May rolls around, something in me lights up.

chapter 37

REED

In the first week of May, I find the courage to do something that is overdue by almost three decades. Something I never felt the need to do until I met her.

My parents' tombstones sit next to each other in muddled soil. Cold, dirty, immobile. Maybe a tree with long branches would do this gloomy corner more justice, but even in death, they don't deserve such kindness.

I once read that cemeteries are places where people go to find peace and tranquility. Where they feel closer to their loved ones who have passed, and the veil is thinner. But looking at my parents' names, forever engraved in rock, I don't feel any of those things.

Before I got here, I thought resentment would take over at the sight of their tombstones. Hatred or even sadness. But standing in front of the place where my parents rest—hopefully, they aren't doing much of that—I feel nothing.

They don't deserve my emotions anymore.

Ginny sniffs around my feet and lies down on a patch of grass when she doesn't find anything interesting to play with.

The plan was to see their tombstones and leave. That was it. I wasn't planning on opening my mouth and speaking to the nothingness in front of me.

"I met someone," I start, unsure of what I'm even doing. But for once, I don't fear it when my heart takes the lead. "She's an amazing woman. So fucking smart. So generous. So beautiful, she takes my breath away. I'd never been in love before her."

Silence greets me.

"And I threw it all away," I conclude. "Because of you."

I'm also not expecting my words to feel like a lie.

I frown to nobody, because nobody is here but Ginny and me. Weirdly enough, I feel the need to explain myself.

"You ruined me," I accuse a pair of ghosts who aren't here to listen. "You abused me, put me in danger, and scarred me forever in countless, cruel ways."

They were heartless abusers, both of them. They taught me that love is a dangerous thing, that I was to blame for everyone's pain.

"You said I would never be able to take care of anyone," I keep going. "But that isn't true—I took care of myself better than you ever did. And I'm taking care of her."

I glance down at Ginny, who looks up at me with her tongue hanging out from her mouth. This little furry thing has shown me unconditional love in a way I never thought I'd experience again from a pet. Because, after what happened to Daisy—after what my parents convinced me I did to her—I didn't think I'd ever deserve it.

Ginny is the savior I never saw coming. Taking care of her and loving her gives me a purpose every day.

So maybe my parents were wrong all along.

"I'm here." I swallow back the unexpected lump in my throat. "Even after all you did to me, I'm still standing. I've made a life for myself—one I'm proud of. You don't define me."

A cold gust of wind hits my face. I keep talking.

"I will always hate you for what you did to me, but I refuse to let you take any more space in my life," I say into the nothingness. "I thought you'd broken me, but Lila showed me the real me was just locked away. I won't let you kill me while I'm still breathing. I survived you once, and I will keep doing it."

Ginny whimpers, glancing between me and the tombstones. I crouch to scratch the spot she likes behind her ears and find myself smiling as she licks my hand.

"I love you, little one. You know that?" I tell her as the puppy keeps licking away. "I hope I'm being a good dad to you."

Her tail starts wagging, which I take as confirmation. Carefully, I pick her up and cradle her against my shirt as I take one last look at my parents' tombstones.

I already know I'm never coming back.

It's taken my heart thirty years to understand it was never my fault. A child is never responsible for their parents' fuckups or for the bad things that happen to them. And I owe that child still living inside me forgiveness and patience.

As I get Ginny in the car and drive back home, my thoughts drift to the woman I haven't been able to forget in the past six months. Because none of this changes the fact that I lost Lila and I'll never get her back.

And it hurts. It fucking hurts like nothing I've ever experienced before to lose the one person I wanted to make mine forever.

Because Lila is mine. Not in a possessive way, but in the sense that she's my everything.

I should've known better than to cross so many lines when I was aware of the consequences. The last thing she needs is for me to come back and make things even more complicated. She deserves to shine again, and she won't do it next to me.

A second realization hits me as I stop the car in my driveway—I will never love anyone ever again. Not in the everlasting, consuming way I love her.

Maybe it should anger me, make me feel scared that now that I've finally discovered my heart isn't broken, I won't get to use it again. But just the thought of loving someone who isn't Lila makes me so sick, I discard it immediately.

Ginny hops out of the car using her three little legs and

follows me home. As I shut the door behind us, my phone buzzes.

Fully expecting it to be a work email, I ignore it and check on Ginny's food and water bowls.

My hours at the youth center have significantly increased in the past few months after I left my job as a researcher. It was about time that ended, anyway. I won't lie—I would've liked to see the project through. That was the plan all along, but I also can't bring myself to regret my choices.

Not when my choice was Lila.

What matters is that the project will go on without me, and those kids will get the funding they deserve. As for me, I've grown tired of hopping between research labs when my calling is to work directly with children. So, in a way, this was the push I needed to reconsider the future of my career.

And while I could never regret my choices, I've finally recognized that I got involved in so many projects, tried to tackle too many jobs at once, because I was trying to fill a void. If I was always on the go, busy and in demand, I didn't have time to dwell on everything that was missing from my life.

I've now significantly cleared my schedule, and I prioritize spending time with Ginny, Liam and Warren, or Haniyah. Checking my work email when I don't have to is no longer something I rush to do.

But after a quick shower, when I decide to check my notifications, I see it was never that.

My heart stops, and I briefly wonder if I hit my head and I'm just seeing things. First, I talked to my dead parents in the cemetery, and now this?

The text is still there when I blink, and it doesn't disappear minutes later.

It's real.

Lila: Hi. How's Ginny?

chapter 38

May 7 at 7:55 p.m.

Lila: Hi. How's Ginny?

Reed: Hey. She's doing well. Just came back from a walk. *picture attached*

Lila: Thanks for answering. I didn't think you would. She looks so cute.

May 12 at 11:03 a.m.

Reed: I hope I'm not intruding. Just thought you'd like this picture of Ginny wearing a birthday hat. They celebrated a party at the dog daycare yesterday. *picture attached*

Lila: Oh my God. She's adorable.

May 15 at 6:27 p.m.

> **Lila: How are things at the youth center?**

> **Reed: Just got out of a session with Cameron. He says hi.**
> **Boxing lessons are paying off for everyone. Melody can now throw a punch.**

> **Lila: Please tell them I miss them and I'm glad they're doing well. Go Melody :)**

May 19 at 9:48 p.m.

> **Reed: How are you doing?**

May 20 at 12:19 a.m.

> **Lila: I've been better. You?**

> **Reed: I've been better too.**

May 28 at 8:01 p.m.

Reed: Ginny did a funny thing today. And by funny, I mean funny to her, not to me. *picture attached*

Lila: Did she... eat that cushion?

Reed: Only disrespected it a bit. I've spent the past twenty minutes picking up polyester from the floor.

Lila: Look at that cute face, though.

Reed: She knows how to use it.

June 4 at 8:25 p.m.

Lila: How are you doing?

Reed: Tired from work. Going to the gym probably didn't help my exhaustion. How are you?

Lila: Just got back from a pottery class.

Reed: Pottery?

Lila: It's a new hobby. I've been
making lots of mugs.

Reed: Can I see?

Lila: This is my most recent one.
picture attached

Reed: The little hearts look great.
Creating beautiful things suits
you.

June 6 at 1:54 p.m.

Reed: Hey. I just wanted to
apologize for my last text. It was a
little weird.

Lila: It's not weird if it made me
smile.

Reed: I'm glad I made you smile.

June 6 at 8:16 p.m.

Lila: I wanted to make you smile
too. *picture attached*

Lila: Hopefully I didn't make you cringe instead.

Reed: I never thought you'd send me a dad joke about academia.

Lila: But did it make you smile?

Reed: I'm smiling right now.

June 8 at 3:14 p.m.

Lila: I just wanted to congratulate you on your project. I read that it was approved last week. It will be life-changing for children.

Reed: Thanks, Lila. I'm glad it went through.

Lila: I didn't see your name on it, though. Did I miss it?

Reed: I couldn't stay on the project after I left my research position. University policy.

Lila: Oh. I didn't know.

Reed: It's okay. What matters is that it'll make a real change.

Lila: Do you know when the foster homes and youth centers will get the new funding?

Reed: Hopefully in October.

Lila: That's amazing. Whether your name is attached to it or not, it was all your doing. You deserve this success.

Reed: Thanks, Lila.

June 10 at 4:58 p.m.

Lila: Any exciting plans for the summer?

Reed: Not really. Staying in Warlington, applying for a few jobs. Hanging out with Ginny, Liam, and Warren.

Lila: What do you mean applying for a few jobs?

Reed: I want to work with kids, not in a lab. I've been thinking about it for a couple years now, actually, but never took the leap.

Lila: Makes sense. Any offers so far?

Reed: I haven't formally applied anywhere yet. I wanted to take a short break and focus on the youth center. What about your summer plans?

Lila: I'm traveling with Mariah for a few weeks. We're going up to this lake town in Maine—Bannport. My aunt and uncle have a cabin up there.

Reed: Sounds great. I'm sure you'll have fun.

June 12 at 9:32 p.m.

Reed: Sorry, I have to ask. Did you get your youth counseling license? You don't have to answer. I don't want to overstep.

Lila: Um, not yet.

Reed: Is it not in your plans anymore?

Lila: It is. I'm not sure if you know, but I was allowed to graduate in January. I went to Norcastle after that with my aunt and uncle. Worked at a café. Did pottery. That kind of thing.

Reed: You needed a break.

Lila: Yes.

Reed: How are you feeling now?

Lila: Better. I needed to find myself. Get to know who I am outside of school and academia.

Reed: And did you do it?

Lila: I'm almost there.

June 16 at 5:02 p.m.

Lila: New mug *picture attached*

Reed: Didn't know orange and pink went together. Looks good.

June 17 at 8:30 p.m.

Reed: Ginny made a new friend at the park. *picture attached*

Lila: Awww. Is that her boyfriend? Girlfriend? Look at their noses pressed together.

Reed: She's not allowed to have boyfriends or girlfriends. She's my baby.

Lila: Protective much?

Reed: Damn right.

June 20 at 6:24 p.m.

Lila: Just got to Maine with Mariah. Isn't the lake so pretty? *picture attached*

Reed: It is. Have fun and stay safe.

Lila: Thank you :)

June 23 at 3:23 a.m.

Lila: I just had a nightmare, and I can't fall back asleep. I don't know why I'm texting you.

Reed: Are you okay?

Lila: Why are you up?

Lila: I didn't think you'd reply.

Reed: It's one of those sleepless nights. Answer me.

Lila: Bossy. It was just a nightmare. Why can't you fall asleep?

Reed: Too much on my mind.

Lila: As in...?

Reed: As in you.

Reed: Sorry. I shouldn't have said that.

Lila: It's okay.

Lila: You're on my mind, too.

Reed: Yeah?

374

Lila: All the time.

June 23 at 8:05 a.m.

Reed: Good morning. Did you fall back asleep last night?

Lila: Yeah, but I didn't sleep very well. You?

Reed: I slept for two hours or so.

Lila: Oof.

Reed: I know. And by the way.

Lila: Yes?

Reed: You're on my mind all the time, too.

June 25 at 7:26 p.m.

Lila: Just got back home from Bannport. Time to start studying my ass off for that license. Any tips?

Reed: Not many. I'll email you

some mock exams.

Lila: Thanks :)

Reed: Good luck. You'll nail it.

June 30 at 11:09 p.m.

Lila: Question.

Reed: Shoot.

Lila: Do you miss me?

Reed: All the time.

July 1 at 10:14 p.m.

Reed: Question.

Lila: Yes?

Reed: Why a café?

Lila: What?

Reed: Why did you work at a café in Norcastle?

Lila: It was the first place that called me back. I wanted a job that had nothing to do with academia or my master's. Not that I don't love working with kids, because I do, but I needed something different.

Reed: Did that job help you find yourself?

Lila: In a weird way, yes. It helped me see my worth outside of my grades. Like I had other parts of me to offer. I had no barista experience, and I was a shitty one for the first couple of weeks, and it was okay. I didn't feel like a failure or take it personally. Sorry, I'm rambling.

Reed: Don't need to apologize. I could read your texts for hours.

Lila: I'm blushing.

Reed: Good.

Reed: I have another question.

Lila: Go ahead.

Reed: Do you miss me?

Lila: All the time.

July 3 at 4:12 p.m.

Lila: It's official. My dad is retiring next month. I don't know how to feel about it.

Reed: Feel free to vent.

Lila: Oh, I'm going to.

Lila: It's just the fact that he's getting old, I think. He's been a tattoo artist all his life, long before I was born. It's part of his identity. It's weird that he won't work there anymore.

Reed: Changes can be scary. What you're feeling is normal. Have you talked to your dad about it?

Lila: Yeah. He's excited about retiring. Says he and my mom can travel more now and do more things together.

Reed: Retirement won't be a bad thing, then.

Lila: I guess not. I just need to get over it.

Reed: It's okay not to be over it. Just text me whenever you want to talk. I'm here.

Lila: Thank you. I'm here, too.

July 5 at 7:39 a.m.

Reed: Happy 25th birthday, little criminal.

Lila: I didn't think you'd remember. Thank you :)

Reed: I could never forget.

Lila: I can't believe my brain is fully developed now. Honestly, it feels the same.

Reed: Any big plans today? Enjoy the new brain.

Lila: I'm going out with Mariah and some friends.

Reed: Have fun, then. And be safe.

Lila: Thanks :)

Lila: Also, I missed that nickname.

Reed: Me too.

July 7 at 10:25 p.m.

Lila: Hi.

Reed: Hey.

Lila: I need to tell you something.

Reed: I'm listening.

Lila: I had fun at my birthday party, but I couldn't stop thinking about how you weren't there.

Reed: Did you want me to be there?

Lila: Yes.

Reed: I would've been there if you'd asked me to.

Lila: I don't trust myself around you.

Reed: I don't trust myself around you either.

July 9 at 10:01 p.m.

> Lila: Reed.

Reed: Lila.

> Lila: Are you at home?

Reed: Yes. Why?

> Lila: Are you free?

Reed: Yes.

> Lila: Can I call you?

chapter 39

LILA

The dim glow coming from my phone is the only light in my bedroom. I'm unable to take my eyes off the three dots dancing on the screen until his reply comes through.

Reed: Of course.

Taking a deep breath through my nose, I ignore the pounding of my heart and tell myself it's going to be okay. This is what I want. What I've been thinking about since that late-night conversation with my aunt and uncle months ago. Even longer, if I'm honest.

I wrap my softest blanket around my shoulders and sit back against the headboard.

The past seven months without Reed have been eye-opening in very necessary but painful ways. The last time we saw each other, I thought I'd never want him in my life again. I wasn't angry at him, not really—I was angry at myself for having lowered my guard after I promised my career would always come first.

Graduating in January was something I wasn't expecting. But once I got my diploma, it didn't feel...right. It wasn't like I'd fallen out of love with my dream of becoming a youth counselor, but after everything that had happened, it didn't feel like the right time. Becoming a Masters graduate in counseling didn't change the fact that I still didn't know who I was. That I saw no value to myself outside academia.

Months of being away from the gossip, my comfort zone, him, slowly started to change my perspective. And when I found myself unable to stop thinking about the calm way my heart would feel with Reed, the easy way I would breathe with him, I simply didn't fight it.

I had no plan when I sent him that first text in May. If anything, the past few months have taught me that plans don't always happen, no matter how badly you want them to. I've learned that it's okay to go with the flow and that I'm capable enough to ride any wave.

Now, I also have no plan as my finger hovers above the Call button. All I know is that I've spent enough time away from everything and everyone to decide what I really want and don't want.

And I want him.

I press the button and hold my breath.

"Hey."

The sound of his voice, so deep, so familiar, makes my knees buckle and my heart flip.

My own only comes out as a whisper. "Hi."

I hear his soft breathing in the background, and it grounds me. *He's here. With me.*

"I wasn't expecting my night to go like this," he admits, a hint of a smile in his voice.

God, I miss that smile. I miss when it was directed at me.

"Any complaints?" I ask, my voice quiet.

"None at all. How was your day?"

I pull my knees against my chest. "I went to a pottery class."

"Any new mugs in the works?"

"I'm going down a cereal bowl rabbit hole right now," I tell him, the shyness peeling away from my voice with every interaction. "I also looked into Spanish lessons for adults. I think it'll be good for socializing, too."

"That sounds incredible, Lila."

The way he says my name sends a thrill down my spine. I hug my blanket tighter against myself, wishing I was in his arms instead. "How was your day?"

"I heard back from a foster agency this morning. About the job."

I sit up, excited. "How did it go? They want you, don't they?"

His chuckle makes me clamp my legs together. *Stop it.* "They sure do."

"I knew it." I beam. "I bet they didn't even read past your name on the application. I mean, who doesn't know *the* Reed Abner?"

"Way to stroke my ego, little criminal."

My stomach does a little flutter at the nickname. "Just telling the truth. Will you say yes? Or are you waiting for any more offers?"

"Honestly, I might say yes to this one."

"Oh?"

"It's, ah..." He clears his throat, hesitating. "The foster agency. It's the same one that handled my case when I was a kid."

My chest constricts. "Talk about meant to be."

"Yeah. I guess it is."

Silence falls, but it's not uncomfortable. I feel him so close, as if he were in the room with me. *I wish he were.*

"Lila," he starts softly.

"Yes?"

"Can you keep talking to me? I miss hearing your voice."

The organ in my chest melts, and I let it happen.

"I miss your voice, too," I admit quietly.

"Yeah?"

I nod even though he can't see me.

"What else do you miss?" he asks next, sounding almost shy.

I take a shaky breath, my heart beating so loud that I'm afraid he'll hear it from the other side of the line.

"I miss..." *Everything.* "I miss Ginny. A lot."

"She misses you too."

Great. Now I'm about to start sobbing.

"I miss the youth center," I continue. "I miss running workshops with you, helping the kids with homework...just being there with all of you. I miss Haniyah and all the volunteers. I miss..."

I miss you.

"Lila." My name is followed by a deep sigh. "I'm so fucking sorry. I'm so sorry I was so careless. I don't know what I've done to deserve you talking to me again."

We're doing this.

We're finally talking about what happened in December.

I'm still scared to because this new me isn't used to taking leaps of faith. I did it once, and it ended up in tears. What will happen if I open up my heart now?

"I'm sorry, too," I whisper into the night, my hands clammy with nerves.

"You don't have to apologize—"

"I do," I cut him off.

"Lila, you don't," he insists. "I'm the older one. I should've stopped us when I had the chance."

"Just let me... Let me say this." I swallow. "Please."

"Okay," he concedes.

All my life, I've been too preoccupied with everyone's idea of me to develop my true sense of self—and I'm not blaming anyone but me for it.

All those months in Norcastle, where I felt free to follow my own path without worrying about anyone's expectations, made me realize something—I've been the prisoner of my own anxiety and overthinking all this time, subject to expectations that weren't there.

I was free to be myself all this time, and I couldn't see it. But I've finally become a woman who refuses to betray her heart ever again.

"We were never a mistake," I tell Reed quietly, feeling the weight of regret leaving my shoulders with every word. "You didn't ruin my career. If anything, *I* ruined it for myself, but it's not... It's not truly ruined. The rumors might follow me around forever, but we both know they aren't true. And yes, we broke some rules, but my value as a youth counselor has nothing to do with my relationships in the first place. I know my worth now, and I know I've earned everything I've got through hard work.

"I'm sorry I said being with you was a mistake, Reed, because you're the best thing that has ever happened to me."

A pause. Then his rough whisper, "Say my name again."

"Reed," I whisper, my lips tilting into a smile.

"Fuck. I missed that," he breathes. "*You're* the best thing that has ever happened to me, Lila. You deserve all the good things that happen to you because you've worked so damn hard for them. But that doesn't change the fact that I will never forgive myself for hurting you."

"We both hurt each other, and we hurt ourselves," I say. "What is done is done."

"And what happens now?"

I throw my head back, eyes lost on the ceiling.

"I don't know," I admit quietly. "Everything is complicated."

According to Eva, the rumors on campus have been going on all year, even after Reed left—that only made them worse. What Karla started will follow me forever, but that doesn't mean I have to be a martyr.

"I understand." His voice sounds so gruff, it sends a thrill to my core. "Maybe it makes me a selfish bastard, but I don't want to lose you. Not again."

"You won't lose me," I reassure him. "I don't want to lose you either."

"You won't."

"Are we friends, Reed?"

"I'll be whatever you want me to be as long as I get to stay in your life, angel."

It's his nickname for me that fills my eyes with unshed, relieved tears.

"I want to call you again tomorrow," I confess. "Can we do that?"

"Of course we can," he says softly. "Whenever you want to, I'm always here."

"Okay."

"Okay."

One step at a time. I can do that.

"Good night, Reed," I mutter with a hopeful gleam in my chest.

"Sleep well, Lila. We'll talk tomorrow."

When we hang up, I look around my dark room and realize something—I feel lighter, and so does the world around me.

chapter 40

REED

Lila and I speak on the phone every July night.

With Ginny sleeping on my lap, I revel in the sound of her calming voice as she tells me about her day, her friends, and her pottery classes.

She teases me that I mostly stay quiet and let her ramble, and I tell her I just missed her voice too much. That I will never get tired of hearing her talk so passionately about the things she loves.

Just the fact that I get to talk to her every night is enough to get me through the day.

I send her a picture of Ginny every other day, and she sends me the occasional picture of a mug-in-progress. I tell her she can text me anytime if she ever needs me, and she tells me to do the same.

During one of our late-night calls, I confess I visited my parents' graves back in May.

"Why did you do it?" She sounds curious, not judgmental.

My fingers tangle with Ginny's short fur. She's peacefully snoring on my lap under the faint glow of the lamp illuminating the living room.

"I owed it to myself to close that chapter," I say.

"And did you?"

I ponder her question and come to the conclusion that, no, I haven't. Not fully.

"I'm almost there," I tell her, mirroring her words from when I asked her if she had found herself.

A comfortable silence stretches between us. We do this a lot during our calls, just sitting in silence. Knowing she's on the other side of the line, breathing, so near me yet so far, brings me a sense of comfort I've never known before.

Until, in the last week of July, she says, "Reed?"

"Yeah?"

"I want to see you."

Her voice comes out as an unsure whisper.

My heart starts beating faster. "Now?"

She giggles. *That laugh.* "I mean...if you want to. I'm in Warlington."

My body and my soul beg me to say yes, to get in my car and drive to her house if that means I'll get to breathe her in again. But I can't ignore the string of regret pulling at my gut, and I know I have to do one last thing before I see her again.

So, I tell her. She says she understands, although the slight hint of disappointment in her voice pierces through my heart.

The next morning, I send him a text.

> **Me: Hey. Can I stop by the shop today at closing time?**

It takes him two hours to answer.

> **Cal: Don't make me regret it.**

⁓৹⁓

The bell chimes above my head as I step inside the tattoo parlor and spot a lone figure at the back of the shop—a man I haven't seen in too long.

"Hey," I call out, my hands in the pockets of my slacks.

I don't sound like I'm freaking out, even though that's the only thing happening on the other side of my relaxed facade.

Cal turns from the station he's cleaning up. "Just a minute."

His voice sounds neutral, which amps up my anxiety levels. Cal is a good friend—he never sounds neutral with me.

Was *my good friend before I hurt his daughter. Now, I'll be lucky if I don't become his target.*

I don't move a muscle as I wait for him at the front. He takes his time clearing everything up, or maybe I'm just on edge. Either way, I don't breathe too normally for the next five minutes.

I sure as hell don't feel any better when he finally makes his way toward me, a serious expression on his face, and the first thing he says is, "I should probably kill you."

I swallow back the tension rising in my throat. "You probably should."

He crosses his arms, frowning. It's the most defensive and pissed-off I've seen him look. "Tell me why I shouldn't."

I'm honest when I say, "I can't think of any reason."

We stare at each other for what feels like a torturous eternity before his shoulders sag with a deep sigh. "Why are you here?"

"I want to apologize to you," I say, not beating around the bush. "The last thing I wanted was to hurt any of you, and I could never regret it enough."

He looks at me like he either doesn't believe me or doesn't want to. And I'd rather be anywhere else than under the stare of one of the most intimidating men I've ever met, but I'm doing this for Lila.

"Lila told us she's speaking to you again." His words sound like an accusation.

Hearing her name makes my chest crack open. "She did?"

His nod is slow, measured. For a moment, he doesn't speak.

"I've had eight long months to think about this whole situation," he finally says. "But I'm not sure how I feel about it yet."

"I underst—"

"My *daughter*, Abner? Are you fucking kidding me?"

"Cal—"

"It's *sir* from now on."

I give him a flat look. "You're joking."

"Do I look like I'm joking?"

He looks one second away from tackling me to the ground. So, no, *playful* isn't an adjective I would use on him right now.

"All right. Sir." Is it me, or are his lips twitching? "I came here to apologize. Grace told me you needed time, but if it hasn't been enough, I'll leave. I'll understand if you don't want to see my face ever again."

"Let's not get dramatic," he surprises me by saying. "Do I want to kill you for hurting my daughter? Absolutely. Do I think you're scum of the earth? No. I've met real scum of the earth before, and you don't deserve to be put in that same box, no matter how mad I am at you right now."

I don't know what to say to that because I don't think I deserve this level of understanding, so I stay silent.

"What are your intentions here?" he asks me, his voice serious. "Aside from apologizing, what do you want? Because I know you want something, and I'm not sure I'll like it."

"Lila wants to see me, and I can't promise to never see her again unless she asks me to."

Cal narrows his eyes at me. "Are you asking for my permission to date my daughter, Abner?"

"No," I say. "I'm telling you I'm going to."

A deafening silence falls over the tattoo shop.

I can't read his face. My own stays blank.

I don't move. Neither does he.

"You've got balls telling me you don't give a fuck about what I think as long as Lila is happy, I'll give you that."

I swallow. "I don't mean to disrespect you."

I don't add *sir* because he might kill me for real this time.

He sighs, shaking his head. "Look, man. All I know is that you hurt my daughter, and she went through hell because of it. But I also know she needed the wake-up call."

I frown. "What are you getting at?"

"I'm saying what happened, happened, and what matters is that you came out of it. And Lila is happier now, more herself. Now that eight months have passed, I can see the little good in this situation. Talking to Lila has also helped. She isn't lost anymore." His stare is hard on me. "You're a good man who fucked up. It doesn't mean I'm thrilled to see you with my daughter, but I won't hold any grudges if she forgives you."

"What would it take to earn your forgiveness?" I ask. "To earn Grace's?"

"We've talked about this, Grace and me. With Lila, too. I've always trusted you with her, and a part of me still does. Maybe I shouldn't, but gut feelings never lie to me. I need some time to get used to...to this whole thing, but Lila is smart—more so now that she's finally living for herself. If you choose each other, her mom and I have nothing to say about it. But if you ever hurt her again, Abner, consider yourself dead."

"I will never hurt her again, Cal. I'd rather hurt myself a thousand times before I let her feel a second of pain."

His face remains stoic, but approval shines in his eyes. "You'd better."

"I want to start again," I tell him. "Whatever I have to do to get your trust again—and Grace's—I'll do it."

He looks at me for a moment too long. "All right. We'll talk about this some other time. Now, if you'll excuse me, I want to close up and go home to my wife. It's been a hell of a day."

"One last thing."

I don't know what takes over me when I open my mouth and say the next words. All I know is that it feels like the final puzzle piece has just clicked into place.

chapter 41

LILA

My leg bounces with anxiety as I glance around my dad's tattoo shop.

This isn't the last time I'm going to come here, but it feels like it. Because I might have found my self-worth in the past eight months, but my dramatic tendencies will always be part of me.

I try to let these feelings go, but one look around me is enough to bring me down again—I'm blaming that *"Happy retirement, Cal and Trey!"* banner hanging at the back of the shop.

Despite how hard I've tried to ignore it, the day of my dad's retirement comes anyway. On this sunny August day, my heart breaks a little as I watch my family, friends, and longtime clients of my dad's celebrate a career of success. A legacy.

As if she can sense I'm about to burst into tears, my mom breaks away from the group she's talking to and sits next to me in the tattooing chair. She wraps an arm around my shoulders and kisses the side of my head.

"Why are you here all alone?" she asks.

Another thing I've learned from my time away is to be generous with my feelings by not concealing them for the sake of other people's comfort. Maybe I would've pretended everything was okay for my dad's sake if we'd been having this conversation last year. But the new Lila doesn't want to hide anymore.

"I'm sad about Dad retiring," I confess. "I don't know what comes next."

"I'll tell you what comes next." My mom hugs me closer to her side. "First, the three of us are going on that cruise your dad wants. I booked it as a surprise, and he doesn't know it yet, so shh."

That makes me smile. "He's going to freak out."

"That's the goal. Then, when we come back, he's going to stop by the shop to check on things because he can't help himself, and I'll have to scold him for it a million times."

My smile widens. "A million times won't be enough."

"Right?" She chuckles. "And then, he's going to do whatever he wants because he deserves to take a break. He's been talking about updating the patio for months now. He might just discover his new passion."

I can't help it—my chest caves in. "I don't want things to change," I admit quietly.

"Because it's scary?"

I nod. "What if what comes next is bad?"

My mom pulls away so we're looking at each other. Whatever she's searching for in my gaze, she finds it a moment later.

"You've gone through many changes this past year," she starts, her voice soft. "It's normal to be scared. But be honest with me, sweetie. Would you rather be who you are now, or who you were last December before everything happened?"

It's not a difficult answer.

"I'd rather be who I am today," I admit.

"Why?"

She knows the reason, but I still tell her, "Because I finally feel like myself."

I'm aware that I'm still a work in progress, and that bad habits can't be shed overnight. But I no longer feel that anxious pull to hide my discomfort, to please everyone but me, to ignore what I want because I'm scared others will find it out of character for me.

And in a messed-up way, it's all because of what Karla did to me. To us. If she hadn't sent those pictures, if she hadn't spread the rumors, if I hadn't been catapulted out of my comfort zone so brutally and forced to face my worst nightmare, I wouldn't have found this new version of me I love so much.

Now I know that, even if the worst happens, I have what it takes to rise from the ashes.

"You had to go through very uncomfortable changes to be who you are today," my mom continues. "But that shows that not all changes are bad. Look at you—you've never glowed brighter. We'll always be proud of you no matter what, Lila."

She kisses the side of my face again. "Did you know Dad tattooed me in this very chair?"

"What? It's *this* one?"

How did I not know this?

She hums, smiling. "Notice how all the other chairs are different? It's because he refused to get rid of this one when they updated the furniture years ago. He usually keeps it at the back and doesn't let his clients use it."

I find myself smiling too. "Totally sounds like something Dad would do."

I've heard the story of how my parents met a million times, but I never get tired of it. How my mom wanted to get a tattoo to resemble her strength but freaked out at the last second. How my dad watched her hesitate right outside the shop, not understanding why his heart had just started beating again when he had never met that girl before.

He turns to us then, and he promptly excuses himself from the group he's talking to.

"What are my girls chatting about?" he asks before kissing my forehead, then my mom's lips.

"I was just telling Lila about our chair," she says.

He touches the worn-out fabric. "I've had this thing for

thirty-plus years. It's a miracle it's still standing."

A sudden lump clogs my throat. "What happens to the chair now? Are you leaving it here?"

"No way," he says immediately. "This is a relic—it's coming home with me."

Why is a chair about to make me cry?

Dad ruffles my hair. "Are you okay, little sunshine?"

I don't know what does it for me. Maybe it's his nickname for me, or maybe it's that I'm finally allowing myself to be openly vulnerable. All I know is that a single tear rolls down my cheek, and then another one, and I don't stop them.

My dad pulls me into his arms. "It's okay, Li."

My mom starts rubbing comforting circles on my back.

"I know." I sniffle. "I'm happy for you, Dad."

"Thank you." He kisses the top of my head. "This only means I'll have more free time to pester you."

I chuckle against his T-shirt. "Can't wait."

And I mean it wholeheartedly.

The retirement party goes on well into the evening, in which some more tears are shed. This time, from my best friend.

Over the past few months, Dad had brought up the future of the shop to me again. So, I told him what I'd been about to say when we first discussed his retirement.

"Nobody deserves to get the shop more than Mariah," I told him, feeling every word in my heart. "Tattooing is in her veins, and she's beyond talented. She's so smart, too; give her a two-month business course, and she'll be running the place like no other."

My dad confessed he and Trey had considered Mariah before, but they wanted to make sure I was okay with it.

"I'm still signing you as a co-owner because Inkjection is my legacy, and I want you to be part of it," he said. "If you agree."

My answer was sincere. "It would be an honor, Dad."

We agreed that Mariah would run the place when the time came, and she'd have to consult with me about any major changes, such as if she ever wanted to sell the shop. Once Uncle Trey agreed—he knew Mariah would freak out in the best way— we decided to break the news at their retirement party.

Just like we predicted, she starts crying tears of joy as soon as we tell her.

"You won't regret it," she says, emotion clogging her throat.

I laugh as I hug her tight—not because I think her tears are funny, but because the fact that she hugs me first, even before she hugs her dad, sure is.

"Nobody deserves it more than you," I tell her. "You're going to do an amazing job. And if you ever need help, you know I'm here."

She plants a loud kiss on my cheek. "I love you, Li. Sisters forever."

"Sisters forever," I echo.

The tattoo parlor clears out a while later, but my parents and I stay behind to tidy up.

They stay at the back while I take care of the front, straightening the cushions on the leather couch and sweeping the floors.

I shut my eyes and breathe in deeply, taking in the moment. Far from feeling sad, a new sense of purpose fills my veins now. Because just the thought that this place that means so much to me now belongs to my best friend and I is something so special, so meant to be, I can't find words for it.

I picture myself walking through the door next year, in five, in twenty, and I only feel calm knowing my dad's legacy will live on.

We'll make sure of it.

When I open my eyes, I'm not expecting to see him on the other side of the windows.

I blink, just in case all the strong emotions from today are making me see things. But Reed is still standing outside my dad's shop, hands in the pockets of his slacks, his eyes on me.

The world stops around us.

It hits me that we haven't seen each other in person since December. I wonder what he thinks as he looks at me. If he can see the changes inside me being reflected on the outside.

This time, every part of my being is sure as I unlock the front door.

"You're here" are my first words to his face after eight long, much-needed months of forcing myself to listen to my heart.

"And you look even more beautiful than the last time I saw you," Reed says.

My heart leaps. "Do you want to come in?"

He nods, not taking his eyes away from me.

I close the door behind us. He takes up so much space; I'd forgotten how imposing he is. Far from making nerves swirl in my stomach, though, his presence soothes me.

My heart recognizes its keeper.

"What are you doing here?" I ask him, my body gravitating toward him.

"Your dad told me I could stop by."

My eyes widen. "He did?"

Dad told me about his conversation with Reed, but he didn't reveal much, so I don't know what went down that day. Reed doesn't have a black eye right now, which I'll take as a good sign.

He dips his chin. "Yeah."

"Why?"

"You're here." Dad's voice comes from somewhere behind me. When I look back, he and Mom are at the front of the shop. "You must be Reed Abner."

Wait. *What?*

"Did you hit your head?" I frown in my dad's direction.

"Dad, you know him."

But Reed doesn't seem fazed. And judging by the smirk on my mom's face, I'm definitely missing something.

He steps forward, holding out a hand in my dad's direction. "It's great to meet you, sir."

Sir?

"Why are you being so weird right now?" I lose it a little when my dad shakes Reed's hand. "What's going on?"

My mom only chuckles, mirth dancing in her eyes. I officially don't understand a thing.

"Pleasure is all mine," Dad says. "My daughter has told me so much about you. You're about to start a new position as a counselor at a local foster home, I heard?"

"All right. Enough." I step between them, gently pushing Reed back with a hand on his torso. My gaze pinballs between the two insane men surrounding me. "Stop being embarrassing. If neither of you tell me what's going on right now, I'm going to scream."

It's Reed who takes the lead. "I told your dad I wanted to start again when I talked to him last week. He agreed."

"So, you're what, pretending to meet for the first time?"

Dad shrugs. "He needs to win me over."

When Mom chuckles, I turn to her. "Are you meeting Reed for the first time, too, or are you a normal person?"

She smiles. "Don't worry, sweetie. I haven't lost it yet."

"So." Dad ignores us, crossing his arms and looking at Reed again. "What are your intentions with our daughter?"

Kill me now.

"I give up," I mumble, hiding my face in my hands. "I'm done with both of you."

"For now, I'd like to take her out on a date," Reed says as if I weren't here at all.

And despite this situation being ridiculous, my heart melts

at his words all the same.

"Are you asking for my permission?" Dad asks.

"I'm telling you what I'm going to do," Reed says boldly, sliding his gaze to me. "If she says yes."

I don't miss the smile on my dad's face, as if they just shared some kind of inner joke I'm not privy to. And honestly, I'm too scared to ask.

"What do you say, angel?" Reed asks, his full attention on me. "Would you like to go on a date with me tonight?"

It doesn't even register that he's just called me angel in front of my parents. I don't care about what they think of him, of us, of any of this. Not anymore.

Reed and I are the only ones who matter right now.

And so I tell him, "I'd love to."

chapter 42

LILA

Reed picks me up from my parents' house a couple hours later.

The city lights blur past us, but I can't peel my eyes off the man behind the wheel. The man I've missed with my whole heart and who I refuse to let go of ever again.

"Stop looking at me like that," he warns me, a playful edge to his voice, as he keeps his gaze trained forward.

"Or what?" I tease.

His hand slides to my bare thigh, riding up the hem of my summer dress. "Or I will pull over and take you in the back seat, which isn't ideal because I want to talk to you first."

My pulse accelerates. "But you're still taking me in the back seat of your car some other time?"

"I was thinking somewhere more romantic, but if that's what you want, then sure."

"You spoil me too much."

"What can I say? Spoiling you makes me hard."

He keeps his hand on my bare leg for the rest of our drive and only pulls away when we stop at his driveway.

"I know this is probably not the date spot you were expecting," he starts, sounding so nervous that it's adorable. "But I wanted us to have a private place to talk. We can go somewhere else if you want."

I give him a sincere smile. "This is more than fine."

And it only gets better when Ginny sprints down the hallway

the second he opens the front door, coming straight for me.

"Hi, sweet baby," I coo, crouching to scratch her behind her ear. It's still her favorite spot. "I missed you so much. You look so much bigger than last year."

"She did get a little bigger," Reed confirms. "Are you going to cry?"

I chuckle, my eyes glassy. "Maybe."

How can he tell when I'm not looking at him?

Gently, he helps me up to my feet and tucks a strand of hair behind my ear. "Why are you going to cry?"

"Because I missed her so much," I say, still looking down at her. "Was she good to you? Did she make any new friends? Did you take her to the vet?"

His hand rests on the small of my back. "I'll tell you all the updates over dinner, all right? But she's fine, and she missed you too, so she's happy now that you're here. We both are."

I shift my gaze to him, to the vulnerability in his eyes. I'm about to tell him that I'm happy to be here, too, when the smell hits me. "Why does it smell so good?"

"Ah, I might have prepared something for tonight," he admits, his cheeks reddening.

"Can I see?" I beam.

With his hand still on my back, he guides me across the hall, through the kitchen. It smells even better here, but it's spotless, giving nothing away.

Until the garden comes into view, and my breath catches.

"It's not much, but I hope you like it," he says, still in that shy voice.

The words get stuck in my throat as I take in the small table with two chairs, adorned with flowers, candles, and fairy lights.

"Did you do this?" I ask, my voice small.

"I might have asked for a bit of Haniyah's help, but yes," he confesses. "What you're smelling is the dinner I made earlier. It's in the oven. I hope you like steak."

"I do." I look up at him, my pulse hammering in my throat. "This is the most romantic thing anyone has ever done for me."

He shakes his head. "You deserve better. And I have better things planned, but tonight I wanted us to talk in private, and this is all I could come up with."

"It's perfect." I get on my tiptoes and press a soft kiss to his stubbled cheek. "Not to sound desperate, but I'm starving."

He chuckles. His blush is adorable. "Let's eat, then."

Throughout dinner, bathed in the soft lights and the candle glow with Ginny begging for some food at our feet, I get the comforting feeling that I could get used to this. To doing this with him, being surrounded by his soothing presence all the time. I *want* to.

As he tells me about his summer and I tell him about my months in Norcastle, I realize nothing else matters than being here, right now.

His voice is a familiar sound that I want to hear forever. I never want to lose his touch again, his warmth, *him*. I don't want the memory of what we could have been to follow me forever. I want him to be my past, my present, my future.

Because I've tried to move on from Reed, but I'm tired of fighting against my heart's instincts.

"How did you like dinner?" he asks when we're done with dessert.

"It was perfect," I tell him with a smile. "Everything is perfect."

He sits back on his chair. "Come here."

His eyes never leave mine as I walk up to him. The warmth of his hands on my hips seeps through my skin, and I hold my breath as he carefully lowers me to his lap.

The comforting sound of crickets takes over his garden. It's like only we exist in this moment.

His voice is quiet as he places a loose strand of hair behind my ear. "I could look at you forever."

My fingers play with the hairs at the nape of his neck. "I could look at you forever, too," I admit.

"Maybe we should do something about it."

"Maybe."

He buries his face in my neck and takes a deep breath. "I'm sorry, Lila. I'm so sorry I made you go through hell. I'm so sorry I couldn't protect you from the pain. I will never forgive myself for it."

"Hey." Gently, I hold his cheek until he's looking at me. The devastation in his eyes is a sight I never want to see again. "I hurt you too, and I'm sorry for it. But I don't regret it, Reed. Not a single moment. These past few months have been life-changing for me. Uncomfortable, yes, but necessary. I wouldn't have found myself without the pain."

"Do you mean that?" he asks, leaning into my touch.

"Every word."

Silence falls over us, the sounds of the night speaking for us. Reed hugs me closer in his lap, and I wrap my arms around his neck, wanting to never let go.

"You once asked me what you could possibly teach me that I didn't already know," he starts, breaking the silence with that deep rumble.

His heartbeat accelerates when I lay my hand on his chest.

"I remember," I whisper.

Back when I didn't believe in myself, not really. Back when he gave me the tools to.

A shiver runs down my spine when he presses a soft kiss to my bare shoulder, then to the side of my neck, then behind my ear. His grip on me tightens, and I melt into him.

"I said you taught me plenty of things, and you didn't believe me," he says. "But you taught me the most important thing of all,

Lila. You taught me how to love."

My hands start trembling. Not from fear or cold, but from an entirely unknown emotion I've never felt before.

"My parents made me think love was something conditional and hurtful," he adds. "I let them define me for so long, convinced they were right. But then you came along and shattered all my inhibitions without even meaning to. It's like I've been sleeping all my life, and now I look at you and see the good of life for the first time."

My eyes get glassy.

"I'm sorry I put you through everything last December and every day since. I tried to fight it, tried to convince myself that my feelings were wrong, that I was sick in the head, that you would never feel the same. And maybe you don't feel it at all, but I still want to say this."

"Reed..." I whisper, the beating of my heart matching his.

"I love you, angel. You're the best thing that has ever happened to me, and I want to take care of you for the rest of my life. If you want me, I'm yours."

His confession slices my chest open in the most beautiful, painless way. It bleeds into my heart, cradles it, caresses it.

I'm finally here. I'm home.

Hiding my face in the crook of his neck, breathing in his familiar scent, I silently thank my destiny for allowing me to live this life. For allowing me to have him.

And when I pull back, the raw love I see in his eyes takes my breath away.

"I don't regret a single thing that happened because it led me to you," I tell him. "You're my dream come true, Reed. I love you. I love you with all I've got."

He cups my cheek, guiding my lips to his.

Home. I feel at home in this kiss, cradled in his arms.

Passion ignites in my stomach, burning me in the most

delicious way. My chest heaves with need that he notices right away because he's *Reed*. Reed, who breaks the kiss only to peck my lips again and again. Reed, who picks me up bridal style to carry me inside the house.

In his bedroom, he lowers me to the mattress and kisses me again. Sweet at first, then with more urgency. I pull him closer by the collar of his shirt and wrap my legs around his hips, urging our bodies to become one.

"Goddammit," he grunts as he grabs my ass, pushing me farther into his bed. "This is coming off."

I chuckle. "My dress?"

"Your dress. Your underwear. All of it."

I bite down on his lower lip, tugging at his collar again. "Then so is this."

"Whatever you want, angel."

He closes the distance between us again, devouring my mouth. But then a sudden question crosses my mind, one I've been wondering for months.

"Reed?"

"Mmm...?"

"Why do you call me angel?"

He takes his time answering. As if he couldn't stay away, he presses a line of kisses on my neck, then on my cheek, and finally a soft peck on my lips.

"I'm not much of a spiritual person, Lila, but I believe you were sent to this world to heal my soul," he says. "And not just mine, as much as I want to keep you to myself. You're a gift to this world. You make everyone's life better just by being near them. You love unconditionally, and I admire you so damn much for it. You're an angel walking among mortals, and I'm so damn lucky to call you mine."

"How are you real?" I breathe out.

"I could ask you the same thing." He kisses my forehead. "I

love you so much."

"I love you too," I whisper, my lips brushing his.

I wrap my legs around his hips a little tighter, pulling him closer. He lifts my body with one arm until my head is buried in his pillow. It smells so much like him, so deliciously familiar I could get used to sleeping here.

"You want to know a little secret?" he whispers in my ear, his voice playful. "I have condoms this time."

When he grabs a new package from his nightstand, I try not to smile but fail. Because the fact that he bought them specifically to use with me makes my desire burn even hotter.

He lets me push him down on the bed until I'm sitting on top of him.

"I like where this is going," he drawls, his hands lighting my skin on fire.

Smirking, I untuck his shirt from his slacks and start guiding it up his torso. I can't help myself as I lean over him, kissing my way down from his chest until I reach the button of his pants.

He grunts. "Are you trying to kill me?"

My only answer is to undo his button. He's rock-hard behind his boxers, so I stroke him through the fabric, getting him even harder for me.

"Lila," he grits out.

"Yes, Dr. Abner?"

"*Fuck*." He throws his arm over his eyes. "Don't call me that while your hand is around my cock."

"Why?" I keep stroking him. "Scared you'll like it too much?"

I take his groan as a yes, which only makes me wetter.

In one movement, I free him from his boxers and take him into my mouth, just like I've been dying to do again since that night at the hotel. There's something about bringing such a powerful man to his knees that gives me unmeasurable pleasure.

"Slow down, baby, or I'm gonna come," he grunts, but he still guides my head up and down his shaft.

I release him with a pop and throw my dress over my head. It falls somewhere on his bedroom floor, just like my bra mere seconds later.

Without taking my panties off, I climb on top of him again and rub myself against him, teasing both of us every time his engorged head presses against the fabric.

"Lila," he grunts, his grip on my hips strong and possessive. "I want to be inside you so fucking badly."

The plan was to tease him for a bit longer, but the truth is, I'm burning so hot, I couldn't take it if I tried. So, I grab his hard length with one hand and pull my panties aside with the other, too blinded by lust to take them off completely.

"The condom," he grunts just as the tip brushes my wetness.

"Later," I breathe out, teasing my slit with his length. "I want to feel you bare."

He curses under his breath, and so do I at the first sensation of him inside me. He's so big, he fills every inch of me, stretching me out until I can't take it, so much so that I need a moment to relearn how to breathe.

"Ride me slow," he instructs in a low voice. "I've got you, baby. That's it."

I find a slow rhythm that fills me with pleasure until my body demands more, and I quicken my pace. He grips my hips and finds a rhythm, telling me how good I feel, how tight, how wet, how long he's been waiting to pleasure me like this. I brace myself on his stomach as I bounce on his cock, using him as I please, and he lets me because he loves it when I take charge.

The feeling of his hardness sliding in and out is almost too much to take. His eyes stay locked where our bodies meet, bare of any barrier, and I curse at myself for not having done this before. He feels like heaven.

Those strong hands lift me up effortlessly, moving me up

and down faster and deeper, and making it hard to breathe. Once again he's taking charge; I don't complain because it feels *so fucking good.*

"Condom," he grits out when my walls start pulsing around him.

I bite my lip as he reaches for it, and I keep moving until he gently guides me off him to put it on. I waste no time climbing back on top of him when he's done, stroking him once, twice, three times before guiding his length back inside me.

We don't last very long after that. With our chests pressed together and his lips on mine, we come down from the high as one, my moans and his grunts filling the silence of his house.

"I love you," he whispers, still pulsing inside me. "I love you, Lila. I love you so much."

"I love you more," I whisper against his lips, riding the last waves of my orgasm. "God, I can't wait to do that again."

He chuckles. "You're an insatiable little thing, aren't you?"

"Only when it comes to you."

He lowers me to the mattress carefully, kissing my forehead. "I have to show you something, but I need to clean up first. Close your eyes."

"Oh?" I smirk but do as he says. "Can you give me a hint?"

I feel him getting out of bed and moving around the room. "Nope. Here, put this on. I don't want you getting cold."

He gives me one of his hoodies, and I put it on because I love being wrapped in his smell. Too tired to get up, I keep my eyes closed and hear him move around. The familiarity of it brings me a sense of comfort I've never felt before, and it's like a part of me knows this is it for me.

He's my destination.

"All right, you can open your eyes."

I do as he says, only to find him standing at the foot of the bed. He's wearing a pair of sweatpants, but his chest is bare. That makes me lift a playful eyebrow. "If this is what you had to show me, I'm not complaining, but I've seen it before."

His shy smile takes me aback. "*This* is what I wanted to show you."

My breathing stops when he turns around. Because his scar is no longer visible—in its place, there's a tattoo of beautiful angel wings half made of flowers.

I stand from his bed, walking slowly to him, as if the wings and the flowers would disappear if I rushed. But they're still there when I trace the intricate lines of each feather with my fingers on his soft skin.

"Your scar," I whisper. "I can't see it."

"It's still there," he says. "But now it's covered by a beautiful thing."

It doesn't escape me that he got a pair of angel wings tattooed. "Is this...?"

"For you." He turns, his hands finding my waist. He's gentle as he rests his forehead against mine. "I hope it doesn't freak you out. But when I say you're my angel, Lila, I mean every word. I want you on my skin forever."

"It's beautiful, Reed." Emotion clogs my throat. "I love it. I love you."

He gives me a short, sweet kiss before he pulls away. "Want to know another secret?" I nod. "Your dad did it."

I don't know why it takes me by surprise, but it does. "The tattoo?"

"I asked him if he wanted to do it when I went to talk to him earlier this month," he confesses. "I was his last appointment."

My heart starts beating faster. "As in, his last appointment ever?"

"Yeah."

"Did you tell him...?"

"I told him everything." He brushes my hair away from my

face. "I told him I love you more than anything in this world and that I wanted all of us to start over. Said I wanted to tattoo these angel wings for you because you taught me to learn from the pain. To free myself from my shackles and fly away."

Tears dwell in my eyes. "That's... That's the most thoughtful, beautiful thing anyone has ever done for me."

He's gentle as he wipes them away. "I would do anything for you, Lila. I will."

And when he kisses me again, I can taste the promise of undying love on his lips.

chapter 43

LILA

One year later

"This is where we found her," Melody says.

"No way! She was down there?"

All three teenagers glance between Ginny—sniffing around the park—and the bush.

Cameron sounds proud as he says, "Yep. Lila got her out."

Julian, one of the new kids at the youth center, gapes at me. "Is that why she only has three legs?"

"We were told she was born like that," I tell him. "But she doesn't have any complaints."

Sure enough, Ginny wags her tail as she starts toward the kids in her little wheelchair. Last year, her vet advised us to get her a doggy wheelchair for her walks so she'd put less pressure on her other legs. And Ginny, being the sweet baby she is, got used to it instantly.

"Ginny is the best." Melody crouches to pet her behind her ears. "She's our mascot now."

I chuckle, knowing how true that is. Ever since Reed adopted her, she's been at the youth center every week, and the kids love her. So much so that whenever she stays at dog daycare instead, there's a collective breakdown.

As Melody keeps telling Julian about Ginny's adventures at the youth center, soon joined by other kids, I search the park for

Reed.

His imposing height makes him impossible to miss. Surrounded by the little ones, each begging for his undivided attention, he's patient as he helps them on the slide one by one. Ike, however, is just happy to stand to the side and chat his ear off.

I smile.

"I'm going to find Reed," I tell the teens around me. "Be good, okay? No leaving the park."

"Can Ginny stay?" Cameron asks, his voice hopeful.

He's changed so much in the past two years—from a sad, angry kid who didn't understand his feelings to a more compassionate, disciplined young man. Reed says he still has a long way to go, but boxing has been a godsend, and we couldn't be prouder of him.

"Sure, she can. If she wants to," I tell him.

"You stay with us, Ginny-girl," Melody says.

I wave at Haniyah, who is standing a few feet away with other volunteers, as I make my way to my boyfriend.

Boyfriend. That word isn't strong enough. Not when he's so much more than that.

When our eyes collide, he winks at me, making my heart flip.

"Hi, Lili," Ike greets me first. "Look."

He opens his mouth to show me one of his missing front teeth. "Oh, wow. Did the Tooth Fairy come to your house?"

"Sure did," he says proudly. "She gave me a real coin *and* a chocolate coin."

"You're a lucky boy, Ikey."

Reed's hand travels to the small of my back. "Hey."

"Hi, handsome," I whisper, watching in delight how his cheeks turn the lightest shade of pink.

He squeezes my waist before going back to helping the kids on the slide.

When I came back to the youth center last year, we agreed to keep it professional around everyone else despite our relationship not being a secret. Haniyah almost teared up when we broke the news, saying she'd seen it coming from a mile away and couldn't think of a better partner for Reed. She's been even more welcoming to me ever since, inviting me along for dinner parties at her house. Haniyah and her husband have a very active life in their community, and since they treat Reed like a son, they were quick to start treating me like a daughter.

Still, to avoid getting teased by the kids—not that they don't tease us to their hearts' content anyway—we decided to keep PDA to a minimum. At times like this, though, when he's being so patient with the kids while looking *like that*, all I want is to climb him like a tree.

And it's like his instinct tells him when I'm in the mood, because his faint touches become more frequent and his eyes on me burn hotter throughout the day.

Luckily for me, the bus arrives to take the kids back to the youth center an hour later, putting an end to our field trip and a much-needed start to me throwing myself at the love of my life.

"What's gotten into you?" Reed chuckles as I pepper his neck, his cheeks, and his lips with kisses once we're alone in the parking lot.

"I missed kissing you."

"I missed kissing you, too, angel." He pulls me closer and pecks my lips. "Come on. Let's go home. You promised to help me with the book, remember?"

"Way to kill the mood," I say, pulling away, but I'm smiling.

Reed has been working on a new book for the past couple of months. He refuses to tell me what it's about, though, arguing that he wants my honest opinion once it's ready. He's working on this one by himself, not with my mom, which makes me even more curious.

My parents' relationship with Reed has gone back to normal over the past year, although it was a slow process at first. He and my mom still collaborate sometimes, and he and my dad are pretty much inseparable. Every time my dad calls to say he's renovating something in the house, Reed immediately offers his help.

He also met Maddie and James not long ago, along with my cousins. They all instantly liked him, although James did threaten him "just for good measure." Maddie rolled her eyes at me while it happened, while my dad gave James a proud smile. They're both clowns, but I love them too much to care.

As he drives us home, Ginny looking out of the window in the back seat, I make a mental list of all the things I need to get done on Monday. I started working at a local school a few months ago, counseling middle schoolers, and it's everything I've ever dreamed of and more.

Turns out that, far from the rumors about Reed and me affecting my career, it's never been better.

One of the attendees of the Youth Counseling Expo recognized my name among the applicants for a position at her school, and she quickly hired me after my interview. She never mentioned Reed once and kept telling me how much of a lasting impression I'd left on her after my presentation.

Now I get to wake up every day next to the man I love, in a house we've made our home, with our sweet three-legged baby, and go to work at my dream job I feel *worthy* of doing.

I couldn't be prouder of myself and how far I've come in the past three years, and I'm equally as proud of the man behind the wheel. Just like me, he gets to wake up every day and make the world a better place. Destiny brought him back to the foster agency that handled his case, and he's now doing the same for other children.

And thanks to Reed's research, Warlington Youth Center—

as well as many others—finally got more funding to hire mental health professionals and plan more activities.

If I'm an angel, he's a god.

When we get home, Ginny wastes no time darting for her food bowl.

"I'll go grab the manuscript," Reed tells me, pressing a kiss to my temple before disappearing upstairs to his office.

I hang my coat and wait for him on the couch, a smile drawing over my face every time I look at the pictures of us and our loved ones peppering the bookshelves. Reed asked me to move in with him shortly after we got together, and I was only too eager to accept.

My heart feels warm and calm, just thinking how this is our home now.

When he reappears in the living room, stack of papers in hand, I pick up on his nervousness at once.

I arch a playful eyebrow. "I've read your writing before."

"Yeah, yeah. I know."

When he doesn't add anything else, I grab the papers from his grip and sit back on the couch.

"Can you read it out loud?" he asks, his voice not sounding completely normal. He doesn't sit down, either, which only adds to the weirdness. "Just so I know it sounds good."

Still not sure what's wrong with him, I clear my throat and start reading.

"There was once a boy who was born in the shadows," I read. *"He didn't know what happiness was, what love felt like, or what freedom tasted like. In many ways, he was a prisoner."*

I look at him again, but his eyes are on the ground, so I keep reading.

"His life was a nightmare he couldn't wake up from. Until, one day, a golden light appeared in his bedroom, making all the shadows disappear. Only it wasn't a light—it was a girl who told him she was

going to be his best friend. The girl took the boy's hand and walked him outside, where he saw daylight for the first time. She taught him to play her favorite games, to smile and laugh. Before he knew it, the nightmare had turned into his greatest dream. That's when the boy realized the girl was much more than his friend—she was his angel."

My heart stops at that word.

I look at him once more, but he keeps avoiding my gaze.

"As time went by, the boy and the girl fell in love. They grew together and tried to keep the shadows away. When the darkness crept in unannounced, they held each other's hand and found the light again. They made a home, full of happiness and love and freedom and all the wonderful things the boy had never felt before meeting her.

"And one day, when their love got brighter than the whole universe, the boy decided he wanted to be his angel's keeper forever. So, he asked her one question."

My gaze is blurry as I look at Reed kneeling before me, a small box between his hands.

"Lila," he starts, his voice so raw with emotion that it makes me breathless. "I think I knew the moment I met you that we had something special. My future had always been dark to me, unclear—I never saw happiness in it. But then you showed me love, real love, and everything started taking shape. I imagined things I never allowed myself to, like having kids and growing old with someone. You are my life, my angel, and I want to spend the rest of my days with you.

"I love you, Lila. More than I've ever loved anything and anyone in this world. Will you marry me?"

More love than I ever thought myself capable of experiencing fills my heart. Words aren't easy right now, so my answer is to throw myself at him, hugging him close until I can barely breathe. He wraps one arm around me, his other hand tangling in my hair.

"Is that a yes?" he asks, visibly less tense than just a moment ago. "Or is this a breakup hug?"

I laugh, the tears running freely down my cheeks. "Of course I will marry you, Reed. I love you so much. So, so much."

"I love you too, angel." He takes my hand in his and gently slides the most breathtaking diamond ring I've ever seen onto my finger.

"Your love has always been worth every bit of pain," he whispers, pressing his lips to my ring. Sealing our promise of forever.

My eyes find his, and I realize how true that is.

Because Reed is my life, and I am his, and nothing will ever be strong enough to keep us apart again.

epilogue

LILA

"Where's my buddy?"

Dad walks into the kitchen, gift bag in hand, his eyes darting around the room.

I smile as I close the fridge. "What happened to *Hello, dear daughter. Are you having a good day?*"

Mom rolls her eyes behind him, giving me a knowing look. "Whatever you tell him now is pointless. You know how he gets."

"Hey, old man." My aunt Maddie walks into the kitchen, barefoot and sipping on Dylan's abandoned apple juice. She points to her hairline. "You have a brand-new gray hair right here."

"Show some respect to your older brother," my dad fake-scolds her, fighting a smile.

"But it's more fun if I don't," she argues. "Hi, Gracie. You look as stunning as always."

My mom laughs. "So do you, honey. Where are Alice and Dylan?"

"Pestering Lila's very patient dog in the garden," she says. "James is keeping an eye on them. And by that, I mean he's taking pictures like a maniac because he insists he never has enough."

Dad turns to me. This time, though, he presses a kiss to the top of my head. "Where's the birthday boy?"

"He's upstairs," I tell him as I kiss Mom's cheek. "He'll be here in a minute."

Just then, the stairs groan under Reed's weight as he comes back down. And I can't help but feel my heart melt all over again when he appears in the kitchen, our son perched on his hip.

"Hey, Grace. Cal. I didn't hear the front door."

He kisses my mom's cheek but doesn't get to shake my dad's hand because the second he sees his grandson, trying to get his attention is pointless.

"There's my buddy." Dad's smile is the biggest I've ever seen. Seeing them together is one of my biggest joys. "Grandma and I got you the coolest birthday gifts. Do you wanna see?"

Sam squeals, throwing his arms around my dad.

When we found out I was pregnant three years after our wedding, it was a surprise. Reed and I had talked about having kids, but we weren't in a rush to start a family. And when we were told we were having a boy, giving him my dad's name felt right to both of us.

"Nobody calls you Samuel anyway," I told Dad the day Sam was born, tears in both of our eyes as he held my son for the first time. "We might as well give the name a second chance."

Sam and my dad have been inseparable ever since, like two akin souls who have found each other after lifetimes apart.

So today, at his first birthday party, it doesn't surprise me that my parents have decided to spoil him with *eight* gifts, each one bigger than the last.

Reed pulls me into his lap as we all sit in the living room a while later, watching our son tear open the gift paper with my dad's help, as well as Dylan's and Alice's.

"Are you having fun, angel?" he whispers, pressing a soft kiss on my neck.

I shift in his lap. "I am. And he seems to love his gifts."

Sam squeals as Dylan helps him unwrap a new firefighter toy. He's very into those these days.

"I love him so much," Reed whispers, a smile on his face. He presses a gentle kiss on my shoulder. "I love you both so much."

At first, Reed struggled with the idea of becoming a father. Not because he didn't want to, but because he was scared to mess things up. But after countless conversations with me and my dad, asking him for advice, he finally felt ready enough.

Turns out he had nothing to worry about. The second Sam was born, Reed stepped into the role as if he had been born for it. He loves our son with all of him, protects him, and makes sure he has the happy childhood he never had.

I thought I couldn't possibly love Reed more—or find him any hotter—but then he became the best father in the world and proved me wrong.

Our son has Mariah, Haniyah, and everyone else in our families wrapped around his little finger, and no one would have it any other way.

I rest my head on my husband's shoulder and look around the room, so full of happiness and love. And I take in the moment.

Sam's happy squeals. Ginny's wagging tail. My dad's excitement. My mom's smile. My aunt's teasing. My uncle's laughter. My cousins' bickering. My husband's arms around me.

And I realize there's nothing, absolutely anything, I would've done differently. Because every painful lesson got me here, to this life that feels so complete.

To the brightest light.

THE END

ACKNOWLEDGMENTS

And with that, The Brightest Light series has come to an end.

To say the past year and a half has been insane would be a tremendous understatement. If you're new here and have no clue what I'm talking about, that's okay—thank you for picking up this book and (hopefully) rooting for Lila and Reed as much as I did while writing their story. But if you've been around since the start, then you've probably read my debut, the first book of this series, *The Brightest Light of Sunshine*, and fell in love with my favorite tattoo artist and ballet teacher duo. That book changed my life in far too many ways to list here, and it's all because of you. Words will never be enough to thank you for screaming about my books everywhere, for your reviews, for your edits, for your kind words. Writing a book is no easy feat, let alone when you're constantly a ball of anxiety and self-doubt, so thank you for caring about the stories I need to tell and for being patient with me while I grew confident in my author voice. This is my dream job, and I'd still be doing it if it weren't a job, but you all make it infinitely more rewarding.

To my late family dog, B. Your memory will always live on with us. We love you and hope you are happy, healthy, and spoiled wherever you are. Ginny is for you.

To Alejandri. Oh look, another book you can't read until you're eighteen. Not much longer to go, so hang in there. You're the best (and funniest) cousin I could've ever asked for, and I'm endlessly proud of you. I love you more than life itself. (Looking forward to those free plane tickets when you become a pilot, by the way).

To Tía. Thank you for being a constant cheerleader in whatever I feel called to do. You're an inspiration for me in many ways, and I'm so proud to be your niece. I love you.

To Alexis. Thank you for your endless patience, for brainstorming with me when I got stuck, and for believing in me when I didn't (aka more often than I'd like to admit). I love you so much.

Para mamá y papá. Todavía me quedan unas pocas sesiones con la psicóloga para que os deje leer mis libros. Paciencia, porfaplis. Menos mal que me queréis y no me lo tenéis en cuenta. Os quiero mucho.

To Fátima. Thank you for listening to my endless voice notes and answering my thousand questions about academia. You also have the best gossip, which helps on the tougher days. I love you, and I love being your friend.

To my editor, Solange Jazayeri, for always being incredibly uplifting. Your advice and insight over the past year have made me a better author. Thank you for allowing me to learn from you.

To Meredith Wild and the entire team at Page & Vine, who made this release possible (and killed it with this gorgeous cover). Thank you for giving this series a home and treating me and my characters with so much care.

To my agent, Savannah Greenwell. Thank you for your constant hard work. Hopefully you already know how awesome you are, but if you don't, here's a reminder! I love having you on my team.

To Keeley Catarineau from Hot Tree Editing. You're insanely talented, and it means everything to me that you love my characters so much. Thank you for being such a joy to work with.

To Aurora, Alex, Zarin, Aleish, and Mahbuba. Thank you for your invaluable feedback and unhinged comments on this story. I don't know how I got so lucky to have you five supportive, brilliant, and extraordinarily hilarious girls in my corner. I hope to give you all a bone-crushing hug one day.

To Ellie from Love Notes PR. Thank you for being such a talented social media manager. Your hard work is the reason I can focus on writing guilt-free, and that's priceless. I'm your biggest fan.

To S, my therapist. This book wouldn't exist without you because I would've given up long ago. Thank you for being a rock star. You won't get rid of me just yet.

Para Tata y Abue, siempre.

about the author

Lisina Coney is a New Adult and contemporary romance author with a weakness for heartfelt love connections and happy endings. She believes in creating complex and relatable characters that will make her readers feel less alone in their journeys.

Besides putting her daydreams into words when the sun comes down, Lisina is an avid reader who is obsessed with French fries and tends to force kisses on her very patient cats.

For more information about Lisina's books (as well as some good ol' bonus content), you can visit her Instagram page @lisinaconeyauthor and her website www.lisinaconeyauthor.com